Praise for Faith Hunter's Soulwood Novels

"Rich, imaginative, and descriptive, Hunter's latest novel in her Soulwood series shines. . . . The intriguing, inventive plot coupled with the bone-chilling tension make this story an unforgettable read."   —RT Book Reviews

"I love Nell and her PsyLED team and would happily read about their adventures for years."   —Vampire Book Club

"Faith Hunter does a masterful job . . . and has created a wonderful new heroine in Nell, who continues to grow into her powers."   —The Reading Café

"Once again, Hunter proves she's a master of the genre."
     —Romance Junkies

"*Blood of the Earth* by Faith Hunter is the best first install- ment of an urban fantasy series I've read in about a decade. Highly recommended."   —Rabid Reads

"There is wry humor, mild levels of snarkiness, cross- pollination with Hunter's characters and events from her Jane Yellowrock series, and passages setting a breakneck pace that may cause you to forget to breathe."
     —Kings River Life Magazine

"A heck of a lot of fun, a neat mix of the supernatural and a police procedural."   —*Locus*

Praise for Faith Hunter's Jane Yellowrock Novels

"Hunter has an amazing talent."   —SF Site

"Readers eager for the next book in Patricia Briggs's Mercy Thompson . . . . Faith Hunter a try."

     brary Journal

Also by Faith Hunter

The Jane Yellowrock Novels

SKINWALKER

BLOOD CROSS

MERCY BLADE

RAVEN CURSED

DEATH'S RIVAL

THE JANE YELLOWROCK WORLD COMPANION

BLOOD TRADE

BLACK ARTS

BROKEN SOUL

DARK HEIR

SHADOW RITES

COLD REIGN

DARK QUEEN

SHATTERED BONDS

The Soulwood Novels

BLOOD OF THE EARTH

CURSE ON THE LAND

FLAME IN THE DARK

CIRCLE OF THE MOON

SPELLS FOR THE DEAD

The Rogue Mage Novels

BLOODRING

SERAPHS

HOST

Anthologies and Compilations

CAT TALES

HAVE STAKES WILL TRAVEL

BLACK WATER

BLOOD IN HER VEINS

TRIALS

TRIBULATIONS

TRIUMPHANT

SPELLS FOR THE DEAD

A Soulwood Novel

Faith Hunter

ACE
New York

ACE
Published by Berkley
An imprint of Penguin Random House LLC
penguinrandomhouse.com

ISBN: 9780399587962

First Edition: July 2020

Printed in the United States of America
3   5   7   9   10   8   6   4   2

Cover art by Cliff Nielson
Cover design by Katie Anderson

To my Renaissance Man,
who always does the right thing,
even when it's hard and hits him back.

ONE

Superstar Stella Mae Ragel and her housekeeper were found dead at her horse farm at ten twenty this morning. According to JoJo at PsyLED HQ, another member of Stella's staff was now dead, more were dropping like flies, and the media was beginning to gather, also like flies.

Because of the speed of the progression of the illness and the high-profile victim, Psychometric Law Enforcement Division of Homeland Security had been called in. My skill set didn't include medicine, forensics, or any form of magic except my own, so I figured I had been requested to do the scut paperwork.

I'd had less trouble getting into a private, top-secret research and development center with government contracts than I did getting onto Stella Mae's property. My personal ID, my PsyLED ID, the sticker on my official PsyLED vehicle, and the fact that my boss' boss had put me on the list kept by the security team at the gate were the only reasons I got in at all. The media people shouted questions at the car through the entire ID and vetting process, most of them shrill and sounding a little rabid. Some demanded to know what drugs had killed the country singer. Some wanted to know if she'd taken her own life. Some seemed to believe she had been the target of a deranged stalker.

The winding gravel driveway to Melody Horse Farm was long enough to keep the house from view by the dozens of media vans and cars parked out front, but I spotted a drone overhead and a helicopter with a newsy daredevil hanging out the side with a shoulder-mounted camera, getting the views. I hoped he was strapped in. I hoped the drone stayed out of his way.

I pulled over to let two ambulances pass me, both units moving slow, not running lights and sirens, so I knew the occupants were not in life-threatening condition, just sick or wounded and needing medical help. Through the rear windows of the last ambulance, the man on the stretcher lifted a hand at me, waving. The African-American man wasn't one of my team, and I didn't recognize him. He was fully dressed out in a sky blue biohazard suit, which was not reassuring. The latest batch of unis had been color coded so we didn't have to read labels in emergency situations, and the sky blue ones meant he was under precautions for everything: viral or bacterial pathogens or paranormal contagion or a combination of all three. We called them P3Es—paranormal personal protective equipment. When our team, PsyLED Unit Eighteen, was called in, there was always a para component.

I pulled back into the drive when the ambulances rolled past. Weaving between several dozen official police vehicles and three more ambulances, I parked and idled, sitting in the sunheated car as I studied the house and grounds. Horses stood at the fence just ahead, watching the excitement, tails twitching, ears at attention. Aside from sitting on a draft horse a few times, I didn't ride, but I'd been raised on a communal farm, so even I could tell these were expensive, well-cared-for, curious, and intelligent equines. They had bright eyes, perked ears, and the glossy, well-conditioned, self-satisfied look of top-notch athletes who knew they deserved the best. I rolled down my window and smelled the farm air: manure, horse, hay; a scent that meant all the good things from my childhood—before I learned what God's Cloud of Glory Church really was and had gotten away from the dangers of the polygamist lifestyle.

"Hey, sweetie," I said to the nearest mare. She was a roan beauty with a six-month-old or so foal beside her. The mama horse flicked her ears at me in interest, probably wanting a peppermint or a carrot, which I didn't have. Flies and gnats swarmed around her face but didn't land, suggesting an application of bug spray. I let off the brake, rolled a little farther off the driveway, cracked all the windows against the day's heat, and touched the button to turn off the car. Which still felt all kinds of strange when, for my entire adult life, I had turned a key.

This was my first day back at work after two off, and I wanted one last moment to breathe in the calm before diving into work. Sitting alone in what was surely the quiet before the investigative storm, I studied the remarkable, well-cared-for, well-funded farm, and wondered how money related to the deaths here.

Stella's place was perched on the back crest of a hill, a large two-story, white-painted clapboard home with tall windows, dark shutters, porches at front and sides, and multiple dormers on each side of the tall, four-sided mansard roof. The house—like the four hundred acres of land—was big, even by church standards, and I came from a background where four wives and as many as forty children lived in one house. Big, I knew. This place was *huge* and extravagant and elegant. The front grounds were landscaped with mixed ornamental grasses and native landscape plants still holding on to summer green. An orchard of fruit trees, yellow-leaved with the season and some still bearing ripe apples, were planted beside the house; a nut tree orchard was in the background; hundreds of maple trees were farther back, bursting with colorful leaves from the short but deep chill that had taken over the region last week before the return of the unexpectedly warm Indian summer. Round bales of hay dotted a recently cut field nearby, and closer to the house, deep beds of well-worked soil were planted with ornamental kales and fall mums.

My fingers itched to dig into the soil, to feel the life in it, explore it with my nature magic, and let my own roots grow. But unless I wanted to be a tree again and perhaps forever, that wouldn't be smart.

The side door opened and a woman wearing a P3E pulled a stretcher across the narrow porch and lifted one end down the three steps to the ground as if it weighed nothing. On the stretcher was a biohazard cadaver pouch (also called a human remains pouch, or HRP). The other end of the stretcher was lifted down the steps by the woman's coworker before they wheeled it to a coroner's transport van. Weirdly, the HRP seemed to hold something boxy, rectangular, not body shaped. I wasn't sure what that meant, but then, I wasn't sure about much of anything. The gag order on this case was already in place.

The only particulars I knew about the crime scene had been told to me by JoJo Jones at HQ before I left. "Three dead, bodies

going to UTMC for full forensic workup. Don't touch the bodies. I've sent you the timeline. Be careful."

There were a whole lotta possibilities in the little I knew.
JoJo's "Be careful" implied the scene was still potentially dangerous. More significant was that the dead on-site would be
transported to the University of Tennessee Medical Center in
Knoxville, which had one of only a handful of forensic patholo-
gists in the United States who also had a secondary certification
in paranormal medicine. Para med was a rare specialty, and
Nashville, which was much closer to the crime scene, had no
such pathologist and no paranormal unit for patients. So, dead
bodies, danger, paranormal, all sounded bad, but the bucolic
setting was peaceful and the calm, measured body language of
the first responders said everything was under control.

Maybe all the bodies were gone by now. That would suit me
just fine. Having grown up at a church that practiced a form of
communal farm living, I'd seen plenty of dead things, and even
knew how to butcher animals for meat if necessary.

Didn't mean I liked seeing dead people.

My phone vibrated and I looked at the screen. It was my
sister Mud, and I let the call go to voice mail, knowing it was
trouble I didn't have time to deal with right now. She'd text me
if it was something really urgent, but it had to involve spurting
blood, active flames, or dead bodies to fall under that category.
Arguments between sisters didn't count no matter how bad they
got. We had tried it the other way around, calling only when
urgent, but I used texts for work, and the constant dinging of
family texts was distracting, so they were used for true emer-
gencies, calls for minor things. If my sisters killed each other,
well, I'd deal with the mess and the cleanup when I got home. I
ignored the voice mail too, though I wanted to bang my head on
the steering wheel in frustration.

The coroner's van trundled behind my vehicle, so I got out,
made sure my weapon was securely seated in its Kydex shoulder
holster, put on a casual jacket, and smoothed the driving wrin-
kles from my work pants. Opening the trunk, I retrieved my
handheld psy-meter 1.0 and did a quick scan of the grounds and
the house. Psy-meters picked up paranormal energies known as
psions, but there was nothing much beyond normal ambient energies present outside. I put the psy-meter away and lifted out

the milk crate that held my faded pink blanket and the potted tree before closing the trunk. "Sorry about the dark on the ride over," I told the tree. "I'll try to get something rigged so you can sit in the sunlight while I drive."

The potted vampire tree was a new addition to my evidence arsenal. I had no idea what English it understood, but I'd taken to talking to it anyway. Plants that were talked to in a kind tone of voice were happy plants. And since the vampire tree species had recently (probably, most certainly) eaten one of my enemies, I tried to be polite. I didn't want it to get mad. I placed the small crate on the passenger seat and locked up.

Scanning the grounds, I walked to the side door, where the body had come from, taking in the scenery behind the house and down the low slope of the hill. There were covered training rings, trails, outbuildings, several pastures, a mechanical horse walker, horse gear, and a barn that was bigger than my house. The horses that were hanging over the fences were muscular and sassy, with slightly dished faces, as if they had some Arabian in the genetic mix. The yearlings and mares with this year's foals appeared to be in one pasture, with geldings pastured separately.

Close to the barn, a bright red bay horse, bigger than the others, stood posed in a paddock, the breeze flinging his black mane and tail. He had black stockings and hooves, and a peculiar lightning-shaped white blaze on his face. He pawed the dirt and circled, prancing, posturing, tail held high. He reared and kicked, showing off. This was a stallion, the only intact male horse I had seen on the property so far. He snorted and burst into a tight, circling run, his mane and tail flying, neck arched, as if he was showing off. He blew a breath of delight and alpha-male satisfaction and tossed his head, the odd facial blaze seeming to flicker like flames. I didn't have to know anything about fancy horses to know this one was *expensive*.

Farther away from the house were a huge white metal shed with three fifteen-foot-tall garage-type doors and a big circular drive. Parked in front of the one open garage door was a forty-foot-long, solid black recreational vehicle with multiple dual wheels, a matching black transport trailer hitched to it. Through the windows in the closed shed doors I could see two more trailers. Big ones. To the side of the RV storage building was a long, very fancy horse trailer. Just looking at the vehicles made me think seven figures several times over.

Dang. Being a country-singing megastar made good money.

An older, pudgy cop standing inside the door stopped me and I had to go through the entire show-and-tell of my ID again. "Not that I mind," I said mildly, "but why all the security?"

"Sheeee-ut. A purdy little media photographer in a doctor's coat made it through the kitchen earlier, following the coroner." Lips pursed between his chubby cheeks, he compared my face with my official ID and my driver's license. He shook his head and returned my IDs. "She looked even younger than you do. He-yell, she even had an official-looking ID pinned to her doctor's coat. Switching her ass at me and smiling like she belonged here. The broad was inventive, I'll give her that. But I got my ass chewed, so full ID protocol it is." He lowered his voice, checking my name off a paper on a clipboard. "The sheriff's my cousin or I'd be in real trouble. You're on the list," he finished. "They're down the hall." He handed me a handful of plastic-wrapped candy. "Here. You'll need these. Extra-strong mints."

"Oh. Thanks." That was ominous. Mints were used in crime scenes where the bodies had been dead a while, to combat the stench and control the nausea that came from dealing with them. I shoved the mints into my pocket. I was pretty sure the sheriff's cousin was checking out my backside as I moved through the high-end kitchen toward the hallway. And yep, when I looked back, I caught him eyeing me. I'd been ogled by churchmen since I was ten, and had little patience with it. I really wanted to smack him with my badge, but that might make waves. I had to be on more professional behavior than I sometimes wanted to be, or knew how to be. I hadn't been a special agent for long and acting like one wasn't second nature to me. I frowned at him, but he just grinned, unrepentant and probably thinking he was cute, or that giving me mints gave him the right to leer.

Before I went down the hall, I took a moment for a good look at the kitchen and the huge room beyond it. There were white marble countertops and an island covered with bags of commercially made bread and buns, wilted lettuce, and tomatoes. There was a huge copper farmer's sink, a heavy-duty bread-maker's mixer, a copper-clad baker's oven, and a six-burner gas stove. The glass-fronted upper cabinets went to the tall ceiling, displaying white dishes; copper lights descended in strategic locations; and the floor was pristine interlocking white vinyl tile.

Through a cracked-open door I spotted private stairs up to the second story. I figured they gave direct access to the bedrooms for midnight snacks.

The gathering room had comfy, squishy green furniture, lots of pillows, and a fireplace big enough to roast a small hog. Stella Mae's home was beautiful, like one in a house design magazine, but everything looked utilized, not just for show, the sink with lizard-skin patina, the copper on the oven showing indications of heat.

The kitchen and gathering room struck a chord of lust in my heart, the sin of covetousness the churchmen always talked about. Thinking about my own home and the discord waiting for me there, I turned down the spacious hallway with natural plank flooring and wide doorways. At the end, near the staircase, the stench of death hit me and I slowed. The smell circulated on the air, ripe, foul, sickly sweet. As if they didn't smell it, there were clumps of chatting LEOs—law enforcement officers—uniformed, plainclothes, and one member of my team. Occam looked up, wearing his cop-face expression, and my heart gave a little jolt of joy.

"Ingram," he said, the smile in his voice telling me he really meant, *Nell, sugar.* The scarred skin pulled around his lips and his amber-hazel eyes crinkled with happiness as he excused himself from the officers and strode toward me, meeting me midway down the hall.

His hair had grown back blonder and he wore it longer than before he'd been burned, to cover up the patchy, hairless scars above his ear. "You made good time from Knoxville," he said softly, his tone saying so much more. "You run lights and siren in your new official vehicle?"

I wrinkled my nose at his teasing. "I did not. But I did discover the joys of cruise control and audiobooks. What we got?"

Occam's eyes went warmer and tender and my middle melted. "You mean between us?" he murmured.

My heart sang at his words and I resisted the urge to rub my curled fingers along his jaw. Wereleopards adored physical affection, and a cat-claiming face rub was especially pleasing to my cat-man. "The case, if you please? And why I'm here?" I managed, sounding far too prim.

Occam's expression slid to business-serious. Softly he said, "Three dead, two days after the end of Stella Mae Ragel's last concert tour. Her band, production crew, manager, and grips were supposed to meet here at ten, unload and organize gear, then eat lunch together and discuss the financial results of the last tour. Which I understand were better than expected."

"Money," I said, naming a common reason for murder.

"Yes, ma'am." His Texan twang was moderated, the way he talked in public, just as my church-speak was moderated. It was a shame, but some idiots seemed to think Southern dialects were a sign of lack of intelligence, when in reality they were a sign of location-location-location, culture, history, immigrant influxes, and location. "Her crew last spoke with Stella at nine a.m. to confirm the meeting time, and she told them she and Verna Upton, the housekeeper, were heading down early to start work."

"Down?"

"Basement studio with work area, lounge, and sound production room. About two thousand square feet of expensive sound equipment, instruments, and liquor. Stella has a stellar liquor collection."

What I knew about alcohol could be written on my little fingernail in longhand, but I nodded for him to continue.

"The crew—band and roadies—started arriving, but no one answered the door. After twenty minutes, they used the hidden key and found the two women in the basement, dead. They called nine-one-one immediately."

"COD?" I was asking for cause of death, still thinking murder.

"No idea. No blood spatter, no obvious signs of trauma, no signs of illness. Looked like they fell where they stood. But they also looked as if they died days or weeks ago instead of an hour."

"Was someone impersonating them on the phone?"

"The band members insist not. They say it was Stella and she sounded fine, which, if correct, means extremely accelerated decomp."

Which provided one small reason why a PsyLED special

agent might have been called in, but there were now three on the premises.

Occam continued. "Within seconds after her crew called the police, Stella's personal assistant, Monica Belcher, arrived and opened a shipping box of new tour T-shirts. She fell, dead when she hit the floor. She was still holding a wad of the new shirts. The bass player and the drummer ran to her but started feeling sick, and the band and roadies evacuated the basement and called nine-one-one again to request paramedics. Local PD, Sheriff Jackett, and Tennessee FBI were all here in less than twenty minutes, and medic units from Nashville in thirty."

That was fast, even for murder. "Fame has its benefits," I said, hearing unfamiliar sarcasm in my tone. I wondered if my derision was a remnant of kitchen-envy. Or maybe farm-envy. Or maybe just pure old envy-envy.

"By the time the first LEOs and medics got here, Belcher's arm—holding the shirts—was showing signs of rapidly advancing necrosis. It looks as if her flesh is rotting in time-lapse photography. Faster even than Stella Mae and Verna Upton."

"Why was someone opening a box of T-shirts when her boss was dead at a crime scene?"

"They say Monica Belcher was one of those people who can't sit still, always had to be doing something. She freaked out when they found the bodies and she started opening and storing gear in a frenzy. There may be more to it. We're still in the early stages of questioning. They're all pretty shook up."

"And the bodies are all three necrosing at an accelerated rate," I said, just to be clear.

"Yup. And listen to you talking cop-speak, Special Agent No-Longer-a-Probie Ingram."

I chuckled quietly, as he surely intended. I wasn't a probationary agent anymore, but since some of my time in the unit was spent as a tree, I was still a rookie. The more experienced unit members still babied and teased me. I teased back, "What more you got to tell me, Special Agent Cat-Man?"

"Only that I'd like nothing better than a beer in that hammock out back, but that's just me." Occam's lips lifted on one side, his still-scarred face pulling down on the other, and his one good blonde eyebrow waggled up and down. "It's a two-person hammock," he added.

"Uh-huh. The case, please?" I said, sounding all starchy.

Occam went on. "Yeah. All three bodies are decomping abnormally fast. So far they only got the housekeeper out of here and she had to go in a cooler. They scooped her up with shovels and spoons."

That explained the stench on the air and the boxy shape in the biohazard cadaver pouch. A cooler. With a rotting body in it. But awful as it was, accelerated decomp was not a good reason for three PsyLED agents to be here. The stench in the hallway suddenly got worse as the air-conditioning came on. Eye-wateringly horrid.

"Why did the locals decide to call PsyLED for a paranormal workup instead of just a biohazard biological workup? And while you're talking, some indication why *I'm* here?" Because I had lots of skill sets that could be done by the agents already on-site, and few that were mine alone: in the office it was paperwork, research, and summations, and in the field it was getting along with vamps and reading the earth. Vamps usually liked me or thought I was amusing, mostly because I wasn't afraid of them when I likely should be. Reading the earth was an arcane ability, part of my nature magic, and was the usual reason I got out of my cubicle.

"A backup singer and musician, one Catriona Doyle, member of the Doyle witch family from Ireland, was here before the local LEOs got here and started a *seeing* working. She's an earth witch, and says there's some funky magic going on in the house. She speculated that a strange kind of *death* working was taking place. That's why PsyLED was called. T. Laine was on the way to Bowling Green for a reading and FireWind hijacked her here instead. She's still downstairs and she says it's magical, but not like any magic she's ever seen before. Something different and real bad. Hence our backup."

T. Laine Kent was Unit Eighteen's resident witch, and doing readings had become one of her specialties: reading DBs—dead bodies—reading crime scenes, and reading other magic users. Using a *seeing* working, along with a psy-meter 2.0—the highly sensitive, upgraded model—and her field experience gained at some really awful crime scenes, she could detect and identify blood magic, dark magic, and Blood Tarot spells better than the rest of us put together.

Occam pulled his phone and read his notes, his face losing its humor, his voice all cop-emotionless. "Along with local hazmat, Kent initiated CBRNEP workup." It was pronounced *ky-ber-nep*, but CBRNEP was the crime scene protocol for chemical, biological, radiological/nuclear, explosive, and paranormal materials, a protocol developed by the Center for Domestic Preparedness. "So far, we're clean on chemical, radiological/nuclear, and explosive causation. Still holding out on biological, para, or combo."

My eyes met Occam's and his one good eyebrow lifted in agreement with my thoughts. Biological causation would be bad. A combo would be terrifying. PsyLED brass and the military had been creating response strategies involving militarized magical energies coupled with all the other elements of CBRNEP. None of the scenarios had resulted in manageable outcomes.

Occam went on. "Kent doesn't have a probable COD yet, but the drummer, male, and bass player, female, who started feeling sick in the basement, are on the way to UTMC-Knoxville for monitoring in the para ward.

"The coroner and Putnam County medical examiner are onsite, down there now with T. Laine, dressed in blue unis, each holding a null pen, debating how to transport the other two bodies. Current plan is to find some null biohazard HRPs for transport to UTMC. Otherwise it's possible the bodies will be fully decomposed by the time they get there."

Everyone, alive and dead, was going to Knoxville. It would be handy to have all the victims—patients and DBs—in one place. Even more than sixty years after the paras leaped out of the para closet, medical professionals who treated or worked on paranormal creatures were few and far between. UTMC had long been on the cutting edge of para studies.

I drew a little circle in the air with my finger. "And why does your face look like that? So unhappy underneath the cop-face mean."

"As soon as the sheriff arrived, he called in the local FBI. The feeb SAC took Catriona in for questioning. In cuffs. She was gone before T. Laine got here."

"Why in handcuffs? Because she's a witch?"

"Witch. Woman. Foreigner. Young. Pick one. Or pick 'em

all. From what I gather, the special agent in charge of the local FBI office hates most everyone."

Tennessee PsyLED and FBI had not healed our professional relationship since the state's FBI director had been outed by us as a *gwyllgi*—a devil dog. Not that they wanted a devil dog in charge, but the FBI embarrassment of having a deadly paranormal creature under their noses and giving them orders had been hard on the whole department. Now it was tit-for-tat at the higher levels of the state organization. The younger feebs seemed okay, but upper management and the older entrenched agents were often a problem. Occam nodded a greeting over my shoulder.

Before I could turn, T. Laine said, "Your hair is gorgeous. I officially hate you."

The hate comment meant she was jealous of my hair—which had gone a strange shade of metallic scarlet a few months back and become wildly curly, thanks to my becoming a tree for a while. The color and curls were fading now, but T. Laine still had hair envy. I stepped at an angle to include her.

Lainie looked tired, her skin pale, purple smudges beneath her dark eyes, and her dark bobbed hair was snarled and squashed flat from the elastic strings of a bio face mask. T. Laine needed another witch in the unit to share the witchy duties, but witches who were willing to go into law enforcement were rare as hen's teeth.

"Update, to make sure we're all on the same page. I drove here and tested the site," she said. "It isn't a typical witch working or curse. I've never seen anything quite like it. Just looking at the scene, it fits some of the parameters of a *death* working but falls totally outside on the psy-meter, and it's everywhere downstairs, especially in the swag storage room, where the third victim, Monica Belcher, fell and died. That room reads so strong of these death energies that, so far, I haven't found a way to stay inside safely, and the two city cops who went in to take crime scene photos before I got here were contaminated. They just arrived at HQ to sit in the null room for a while, in case that helps."

"What kind of psy-meter reading?" I asked. Every species of paranormal creature had its own specific levels, even me. And magical workings and magical energies always read on the psy-meter.

"All four psion levels are up, but they bounce up and down, as if the energies are being affected by something else, like compasses going haywire over the Bermuda Triangle. Almost everything in the basement is showing signs of disintegration, not just the bodies." T. Laine rubbed her hand through her hair, a gesture that was part frustration, part something else. Maybe headache. "I've never seen anything like it," she repeated, "and I don't know where to look to help me categorize it since no one up-line has answered my calls yet."

Her eyes cleared slightly and she gave me a wan smile. "No maggots yet, though."

"Ha-ha," I said. Vampires called me Maggots or Maggoty, or Little Maggot Girl. The nicknames were a thing of perpetual amusement to my coworkers. "What's a swag storage room?"

"It's storage space for promotional merchandise and display stands."

"What do you need me to do? Why am I here? This thing is in the house, not the earth."

"FireWind requested you on-site."

"Oh." FireWind was the new up-line big boss and he scared the pants offa me. Being scared made me mouthy and so Ayatas FireWind and I had not gotten off on the right foot, if there *was* a right foot with him.

"FireWind is on the way from New Orleans. For now? Familiarize yourself with the site. Then you can start organizing the electronic file tree for PsyLED's inquiry, take photos and notes, hand draw the crime scene, and start the prelim witness interviews." She took a breath that ended in a frown. "Let's take a quick tour of the basement. That's a vision that'll melt all the red off your lollipop."

I would never understand what lollipops had to do with dead bodies. I followed Kent through the gaggle of officers at the end of the hallway and down the stairs to a landing where the stairs turned. There was a narrow window there with three house-plants on the ledge, and a table stacked with sky blue unis. Under the table was a huge plastic container for contaminated unis. I opened one of the super-strong mints and placed it on my tongue before we both dressed out in the null P3E unis. The one-piece biohazard uniforms had been designed for contact-based bio-logical pathogens and had then been altered and spelled by the

Seattle coven against magic. They covered the wearer from head to toe, starting at the oversized booties, rising up our legs to a waist that never fit, to the head cover that could be cinched over forehead and chin. To go with the unis were extra-thick spelled nitrile gloves and darker masks, which could be fitted to our faces to create a seal so that all air exchange had to pass through the specially treated null cloth.

The stench coming up the stairway was enough to make me nearly gag, even with the mint. Some people said they breathed through their mouths when they encountered bad smells, but that left my tongue coated with a nasty smell/taste sensation. That perception lasted longer than the smell alone and made me not want my dinner.

On Unit Eighteen I had gotten sort of used to foul smells, but this stench was in a category all its own. If I could have stopped breathing entirely, I would have. The scent was a sweet, sick reek of advanced rot mixed with . . . I didn't know what. Mixed with other things I couldn't identify. When we were dressed, T. Laine handed me a null pen to protect me from the paranormal energies and a cloth handkerchief with mentholated vapor rub on it. I took both and tucked the cloth inside my mask, near my nose, and the pen into a chest pocket of the uni.

The stairway ended in a landing centered in the tan-carpeted basement. Musical instruments were everywhere, hanging on the walls, on stands in rows along the walls, in cases stacked in a corner. Set up as if to play or practice were three sets of drums and several types of cymbals; a rack of things that looked like kids' rattles; three electronic pianos and organs; a series of bells, xylophones, and glockenspiels; and a white baby grand with the Bechstein logo above the keys. There was a body in a spreading wet circle in front of one case of instruments and a larger wet place in the carpet near her, the dampness extending beyond the taped outlines applied by the local LEOs.

"Stella Mae Ragel," T. Laine said, identifying the DB.

I walked closer to the body and paused before taking three steps back. I did not need to see it again. It reminded me of bodies pulled from rivers, the skin slipping away from gooey, almost soapy tissue beneath.

Avoiding the wet spots, my bio-suited feet *shushing* on carpet that puffed with dust, I moved to the wide double French doors and partially opened the closed shades that covered the multipaned windows. Beyond the doors was a pea-gravel drive. I pretended to study the view, though that was more to give myself time to process what I had seen than to look out. Beyond the glass-paned doors I could see part of the barn, a large watering trough, the horse walking machine, and a length of four-board white-wood post-and-rail fencing. There was also what looked like a swimming pool with a horse in it, and two young girls standing on the cement edge, attending it.

The horses had a swimming pool. I shook my head.

Five teenage girls were sitting on top of the fence, watching the house. I made a mental note to get their names, get the names of everyone in or near the house in the last two days since Stella Mae got home from her tour.

With my stomach back under control, I closed the blinds and rejoined T. Laine, who was still standing near the body. It looked as if it had been dead for days, maybe lying in a steam room. She was wearing a three-quarter-sleeved T-shirt and jeans and was lying facedown, her hands under her torso as if she had tried to catch herself when she collapsed. The flesh I could see was at the neck, jaw, one elbow, the bottoms of her bare feet, and her dried crinkled hair. The body was swollen, stretched, dark with lividity, the skin bubbly under the surface. I couldn't see her face and I was glad of that.

I took one last look at the body and turned away, sucked on the mint. Tried not to breathe. Tried not to see the body on the back of my eyelids every time I blinked.

Pointing at the tape outline and the wet carpet, T. Laine said, "The housekeeper was there. Sound booths and production room are this way."

Breathing through the handkerchief in my mask, I followed her to the side and saw two tiny booths, not much bigger than my new shower at home, with a single metal chair, microphones, music stands, and headphones. A third room was larger, with a drum set and an electronic keyboard inside. Across from them was a room with a computer and a board with switches, sliders, and knobs, like I had seen on TV, except smaller and more compact.

Reading my mind, T. Laine said, "Brand-new soundboard with all the electronic bells and whistles, installed while Stella

was on tour. The bath was upgraded too—Carrera marble all
the way. The carpet in this entire lower level is spanking new,
created specifically for deadening sound."

"It's awful dusty."

"No. It's disintegrating."

"Oh. Okay." I thought about the site and how much we didn't
know. "So people were in here while she was gone? Doing construction?"

"Yes. Dozens. They finished two weeks ago. I'm trying to
get a list and find out if any of the construction crew are sick or
missing, if anyone was a practitioner of some kind of arcane
arts. The other body and the tour swag are in here."

I still didn't understand what swag was, but I followed T.
Laine to the open door of a storage room, where she put out an
arm to block my way. The stench that boiled out was worse than
that in the main studio area. "The deputies got still shots, which
I've uploaded to the case file, but we don't need to spend time
in there unnecessarily, even with the null pens."

"Oh," I said again. I managed to swallow my tongue back
into place and not embarrass myself by vomiting like a probie.
"Yes. I see why."

From the entrance I could see rusty metal racks with a few
electronic gadgets on them, a rack of small speakers printed
with a guitar and Stella's name in a fancy font, a few hats and
belt buckles with the same logo. On the far side of the room
were a stack of flattened empty boxes and three half-empty
boxes, each marked with shipping labels. In the middle of the
floor was one large box filled with T-shirts. Except for the T-
shirt box, the room had a depleted feel, as if the band had sold
all the goodies that might have been stored here before the tour.

I forced my eyes down to the dead woman on the floor. She
was on her side beside the T-shirt box, the words *Merry Promotions* printed on the sides. One hand was draped up over the box
edge, holding a handful of shirts. She was wearing a short-
sleeved dress and the arm I could see appeared to be covered
with small greenish soap bubbles spread across the muscles.
The bones in her green-fleshed hand were exposed where she
still gripped a handful of shirts, though the shirts seemed fine,
not rotted. Her face was awful. Her mouth was pulled away
from her teeth, her gums blackened. Her eyes were whited out,

like small boiled eggs, but leaking greenish bubbles. Her legs looked damp and pale and were lined with reddish lividity on top and much darker purplish lividity below, where gravity had pulled the blood down.

"I wish I could try a reversed *hedge* working around the bodies," T. Laine said, "but the Knoxville covens are still not answering my calls and I can't do much alone."

While some of the witches were not averse to helping us, the leaders of the Knoxville covens were no longer agreeable to helping PsyLED. Not that I blamed them. I asked, "What would happen to the bodies if we got them into the null room at HQ?"

"I don't know. I did toss a null pen into the cooler with the one DB we got out of here. If there's anything left inside when the transport vehicle gets to UTMC, we'll try sending the others." She considered and added, "If the transport vehicle makes it."

A finger on the body twitched. It was not an indication of life or zombification. I knew that. It was still creepy and gross. And the smell was suddenly worse, overpowering the mentholated salve on the handkerchief. "You think the vehicle will be affected by the energies?" I asked, pressing the mask and the hankie inside it around my lower face. Which was doing nothing at all against the rot stench. I sucked on the mint, but my mouth was coated by the stink in the air.

"It's possible. The carpet under the bodies is rotted through. The bottom of that box is showing signs of disintegration. The piano's finish is crackling and the lid over the strings, or whatever you call it, is split. The guitars closest to this room are falling apart."

I glanced back and saw the destruction I hadn't detected until she mentioned it. One guitar body had separated from the neck and was hanging by the strings. There were half a dozen guitars hanging near it, all showing signs of dry rot. The percussion equipment was dull and powdery looking. I remembered the RVs out back. The purpose of the band and crew lunch had been to unpack the tour gear. That probably meant there were more instruments and equipment out there. "Did you say the deputies got photos of the room earlier?"

"Yeah." T. Laine's jaw tightened. "The piano and the guitars looked fine when they arrived. Come on. Let's get out of here. Even with null pens we've been in here long enough."

As we walked back upstairs, a tension I hadn't noticed fell away from my shoulders. I guessed it was death energies pushing on me, but it didn't feel like witch magic. It felt scratchy and cold and odd, but not in a way I could put words to.

On the landing, we changed out of the blue unis and put the contaminated gear into the disposal bins for crime scene workup. I returned the null pen to T. Laine and tucked the handkerchief into my pocket for later use. I crunched the mint and let the flavor flood my dry mouth.

As we climbed the last steps, T. Laine asked, "You glad to be out of the office and away from the search for the Blood Tarot deck?"

"Until I got a whiff a this place, I was. Now, not so much." I pulled my jacket lapel out and took a sniff. "I don't think I'll ever get the smell out of these clothes. I might have to burn 'em and that goes against the grain for a ch— for me." I'd almost said "for a churchwoman," but I wasn't one a them anymore. "But yeah. I'm happy to stop the Blood Tarot search for a while. Don't tell JoJo, but it's boring."

JoJo Jones, the special agent who sent me here, was the unit's second in command and our highly prized former hacker. Or not-so-former, sometimes. JoJo loved research better than anything else in life.

The Blood Tarot was one of three black magic tarot decks known to be in existence and it had been missing since our last big case, possibly destroyed. Possibly not. We hadn't been able to prove either possibility, and it was too powerful an object to be forgotten, out there, somewhere, tempting someone to use it. I wasn't having any luck locating it in a pawnshop, on the Internet, on the dark web, or on the magical black market.

In the kitchen, someone had made a pot of coffee in Stella's fancy Braun. It was probably against regs to make and drink coffee in a victim's house, but it smelled fresh and there were stacks of paper cups to the side, so I took that as an invitation. I slid a paper cup out of the plastic sleeve and poured coffee. The effect of the mint was gone and I needed to get the taste of rot out of my mouth and breathing passages. T. Laine and Occam, who had been talking to the uniform guarding the door, poured cups too. The uniform, a different deputy from the sheriff's cousin, was a substantial black man in his fifties. He took a cup and went outside to talk to someone approaching the house.

I sipped, breathing the rich scent, and leaned my back against the edge of the fancy stone countertop. Only the sound of murmuring voices disturbed the quiet of the house. Every time I blinked, I saw the soapy greenish flesh and the bones in the hand holding the black tour T-shirts screen-printed with white and scarlet in words and images.

In spite of the death, the afternoon sun was warm through the windows and there was an illusion of peace in the kitchen. Two people sat on the sofa in the gathering room, their heads together, speaking softly. I rose up on my toes and made out two young, tattooed white women with spiky rainbow-colored hair, wearing trashed jeans and sweatshirts. They had been crying, their makeup smeared and faces chapped.

In a mutter, T. Laine said, "Okay. Five-minute break's over. I originally requested this site be treated as if it was a level three biohazard/spelled site, but I didn't get to follow through. Since the site didn't read like typical witch *death* energies, and because I couldn't *prove* it was a crime scene and not an accident, and since the family had driven up and were demanding access to the premises, the sheriff elected to downgrade it to level two."

"Family? Where?" I asked, looking at the two women.

"Outside for now," Occam said. "In Stella's RV, which I cleared and released to them, per FireWind."

"He's taking a strange interest in this case," I said.

"He's a fan," T. Laine said, shaking her head. "I'd never have guessed. Anyway, whatever is causing this accelerated decomp isn't decelerating like I expected, probably because I was treating it like witch magic and it isn't. I may have to pull rank on the sheriff and upgrade the threat level. Thoughts?"

"I'm leaning toward an upgrade," Occam said. "At this rate, with the accelerated decay, I doubt we'll even get PMs. I—"

The two women on the couch slumped and toppled over. I dropped the cup on the counter. At a dead run, I leaped for the women. T. Laine snagged my shoulder and yanked me back. "No!"

"But—"

"No! They're with the band. Backup singers." Meaning they

might be contaminated with something we couldn't see. "They were downstairs when the LEOs arrived," T. Laine said, "without null pens to mitigate the . . . hell. The *death whatever-this-is*."

"Right," I said, my heart feeling like it might bust outta my chest. "*Death whatever.* We have to call it something."

T. Laine gave us each a null pen and we approached the women slowly, keeping a good ten feet away. The women were unconscious, barely breathing. A door to our right rammed open and a man stumbled into the kitchen from a set of stairs leading to the second story. He reeled against the wall, bounded off, and fell.

Lainie grabbed Occam's shoulder and my wrist, shoving, backing us out of the gathering room. She shouted, "Clear the house! Clear the house! Level five containment protocol. Clear the house! Clear the house! Level five containment protocol. We got a problem, people!" To us she said, "The locals locked down only the crime scene, not the upper floors, so people on Stella's approved list have been up and down for hours. Stupid star-struck sheriff."

Law enforcement officers boiled out of the hallway leading to the basement and rushed outside. Standing to the side of the door as people raced past, T. Laine said, "I want everyone quarantined. I have a feeling this is getting worse instead of better."

Three more civilians rushed down the stairs from the second story and T. Laine called out, "Special Agent Kent, PsyLED. Outside, all of you. Occam, keep them together and don't let anyone leave, law enforcement included. Nell," she shouted, though I was right beside her, "get the quarantine tents out of my vehicle." She placed her keys into my hand and said softly, "I'm calling FireWind for an ETA, and to bring a warrant for the entire house. The locals only got one for the basement, which was stupid beyond stupid," she practically spat. "I want full access and a full crew."

"You won't get LaFleur and Racer," Occam said. "They're still in Chattanooga."

T. Laine cursed. "You!" She yelled and pointed at a woman in a sheriff's deputy uniform. "Get a team together and clear the house. Wear gloves. Touch *no* one, *no* thing, not one person, with your bare skin, not a doorknob or chair, no matter what, and get out fast. I want to make absolutely certain this place is empty."

"Yes, ma'am," she said and started issuing orders.

"We need a null room on-site," T. Laine said. "I have some calls in to find—"

Outside, a man hit the ground. Then another. T. Laine raced to the door and whispered, "Those two. They weren't here when the bodies were discovered, but they did go down to get a look before the local law got here." She turned and stared into the room, her eyes focused on something terrible that only she could see. "It's not decelerating," she repeated, her tired face growing even paler. "It's growing."

The victim list was now nine dead or down, and I wondered if the entire crew who had traveled with Stella on the tour had been affected by the *death whatever*. I had no idea how T. Laine would contain the energies and help the victims, but her being in charge of that meant the investigation was on Occam and me. I still had no idea why the überboss wanted me here, but for now, I needed to work.

TWO

More bodies fell, all of them people associated with the band or who had been in the basement. Some were struggling to breathe; some were unconscious. "Leave 'em where they lay," T. Laine shouted, racing outside, her hands and body position suggesting that she was using a *seeing* working to explore the magical energies around the house and the victims. "A portable null room is on the way."

"But they need our help," an EMT said, his eyes tracking the victims lying on the lawn.

"Not until we know what we're dealing with," T. Laine said, "and not without responders wearing blue unis." She pointed at Sheriff Jackett. "This thing seems to be expanding and growing, not decreasing. Maybe even jumping from victim to victim. I'll cover them all with null blue aprons, but keep your people away or you can deal with this on your own. I swear to God, you make my job any harder and I'll leave." Which was a lie, but the sheriff didn't know that.

"Why not just give EMTs unis and one a them null pens and let them help?" the sheriff asked.

"The null pens all need to be recharged except for two, and I'm low on unis," she said. "Without a null room, we have a bigger disaster in the making."

He gave a slant-eyed grunt. "Roger that. Back off, people," he said, louder.

T. Laine looked at me and murmured, just for my ears, "I pray to God I really do have a null room on the way. I haven't heard back from the North Nashville coven, but rumor says they have a portable one."

Running into the face of danger was second nature to first

responders, but so was using the correct equipment so they didn't end up making things worse. As long as more help was coming they were willing to wait.

The first responders watching, T. Laine and Occam dressed out in fresh blue unis and started quartering the yard, covering the victims with blue aprons made of the same materials and coated with the same spells as the unis. Together, they turned victims on their sides, leaving bottles of water with the ones who were conscious, pulling them into shelter as quickly as I got the tents up.

Making trips, sweating, I carried the heavy quarantine tents to the backyard and the deputy who was the sheriff's family—Alvin Hembest—and some of the local LEOs helped me assemble them. The tents were a simple design, but erecting them wasn't a one-person job. I shed my jacket, pulled my springy hair back in an elastic, and put a baseball hat over it. I still sweated through raising three tents, the late fall sun bringing the temp to a humid high eighties. My small team and I also set up awnings and inflated air mattresses, covering them with disposable plastic sheets from the county's biohazard unit. It was a huge van supplied with everything, even a water tank and outdoor shower for washing down contaminated victims. But the county had extremely limited supplies for paranormal contamination, and showering couldn't wash away the effects of weird magics.

T. Laine would have made a great general, giving orders and dividing up supplies. Once all the victims were covered, and the conscious band members dressed in biohazard unis, she assigned four to a tent in a sort of triage, giving her limited, nearly drained null pens to the ones who appeared to be the sickest. Once she had the site as safe as she could make it, she let the first responders dress out in her dwindling supply of unis and render aid. They started oxygen and IVs and took blood pressures.

She assigned Alvin and me to start a database record of the victims and their symptoms and where they had been, and when, from the time they arrived at Stella's house. We used paper pads because I was afraid the *death whatever* energies could potentially ruin electronics. They would rot paper too, but we could take pics of our notes later, giving us backup.

As more and more emergency vehicles rolled in, many from surrounding counties, the local citizens kicked in, dropping off food and supplies at the gate: hot coffee and donuts came from a coffee shop and bakery, a local convenience store donated drinks and ice, a church delivered fried chicken and fixin's from a local Krispy Krunchy Chicken. A portable toilet was offered by a contractor but wasn't needed because there was a human-bathroom in the barn. A pharmacy provided sunscreen, bug spray, tubes of lip protection, Tylenol, Tums, and assorted such things. Bags of chips and protein bars were delivered from a local grocery. Another church delivered bottled water, bleach, paper towels, and toilet paper. Bringing in food and supplies was good advertising for the local stores and churches, as the media sent out footage to the entire nation. Stella Mae Ragel was a national treasure.

Her death also meant unwanted publicity for anyone who got into camera range. Except for the time I erected tents, I kept my jacket on, a unit baseball hat on, and my face turned away from drones and telescopic camera lenses.

Once the quarantine tents were set up and full of people, Alvin and I took a break. Sitting on the steps to the side porch, we drank water and shared a bag of pretzels. Nearby, T. Laine begged for help from Tennessee's witches, calling from her super-secret witch databank. Ending one especially frustrating call, she muttered, cussing under her breath.

Alvin said softly, "I feel sorry for her. Purdy li'l thing like that, having to be in charge of all this."

"Alvin. You do know she does this all the time. It's her job. She loves it. She's good at it." When he looked puzzled, I said, "She isn't doing this job to snag a husband, quit work, and raise babies."

He looked truly confused. "Every woman wants babies."

I closed my eyes. Breathed. Though I feared the stupid might be in the air, something contagious. "No. They don't. Lots of women don't want kids."

"Well, sheeeit. These modern women jist don't make no

sense." He shook his head and looked over my shoulder. "Incoming," he said.

I looked where his eyes led, to see Sheriff Jackett striding toward us, between us, and up to Unit Eighteen's witch. T. Laine had just dropped into a chair on the side porch, frustrated, tired, and worried, pinching the bridge of her nose between two fingers, eyes closed. "I want access to that basement," he demanded.

T. Laine dropped her hand and looked up at the sheriff. She said nothing. I had a feeling she was counting to a hundred. Or mentally using the sheriff as target practice for ninja throwing knives. "Oh?" she said.

"Wiggle your nose or blink hard or whatever you do. But make it safe to enter. We need our crime scene."

It was an insult based on old TV shows. Softly, T. Laine said, "Really." Her face was cold, expressionless.

"I can't see that you're doing anything at all but wasting my time."

Occam, sensing or hearing the ruckus, appeared from a tent and ambled closer. Unit Eighteen closing ranks.

Lainie stood and pocketed all her null pens. Every face in the yard was turned to her, waiting as she arranged things in her pockets to her satisfaction. I couldn't see Jackett's face, but his body language suggested he was getting riled. Ruminatively, T. Laine said, "While you've been running around glad-handing, getting ready for the next election, and chatting with the press despite your own gag order, I've been evaluating the efficacy of the spelled unis and the null pens against the things happening in the basement. I think I'm close to a conclusion, but I'm not there yet. You got spelled unis? No. You got null pens? No. You don't. So, go on in, but you and your deputies go in without my gear. Which means your people may die. Otherwise, you'll wait on my evaluation. Now. Get outta my face and take your insulting witch comments, and let me do my job." T. Laine pushed past Jackett and gestured to Occam and to me.

We met in the grassy area and I said, "You are my hero." It was something I'd heard people on TV say to anyone who stood up to unfairness.

T. Laine blew out her frustration. "I look like I'm wasting time, but I'm taking readings every five minutes. Which is what

I should have told him instead of mouthing off." She shook her head. "Men like that push my buttons. Anyway. It looks as if the unis and null pens, when used together, create a narrow circle of protection around the wearer/holder. But the pens drain fast and need a three-person coven to recharge them, which I don't have, and I'm down to one box of unis. I haven't yet determined how wide the protection is, if it totally encircles the wearer, how long the protection lasts, and how much gets through to responders the closer we get to the victims and the bodies. I'm thinking about limiting access to the patients and the basement to twenty minutes, with a sixty-minute break between stints, unis hanging in the sunlight, to reduce recontamination. Then, after sixty minutes total in the house or with victims, the wearer and his gear have to spend time in the null room. If it ever gets here."

"The North Nashville coven said yes to bringing a null room here?" I asked.

"Yes. But now I can't raise them on their cells, so I don't know what to do next or if help is really coming."

I said, "Maybe pulling a null room messes with the signal?"

"A better answer than them not coming." She took a deep breath, pulled a water bottle from a pocket of her uni, and drank it down. "And I have to keep everyone away from the basement until I know I have a way to treat their contamination. Stupid-ass sheriff."

"Your plan sounds good," Occam drawled. "Sounds like the appropriate thing to do, if not the politically correct way to do it."

T. Laine made that breathy irritated sound again. "Politically correct? Are you saying I need to apologize?"

"Hell no. He was an ass."

T. Laine grinned and looked at me. "You got a good one here."

Occam propped his hands on his hips and agreed. "I am a right fine specimen of manhood."

T. Laine gave a soft snort.

I fought a smile, looking down at my hands, clasped in front of me. Occam was . . . Occam was my cat-man. Accent on the word *my*.

"Jackett," T. Laine called out. "I have a compromise between speed and safety."

Jackett ambled over, his face saying he wasn't sure how to act but didn't want to look as if he was being difficult *or* as if he was giving in to a federal cop and witch.

"The unis we've been using," T. Laine said, "are antispelled unis made by the Seattle coven especially for law enforcement and crime scene techs at paranormal hazardous crime scene sites. They are expensive and hard to come by. We went through an entire yearly supply of them on the last big case we worked and after today, I'm dangerously low. I have twenty null pens and they drain fast. I need a coven to recharge them, and before you ask, no, they can't be charged with electricity. Your agency does not have access to a coven, correct?"

"Correct. I'm listening," Jackett said.

"I've determined the most likely time parameters to keep the gear working and the people safe." She explained the time on, time off, and time in a null room protocol. "That's based on us having access to a portable null room, which is supposed to be on its way from Nashville. If it doesn't arrive, then your people will have to drive to PsyLED Knoxville and sit in ours, according to the protocol I've outlined."

Jackett nodded, still listening.

"While we're talking supplies, equipment use is specified and coded by budgetary demands. PsyLED's eastern regional director is talking to the governor to declare this an emergency, which will free up people and equipment, but I haven't heard back and I need to order and overnight more unis and equipment for this scene. We need to talk jurisdiction and money."

I was inordinately proud of T. Laine, standing up to male authority figures without getting all prickly. I wanted to give her a hug, but I figured that should wait.

Jackett looked out over the property, clearly seeing a high-profile situation he wanted to be part of but didn't have the resources to handle. He frowned, thinking. "I ain't ready to turn over full jurisdiction just yet. Hell, my own investigators ain't even sure this is a crime, and my hazardous materials response team ain't sure what this is either. Let's keep working together. I got a budgetary line item for paranormal investigations I can put toward the supplies. It's never been used, since we don't have witches or weres or fangheads in this county." His tone said that made his county superior to others.

T. Laine took a slow breath, holding back her annoyance. "Fine. Here's my deal. You reimburse PsyLED Unit Eighteen for the unis your people wear and the cost to recharge the null pens they use, you agree to make sure your people spend the proper amount of time in a null room, no matter where they have to go, and you can get in there."

Jackett rubbed his chin as if it itched. "That's agreeable to me. Send me a text with the itemized costs. I'll approve it and get the paperwork to your HQ. If it does become a federal PsyLED case, I'll eat the cost of unis used now and during the paperwork transition." He dropped his hand. "And I'm sorry I used inappropriate words about the witch situation. One of my deputies informed me why they were ill chosen."

T. Laine took a moment to let the words sink in between them. Stiffly, she said, "Sorry I mouthed off. I don't know what these energies are, and I need to make sure all our people are safe." She stuck out a hand. They shook. "Oh," she said. "No electronics inside. I can't protect them."

Jackett nodded agreement before he turned and started shouting orders. To us, T. Laine said, "And that, boys and girls, is how to smooth troubled waters and ruffled feathers, lessons courtesy of SWAT's Gonzales." I wasn't sure who had soothed who, but I didn't disagree.

Two deputies, who had already been inside and knew the protocol, requested gear and null pens. Dressed out, they started manual timers, as opposed to electronic ones, and went inside. The stench in the house puffed out each time the door opened, and I reapplied mentholated rub to my handkerchief and kept it folded inside my shirt collar.

Around us flies buzzed, the biting kind, and the sun beat down, making me miserable. At least the sound of horses and birds in the distance was pleasant.

I still didn't know exactly why I was here, but I knew how to make myself useful. Sitting on a deck chair in the shade behind the house, I expanded my database, this time on my laptop, exporting it every few minutes to HQ in case the paranormal energies of *death whatever* messed with the electronics. Along with Occam, I initiated prelim interviews with the victims who were still conscious, and stayed out of the way of the paramedics.

* * *

By midafternoon, the sickest victims had been transported to UTMC for evaluation and treatment, we had indications that time in HQ's null room had helped mitigate the two cops' minor symptoms, and the media furor had reached a fever pitch. Rumors that witches had attacked Stella Mae were rampant. Photos taken by some of the band members were making their way to the Internet and going viral. Public hysteria was building. And we still had little idea what was really happening.

As we worked, Alvin kept a sharp eye out and caught two reporters sneaking in through the back acreage. They were arrested on trespassing charges, but the arrests did nothing to stem the tide of nosiness. More and more media vehicles were lining the road out front. At one point, I counted six drones and two helicopters filming overhead.

Most importantly, the Nashville witch coven finally showed up, two cars and a van pulling a cargo trailer down the road. The trailer was the portable null room, which the LEOs, the paramedics, and the remaining human victims on-site needed badly. T. Laine had to request a police escort to get the witches onto the grounds, but their faces were apparently known to the locals because their movements were followed by a Primitive Baptist preacher with a bullhorn.

The preacher seemed to feel he had a right to give everyone migraines while he assigned every soul but his own to hell. He was stopped at the entrance to the drive and turned back, but even so, things weren't copacetic with the witches, and the media drones were making sure everything went out to the public.

I watched as they pulled up, parked in the middle of the driveway, got out, and—in unison—slammed their vehicle doors. They were all wearing long black skirts and black shirts, like tropes out of a novel about witches. There wasn't a smile in place as they spread out in a semicircle across the lawn, seven of them, a good number for a coven. They approached the house and the quarantine tents like hunters flushing game. They seemed to have a collective mad on, their eyes taking in everything from the tents to the victims in the unis to the law enforcement types, who were watching them back with penetrating curiosity and a measure of hostility.

I moved closer to get a better view and ended up near Officer Alvin Hembest, who stood with one hand on the butt of his service weapon. It wasn't a very calming stance, and it was echoed by the other LEOs. Putnam County and the surrounding environs appeared unwelcoming to the witches who'd come to save them.

When the witches stopped, every eye was on them and the officers were silent, watchful. The witch in the middle was a short woman with shoulders like a linebacker. She was clearly the leader, and she raised her voice, shouting, "Why should we help you, when you took one of ours into custody?"

"One of yours is in custody?" T. Laine asked, her tone practical and her volume moderated. Though she surely knew the answer to her own question.

"Catriona Doyle," the leader said. "The FBI took her into custody as a person of interest and they won't let us see her. The agent sent social services to pick up her kid. *At school.* Her *child* has been remanded into the system instead of to her sister or to one of *us.*"

"The child's other parent?" T. Laine asked.

"We've attempted to notify the child's father, but he and his second wife are on a documentary photoshoot somewhere in the Australian outback. Doyle's sister showed social services notarized papers giving her custody in the event of problems. Social services and the FBI refused to even look at them."

"Sheriff Jackett," T. Laine said, without looking away from the witches. "You know anything about that?"

"I don't, Special Agent Kent. The FBI shares office space with the Cookeville PD. The chief agreed this scene was outside his jurisdiction, and he left around noon," Jackett drawled, his voice a familiar-sounding Tennessee cadence. "I'll find out what's happ'nin', but I got to say, what the witch is describing is all by the book. It ain't uncommon to hold a person of interest and, according to established protocol, to make sure any children are safe for the duration. Social services will hold a custodial ruling as soon as possible and see that the child is returned to the rightful family member, but short term, the safe place is with a foster home."

"I don't think so," the leader said. "Foster homes are notoriously dangerous, especially to children of witches."

"It's protocol, ma'am," the sheriff said, his tone composed and unemotional.

"Really?" T. Laine said. "Protocol can be interpreted. This sounds like extreme measures to me. Measures that might suggest Catriona is dangerous just for being a witch, measures that would pit the magic workers we need at this scene against us in law enforcement, at a particularly bad time. We are not looking at a *death* working or curse. You aren't even certain that this isn't an accident of some sort. Catriona isn't a death witch, so she isn't a suspect."

"Maybe, maybe not," Jackett said, equably. "I ain't here to argue. But in the interest of interspecies harmony, I can make a call."

"We aren't different spe—" she started.

Occam stepped up to the sheriff, all man-to-man, a hand on the older man's shoulder. The change in the sheriff's demeanor was immediate: his shoulders relaxed and his face lost the hardness he'd worn when watching all the womenfolk.

I'd seen just that reaction among churchmen. Fear of women created a need to control them, especially among weak men who didn't know their place in the world and feared anything that might take their little bit of power from them. T. Laine's eyes went narrow and hard at the obvious body language. Occam's tactics would not have worked for a woman. Had Lainie stepped up all backslapping bonhomie, a man like Jackett would have been put off. Of course, had Jackett been a woman, Lainie might have had the best results. Sexism was a peculiar thing.

Occam pulled Jackett back into our little group and said, "From what I've heard of him, FBI Senior Special Agent Macauley Smythe is a racist, a misogynist, and a witch hater. Everybody here knows it. Most all your people saw it when he handcuffed the witch in question and hauled her away. He was not gentle. He enjoyed it a mite too much." Occam looked around, as if to point out the numbers of people who had seen the unprofessional and unnecessary tactics. "I think you might want to do more than *call* the chief of police and the FBI office. Maybe you would consider a personal appearance and make sure nothing untoward is happenin' to Catriona Doyle, a woman currently living in your county. A citizen of Ireland, with rights under U.S. and international law. A citizen protected by her

embassy. Your cooperation and assistance might make the
Nashville witches a tad more willing to assist us. And we *do*
need their assistance to keep all your people and our people and
the civilian victims here alive."

Jackett was a middle-aged man with a paunch that moved
when he took a deep breath. He didn't look happy at being maneuvered into doing anything to help the witches, but sheriffs
are political beings. They want to keep the voting public happy
and anything that got in the way of finding Stella Mae's killer
would be bad for Jackett's future occupational and happiness
factor. "I reckon I can do that for you'uns."

I jerked at the familiar church-speak, but no one else seemed
to notice.

"And woe betide the man or woman who harms her or her
child," the coven leader said, loud enough to be heard.

"That a threat?" Jackett called back, not sounding as though
a threat would bother him much.

"Never," the witch said. But the smile she sent the sheriff
said otherwise.

Sheriff Jackett hesitated, watching the witch, before he pulled
his key fob from a pocket and walked to his car. No one spoke
as the official vehicle departed. Into the uncomfortable silence,
T. Laine stepped forward and extended her hand to the coven
leader. Softly she said, "Special Agent T. Laine Kent, of the Kent
witch clan."

"I didn't think they let witches in to PsyLED."

"I was one of the first."

The coven leader made a humming noise, then took her
hand, and the two women shook. "Astrid Grainger, of the
Grainger clan, coven leader of the North Nashville coven."

"We can use some help," T. Laine said. "And that null room
you trailered in is desperately needed." Gesturing us to the side,
Lainie lowered her voice and we all gathered around her as she
filled the coven in on the situation. She ended with, "I can't
guarantee full funding for your services, but I can guarantee
you great PR."

Astrid gave a mighty frown and T. Laine pushed on, fast.
"You need something to work past the long-standing witch pho-
bia in the rural parts of this state. This case could be it. It's
garnered national media attention and, if witches are part of

solving it, part of saving the victims and deputies, you'll be heroes. We need you. The site's not reading like witch energies and we don't know what it is or, frankly, if there's even been a crime committed. Needless to say, that part can't reach the media. Not yet."

Astrid Grainger made a harrumphing sound that conveyed a sour acceptance of what couldn't be changed, but her shoulders relaxed. "First let's set up a circle and recharge the null room, which it needs after travel. Then we'll see if we can spot anything clinging to the humans." She waved her arm at the band members peering out of tents. "They'll have to remove the null suits and aprons. If something magical's clinging to them, we can then decide if a stay in the null room would help or make things worse. And then we can recharge the null pens, if you know the working."

"I do." T. Laine pointed to a flat place on the back lawn, away from potential horse droppings, a spot that would make overviewing by drones difficult. "Circle there?"

"Good," Astrid said. "I'll take two of my people and recharge the null room trailer. Etain," she said, louder, "get the chalk, the chalk spreader, and the implements."

"Aye," one of the witches said. With the single word, I knew she wasn't from around here. "String and stick, bell and candle too?" She was Irish. I had never met an Irish person before and I loved the way the lyrical sounds fell from her mouth. She had freckles the color of light brown sugar, pale skin, and straight brown hair with just a hint of red. She was wearing a black Stella Mae tour T-shirt, with the white and scarlet logo of a silhouetted Stella Mae and her guitar on front and the tour dates and cities on the back.

Astrid waved a hand in a *whatever* motion and, except for Etain, the witches followed her away. I bent back to the timeline database I was building. There were dozens of names already attached to the potential crime scene. One of the pitfalls of Unit Eighteen covering such a large region was that we didn't know the law enforcement officials or the microculture of the small towns we visited on official business and we were always playing catch-up. It meant starting from scratch with each out-of-town case. Databases were the stuff that kept us on top of cases.

"Ingram. Hang on," Occam called out, loping from the direction of the barn. I hadn't even noticed he had slipped away. Cat stealth, cat grace. He looked so much better than he had. Hunting every full moon on Soulwood meant each time he shifted back to human he was more healed. "We got company," he murmured. He nodded his head toward the car moving slowly up the drive. "One of the deputies says that's FBI from the local office. Evidently he was here with the feeb senior special agent earlier."

"Then he'll know about ma sister," Etain said, stepping away from Astrid's trunk, her face going hard.

He was driving an older-model government car, a skinny black man with close-cropped dark hair, a thin mustache, and a goatee shaped like an arrowhead pointing at his chest. The door opened and he lifted a hand in a wave as he left the vehicle. He looked fit, determined, and tense as he strode to Occam and me, perhaps because of the way the deputies on-site were watching the newcomer. Like he was dangerous. Or particularly unwelcome.

Etain, Occam, and I met the new arrival in the open area between the parking and the house. The tall man extended his FBI ID. "Special Agent Gerry Stapp, FBI."

"Special Agent Occam, PsyLED." Occam thumbed at me. "Special Agent Ingram, PsyLED."

"Nell," I said, smiling, because Stapp looked nervous and I wanted to put him at ease in case his nervousness was due to us being Unit Eighteen, the only PsyLED unit known to be mostly paranormals.

"Etain Doyle," the Irish witch said. "Catriona Doyle is ma sister and you people took her." Etain's voice went higher. "And you kidnapped her child."

"If you'll excuse us, ma'am," Gerry said to Etain, "I need to speak with the special agents."

"I'll be staying right here, unless you plan to cart me away too." When Stapp started to protest, she raised her chin and added, "You send me away, I'll cast a *hearing* workin' and listen in anyway."

I hadn't known that was possible, but it made sense. I wondered if the media had witches capable of that particular magic. That would be bad. I dragged my attention to Gerry.

None of us shook hands. Gerry looked over our shoulders at

the other law enforcement officers before returning his attention to us. "I'm sorry about your sister being taken in," he said softly to Etain. "It wasn't my idea. And I didn't know about the child until it was too late."

To Occam and me, he said, "I don't have much time, so listen fast." His words were rapid and low, so his voice didn't carry. "I'm here to cause trouble and make a stink, per orders of the senior special agent, Macauley Smythe. In a minute I'm going to act like an ass and you're going to tell me to go to hell."

"Why's that?" I asked. "Why are you going to make a stink?"

Still soft and fast, he said, "Because Smythe is my boss and he said to. I toe the line for two more months until he formally retires. Everyone knows he hates anyone who's not just like him. I'm black, I'm gay, he hates me, and he likes making my life a living hell. And before you tell me to write him up, his sleeve is checkered with racist incidents, use-of-force violations, and, way back when, at least one witness-tampering incident. He was always reprimanded up and promoted into a more rural sector. Either no one cares what he does or he has a protector up-line. These days, he has illusions of an easy retirement as a county sheriff or PD chief around here. Anything he can do to stymie your investigation and make the witches look responsible, he'll do. Two months more and I can take over this office and make things right, so I'm following orders." He made a little snorting laugh. "And because I've heard that Unit Eighteen are mostly paras, I'm hoping that will keep you from reporting me for talking against my up-line. That enough reasons?"

"Not gonna happen!" Occam said loudly, stepping between Gerry and the onlooking LEOs. He bunched his fists and stuck his head forward, for all the world as if he was mad. I hadn't known he could act that well and a little churchwoman voice inside my head called it lying. I knew it wasn't lying. But my brain and my history didn't.

"We have Catriona and you have the property," Stapp said, loudly. "Smythe wants info. He wants this site and he wants PsyLED off it."

"Not gonna happen," Occam said again. "He isn't equipped to work it up."

"And no one is gonna be able to work it wit'out us," Etain said, joining the play. "I can feel the bizarre energies through ma boots."

I slid a look her way. I had felt nothing. But then, I hadn't tried, not with so many people around.

"He'll keep you from Catriona Doyle no matter what it takes," Stapp said. Softer he added, "He's started on the paperwork to charge her with multiple counts of first-degree murder by magical means. Whoever you have up-line needs to get on this now, not tonight, not tomorrow. *Now*. Before he can push the paperwork through. Before it hits the media."

"Even if it gets thrown out, if he gets an arrest this early in the investigation, the media firestorm would be huge," Occam said, his eyes moving to the road where the news vans were parked.

"It's already huge and Smythe intends to fan the flames," Stapp said.

"I'll curse him and turn his pecker into a toad," Etain said. She had an impish face, but she looked anything but cute now. She looked dangerous.

"You can do that?" I asked.

"No. But he doesna know't."

"No threats," Gerry said. "Anything you do along that line will play into his hands. Get someone up to Cookeville, to the city police department at the corner of East Broad Street and Walnut Avenue." He raised his voice. "This is our site! Paras can't fairly and honestly investigate a crime committed by paras against good, God-fearing people like Stella Mae Ragel. That's a job for humans."

"The sheriff is on the way into town now to intervene," Occam said quietly.

"Not enough," Gerry said just as softly. "You need to be able to pull rank hard and fast."

"You ain't getting to pull lead on this one, Feeb," Occam said, loudly. "And anyway, from what I understand, Smythe's mama was a *witch*. So what makes him any more capable?"

I managed to keep the surprise off my face. How had Occam learned that? And then I realized he was still lying and planting seeds to discredit Smythe. It was quick-thinking and mean and . . . and the churchwoman voice shut up. The new me, the

PsyLED special agent me, kinda liked it. I raised my eyebrows in approval at my cat-man. His lips twitched.

"A witch?" Gerry said, sounding stunned.

Occam said, still loud enough to carry clearly, "We'll provide interdepartmental cooperation when and if we get access to Catriona Doyle."

"And have you paras prep her? Ain't happening."

"We'll get the PsyLED special agent in charge of the eastern U.S., Ayatas FireWind, involved," I said quietly. "He'll provide pushback."

"Hope it's not too late," the feeb said softly. Gerry Stapp turned on a heel and strode back to his car, the epitome of outrage.

Etain said, "Him I like. He's a right sneaky bastard." She slanted her eyes to Occam. "So are you, cowboy. You happen to be available tonight?"

I flinched at what sounded as if she was asking him for a date, but she went on.

"I could use help to kidnap ma niece back and break ma sister from *príosúnacht*." She sent him a saucy grin. "We could have a pint and a bit of fun after, to sweeten the deal."

It sounded like a churchwoman bargain, help in return for sex. And I did not like it one little bit.

Occam grinned at her, a lazy twinkle in his eyes. "The rescue part sounds like fun, but I'm taken." His gaze slid to me. "And she's dangerous."

"Oh," Etain said, looking back and forth between us. "I see how the wind blows. If I break Catriona out, I'll have to do it on ma own, then." She sighed in frustration and went back to removing gear from Astrid Grainger's trunk.

I had a feeling Etain wasn't joking about the jailbreak, but Occam didn't look worried. He showed teeth in a grin and called FireWind on his cell, telling the big boss that we had political troubles—not an uncommon thing these days—and rerouting him directly to the Cookeville PD and the recalcitrant FBI special agent in charge.

But unless FireWind had favors he could call in, things were pretty much what Gerry Stapp had said: We had the site. Smythe had Catriona.

I shook my head and left my cat-man talking, putting politics and pretty, flirtatious, desperate Irish girls out of my mind. My job today was database work, talking to the local law, and questioning the band members about where they were, and when. Politics were the problem of the more experienced team members.

Events at the scene crawled on. Deputies and the remaining victims were read by the witches. They all had some measure of the *death whatever* on them, so groups were herded into the null room trailer.

As the band members finished their half-hour stint in the portable null room, I began to expand on the prelim questioning for the timeline, talking to as many as I could. It was an ethnically diverse group, which I learned was an oddity in the country music scene, including three backup singers, all female, one African, one Asian, and one Caucasian, and Cale Nowell, the tattooed African-American guitarist. He had been one of the first on-site that morning and was with the first group that found Stella, along with the drummer. He turned out to be the man who had waved at me from the ambulance when I arrived. The entire band was visibly shaken and not overly helpful. No one knew anything about how or why Stella died. She seemed to be universally loved and respected.

Initial interviews were usually interesting and challenging, but this time it was sweaty work, outside, in the afternoon sun, in the last hot spell of fall. My clothes smelled like *death whatever*; I was getting nowhere; I was feeling marginally gripey; and I was wondering when Tandy would arrive. He was the unit's empath and was normally present at questionings, but he was nowhere to be seen yet. Not that anyone was telling me anything. I might no longer be a probationary agent, but it was taking far too long for the stigma to wear off. Hence the gripey.

I worked until T. Laine called to me. "Ingram? Your turn to be read by the witches."

The air had cooled in the late afternoon, but it wasn't cold enough to create the shivers that suddenly quivered along my bones and pebbled my skin. My feet felt leaden as I crossed the lawn. It was all I could do to step through the witch circle and not run before Astrid could close the circle behind me. I was all kinds of self-conscious and crossed my arms, holding my elbows as I took a place in the middle of the witch circle. The coven and T. Laine looked at me. That was it. They looked at me as the wind cooled, sharpened, and blew through the horse farm.

Standing in the chalk circle, witches looking me over, brought slivers of odd memories to the surface, one of me standing in the middle of a circle, long ago, as someone decided I wasn't a witch. The next memories were an overlapping batch: the sound of a man's voice as he demanded me for his bed; the same man reaching for me in the greenhouse; the smell of fresh-baked berry pie on the air where I hid in the kitchen as that voice informed Daddy for the third time that I was "ripe" and that he wanted me; the fear that clotted my heart as my father calmly said he would think about it. I had been twelve.

"Nell?"

I flinched and looked up. Tried to focus past the memories and into T. Laine's dark eyes. Dark hair, nearly black, caught the wind, tangled in her eyelashes. I caught a breath and it sounded strange, squeaky. My arms were aching and my fingers were stiff as I peeled them off me. I was shaking.

"Nell?" she asked softer. "You okay?"

I nodded before I thought. Because no. I wasn't okay, and my friend knew it. "Memories," I managed. "Bad ones."

She gave a slight head tilt that meant she heard me, and that others were listening. She took my arm and led me from the circle, away from the witches. "We should have a girls' night out and blow off some steam."

"I don't know how to blow off steam," I said, blinking away the dryness that burned my eyes. "Churchwomen don't blow off steam, we—they—redirect it."

"I'll bet they do," she said, sounding grim. "But you broke that mold. You, JoJo, Margot, and me? We'll have a few, maybe do some line dancing, and indulge in girl talk. Soon. For now"—she glanced at the driveway—"you need time in the null room. You're covered with what we're currently calling *death* energies."

My heart went all aflutter. Death energies was more specific than *death whatever*. Death energies sounded like a new thing. Not witch magics. Not . . . not anything I understood. I couldn't go home with *death* on me. I might harm my sisters, could damage Soulwood.

"So am I," she continued. "The coven wants us both inside the null room for ten-minute segments, with readings in between, to see how long it takes to break down the energies on nonhumans. We can talk."

"I don't want to talk," I said.

"Then we can just sit there in silence. Come on." She plucked at my sleeve and I followed her to the portable null room trailer, up the back ramp, and inside. Someone shut the door behind us, leaving me with T. Laine and six chairs. She pushed me to one and took another, sitting. She glanced at her watch and back up to me. I had been afraid we'd be in the dark, but there were lights in the ceiling and someone had run in an extension cord.

The cold of the *null* workings impregnated into the plywood walls of the six-by-twelve windowless trailer sent sharp shafts of ice into my veins. "I get that witches know I'm not human," I said. "They got *seeing* workings. But it seems odd to use me as a test subject, as I'm the only one of my species on-site."

"Null rooms are easier on us than on Occam, and they already tested it on the humans, reading them, trying to find a safe minimum time to erase the energies clinging to their skin. Sit."

The null room at HQ made me feel a little nauseated. This portable one was less powerful but more . . . spikey? It felt a little like the way my arms had felt the day I insulated the upstairs bedroom walls with rolls of pink stuff. The room also was affecting my ears and I caught myself on the back of a chair.

"Nell?" Worried tone.

I waved at her and sat. "Sick at the stomach," I said. "A little dizzy."

"Okay. Good to know. You need to hurl, I'll push you outside. And we'll get barf bags for the next batch. You get any other symptoms, tell me."

"Batch?"

"Half an hour seems to be enough time in the null room to clear most humans, but five still read as contaminated, even after two stints in here."

"Oh. Right." I swallowed down the sick feeling and sat.

"You want to talk about it? About what made you look so terrified a few minutes ago?"

I firmed my mouth, thinking through how much of my childhood I wanted to share. "My mama . . ." I stopped. "My mama had me tested to see if I was a witch when I was little. Because I could make things grow so well in the communal greenhouse. There'd been . . . talk." I gripped my arms again, holding myself. "You know that part. I remembered standing in a circle. I was nine? Ten?"

"Okay." T. Laine looked calm, compassionate. Ordinary. And in spite of her exhaustion, strong. As if I could tell her anything and she wouldn't bow under the weight.

"That memory brought up some others. The sound of Colonel Ernest Jackson's voice in front of the whole church, when he stated his intent to take me as his concubine."

Lainie's eyes narrowed again. It was her "going to battle" look.

"I had just started my menses. To a churchman, that meant I was a woman grown. That was the first time he demanded me for his bed. The second time I was in the greenhouse, encouraging the basils to grow. I was good at growing basil." I flapped a hand to show I knew I was vacillating. "I was working one afternoon and he grabbed my arm. Tried to pull me away." I rubbed my arm where his hand had gripped it so hard it had bruised purple and black. "Mama Grace stepped in and talked his ear off about the church social coming up. He left. The mamas all came and we walked home together. Then that night . . ." The rich sweet scent came to me. "Mama Grace had made me a blueberry pie and we had just cut it, when the Colonel walked in. Didn't knock. Just walked in like he owned the place. I ducked behind the counter and curled up in a ball. The Colonel informed Daddy for the third time that I was 'ripe' and he wanted me for his wife or concubine. He didn't care so long as I ended up in his bed. My father said he would think about it." I met T. Laine's eyes again, hers black and stormy. "I was twelve. The next Sunday in church, I told him off in front of the entire congregation and that's when I left with John and Leah Ingram. Went to live with them. Married into their family."

She said, "I'd burn that church to the ground and every man on the premises if I could, and take the jail sentence as worth it."

"I thought my family had abandoned me. But they went in secret to the Ingrams and negotiated me a safe haven, living off church grounds, but still within the church membership. If I'd left the membership, the men might have found me and taken me back. Daddy and the mamas? They kept me safe as best they could, as best they knew how."

"Sure." Her tone said she didn't believe it.

Years later, I had killed someone who attacked me on the farm. I had never known who it was, never seen his face in the twilight. And then, even later, and much more recently, I had killed one of the worst churchmen. He was dying. I could have healed him. But I killed him and I fed him to the land, every scrap of clothes, shoe leather, skin cells, and eyebrow hair. Maybe it was the null forces beating into my brain, but for some reason I wanted, needed, to say the words, to confess my crime. But I didn't. My need to unburden would, in turn, burden my friend with my sin and evil. And then she would have the additional burden of turning me in for a crime that could never be proved. So for now, I kept it to myself.

She grinned at me. "You ever need help going after the churchmen, I'll help you bury the bodies."

"Bury," I murmured. "I have no need to bury bodies." The land itself took care of that.

T. Laine looked at me oddly.

"Change of subject," I said. "Have you asked for help from the national witch covens or whatever they're called?"

T. Laine snorted in derision. "Bunch a pansy asses. They wouldn't even take my call." She scowled and said, "I mighta burned some bridges recently, when we were trying to locate the Blood Tarot."

T. Laine had a temper. I had heard that it could sometimes be spectacular, though I hadn't seen evidence of it yet. Innocently, I said, "Oh?"

She laughed. "Yeah. Well. Okay, so a few weeks ago I called the acting leader of the United States Council of Witches for help with closing the hellmouth and shutting the demon away permanently. She refused. I reminded her that spells used against humans fell under witch council purview. She refused again. I might have used some colorful language. She hung up on me."

I tried not laugh, but I couldn't hold it in.

"Right. Yuck it up," she said ruefully. "Ten minutes are up. Let's go be read again." She stood and rapped on the door. It opened in a slit of blinding red sunset, shockingly bright after the dim lighting of the windowless room. Squinting, I followed, one hand on the wall and then on the less-than-sturdy railing to keep from falling and tumbling to the ground.

T. Laine and I stood together in the center of the circle and the coven pronounced us clean. I went back to the laptop and stood over it, my hand on the cover, thinking. Recently, after the Blood Tarot case, I had confessed most everything to Rick La-Fleur, Soul, and FireWind. Everything except that I had a sentient tree and sentient land and that I'd killed people. And had bloodlust. If I revealed all that, I could go to jail. It was getting hard to keep track of who knew what.

I opened the laptop, signed in, and converted paper notes to files, then went back to interviewing victims of the *death whatever* energies, talking to them through tent walls, fleshing out the timeline, tracking the band's movements and gigs—which meant music shows and events—on their tour. And *not* thinking about the fact that so many people knew various parts of my secrets.

THREE

Over the next hour, the sunlight failed and the landscape and security lights came on. Mosquitoes appeared. Unit Eighteen made progress and learned things, not all of them good.

The not-so-wonderful part had started when the driver of the vehicle transporting Stella's housekeeper—the one in the cooler with the null pen—started feeling sick outside of Farragut. The vehicle itself broke down minutes later on I-40. The rubber parts of the engine and tires disintegrated all at once in a massive failure that nearly resulted in an accident. Within minutes of the near accident, the cooler cracked and dissolved, slopping the contaminated human remains all over the back of the vehicle, which was now on the shoulder of the interstate, surrounded by caution cones and Highway Patrol officers and a biohazard vehicle, all keeping way back.

T. Laine feared it would start breaking down the interstate there and the foundation of the house here, and then the energies might begin to leak into the ground beneath. That situation tied up T. Laine and the witches, trying to figure out how to contain or neutralize the energies that were destroying everything they came into contact with. There was no way to safely transport dead bodies, not without time spent in the null room and we needed it for the living.

To figure out how to fix the *death whatever* energies, T. Laine requested a visit inside the house by the entire coven of the Nashville witches. This would use up almost all of the unis, until the delivery in the morning, but Lainie convinced everyone it was necessary. I would be joining them in the basement studio to video and photograph everything, though my presence was more along the lines of an order, not a request.

As darkness fell upon the low hills of the horse farm, I wove a recharged null pen through my bra strap, dressed out in a clean blue uni, stuffed the handkerchief coated with mentholated gel into my mask, and put a mint into my mouth. Not that anything helped. Trooping inside and down the stairs, trying not to breathe the death stench of the house, I carried three cameras in my pockets: a mechanical 35mm autofocus camera that used real film, an old video camera, and a sturdy digital camera. "My mama had one of these," I grumbled, holding up the film-based Canon.

"Which is why you're down here with us," T. Laine said cheerfully. "Among your many talents is the ability to use old-fashioned equipment. Competency comes with repercussions."

"Do not ask me to milk a cow or darn your socks."

"You know how to do that?"

"No," I lied, stern faced. T. Laine laughed as if she knew I was lying. I hadn't spent a lot of time lying, so she probably knew. I took a breath and the stench was horrible; it was all I could do not to gag even with the air-conditioning turned on high. The stench was also a problem for the witches. They were showing signs of eye-watering gastric distress, which made me feel better if only because I wasn't alone in my misery. Working hard at not vomiting, I grumbled, "Can't you cast an *antiscent* working down here?"

From the bottom of the stairs T. Laine answered, "Not with powerful energies already on-site. And the null pens make it impossible to use personal wards against the smell. So in case you think I'm holding out, no. I'm not dealing with this reek any better than anyone else."

Feeling as green as the witches looked, I joined T. Laine in the basement. I wondered how much face I'd lose if I upchucked in the corner. I wondered if zombies stank like this, not that zombies existed. So far as I knew.

Stella Mae was no zombie. She was greenish mush and brittle bones and horror. The carpet under Stella had dusted and slimed away and the concrete slab beneath was cracked. I took photos as the witches set a protective circle around the body in preparation for a magical *wyrd* that they would speak once the null pens were gone. They were talking the arcane math of spell casting, which had never made any sense to me beyond the basics I had learned in Spook School. Geometry. Math. Not my forte. Astrid suggested a shield to contain the energies, until they could learn how to take them apart.

A shield sounded like a good idea to me.

As they worked, a guitar snapped and fell down the wall with a discordant twanging, leaving the instrument in pieces. The piano looked as if its legs had been attacked by termites and would collapse at any moment.

Unlike the witches, I had a specific job and didn't have to stay down here once the photos were taken, so I worked fast. My fingers clumsy through the null nitrile gloves, I took pics of everything with the old Canon, changed out the film, and took more. Then I videoed everything. And then I took digital photos, sending the digital shots to JoJo at PsyLED HQ every few minutes. Jo would compare the timed shots with similar shots from when the first LEOs arrived and with those taken by the early arrivals of Unit Eighteen. If the cameras worked. If the energies didn't degrade the digital shots. If Wi-Fi still worked down here.

In the room for swag, the racks that once held hats, MP3 players, and small speakers were now rickety, rusted metal. The swag on the racks was rotten, riven, plastic cracking. The empty shipping boxes were crumbled, except for the plasticized labels, which were, so far, merely curled and yellowed. The T-shirt box in the middle of the floor was decaying into crumbled rot, but the T-shirts inside were decaying more slowly, which seemed odd.

But worse was the DB. I concentrated my cameras on Monica Belcher's body. She was mostly dissolved, except for the smell, into thin brownish bones and minuscule green soap bubbles that sludged across the floor. I took shallow breaths through the mask. It didn't help. As fast as humanly possible, I finished my photography and raced away, up the stairs. Gagging.

T. Laine didn't try to keep me in the basement, thank goodness.

On the upper landing, I stripped off the uni, put it in the bio container, and made my way outside. The fresh air was such a relief that I nearly threw up anyway, just getting out of the reek. Crunching my mint, I made my way to a camp stove one of the sheriff's deputies had set up and poured coffee from an old metal percolator into a foam cup. It wasn't the thick black sludge for which cop-shops were known, but strong, aromatic coffee. I breathed the steam and scent.

Holding my cup under my nose, cameras in the crook of an arm, I retired to my car to write up reports, package the film for mailing to the lab, and send the last photos to JoJo. Too sick to actually drink the coffee, I popped another of the super-strong mints and sucked on it for a while to take the stench out of my mouth and calm the nausea. When I could hold down the brew, I sipped, studying the photos. I was halfway through the cup when I noticed some odd things, small incongruities, but any peculiarity could be important. Cases were often solved by small observations and irregularities.

I went back and forth, comparing the digital photos submitted by the first LEOs on the scene to the ones I had just taken. There were opened boxes of swag in the room, one of them T-shirts. It was the only full box. Why full? Why not half-full? Or nearly empty? Did that matter? Was it important? And . . . all the empty boxes in the corner were marked with plasticized shipping labels. But in the original photo, the box beside Monica Belcher had no label. I went through dozens of cop-photos from every angle, to make sure. No shipping label, not even fallen on the floor. Had the label been torn off when the box was opened? Or maybe it was on the bottom. That made sense.

In one photo taken by a cop of the inside of the box, there was a second oddity. Resting on top of the shirts was a green glass bottle holding a length of wire, like coat hanger wire. In the bottom was a skim of what looked like pale green liquid. The shirts were not folded or neat, but crushed and wrinkled, shoved into one corner as if to hold the bottle upright.

I compared that photo to mine. Sitting amid the T-shirts, upside down in mine, was a bottle, but in my photo the glass was blackened, the color hidden among the black shirts. The wire was a corroded black twig. The clear, pale green liquid was gone.

I edited out a section of the pic to show only the T-shirts and went to find a band member. Instead, I found Etain. The witch was draped across the four-board fence, her head resting on her arms, breathing through her mouth, carefully not moving.

Horses' hooves pounded in the darkness, moving upwind and away from the stench of death we both carried.

"This helped for me." I held out one of the extra-strong breath mints. I wished I had candied ginger, but hindsight was useless.

She pushed herself slowly away from the fence, took the small package, and opened it, the plastic crinkling. Gingerly, she put the mint on her tongue as if she feared even that much might make her vomit. "How d'ya stand such a sight an' stink wit'out puking up your guts?"

"I don't stand it very well. Hence my ignominious rush from the basement and a pocketful of mints."

"Och." She met my eyes, hers rueful. "I *vomit teilgthe* all over the garden," she said, the words clearly Irish. "Probably killed whatever I puked on. Have you another mint?"

"Crunch it," I advised, holding out more.

Etain took several, her teeth crunching the first. She lifted a water bottle from the third fence rail, swished her mouth with water, swallowed, then crunched again, and swished some more. "Brilliant," she said.

"Your sister is with the band, right?" I asked.

"Aye. Besides her lovely voice, Catriona's a whiz with traditional Irish instruments. Stella Mae hired her for some sessions last fall and she fit in with the band like a hand in a glove. Stella asked her to join the band for the whole tour. Cattie was ecstatic. I've never seen her so happy." She opened a new mint and put it on her tongue, this time sucking slowly.

"What does she play?"

"Both kinds of Celtic harp, tin whistles, the bodhran, which is like a wide, flat drum. The Irish bouzouki, which is a bit like a mandolin, but not. Fiddle, a-course. Banjer and guitar. She can also play piano, organ, most anything. Cattie's got all Da's musical talent and only a little of Ma's magical. I got none at all of the musical and the greatest part of ma mum's magical." She looked at me, her expression droll. "I was always jealous that she got the gift of music and I didn't. And she was jealous that I had more magic than she did. Fought like two cats in a sack, we did, when we were young." Her amusement fell away. "And now she's in the hands of a cop with a heart full of witch hatred. *I* could zap him. *She's* at his mercy."

"We'll do our best to keep her safe."

"I'll owe you."

"Just part of the job. But I do have a question." I held out the tablet with the pic of the T-shirts. "Are these T-shirts the tour tees? Like the one you're wearing?"

Etain studied the pic, which was grainy and out of focus. "Looks to be. Why do you ask?"

I sighed and shrugged, putting the tablet into my pocket. "I was hoping they might be something else. Something unexpected."

"Like a clue. Evidence pointing to a murdering death-practitioner."

"Something like that. Since it isn't witch magics, I don't know what to look for."

"It doesna match anything I ever felt either, but I know it's death."

The side door opened and three witches raced from the house, two of them falling to the ground and gagging. Three more witches followed but simply sat on the narrow side porch, heads in hands. T. Laine came out last and she looked as green as I had felt. Her misery made me feel better, which likely made me a bad person.

"How about this?" I showed Etain the photos of the green glass bottle and the later ones, where the glass was blackened.

"Oh now," she breathed. "This thing here—" She pointed. "You may have something. But . . ." She curled her index finger down and stepped away from the photo on the screen. "I'd rather no one had ever found that."

"Why?"

"Because that there"—she pointed again—"is a witch working. And it will point at us, damn it all to hell 'n' back." She called, louder, "Lainie girl. May we trouble you for a bit of time?"

T. Laine stood slowly, found her balance, and made her way from the stoop to the fence. "What?" she asked, her tone breathless and curt at all once.

Etain jutted her chin at me. "Show her."

I angled my tablet to her, showing the photos of the box of T-shirts, taken over the course of the day. "Inside the T-shirt box."

T. Laine flashed through several and narrowed them down to two she thought interesting. She went back and forth between photos, whispering comments about spoons and sex, which made Etain smile wryly. Finally she looked at Etain, her eyes wide in a face that was still too pale. "It's a trigger?"

"Aye. A witch-made trigger, I'm thinking. A trigger not a one of us would be willing to touch, for fear it might be weaponized to explode."

T. Laine said, "I've been operating on the idea that because the energies weren't typical witch energies, it meant witches weren't involved in the creation of it. *Death* energies, yes, but no *witch* energies, no witch workings or curses. Yet now we have a trigger that is probably a witch-made device and working."

"Or we may not. This thing might be something other than a trigger. Everything in that basement is disintegrating," Etain said, "including the maybe-trigger, maybe-not-a-trigger." She looked into the night, her attention on her coven, watching the latest member with compassion, but also with a good dollop of amusement, as the woman vomited into the grass. Etain chuckled under her breath as the witches tried to get over their reactions to the stench, all breathing deeply, one lying on her back, facing the sky, breathing through her mouth, making little *erp* sounds.

"Trigger?" I asked. "Like a handgun trigger?"

"Ummm." Still talking to Etain, T. Laine said, "Okay. So . . . the *death whatever* energies were in the box, but contained? Perhaps with a secondary *null* working over the shirts to protect them?"

Etain shrugged, her black T-shirt barely moving in the dark. "That theory weighs with a bit of logic, since the T-shirts have decomposed more slowly than anythin' else."

"Either the band left the box here, untouched," T. Laine said, "or it came after the band left for the tour. But it couldn't have come through the mail prepared to detonate. If this thing is a trigger, it was carried in and positioned on-site. It would never have survived shipping intact."

"It woulda been tilted and turned over at some point, and the *death* woulda begun spreading," Etain agreed. "But it's far more than death energies."

"But why didn't Stella or her housekeeper come downstairs in the two days before they died?" T. Laine asked. "She had a brand-new studio. You can't tell me they didn't come down here."

"Coming to admire is different from coming to work," I said. "And she had been away from her horses for weeks."

Something tickled at the back of my brain and I frowned. "It's death *and* it's decay."

"A double whammy," T. Laine said, shoving her hair up and away from her eyes.

Etain's mouth opened in an O and she shook her head. "I never saw such a thing."

"Explain, please," I said.

T. Laine waved a hand to shut me up, saying, "We're brainstorming." To Etain she said, "A double whammy. The energies—we'll call them *death and decay*, for now—were fully released when the box was opened. But if the condition of the studio is an indication, it had been leaking for some time, the energies accumulating above the shirts but not harming them."

"Against the laws of physics, unless the shirts were beneath a barrier of some sort," Etain said. She pronounced it "barer," but with a strange burr of sound. It took a moment for me to figure out what she meant.

"Yes. Right," T. Laine said. "So maybe a ward over the shirts, keeping the energies above them until the energies accumulated enough inside the box to begin to waft out. Then moving out of the box, and along the floor, like some gases are heavier than others and stay at ground level."

"Until they are stirred up by passing people. A witch created that trigger," Etain said, sadly, "and most likely the barrier."

"Yes," T. Laine said, her fingers sliding from photo to photo. "I agree. Could be a witch-for-hire who made amulets charged with a one-time working without knowing how they might be used."

"We can hope. No self-respecting witch woulda done something like this, killed and injured all these people."

T. Laine grunted. "I've been in law enforcement long enough to disagree. There are evil people everywhere. I think I've got it figured out."

Etain leaned in to hear better.

"The person who set the trigger—as opposed to the person who designed it—inserted a silver wire between the paper sides of the cardboard lid, with the wire's other end trailing down through a tin lid and into a glass jar. There was a hole punched through the tin lid and the wire rested in the bottom of the jar, bent into a triangle. There was likely an amulet there, though we didn't find one."

"Here." I leaned in and paged through my pics to the jar with the clear, pale green liquid in the bottom. "Can an amulet be made of liquid?"

"Well. Wouldja look at that." The witches exchanged glances. "Mind if I show this to the rest of the coven?" Etain asked T. Laine.

"Might as well," T. Laine groused. "I'm going to get canned for letting the coven take part in trying to stop the working and therefore messing up a potential crime scene anyway. Because God knows, if that's a trigger, this is clearly a crime scene."

"Unless the *death and decay* is something different," I said, "and unrelated to the trigger and the box of shirts. We have a theory, not indisputable results."

T. Laine blew out a hard breath and slapped at a mosquito, looking out over the dark grounds, frustration etched into her face.

"What if it isn't a curse?" I asked. "What if it's just nature speeded up."

T. Laine stared at me, her expression intent. "Go on."

"We all die and decay. What if this is just normal, natural things speeded up?"

"That . . . makes sense," she said.

"Astrid," Etain called out. "Come 'ere. The earth spriggan has a photograph of what might be a peculiar trigger amulet."

"Earth *what*?" I said, startled.

"Spriggan." She looked me up and down. "But you're too pretty be a spriggan. More a sprite, I'm thinking. What? You can't tell me ya didn' know." A line formed between her brows. "A sprite is a supernatural, like a fairy or elf. An ethereal entity. You *did* know?"

"I was called a *yinehi* by a Cherokee woman. She said I smelled of earth and the little people. Or a brownie."

"Well then," she said, as if that explained everything. "But y're no' a brownie."

"What's the difference between a spriggan, a sprite, and a brownie?" I asked, curiosity shooting through me. Curiosity and hope. This woman might know what I was.

"A brownie is a household paranormal who does chores in return for a safe place to live and food to eat."

I stilled. That sounded like what I had been when I lived with John and Leah Ingram.

"Spriggans are bug-ugly haints. Sprites are fairy creatures." She tilted her head. "Yeah, so you're a sprite." She took the laptop from my fingers and showed Astrid. "Greenish liquid." She pointed to the last photo. "Do you be thinking the bottle burned and the liquid was used up in the energies?"

"Interesting," Astrid said. "A trigger. This may explain everything."

"Not to me," I said, wanting to return to fairy creatures and sprites, but the conversation had moved on. I would have to add those terms to the list of research into what Mud, Esther, and I might be.

"If it's a trigger, then it was set to discharge, if you will, when the box was opened," Astrid said. "However, before the lid was opened, some of the liquid amulet could have evaporated through the hole in the lid, coating the silver wire, which is why we're seeing the low-level but widespread decay and then the fast-acting decay later. The curse slowly entered the air and the first women who went to the basement this morning breathed it in for, what? Over an hour? Then died. The ones present when the box was opened got the highest concentration of the energies, but for a much shorter time."

"Monica Belcher got the pure dose," I said.

"When Belcher opened the box," T. Laine said, "she was hit with massive energies."

"A *preservation* working, to keep the box and the shirts in a form of stasis," Astrid suggested. "A *preservation* working could have been calculated to not break down the shirts *or* the box until the trigger was activated. If a witch did this, if it was a witch-made trigger, it's a very sophisticated, layered mechanism."

"But the shirts are still breaking down more slowly than anything else in the room," I said. "Things were breaking down before the box was opened. So . . . it's in the air." Dread filled me.

"You're saying that *death and decay* was in the air we were breathin'," Etain said.

"Breathe in and out," T. Laine commanded me. She looked me up and down, using a *seeing* working as I breathed. Etain joined her, both of them silent. "I missed it. You're right," she said to me. "It's in us, small odd little magics on each exhalation." She looked around. "So that means those of us who spent the most time in the basement need more null room time. It's magic, but I don't know what kind." She shook her head. "Maybe it's speeded-up nature, like you said."

"It's glad I am that I'll be spending more time in the null room, then," Etain said, "but ma sister is in jail and has no access to the null room and she was down there, in the basement." She looked at her watch and blinked away sudden tears.

"I'll find a way to get her a null pen," T. Laine said. "We also need to find a way to get the T-shirts and the potential trigger into the null room," T. Laine said, "along with what's left of the bodies. We could put them in coolers, but there's no way to carry all that safely up the stairs."

"Open the French doors and back the trailer inside the basement," I said. "Shovel it all into the null room."

"Well, slap me silly," Astrid said, whirling and striding away, her black skirt flaring wide.

"What just happened?" I asked Etain.

The girl laughed. "That meant we witches should ha' thought of it, though I never knew there were doors down there. I thought it was all windows. Come on. Let's get your cowboy and go stand in the null room again together. Like a threesome but without the fun. Maybe he has a brother?"

"No," I said. "He doesn't. And he's taken and we aren't interested."

"No ring on your finger says different."

I scowled at her, my very best churchwoman scowl, and Etain grinned.

"I'm teasing you. I admit it's mostly to keep ma mind offa ma family. I promise not to poach on your man. Or on you, though you're cute as a bunny when you frown."

* * *

All the witches agreed that *death and decay* wasn't witch magic, not that local law enforcement understood the difference. They were more prosaic. If it walked like a duck, paddled like a duck, and quacked like a duck, it was a duck. As stars came out, small groups of deputies, investigators, hazmat people, paramedics, witches, and band members spent crowded half-hour intervals in the null room to remove any lingering traces of the energies we had breathed in, potential internal effects that didn't register on an outward scan of our bodies with either a typical *seeing* working by the witches or use of the psy-meter.

Etain got her wish and the three of us spent a crowded half hour together in the null room with the other Nashville coven members and T. Laine. A very uncomfortable half hour. The Irish witch seemed to have come to a conclusion and might have been flirting with me. She tried flirting with T. Laine, who rolled her eyes and told the young witch to find greener pastures, whatever that meant. And then, as if she couldn't help herself, Etain looked from her watch and her cell and once again eyed Occam.

While she made eyes at my cat-man, I went green in the deeps of my heart, jealousy green. That jealousy poked at old memories, old sorrows like bruises on my soul, reminding me what it had felt like to be married to John. In the eyes of the church we had been wed, but I had known that Leah was his wife for real, the woman he loved. Sharing his bed. Being the female head of the house. Even though I hadn't loved John in a romantic way, even though I hadn't wanted his physical attention, I had always been the second wife, the lesser wife, the wife who came to them with nothing—or so I had thought—a beggar with no way out.

That lesser position had created feelings in my twelve-year-old heart I hadn't understood then and still didn't now—a strange type of impotent jealousy built of enforced subjugation and insignificance. It was the recognition of lack of power and lack of value and importance in our shared household, in my small world.

Etain was clearly an inveterate flirt, perhaps made worse because her family was in trouble and she was distracting herself. Her flirting likely meant nothing to her, but in my mind she was indeed poaching on my cat-man. And in a small way, I hated her for that. And hated myself for hating her because I knew the jealousy was a weakness inside me.

After our half hour of enforced close proximity and my greenness, Etain and the others took off to do witchy things and Occam and I went to my car. Silently, I shared a packet of commercially packaged salmon jerky and some of my homemade fish-flake protein bars made for the werecats. After the stench of Stella Mae's house and the uncomfortable time in the null room with a witch who was looking for a companion or two to break into the county lockup and then spend the night with, I wasn't very hungry. I nibbled. The salmon was pretty good. The protein bars needed more salt and I'd adjust the recipe next time. Occam added a packet of ketchup to his and thought it was delicious. *Cats.* He grinned at me in the dark, his scarred face pulling up on one side. "You should try it," he said, knowing what I thought of ketchup. "It's good on eggs with Tabasco, good on burgers, good on anything."

I made a face that said plainly, *Gross*, and he laughed. And added another packet of ketchup to the bar.

As we ate, we watched the witches back the null trailer around the house and inside the basement entrance where T. Laine and Astrid, wearing all the null pens and the very last two unis, would attempt to shovel the T-shirts inside. The hope was to break the *death and decay* so the coven could study the suspected trigger, prove this to be a crime scene, prove the deaths were intended and not an accident.

I discovered later that the energies in the T-shirt box were so powerful the shovel fell apart halfway through the chore. The bodies were mostly mush and bones scraped into coolers and tossed into the trailer with cut scraps of carpet from where they had lain. After handling the remains, the two witches also had to sit in the trailer. Astrid and T. Laine emerged deathly ill from the stink, but free of contamination, and once they were free, the coven sealed the null trailer and set a twelve-hour timer to completely deactivate the shirts, carpet scraps, and bodies.

As we ate, deputies and witches ran around like ants. Overworked paramedics took the last of the patients to UTMC. Law enforcement changed out shifts except for us; we had no replacements. Official vehicles drove away. Etain flashed across the driveway, modern and trim and everything I wasn't. I looked down at my hands in the dark: square, hardworking hands, calloused from gardening, hauling dirt, splitting wood, and shoveling snow. My woody nails. Occam said, "I reckon we should go see what's happening, but"—he took a deep breath—"I'm too tuckered out to care right now, Nell, sugar."

"I don't care either," I said, because I was busy thinking about the green footprints tracking through my soul. As I watched Etain dart across again, I was aware that Occam watched me.

Occam pushed the vampire tree's crate to the middle of the dash, out of the way, and said, a soft cat-purr in his voice, "I love you to the full moon and back, Nell, sugar." Which was exactly the right thing to say.

It reminded me that Occam had given me his heart and my own melted. But . . .

"You got something on your mind, woman," he said softly, the entire state of Texas in his drawl. "Spit it out."

I frowned, thinking. There were so many things that could or might get in the way of our relationship. Simple things like me being jealous. Or growing leaves. Or him being moon-called and needing to mate with a female werecat. Did he want that? A werecat woman?

I swiveled in the seat to face him, bending one knee under the steering wheel. "I come from a polygamous background, Occam. Jealousy was a prevalent and pervasive problem, and some men used it to keep their women in line. I understand that a lot of men need to feel attractive to younger and prettier women, and I know I ain't a cat-woman and that you might want one someday. And I know that mating urge might, or could, maybe, be stronger than usual in you right now since you been so puny looking for the last few months and I—"

Occam coughed out a cat laugh, stopping my words. "Nell, sugar, forgive me for interrupting, but I gotta say this before you say anything that might be the beginning of our first argument." He leaned in slightly and took my chin in his hand, turning me to face him. He stroked along my jaw with the pad of his thumb, his fingers heated and gentle. He held my gaze with his. Something that might have been lust filled his eyes and they glowed pale gold. His voice a cat growl, he said, "Puny looking? I looked like a horror movie for the last few months and it never bothered me one whit."

"No?" I managed as a whisper.

"No." He leaned closer to me, his nose only inches from mine, his eyes glowing the gold of his were-creature. His voice went all scratchy, like a mad cat. "More importantly, it never bothered *you*. In fact, it wouldn'ta bothered you if I'da stayed as scarred and hairless as I started out. That right there is worth more than gold to me. So you listen and you listen good. I don't now, and I never will, as long as the moon is in the sky and breath is in my lungs, need the attention of any other woman or werecat."

His voice dropped lower, a full-on growl. "'Doubt thou the stars are fire; / Doubt that the sun doth move; / Doubt truth to be a liar; / But never doubt I love you to the full moon and back.'" His lips twisted wryly. "That right there is a little bit of slightly mangled Shakespeare. I learned it because I know you love his writing. I don't understand every word, but I understand the meaning. And I never have, and I never will quote them words to another creature as long as I live."

Tears had gathered in my eyes and my mouth had opened as he quoted poetry to me, and it formed an O as I said, "Oh."

"I said," he said firmly, "I love you to the full moon and back. Do you love me?"

"Yes," I whispered.

Occam's human nose bumped mine. "I don't play games like your churchmen. I want you and only you, always and ever," he said, our noses touching. He tilted his head and pressed his lips to mine, a kiss that quickly became more as the hand on my chin curled behind my head and he pulled me in. Tongues met and twisted together and things in my middle went all tight and hot and—he pulled away. He was breathing fast. So was I. He managed a deep shuddering breath and rested his forehead against mine. "Dayum, woman."

I laughed, a strange sound filled with longing. "I wasn't jealous. Not really," I said, lying, but wishing it was the truth.

"Maybe not consciously. But you grew up with certain expectancies about relationships. Those childhood expectations influence who you are now. Just like my childhood can and does affect who I am now. Our childhoods can screw with our minds like nothing else. So know this, with the part of you that's all thinking and logic. I don't need nothing from another woman," he said. "I jist need you. For the rest of my life. Now." His yellow-glowing eyes met mine. "I have a need to hear you say it again. And often. Do you love me?"

"Yes," I said. "I love you to the full moon and back."

He leaned in and kissed me one last time, hard and quick. He pulled away, opened the car door, got out, and pushed the door shut. The night pressed against the car windows like small, clawed paws or like serial killers in scary movies, not that I was scared.

Carefully, I tried on the words, "I'm good and ready for us to be together forever." A peculiar heat washed through me, longing and wanting.

But Occam was gone, covering the ground in a cat-assisted lope to reappear near the house, silhouetted by the lighted windows.

Softly, I whispered, trying out the words for the very first time in the silence and isolation of the car. "Will you marry me, Occam?" The words felt strange on my lips, full of hope and fragile trust, a trust I had abused by jealousy over Etain. I had to stop letting my past, my upbringing, get in the way of Occam and me. "I'm so stupid," I sighed to the vampire tree. Fortunately it didn't answer.

I locked the car and went back to work.

T. Laine negotiated with the witches to pull the portable null room to Knoxville as soon as possible and offer it to the doctors and patients. It would be excellent PR, mitigating some of the negative social media reactions to Stella Mae dying from what an unnamed source had reported to be witch magic.

Unlike the standardized protocols for treating mundane disorders, medical treatments for magical ailments tended to be looser, more of an art than a science, and to involve arcane treatments in addition to traditional methods. Though Jo had made an offer to UTMC for patients to use the null room at HQ, no one had come yet except the two cops, possibly because it would be difficult (and a liability) to transport patients. Having the null trailer at UTMC would make it much easier for the doctors to utilize the treatment. Not all patients would be willing, distrusting anything that hinted of witches. The churchfolk weren't the only people who thought all witches should be burned at the stake.

Spotting me, standing half-hidden in the dark, holding my tablet under one arm and wearing what I'm sure was a forlorn and woebegone countenance, T. Laine called me over. "Whatever it is that has you moping, put it away," she said. "Now that the bodies and the carpets are in the null room, Astrid has sounded the all clear. I need a full and comprehensive evaluation and photographs of the rest of the house. I want photos of anything that grabs your attention even if you don't know why it grabbed you. If you spot family, who went inside as soon as Astrid said it was safe, feel free to initiate basic Q and A. Go on. You got this." She patted me on the arm and went back to whatever she had been doing.

"I'm not moping," I said. Though that might be a little lie. I looked around for Occam and didn't see him. Feeling more like a churchwoman than I had in a long time, I squared my shoulders against old emotional habits and went back into the house, muttering to myself, "I'm a special agent. I am *not* a churchwoman. And I am *not* moping."

FOUR

The ground-floor windows were open and night breezes blew through, airing out the place, decreasing the scent of *death and decay*, if not totally neutralizing it. The smell had been lessened by the removal of the contaminated items and bodies.

Upstairs, my tablet under my arm, I followed the sound of voices along a six-foot-wide teal and aqua hallway, a luxurious floral carpet runner underfoot in shades of persimmon and peacock. It muffled my footsteps as I stopped outside a bedroom, standing in the shadows, watching through the cracked-open door, listening in on the conversation inside. Three women were sitting on an oversized bed—way bigger than a king bed—a woven turquoise coverlet and piles of teal and persimmon pillows bunched up around them. The walls were the same shade as the hallway and green and blue vases and fancy bowls sat on tables, a white tufted chaise lounge near a window. Opulent. Decadent.

It must take forever to dust the room.

The women were crying and talking, an older woman rocking back and forth.

"I know, Mama," one of the younger women said. "I know. You want a private service, but nothing we can do will make that happen. We have to have a public funeral and let the fans grieve along with us."

"We ain't got to do nothing until we get Stella Mae's body back," the mother said.

"We ain't got to do nothing until we know about Catriona and if they charge her," the other young woman said. She had a rounded belly with an outie belly button pressing on the fabric of her shirt, looking heavily pregnant. "Gimme another pillow. I been sittin' in that RV so long I can't feel my feet no more."

The older woman was Stella Mae's mom, Tondra, and the other two looked enough like Stella to be her sisters, pointy chins, dainty noses, narrow shoulders, long legs. I checked the names on the file that was being put together from reports sent to JoJo at HQ and found the names Sophee Anne Ragel and Josette Lynn Ragel Jenkins, and photos to go with the names. Sisters. Josette was the pregnant one.

"Yeah," Josette said, stuffing pillows behind her lower spine. "That feels good. Them car people lie when they say their seats give lumbar support. Not for a preggers they don't."

I might shoulda felt bad for eavesdropping, but if they wanted privacy, they should have closed the door. Being nosy was in my job description.

"Catriona's been with Stella Mae for a solid year," Tondra said. "You'uns know there ain't no way Catriona is responsible. She loves my baby."

The dialect threw me again. Intellectually, I knew that the accent I thought of as strictly church-speak was a regional accent across large parts of rural Tennessee, but it still made me feel odd to hear it on a case a hundred miles from home.

"There's love and then there's *love*, Mama," Sophee Anne said, something odd in her tone, "and love don't mean the same thing to Stella as it does to us. You know that."

"Don't you'un be talking about the departed with a lack of respect. I won't have it, not here in her own house. Stella was a God-loving, born-again Christian, and she told me she was now adhering to the straight and narrow."

"Stella wasn't perfect, Mama. And when the cops and the press fin—"

"Stop right there, Josie Lynn. That girl supported us and made sure we'd never hurt for nothing. She was a good girl." Mama Tondra burst into tears and fell on Stella's mattress, crying into the pillows.

I backed down the hallway and made sure my feet hit the wood to the side of the carpet runner as I returned. I hated to burst in on a moment of family grief, but that was my job, so I tapped on the doorjamb, stuck my head in, and turned on the church-speak. "Hey. I'm sorry as I can be for interrupting. But if you'uns all feel up to it, I got some questions for you'uns?" I made it a query instead of a demand so I sounded simple and uncertain. People's emotional guard went up at demands, but they were a mite less recalcitrant with apparent uncertainty. "Special Agent Ingram of PsyLED?" I held up my ID.

Tondra sat up, waved me in, and blew her nose on a tissue, wiping her face. "Come on in. I'm sorry I'm such a mess," she said. "But this is so hard."

"I know it must be," I said, crossing the room. "May I sit?" I gestured at a poufy, ultrafeminine, tufted, fringed velvet chair near the bed. As I walked, I took in the entire room, from the closet that was bigger than my entire bedroom (and that looked as if it had been trashed by a robber) to the burled wood furniture, to the marble-tiled en suite bathroom visible through a partially open door.

"Why not," Tondra said. She rewiped her face and tugged the thick coverlet over her legs and feet.

I pulled my tablet and sent a quick text to T. Laine, telling her I had come upon the family and would initiate the preliminary questioning. I moved the chair a bit and sat so I could see into the closet and the mess on the floor. A pile of clothing had been dropped and all of it was a rich shade of fuchsia pink. Hanging on the rods were clothes of many colors. But all the pink was on the floor. Odd. Unless Stella Mae wore pink on the road? Onstage? I'd need to check that out.

I wished I had the unit's empath, Tandy, or Margot—a former FBI agent, currently PsyLED probie special agent, who had truth-sensing abilities—with me. Both of them were better at questioning people, but I had orders to get things started, and T. Laine, who was a higher pay grade than me, had told me to start up a chat if the opportunity presented itself. I looked up and sighed. "I hate this part a my job. Trying to talk to family when they're grieving."

"You catch the monster what did this and you can question me all you want," Tondra said, curling upright and crossing her legs into a yoga position beneath the covers. She had to be nearly as old as my mama, but she was as limber as a child, and her hair looked expensive, as if it had been styled and colored by someone from Hollywood. She introduced her daughters and herself and said, "Shoot."

"Thank you. Some of these questions might sound personal, but I promise I'm not asking for no reason. First, have there been any threats on Stella's life? Any harassing e-mails or letters or texts?"

"Dozens every day," Josette said, her fingers scratching lazy circles on her belly. "She hired a security firm last year. They handle everything: tour security, electronic threats, and making sure the property is safe. And that includes making sure the horses are safe. The house has security—cameras, lasers, that kinda thing—mostly for when Stella was out of town. The barn is wired too."

"I've got a card with the firm's contact info in my bag somewhere," Tondra said, pulling a leather purse to her and delving inside. Papers crinkled and heavier things rattled and scraped. "It's here somewhere. I've done sent word to the company that they're to be completely open with you on everything."

Josette started to speak and stopped. I wondered why. "What about a will? Life insurance?" I asked.

"Stella Mae's lawyer has all the legal documents. We're the heirs," Stella's mama said, "and Catriona."

I couldn't keep the reaction off my face. "I thought she just met Catriona."

"Last year. We've practically adopted her. She's like family," Tondra said.

Last year was the same general time frame that the security firm had been hired. I made a note about that and said slowly, as if thinking it through, "The FBI might consider her being an heir a possible motive."

"No. Not Cattie. She's had everything she wanted. She's family," Tondra said, tearing up, grief washing down her face, scalding her chapped skin. I wasn't an empath, but I knew Tondra was speaking the truth as she knew it.

"And besides," Sophee Anne said, "financially speaking, Stella was worth way more to us all alive than dead, even with the coffin-rider sales. No one had a reason to want her killed."

"Coffin-rider sales?" I asked.

"Sales that come when a singer dies," Sophee Anne said. "People download so much music it actually makes money. Sometimes a lot of money. But not enough to replace the take from touring and not enough to replace *her*. Not enough to kill for."

"Life insurance?"

"Life insurance is for poor people," Josette scoffed.

I couldn't help my eyebrows going up when I said, "Poor people?"

"To pay off outstanding bills and provide for the family," Tondra said. "Stella done all that already. My girl always thought ahead. Planned ahead. She don't owe a dime to nobody. The only insurance she has is on the property and the horses."

I let that settle inside me, realizing that I needed life insurance to provide for Mud. And a will . . . "Okay. That makes sense," I said, mostly talking to myself. I hated that I no longer lived off the grid, that I had to think like townies, like city folk. To them, I said, "What can you tell me about Stella's romantic life?"

Tondra stiffened and shot a sharp glance at her daughters. I knew that look. It was a mama's warning to keep their mouths shut and let her do the talking. "My girl's a good girl."

"I'm not saying she isn't," I said, softening into a smile.

"Stella ain't been dating no one in particular," Tondra said. "She takes a different singer to every event, like the CMAs, but she ain't picked a man to settle down with."

The sisters glanced at each other but didn't comment.

"One of the gossip magazines—which I do not read, in case you'r'un wondering—says she's been dating Clyde MacMahan again," I said. "The race car driver? She dated him before?"

"Lies. Her'n Clyde's been friends since they was in middle school," Sophee Anne said, ignoring her mother's glared warning. "They dated a couple years back, but there wasn't no passion, you know? Stella said it was like dating her brother. 'Cept she ain't got a brother. It was a joke a hers. 'Like datin' my brother, 'cept I ain't got one, so wha'd I know?'"

At the shared memory, all three women teared up again. I waited while they passed tissues and wiped their eyes.

"She broke up with him?" I clarified.

"Yeah. But she took him to an award ceremony last spring and the press went nuts. Clyde's datin' that actress what's in the new Disney movie. Don't bother looking his way," Sophee said. "He ain't no witch. He's a man through and through." Most people didn't know witches could be male. And that was our problem. Whoever our killer was, she—or he—either was a new kind of witch or had obtained a trigger from a witch to power unknown magical energies. We hadn't released that. So far as I had been informed, the coven hadn't let it slip either.

"Ain't no special man in her life right now," Tondra said. "But if you'un don't mind, can we talk later? It's jist so . . ." She burst into noisy weeping. Her daughters joined her and they all piled up like puppies. I said my thank-yous, told them they'd likely be asked questions by other agents, and to not take it personally if the same questions were picked at again. I wasn't sure they had heard me until Tondra handed me a business card with the security firm name and contact info. She said, "Like I said. You'uns find the murderer who kilt my baby. That's all we want."

Stella's sisters nodded.

I slipped outside the room and down the hallway, taking photos, looking for other people, and generally snooping. As I worked, I wondered how Tondra and her girls would fare in an interview with Tandy or Margot. Because I had a feeling they hadn't been particularly honest with me about Stella Mae's love life.

I was slumped at the kitchen bar, my laptop open and a pad and pen at my elbow, typing up my report when I felt a prickle on my skin, like a cold rush of wind followed by the stillness preceding a lightning strike. Wild magic. I knew it was my boss before FireWind blew toward the house. His emotions and magic were riding high, electric, contained but explosive, like a bomb, primed and ready but confined behind steel walls.

I sat up straight, going on guard, and was watching the door, meeting his eyes as he entered. My up-line boss was a Cherokee skinwalker, soft-spoken, controlled. The frozen gust of magic rolled back and vanished, leaving him just a man, but paler than his normal golden skin tones. Hungry looking.

"Ingram," he murmured in his almost-a-whisper way. And as usual, that was all the greeting I got. He dove right into business. "Update. I understand you have spoken with the family."

"I have food in my car if you want. And while someone stopped using the inside coffeemaker due to *death and decay*, there's coffee in the percolator on the camp stove outside," I said, knowing he had to have seen the command center, as I scratched a note on the pad and passed it to him. It read, *Security system. Family upstairs.* Meaning they could listen in.

He paused the barest moment and gave me a single downward bob of his head, a gesture just like his sister used, economical and yet graceful. Jane Yellowrock was the most wild, untamed, yet decisive person I had ever met. She was the definition of scary. Her brother fell into a similar category, but while Jane trembled on the edge of violence at all times, FireWind was more constrained, reserved, a targeted weapon, which was scary all on its own. "I'd like something to eat," he said. "Seven hours in the car, a discussion with the DOD and a para-hating, right-wing governor, and an interview with the local FBI senior special agent has left me unpleasantly hungry."

I wasn't sure how one could be pleasantly hungry, but I closed my laptop and led the way outside to the camp stove.

The security lights were on at the barn and close to the house. Occam loped in from the shadows and joined us as we poured coffee. T. Laine appeared from the back of the house, where the portable null room was sitting, hopefully stopping the working on the contents. Astrid and Etain followed her halfway, but stopped when they saw us, their eyes on FireWind. They turned and walked away from the big boss. He had that effect on people, drawing eyes everywhere he went, but making people pause and reconsider any possible interaction.

FireWind had golden skin, peculiar yellow eyes, and long straight black hair, currently in a single braid down his back. At six-three or more and very slender, he was gorgeous, according to the others in the unit, but not my type. Nothing like Occam. "My car for debrief?" I asked when we were all in hearing distance.

"Yes," FireWind said. "Flights would have taken me until midnight to get here from New Orleans, so I rented a car and drove. The only rental was an older Honda Fit, which will not *fit* us all. It barely *fit* me."

"Yeah, well, the first person to spill something in my car has to detail it." I looked at the big boss. "You too."

He gave me a small smile. Some time ago, FireWind figured out that he terrified me, and that my way of dealing with terrifying men was to attack first, not back down, and refuse to apologize later. He put up with my insecurities and my social awkwardness, which I appreciated, albeit wordlessly.

As T. Laine filled the night air with a sotto voce update, we trooped through the dark to my car. FireWind reached for the driver's door, his body language saying that position of power was his by right. As he opened it, I swooped in front of him and inside, said, "Why, thank you," and pulled the door shut. My boss blinked and tried to regroup. I lifted the potted tree from the passenger seat and placed it on the dash. FireWind walked around the car, took the now-empty passenger front seat, and closed his door. T. Laine was trying to hide a smile. Occam looked cat-complacent as he joined her in the backseat.

Silence settled in the enclosed space. FireWind's eyes rested on the tree in its pot, but he didn't comment on it. Occam extended a box of donuts toward us, but FireWind shook his head. "Ingram, I understand you might have some protein bars? Something you made?"

I dug in the side pocket of the car and handed him the zipped plastic bag. Inside were the rest of the commercial salmon jerky and my homemade bars, two made with dried fish flakes, cornmeal, and dried fruit, one made with peanut butter, oats, and powdered milk, one made of nuts, seeds, honey, dried fruit, and salt. He broke all the bars and the jerky in half and offered them to us. It was a formal gesture, like breaking bread at a peace treaty or something. I should have felt bad about beating him to the driver's seat, but I didn't. It was my car, after all, and just because he was a man didn't mean he got to take over my stuff. I took half of the peanut butter bar. T. Laine made a face and shook her head. Occam accepted a fish-flake bar and a salmon jerky strip. We all watched FireWind as he sniffed the ones he had left.

"This one"—he held up half a cornmeal bar—"is like something the Tsalagi would prepare in autumn. Traveling food. Dried fish and cornmeal and dried berries. Every clan and every family had its own recipe." He bit in and tasted, chewing slowly. "I like the taste of sweet and salt together." He inclined his head at me.

I inclined mine back and said to FireWind, "We have a lot to tell you, and I know you stopped at the police department on the way in, but for everyone here, I recently finished a prelim question and answer with the mother and the two sisters. Heirs to Stella's land, personal properties, and liquid assets are the three of them and Catriona Doyle, who Stella knew for only a year. Catriona is a very weak witch, a musician in the band, and her sister is the stronger witch, Etain Doyle, currently allied with the North Nashville coven."

"Yes," FireWind said, licking his knuckle to get a salmon crumb, an unexpectedly inelegant gesture, but one that made me like him more. "Money, power, and passion, the roots of all murder. I spent an hour watching Catriona's interrogation through an observation glass and she keeps her secrets well, though I gathered that there was something more than friendship between Catriona and her employer. I am currently assuming that they were lovers, not something she needs to hide in this day and age, but not a relationship that Stella's more right-wing fans are likely to approve."

Surprise flashed through me. Stella and Catriona were lovers? The odd comments by her mother and sisters suddenly made sense. I was an idiot for not understanding them, but homosexuality was severely punished in the church. It wasn't the kind of relationship that was easy for me to recognize, falling into the unfamiliar.

He tilted his head, musing, "The Tsalagi have never understood the white man's needs to regulate sexuality. My impression was a gut reaction and is perhaps incorrect. We'll need Dyson and Racer to sit down with her." He wanted Catriona truth-read by the unit's empath and the unit's probie truth-senser together. It would be impossible to hide anything from them working as a team.

FireWind met my gaze. "Thank you for sharing your food. It will hold me until we leave here for the night."

"My pleasure." And it was. FireWind was overbearing and aloof, a reserved man who was still deeply affected by mores, tribal culture, outdated social standings, and the way the law was interpreted and enforced during the long years of his personal and law enforcement life. Most of the time, I didn't like him. But then he'd do something charming and my perceptions flipped. Besides. I liked feeding people. It made me happy.

He continued, "Catriona is a complicated woman. She, her sister, and her child are here in the States on visas from Ireland.

Catriona keeps secrets. She is grieving her friend and perhaps
lover. And because we have not completely ruled out death
magics, she *will* be charged with multiple counts of premedi-
tated murder by magical means in the morning, and likely Etain
as accomplice." He stared at the potted tree and added, "Unless
we have found highly exculpatory evidence, or unless the sheriff and I provide means forcing Smythe to postpone bringing
charges."

"Smythe is an ass," T. Laine said.

"True," FireWind said. "However, can you absolutely, con-
clusively prove that this working is not from a death-witch
curse, and that Catriona is not a death witch?"

"Not yet."

"Then we must let it play out until we can prove or disprove
those things," FireWind said.

"I'd like to observe when Tandy or Margot talks to Catriona," T. Laine said. "I want to say that she isn't a death witch
and these magics are not death magics, but there aren't any
studies on death witches, and we don't even know what *death
and decay* is." T. Laine's face pulled into a peeved expression.
"In the distant past, all witches were burned at the stake by
humans, but death witches were put down with extreme preju-
dice by whatever coven was capable of it. More recently they've
been immediately placed into null room prisons for the good of
the people around them."

"Not always," FireWind murmured, a small smile on his
face.

"Whatever," T. Laine said. "So we have no studies and no
cases where death-magic energies were read by witches or a
psy-meter. What we know from oral histories is that death
witches lose control of their magics and end up killing their
families. Sometimes their entire towns. From what I've observed, Etain's a vanilla witch. Her magics are ordinary and
controlled. She isn't capable of a magic working as complicated
and original as this one, and Astrid says Catriona has less magic
than Etain. No. Not death witches."

"Original?" FireWind said, picking out one word from
T. Laine's comments. He hesitated, seeming to choose his
words. "It was my understanding that most workings were built

upon others already in use. Even the unusual ones *you* used recently were built upon older, existent workings."

"Yes. Workings are almost always based on previous workings, even inside the strongest covens," T. Laine said. "What I meant was, it's supposed to be impossible to control or contain *death* workings. And while I've seen plenty of triggers, I've never heard of a trigger being used for a curse *and* I've never seen or heard of a trigger like this one. Triggers are for simple workings, very simple, like turning on your lawn-watering system. Not for big magic. This trigger? It's complicated, a complete mystery to the coven and to me. Maybe the Doyle sisters brought it from Ireland, but I'd be surprised." She described the trigger to FireWind. "The amulet was liquid based and its residue smells like licorice, aniseed, and strong spirits."

FireWind turned in his seat and looked out the windows. Occam turned to FireWind, who held up a finger. I understood nothing about the exchange except that something was up. FireWind said softly, "Absinthe?"

I checked the term *absinthe* on my cell and discovered that it was a grain alcohol made by macerating herbs and spices: fennel, anise, and wormwood, among others. Until recently, it was completely banned in the U.S. and most of Europe, but the herbs made it sound like a medicinal, like something Daddy would rub on a workhorse.

T. Laine lifted her brows, thinking. "Absinthe. Could be, but it's hard to find in this country even now."

"Is it legal in Ireland?" he asked, stretching his body to look out the windshield and above the car.

I tapped on my tablet, searching. "Yes," I said, and read the names of several shops that carried it in Ireland. "The reviews are mixed as to its taste and efficacy."

"It isn't likely that anyone devised a working elsewhere and then refined and used it here," FireWind mused. "The Irish covens are quite straitlaced and tend to oversee their younger members with an iron fist." He sat back in the seat, one knee up over the console, invading my space. There was nothing unkind or deliberately baiting about it, but simply because he was so tall and his legs so long. Unlike his usual office attire of black dress pants and white dress shirt, he was wearing black denim and a white button-down shirt with a lariat tie. A silver clip with a tiny yellow stone held the tie together.

I had an insane desire to ask him if he got animal hair on his clothing when he shifted into an animal form, but I swallowed it back. I was developing a big mouth, and while it could have gotten me a backhanded slap in the church, here it could result in professional difficulties that could impact my career.

My brain froze. *I have a career.*

"Ingram?" FireWind was talking to me.

Distracted, I had missed something. I moved my eyes to him, aware that they were too wide, too large. *I have a career.* "Huh?"

"Do you have something to add?"

"No. Not a thing."

He looked amused. "Would you be so kind as to introduce me to the Ragel family?"

"Huh?"

"The Ragel family. The victim's family. Kent is busy. You've met them. I would like an introduction." He was laughing inside. I could practically see it leaking out of his pores.

"Sure."

"Now," FireWind said to Occam.

Occam turned in his seat, opened the door, and leaped out. A drone veered away and Occam raced into the dark, following its trajectory.

The drone had been hovering over the car. Someone was watching, perhaps listening to us. And FireWind and Occam had known.

FireWind exited on the other side and said softly, "Well. That was interesting."

"Yeah. Fu—freaking press," T. Laine said.

The big boss smiled at her quickly recalibrated speech.

Inside, I took FireWind on a tour of the house's main level. When he motioned to the basement stairs, I said, "If you want, but there's a few things you need to know. You'll need to sit in the null room for a while after you get done, and right now it's full of dead body stink. You'll have to dress out and we're out of unis.

The basement should be T. Laine's to explain. And you might want to talk to the family first?" At the last moment I made that one a question, hoping that it changed my suggestions—orders?—into something less dictatorial. He really did bring out the elder-churchwoman-bossy in me.

He tilted his head and his eyes down to me in the formal way that did such a good job of keeping people at a distance. His braid slid over one shoulder to rest across his chest. "As you wish. I informed Kent that I brought a box of blue unis."

"Oh. That's good." Of *course* he had been contact with T. Laine. And had brought unis.

Together we trooped up the back stairs and I gave him a tour of the second level. The master suite was empty and had been tidied by someone, likely the family, especially the huge closet, its door partially open to show the bare floor. I peeked in and there was nothing pink hanging or shelved. I had looked online and discovered thousands of photos of Stella Mae Ragel on-stage. She never wore pink. Someone had removed pink clothing from Stella's closet. I murmured all this, and FireWind made a *hmmming* sound.

We pulled on nitrile gloves and rummaged through the closet, opening drawers, and I found three photo albums and a bunch of loose printed photos, which FireWind estimated were ten years old. We took them in as evidence, placing them in oversized evidence bags he carried in one pocket, just in case something from Stella's past was important to the case. I started the chain of custody forms for things we would remove from the house.

Together we walked around the bedroom, being nosy, the way special agents were supposed to be. There was a tall vase on the bedside table, with a pretty fuchsia bow tied through its two handles. It was maybe eighteen inches tall and it looked old, one of those antiques rich people collect for flowers and display. The vase had a teal bottom that got lighter near the top, the color at the rim a bright pink that nearly matched the bow. A yellow sunflower and green leaves were molded on the front, and a small card was folded at the base. FireWind said softly, "Roseville, the sunflower pattern."

I raised my brows in question. "You don't look like the kinda

man who'd know about pottery. Antiques, yes, because you're
so old, but not fancy pottery." As soon as the words left my
mouth I was horrified.

He looked amused and then his face softened. He said, "My
wife and I visited San Francisco once. She had a particular liking for Weller and Roseville pottery, which she discovered in a
storefront near the bay. She spent many hours there, talking to
the owner, learning the different styles and patterns, and when
we left, I bought her a small tea set to take with us. She adored
the green magnolia pattern and the apple blossom pattern." His
forehead creased and he said, "I believe that I still have the tea
set somewhere, in storage."

I opened the tiny card and on the inside were three words
and a date. "'I love you,'" I read aloud, "and this is dated three
months ago."

"Bag it," FireWind said, meaning take it into evidence. He
shifted the photo albums to his other arm. "Come. Let's see
what the rest of the floor shows us."

We went on, glancing into the rooms, following the soft
sound of voices into a gathering/media room. This room was
furnished with leather-upholstered recliners and sofas arranged
to view the oversized movie screen, and two square tables with
chairs for playing cards or eating. There were black end tables,
a kitchenette and minibar with a full-sized fridge, a two-burner
stove, a microwave, and a large selection of liquors on shelves.
As we pulled off our gloves, I knocked on the door and the occupants turned, going silent. "May we come in?" I asked.

"Is that the FBI agent who took Catriona?" Tondra asked, her
face taking on a pugnacious appearance.

Without stepping inside, he displayed his ID. "I am Ayatas
FireWind, PsyLED, regional director in charge of the eastern
seaboard, not FBI." He smiled and his entire face transformed
into something peaceful and kind and understanding. It ratch-
eted up his gorgeous factor about six notches and was not a look
he shared with his team. The unfamiliar expression faded into
compassion. "I have always been a great fan of Stella's work and
music, from the time she released her first single, 'Show Me
Every Day.' The guitar licks were unique, the harmonics were
utterly bewitching, and the first time I heard her voice I was
captivated. Please allow me to express my deepest condolences

on your loss." He bowed slightly. FireWind was either a class-A actor or he really felt everything he was saying.

"He's here to help," I said.

"If you'r'un wanting to help"—Tondra lowered the footrest of her recliner—"then you can get Catriona outta jail. She did *not* do this."

FireWind gave the evidence bags to me and tipped his head as if in agreement with the statement. "We are working on that. Special Agent Ingram"—he nodded to me—"has asked questions, but if you are willing, I'd like to ask a few more."

Tondra gave him a frown worthy of an elder churchwoman but gestured to one of the square tables. Her daughters followed her there, their eyes on FireWind. They took seats at the table, leaving only one. It placed FireWind's back to the door, deliberately I would assume, by Tondra's fleeting expression.

Most law enforcement officers hated to sit with an open door at their back, but FireWind smiled and I felt electric tings on my skin. There was no question that FireWind had some kind of passive magic. It was like a slow breeze blowing over long grasses, rippling them gently. Almost a vampire mesmerism in its overwhelming calming. It practically demanded for the human women to trust him. I didn't like him using it on them. Not that my opinion counted for anything. He placed a recording device on the table where no one could miss it and turned to me.

"Jones has sent you the address of the hotel where PsyLED is staying. The ninety-minute drive to Knoxville is too difficult for an every-day commute, and we can expect to pull long days for a bit. You may tell the unit to check in and get settled. We'll hold an abbreviated debriefing when I arrive."

It wasn't the abrupt dismissal that a vampire might give, but it was thorough.

He turned his back and took the vulnerable seat.

I realized for the first time that, with FireWind being a big Stella Mae fan, he intended to run the entire scene. He intended to *micromanage* (a wonderful and horrible term I had picked up from the unit) the entire case. And that meant FireWind would be staying at the hotel with us, would be here every moment, peering over our shoulders.

Shaking my head, I carried the evidence bags downstairs. This was going to be a very unusual, high-profile case because of Stella Mae's stardom and rabid fan base, but for Unit Eighteen it would be especially distinctive, with Ayatas FireWind running things. Rick LaFleur, who was stationed out of Knoxville HQ, actually ran most of the southeastern states, which was why he and Margot Racer, the unit's sort-of-probie, were in Chattanooga on a crime scene. We'd be without them, at a time when Margot's reputation as a star interviewer and her history in the FBI would have been helpful. I missed things being run the way I was used to. I might not get along with him all the time, but being healed by Soulwood had changed Rick LaFleur. He was, by far, the more comfortable boss to have around, which was saying a great deal, since I had kicked him in his testicles not long after we first met.

Downstairs, I discovered that the PsyCSI team had arrived from Richmond and had set up their equipment in the gathering room off the kitchen. They and the Nashville coven were dressing out in spelled unis as I passed by, T. Laine giving them instructions on limiting time in the studio since they wouldn't have access to the null room until morning. The crime scene team would soon clear the house so they could work through the night, though what they might find was in question since we had trampled through the house and most everything in the basement was decomposing.

I passed FireWind's message about the hotel to T. Laine, glad I wasn't part of CSI, forced to work straight through tonight. I needed sleep—and I had to deal with the situation at home. There had been more calls with voice messages from my sisters. Both sisters. I had been too cowardly to listen to their complaints, but the list of calls showed that the last three had been within minutes of each other, so I couldn't put it off much longer. I was afraid that Mud and Esther would kill each other if I continued to disregard the war simmering between them.

While everything was fresh in my mind, I stopped in the kitchen and wrote my reports, sending them to HQ. I also read reports filed by some of the others. I was avoiding the car and the privacy I needed to call my sisters. Cowardice, pure and simple. When I had dithered as long as I reasonably could, I left the house and trudged to my car.

The house and grounds were brightly lit, patrolled by private security as well as deputies. That was probably smart, based on the numbers of lights, cars, cameras, and generators at the far end of the drive. I didn't see Occam, so texted FireWind's message about the hotel, and he text-promised back to be along shortly. I stopped at FireWind's unlocked car, placed the evidence bags containing photo albums on the passenger seat, and locked the doors.

As I closed the door, I caught a glimpse of something pale in the darkness. I squinted against the security lights to see FireWind standing in a paddock, his white shirt the pale thing that had attracted my attention. I hadn't seen him leave the house and wasn't certain how he had gotten past me. He was utterly still, both arms out to his sides, his head down, his hair loose. A horse, one whose coat was too dark to identify in the night, flowed around him, prancing, tossing his head. As the light caught him, I recognized the lightning-blazed stallion. I stopped and watched.

The stallion danced, whirled, raced around the paddock, hooves pounding. He reared on his hind feet. A challenge. He pounded down. He snorted.

FireWind didn't move.

The stallion raced again, around the entire paddock. He bucked. Kicked out with his back hooves. He stopped, snorting like a bull, pawing the earth, his head going up and down. Then he charged. At a dead run he raced, attacking FireWind. My breath caught in my throat. The horse stopped fast, sitting back on his haunches. He whirled away, dancing around FireWind. Closer. Closer still. Around and around. Blowing and snorting and making sounds I couldn't identify but which were scary and mean. The stallion stopped. Man and horse in the same space. A man who . . . who likely didn't smell like a human.

Because FireWind was a skinwalker.

The horse pawed the earth. The man didn't move.

The horse tossed his head. The man didn't move.

The horse took a step closer. Until that moment I hadn't realized how curious horses were. Cat-curious. The stallion stepped closer. Kicked out with back hooves. Stopped. Took a step closer. He was within two feet of FireWind's left hand.

Stretching out his neck, the stallion sniffed the hand. He

breathed on FireWind's hand. A stillness followed, man and horse holding position. Slowly, the blaze shifted lower, down to touch FireWind's palm.

The hand slowly cupped around the muzzle, stroking. The horse blew out, pranced, and moved up to FireWind's elbow. To his shoulder.

The two seemed to curl around one another, FireWind's arm circling around the stallion's neck. His hands caressing beneath the mane. They stood still, in the dark, entwined. The stallion whickered.

Feeling as if I was encroaching on something private, an intimate experience, I turned and found my car and drove away. Turned into the street. A memorial of flowers, dolls, and teddy bears had been started and had grown into a long row at the fence line. Cameras and cell phones were everywhere, reporters trying to get a shot of my face through the car windows, and probably succeeding. The press had been joined by what looked like hundreds of cars as Stella Mae's fans continued to gather, standing in small groups, staring at the entrance and at me as I drove down the car-blocked, increasingly narrow road in front of the horse farm, toward Cookeville. As I drove, I called JoJo Jones at HQ. She answered, "Hey there, country hick chick. How you holding up, girl?"

"I'm more a plant person than a baby chicken, but I'm doing good."

She laughed and I updated her on the case.

JoJo told me about the media frenzy over the death of one of America's best-known country singers. "I spotted y'all in a few of the aerial shots," she said. "You're famous."

I groaned. She laughed again. And some of the weight I had carried all day began to lighten. It was half gossip session, half debrief, as if she knew I needed the reprieve from the *death and decay* of decomping bodies.

JoJo told me all about last Sunday dinner with her mama and grandmama and great-grandmama, and had me laughing and commiserating with the multigenerational complaints and arguments of a bunch of women in JoJo's tiny, ultramodern kitchen. Talking to her was a little like home, and somehow made me feel ready to talk to my sisters.

* * *

PsyLED had booked rooms for us in the Hampton Inn, off I-40. I remembered my reaction to the first hotel I had walked into, back when I signed on as a consultant. I had never seen such fancy carpeting, shiny stone floors, ornate décor. I had changed, or I was just exhausted. I didn't hardly look at the place as I checked in, instead going straight to the elevator and up to our rooms, carrying my gear gobags and the potted rooted sprig from the vampire tree. I carried it with me because when I had to read the ground deeply, it let me do so safely. It seemed to keep other plants from trying to root and grow into my body, which was strange and complicated. The tree back home and the potted mini vampire tree were both sentient or near enough not to matter. Not that the tree or I had shared that secret with many people. Tandy knew, but Tandy would never share that.

On our last big case, the tree had named itself the Green Knight, and had chosen a job—to protect me. It also had to be fed occasionally, and it wanted living creatures—mice, squirrels, birds. Also not shared. I wasn't used to keeping lies straight, so I managed by not talking about anything much at all. But it was getting hard to keep it all silent.

JoJo had booked three rooms, one a large suite for FireWind with a king bed and a work area, and the others two regular hotel rooms with two queen beds. If we double bunked, we could sleep four to a room. I hoped the CSI team would be put elsewhere. I didn't particularly enjoy bunking with strangers.

I chose the room farthest from FireWind's corner suite and fortunately my room had a south-facing window for the tree. I tossed my bags onto the bed closest to the window. The view was not much a nothing, but the tree would be happy come morning. I stuffed my *death and decay*–stinking clothes into a large zippered plastic bag, showered fast with my strong-smelling homemade lavender soap, and groomed my leaves—tightly curled leaf buds along my hairline. This was a part of my daily toilette, and if I forgot, the leaves stuck out. I had been classified in Spook School and was listed on my personnel records as nonhuman, paranormal, undifferentiated.

I dressed in sweats and unpacked my four-day gobag. I didn't travel with much. A change of pants, three shirts, the sweats (which I wore when working in a hotel room when business attire would be uncomfortable), sleeping clothes that were really yoga pants and a tank top in case I had to be seen in the middle of the night, undies, extra socks, field boots, jeans for field work, a plastic bag of travel-sized toiletries, extra mags and ammo, and a speedloader. Unpacking took all of twenty seconds. I unlocked and cracked open the connecting door between the other room and this one so Occam would know I was here.

My cell rang. Again. It was Mud's number. Sighing, I sat on the bed and stretched out, propped by the pillows. I hit the accept button for the overdue call with my younger sister.

"Hey, Mud."

"You'un ain't called us all day. We'uns been calling and calling and I'da thought you was dead if I hadn't called JoJo and asked her." Her voice went up in pitch, echoing in the house around her on speakerphone. "You'uns out of town and I *need* you! Esther wants to kick Cherry outta the house!" Her voice went louder. "She's my dog and I say she's an inside dog!"

Esther was taking care of Mud while I worked. It had sounded good in theory. It wasn't working out as planned.

"Dogs and cats is *not* inside critters," Esther shouted. "They belong outside and not in here with people!"

"I thought that since I didn't have school today we'uns could go shopping. Instead I been stuck with *her*! Where are you and when are you coming home so Esther will stop *bossing me around*?"

Rubbing my forehead and the headache that throbbed just behind my eyes, I said, "I don't know."

The silence was absolute.

Then Esther shrilled, "What do you mean you don't know?"

My older sister, who was a tree-creature-in-hiding like Mud and me, was a holy terror. She was pregnant and growing leaves and having marital problems with her husband-by-the-church. Meaning she had never legally married him but was church-married, and in God's Cloud of Glory Church women traditionally had no property, no money, no authority, and no say in anything. She had moved in with us a week past, following a spat with her husband. Daddy and Mama wouldn't take her in, and my older sister Priss had told us, "Flat-out no," so that left me, the rebel who had walked away and survived to tell the tale, as the one with a visitor. I had been willing—even eager—to help any of my sisters, and Esther's watching Mud had sounded great. But Esther's constant whining and snipping had burned me down to a low simmering anger.

I closed my eyes tight, took a steadying breath, firmed my resolve, drew on about half the church-speak I needed to make my point, and said into the silence, "You'uns both listen to me." My heart went hard and my voice went harder. "Esther, there's nothing I can do to help you with your messed-up marriage, the fact that you're growing leaves, your relationship with the church, or your baby. *Not a dang thing.*"

Mud tittered at my cussing.

"You have to figure out your life and what you want and how you intend to get there. If you're gonna fight, then fight, but pick adversaries and battles you think you can win and accept that you may lose. You fight the church, you fight your husband, I'll be at your side to help, but *I cannot fight for you.* And. You need to remember this. If you argue and fight with me and Mud, in my home, on my land, then the only ally you have will turn her back on you. 'Cause I ain't gonna live in misery and disharmony like what you'un and Jed live in."

Over the connection I heard Esther take a shocked breath.

Well, truth was hard to take. Esther had problems, no one was denying that. But some of her problems had been made worse by her attitude. Feeling tired and resentful and worn to a frazzle, I pushed on. "Mud, you have to figure out how to get your sister help, or kick her out, or call Daddy and Mama and have her removed according to church practices. But whatever you do, you need to remember it has repercussions. You help her, you might be stuck with her. You kick her out, you got to live with the knowledge that you made your sister and her baby homeless. You bring in the church, that might get her burned at the stake because she's got leaves. Lots of leaves, thanks to the baby hormones. That path will drag us all into the church spotlight. And it will prove to the church that womenfolk can't live without the stern controlling *man* at the reins."

Mud said, "But—"

"Hush," I said. "I'm talking. According to the church, you're a woman grown and capable of thinking and acting like one.

Now, I know you're just a kid, but you ain't uneducated or stupid or foolish. You got a smart head on your shoulders. You both know how to have a dialogue. That's one good thing the mamas taught all a us—how to talk through problems."

They had fallen silent.

"I can't be there to fix it for either one a y'all tonight," I said. "However, Esther, understand this. That's my house. The dog and cats live there. Inside unless they been skunked. Let them in. *Now*.

"Mud, stop picking at your sister. 'Cause I *know* you been picking and she can't take it right now 'cause a the baby. When I get home, we three are going to have a come-to-Jesus meeting and it ain't gonna be pretty."

A come-to-Jesus meeting meant a meeting that would result in judgment to right the wrongs and change things. It wasn't a meeting I demanded lightly and even Esther knew it. She said, "But—"

"No buts." My voice went hard, cold, and intractable. "My house, my rules." I hit the end button, wondering if I had just ignited a fuse or put out a fire. And knowing that my last few lines had been the exact sort of thing a churchman might say to churchwomen having an argument.

Rules. I had just set boundaries, demanded actions and attitude changes. Like a churchman demanded of his women. Shame curled inside my heart. "Well, dang," I muttered.

"That was impressive, Nell, sugar."

I opened my eyes to see Occam in the open doorway between our rooms. I hadn't heard him come in. He was leaning against the jamb, ankles crossed, arms loose, damp hair hanging forward and curling under his scarred jaw. He had already showered and changed into faded jeans and a long-sleeved Henley tee in a soft faded purple shade. I always looked at his neatly trimmed nails, and he smiled when my eyes dropped down to his toes. He scratched them into the low-pile carpet, much like a cat might scratch on a post, letting me look. They were so different from my deceased husband's old beat-up feet and long thick jagged nails. Something in my middle flickered, heated, and spread, bright and quick, like fireflies in the night, calling to one another. My cat-man was here. Feeling light as a . . . as a sprite, maybe, I stared at him, taking in his damp hair, his slightly scruffy face, at the way the Henley conformed to his long, lean chest, committing this image to memory, so I could pull it up again, anytime I wanted. The fireflies in me multiplied and I placed the cell facedown on the bed.

"I didn't mean to eavesdrop," he said, "but the door was open. I only heard the last bit."

"I was pretty loud. I reckon I didn't care who heard me." I looked from the phone back to him. "I love you, Occam," I said.

His eyes began to glow the yellow of his cat.

"I apologize for my jealousy," I said. "I renounce the church and the fear and the jealousy that made me react to Etain's interest in you. I also renounce treating my sisters like churchwomen instead of equal partners. Sometimes I'm just all kinds a stupid."

He had begun to grin as I listed my sins. It was the kind of grin that said he thought I was cute as a kitten. Adorable. Even when I got all thorny and prickly. One hand had been held at his side, slightly behind his hip. He drew it forward and in his fingers was a single, long-stemmed lavender rose.

"It's called Sterling Silver," Occam said, as its fragrance filled the space between us.

John had brought me wildflowers, but never anything so magnificent. Something bittersweet and urgent and needy flooded into the fireflies within me.

Tears caught at my eyes; my chest twisted into some impossible spasm of delight. My words shuddered when I said, "I love you and I know you love me."

"With all I am and all I ever shall be. With all my heart and soul. With my claws and fangs and with my human body. With your leaves or without. With thorns, like this rose, or smoothstemmed like an oak. To the full moon and back."

"Oh. My," I said, the strange tears spilling over. "So. Catman-who-loves-me. Where are T. Laine and FireWind?"

"Busy," he growled. "At least an hour behind me."

I had thought my question and his answer were an invitation, but he didn't move. Didn't say anything else. But then, he had placed our entire relationship at my feet, in my hands. And . . . we had an hour. A whole, entire hour. Alone. I got up and walked to him, touched his chest with one hand and touched his hand, holding the rose, with my other. His skin was cat-man heated. He smelled of hotel soap and shampoo and I curled my fingers around his. Pushed him gently into his room. I shut and locked the door to my room, the one I would share with T. Laine. Slowly, I spun us and pulled him after me, crawling up onto his bed, and patted the plump pillows. "C'mere, cat-man. I got some making up to do, and I plan to do it in this here bed."

Occam purred, a full-on throat-vibrating purr. He pulled off his Henley. Balled it up and tossed it across the room.

FIVE

FireWind texted us to gather in his suite for an EOB—
end-of-business—debriefing and dinner, as soon as he and
T. Laine had a chance to shower off the death stink and change.
When we got there, we found pizza boxes with the logo for Bel-
lacino's Pizza & Grinders. The four of us fell on the pies as if
we were starving and the pizzas took a hurting in just minutes.

Maybe it was the fact that I'd only eaten donuts, coffee, and
my protein bars all day, but I was pretty sure this was the best
pizza I had ever eaten. Maybe the best meal I had ever eaten. In
my life.

"So good," I said midway into my third and last piece. Even
my leaves, trying to curl into my hairline, were happy.

FireWind took a slow bite and chewed as he watched us
eat, his gestures formal, a ritual, as if eating take-out pizza was
a ceremony of breaking bread. Maybe in his world it was.
Maybe I should ask that. Maybe I should have already asked.
Had I insulted him? I concentrated on my slice, trying to figure out the proper social words. I settled on something that
Mama might have said to the senior wife of a church elder. "I
thank you for the meal, the drinks, and the cheesy goodness. It's
delicious."

T. Laine and Occam chimed in with thanks and FireWind
inclined his head, still formal but a bit less distant. "You are
welcome."

JoJo and Tandy, back at HQ in Knoxville, were on the Internet with us, their faces on FireWind's computer screen in the
middle of the table. It was PsyLED's version of FaceTime but
with added security. They were eating salads and grilled salmon
with some kind of fancy sauce, and I didn't know whether I was

covetous or not. Considering my pizza-swollen belly, I decided envy was out of place.

I asked, "Why's Tandy not here to help with the interrogations?"

"Dyson did the preliminary questioning of the victims sent to UTMC," FireWind said, using the law enforcement SOP of last names only, which I still wasn't used to, "and he experienced a negative reaction to the presence of the *death* working."

I looked at the screen in surprise. The last time magic had affected Tandy he had misused his gifts to sway the thoughts of others. I wondered if that had been a problem this time. He shrugged uneasily and slid his eyes to JoJo, saying, "I had no ability to read emotions. It's nice to not have other people's emotions pressing on my mind, but it made me no more effective than a human." JoJo's expression didn't change at all, but I had a feeling there was more to it than that.

"*Death and decay* energies," T. Laine said, correcting her boss. "It's not a witch working. All we know for sure is it's directed paranormal energies." She was using a tone of voice my mama woulda called sassy and swiped my bottom for using.

FireWind didn't react to it, merely gave a single slow nod. "Interesting distinction. When Ingram returns to Knoxville, and the *death and decay* energies have been neutralized, Dyson may be joining us here, for a limited time, in situations where he isn't negatively affected. I want two people available at HQ at all times."

I didn't look at Occam, but I figured that meant we'd have no more hotel alone time. While we were still finishing up the last bites of pizza, T. Laine opened the EOB by calling on Clementine to record and transcribe the meeting. Clementine was the software that saved us from having to take meeting notes, but it was confined to HQ and only available now because we were essentially live.

T. Laine gave the time, the date, and the names of all present, repeating to the group that she had been on the road to Bowling Green for a read when FireWind redirected her to Stella Mae Ragel's property. Using one clean fingertip to page across the notes on her small electronic tablet, she walked us through the events of the day, and caught us all up on the condition of the transport vehicle that had been taking the body of

Stella's housekeeper to UTMC in the cooler. "It's still stalled in the middle of I-40. The *death and decay* is working much faster in the vehicle than at the studio, probably because the concrete floor of the house is more substantial. The energies have eaten through the cooler, the floor of the vehicle, and the asphalt underneath it." She licked tomato sauce off a finger and tucked her hair back behind an ear with it. "Traffic is backed up for a good seven miles and has been rerouted to back roads, which are bumper-to-bumper. The Nashville coven is heading to I-40 now to set up a circle around the transport vehicle and try to neutralize, or at least contain, the energies. I don't think the vehicle can be salvaged. Frankly, I think it's a total loss. The county will have to replace the transport unit and the state will have to repair the interstate, that is, *if* we can find a way to neutralize the destruction.

"For now, the coven has the worst of the energies at the house shielded and they aren't leaking into the water table. Come dawn, Astrid and a few of her younger witches will be back at Melody Farm to see if the T-shirts and the thing we think might be a trigger for the *death and decay* are clean after being in the null room all night. Overall, the North Nashville coven is working well with the locals, so that's a good thing."

"I'd like a cost-benefit analysis of purchasing twenty portable null rooms," FireWind said, watching T. Laine with the steady gaze of a hunting cat. "We currently have twenty PsyLED units throughout the contiguous states, and are getting ready to open one in Alaska and one in Hawaii. The cost of the null room at Unit Eighteen HQ was twenty-seven thousand dollars, inexpensive because all we had to do was insulate the walls properly so the Richmond coven could apply the working. However, we are limited by its permanent location. It seems wise to provide a portable null room for each unit, if the cost can be included in next year's budget."

"Witches make them, you know," she said, her tone aggressive, staring back at him, her eyes seeing something I was clearly missing. "Including witches at Spook School. You should ask the Spook School coven for a price. But one thing to keep in mind. The trailers have to be tuned up periodically. Like, every time they're moved. And it takes a coven of at least three to do that."

FireWind said, "Tune-up," sounding faintly amused. He used a paper napkin to clean his already meticulous fingers. When he was done, there was no grease on the paper. At all. Had the big boss just used a stalling technique? "I would prefer to keep this outside of the witch covens in Richmond and Baltimore. And away from the Seattle coven as well."

"Really," T. Laine said, her tone too cold to be called deadpan.

"Yes. All three of the major covens have benefited financially and politically from their relationships with the military and federal law enforcement. It's time to expand PsyLED's contacts with other covens in the paranormal world."

"Past time," T. Laine said. Something in her tone suggested that she had said these same words recently.

"I have recognized the benefit of consulting with covens in each city where a PsyLED unit is located. Would you be willing to fly out with each portable null room delivery and give a tutorial to the PsyLED units in the use and upkeep of such a tool?" He was staring at T. Laine, watching her, evaluating. "And, while there, would you consider negotiating with local covens who might be willing to consult with and partner with the human units, providing assistance with the trailers when they are moved?"

T. Laine had gone very still as he talked. "Sure. Bet that would make the entrenched old dudes on the units happy," she said, her tone saying the opposite. "Is this just chitchat or is this a real thing?"

"I have sent a report with an urgent needs request to the director of Homeland. I'll need to provide an additional protocol and budgetary request for the twenty portable null rooms and coven consulting fees. Yes. It's a *real thing*," he said, his voice taking on its first emotional content.

T. Laine sat back, her jaw forward, pugnacious as ever, but her body language looser. It was quite clear that something very unpleasant had happened between the two while I was off the last two days.

"You read my report," she said, accusing.

"I did. It was passed along to me by Soul. In future, I would appreciate being apprised of any reports before they are sent up-line to the assistant director of PsyLED."

My eyes went wide. It sounded as if T. Laine had gone over his head with something and FireWind was ticked off.

"Happy to," she said. "But just so you know and so you can get your tail feathers out of that twist, that report and letter went to LaFleur and up-line to the assistant director before you were appointed to your current position." T. Laine leaned in to FireWind, holding his eyes with hers. "I didn't go behind your back or over your head. Sir."

An uncomfortable silence built in the room, and I was aware of Tandy's and JoJo's interest. They weren't even tapping on keyboards. "And next time you want to reprimand me for something you think I've done, let's talk in private first, so I don't have to bust your balls in the middle of a unit meeting."

FireWind blinked. T. Laine didn't.

Occam drawled, "I'da brought popcorn if I'da known there was gonna be entertainment."

"I just stuck a bag in the microwave," JoJo said from HQ. "This is fun."

FireWind sat back in his chair. T. Laine didn't. "I think that is a fair way to proceed from this point," he said.

"Uh-huh. And I accept your apology," she said.

FireWind smiled, one of those rare, wide, truly happy smiles I had seen maybe twice in all the months we had worked from the same office. "I didn't offer an apology," he said, amusement heavy in his tone.

"Should have."

FireWind chuckled. "Yes. I suppose I should. Please consider it simply late, and not a lack of social graces. I apologize for the incorrect assumption and for not discussing this in private first."

T. Laine remained unmoving, leaning forward for several seconds, before she sat back in her chair. She was wearing an oversized gray shirt and sweatpants and bright pink socks. She still looked tired and pale. "JoJo," T. Laine said, continuing the meeting. "Update us on the lab work I collected on that green stuff on the bodies, please."

The realization hit me. T. Laine had taken charge of the meeting. It should have been FireWind in charge. He had baited her and she had baited him back. The undercurrents in the room were as tangled as any in the Nicholson home back at the church, and surely had more causation than the back-and-forth I had just seen. These two had been in an argument, or something worse, and everyone in the unit knew about it except me.

JoJo said, "The substance is a complex mixture of proteins, sugars, tissue breakdown products, and enzymes, none of which are normal for living humans or in decomping humans. I sent the values to everyone with the comparable healthy living values. I sent samples to the CDC lab for bacterial and fungal cultures and possible virus identification involved in the tissue breakdown. But for now, all we have are the chemical lab values."

I opened the file on my laptop, glad to focus on something other than the undercurrents in the room. There were things like glucose, BUN, sodium—dozens of chemicals. None matched the normal values in live humans. But then the people had been dead so maybe that was to be expected.

JoJo talked a lot more about chemistry, not a lick of which I understood. When she finished with test results, she said, "As soon as you can transport any bodies safely, the paranormal forensic pathologist at UTMC is ready and waiting. She's seen the pics with the green-tipped fingers and she wants a look-see inside the bodies, especially as the hospital has live patients to treat. So far the hospital is just treating their symptoms. The hospitalists want answers and a way to devise a more comprehensive treatment plan."

"The decomp is so fast, I doubt they'll get to see bodies from this scene," T. Laine said. "Probably just more sludge. But we'll know more tomorrow, after we get them out of the null trailer."

JoJo said, "What do we know about Catriona and the FBI guy, Macauley Smythe?"

T. Laine lifted her head from her laptop and spoke to FireWind. "Sir."

FireWind took a swig of his cola and crossed one ankle over the other knee. He said, "Catriona Doyle asked for an attorney and has refused to answer questions. Macauley Smythe plans to charge Doyle with three counts of first-degree murder by magical means, and multiple counts of attempted murder. He intimated to the sheriff that he may ask for a grand jury with the intent of charging the Nashville coven for multiple counts of attempted murder by magical means since she's a member there."

"That's stupid. It'll never hold up in court," T. Laine said.

"I don't think he cares," FireWind said. "As several of you have pointed out, he intends to parlay this short-term renown into a secure job future when his twenty-five are up. The new national FBI director is not returning my calls, though I have spoken with his staff about the imprudence of such charges without sufficient evidence. I do not believe that Catriona Doyle is a death witch. However, with several people in the hospital, and the beginning of a national antiwitch, antiparanormal hysteria, it would be wise to do everything in our power to find the perpetrator and wrap up this case quickly. Jones," he said to JoJo, "you contacted the paranormal ward at UTMC and offered them the null room at HQ and any assistance we might provide. What was the response?"

"The person I spoke with said they had the patients stabilized but they'd let us know if they needed to bring anyone to the null room," JoJo said. "She was not enthused at the prospect, but she said thank you."

FireWind said, "You were on scene all day, Occam. Thoughts on the suspect's methodology?"

"At this point," Occam said, "I think someone got into the house and set the trigger into a box of shirts—assuming it was a trigger—with the intent of killing whoever opened the box."

"Not Stella Mae specifically?" FireWind asked, leaning forward and holding Occam's gaze.

Surprised, I said, "Why would anyone think Stella would open a box of swag?"

"An assistant or a grip or a low-level flunky would open boxes," Occam said, agreeing. "Stella was the star, not the paid help."

"Hmmm. Indeed." FireWind sounded surprised. "And the shirts?"

"Somehow missed or simply not taken on tour because the buses were full?" Occam suggested. "I talked to the driver of Stella Mae's personal RV. He said every square inch of space in both vehicles was packed the day they left. He said he saw several boxes still in the swag room."

"Everyone I spoke with said the shirts look like real tour tees, not some fake batch put there just to load up a spell or a curse," I said. "And with the construction, the trigger had to be set in the last two weeks."

FireWind propped an elbow on the chair arm and rubbed his chin.

I swiped through the still shots of the swag room taken by the first LEOs on the scene. "There were open shipping boxes containing promotional material when the deputies got there. Two had been open long enough that there was dust on the contents." I pointed to a photo indicating dust. "The tape on the box of shirts was freshly cut. Monica Belcher had been putting away things, opened the T-shirt box, grabbed some shirts, and fell." I pointed at a photograph I had taken and said, "I didn't notice it until later, but that looks like the handle of a box cutter in Monica's hand. It's mostly hidden by her body, but it's the right shape." The others leaned as I expanded the image to show a rounded handle.

"The tape could have been cut at some point previous and reapplied when the witch trigger was set," T. Laine said, leaning to get a better look at the photo of the box, "assuming it was a witch trigger, assuming this was a murder, a designation we have yet to officially make." Her face said she was tired of dancing around making this a murder scene, was prepared to call it a witch trigger and start looking for suspects. "But FireWind didn't call it that at the five p.m. press conference and"—she looked at the big boss—"you kept the sheriff and chief of police from doing so too. That was some impressive dancing you and the press did, by the way."

"It kept SAC Smythe from saying things he might have regretted and it bought Catriona Doyle another day without charges. I've read over Ingram's data," FireWind said. "She has specified where everyone was today at the farm, when, and for how long." He looked at me. "Good work getting so many of the social media links for everyone too."

I felt my face warm. I wasn't used to praise.

FireWind leaned forward and clasped his hands together between his knees. "I want a level three background check on every single person who had access to Stella Mae's basement for the entire duration of the tour and level four checks for everyone the two days Stella was in the house after the tour, followed by in-depth interviews, with a close emphasis on the last two weeks. Concentrate on the dead and work out from there. We are looking for a witch, a magical practitioner, or someone with the funds to hire such. We are looking for someone with a grudge against Stella Mae Ragel or one of the band members.

"I know it does not need to be said, but we talk to no one outside this unit, and we guard our words anywhere we might be overheard. The media is everywhere, following LEOs, sneaking onto the property, trying to get inside to take photographs of Stella Mae."

"Worse," JoJo said. "Turn on your TVs. The media just posted breaking news, based on unnamed sources close to the case, that Catriona Doyle will be charged for the murders. Dollars to donuts the feeb, Smythe, released the info."

Occam turned on the set and we watched the news scrolling by on CNN and then on Fox. They were both naming Catriona Doyle as a suspect in the deaths and showing aerial footage of the investigation at the farm.

Without taking his eyes from the screen, FireWind said, "Ingram, I need you to go back to the farm and read the land. I had hoped to wait until tomorrow, but, with this"—he gestured to the TV—"I want it done tonight, not in the daytime when the drones might take footage of you. Since nothing reads specific on the psy-meter, I want you to see if you can tell what the *death and decay* energies are, whether it's speeded-up natural progression or a witch curse or even something else." He hesitated and I thought he might say more about the "something else," but he didn't. "If possible, I'd like you to determine how it got onto the property: via the drive, the front door, the back door, or a trail in." He looked at me. "You were able to determine that with the salamanders, yes?"

FireWind was talking about the things that had nearly killed LaFleur and had killed Occam. I could discern their passage over the land when I read it. "I can try," I said, hesitant. Every time I used my gift of reading the land deeply, I risked losing myself in it and becoming more plant. I had been practicing at Soulwood, and I had gained a little control over reading and the unintended results, but I still couldn't read the earth for more than a few minutes at a time or I set down roots. Literally.

I didn't want to be a tree again. I liked being human.

"We know that three reporters made it from the connecting road overland to the house," FireWind said. "I want you to rule out anything you can, tonight. Tomorrow, after you get some sleep, I want you back at HQ to help Jones on the deep backgrounds."

Deadly danger, followed by paperwork and scut work, I thought. With new probie Margot gone, research fell back to me. Worse, I'd have to face my sisters sooner than later. I held in a resigned sigh.

"I know you are trying to locate the Blood Tarot deck, but put that on the back burner." As if he thought that was why I was hesitating, he added, "The Blood Tarot is a vital piece of evidence from the last case, and when this is wrapped up, you can return to it. Or sooner if we receive evidence that it's being used in blood magic."

T. Laine said, "Nell can't read the earth alone."

I looked down at my laptop. I didn't like it stated quite so baldly, but it was the truth.

"Ah. As we are several days out from the full moon," FireWind said, "I'd like Occam to go with her."

"I can do that," Occam said.

FireWind met T. Laine's eyes. "If this meets with your approval."

T. Laine flushed faintly but nodded.

"A few final, unrelated particulars before we dismiss," he said. "Jones. Originally, the third floor was intended to be set up for a PsyCSI lab, but the engineers say the equipment needs to be on a concrete slab on a ground floor to protect it from magical energy interference and to provide weight bearing for heavy equipment, so the lab will be elsewhere, though close by HQ. Within a few months, we will no longer have to transport in crime scene techs and transport out all testing. HQ's third floor will eventually become the expanded regional administration offices of PsyLED under my direction, and my office will be moved upstairs as soon as construction is complete. Unit Eighteen will continue to be run by Rick LaFleur and Jones, with Jones also responsible for setting up IT for the regional office and meshing the system with the national office systems. Jones, congratulations. You have been moved up a pay grade, but without the onus of moving to another state. You will have your choice of two IT people to work with, and reasonable funds to set up the computer systems."

On the screen, JoJo's mouth was pursed in shock. Carefully, as if he was holding out chocolate and might jerk it back, she said, "I can take Tandy? And train my IT people myself?"

"Yes. I had assumed that you would take Dyson with you upstairs."

I was pretty sure that everyone was as surprised as I was. Maybe more. They all looked . . . stricken was a good word.

FireWind was dour and distant as he looked around at us, including the screen with Tandy's and JoJo's faces. That totally disarming smile flashed before disappearing back into that solemn expression. "Regarding our relationship discussions this previous week, I wish to consider the emotional and practical needs of this unit. In fully human units, fraternization results in transfers and can be means for reprimand. Because Unit Eighteen is composed primarily of paranormals, I am granting leeway where personal relationships are concerned, as long as no personnel problems arise, as long as you are discreet and you continue working well as a team. Should problems develop, offenders will be sent to other units and possibly demoted as required."

It was a gift and a threat.

FireWind went on. "I'm thankful to all of you for the excellent work and hard hours you put in today. Especially Kent, who has done an outstanding job taking lead on this investigation, and who has been the principal individual bringing this region of PsyLED into the twenty-first century. Despite a hasty tongue and hot temper, over the last year, she has developed what I hope will be ongoing relationships with other paranormals, including the unit's weres and Knoxville's Mithran vampires, and has found ways to utilize and work with multiple witch covens over the course of every case.

"Kent." He addressed her. "The paperwork went in yesterday, and at your next evaluation, you also will move up a pay grade, and you will be offered the responsibility I outlined earlier, to travel to each of the other units to train their humans and to negotiate with the local covens for contract work on a consultation basis." He sent her a quick look of chagrin, which was totally unexpected. "That is, *if* you can keep your mouth shut and not annoy your up-line SAC for his cultural oversights and accessional gaffes.

"That is all for tonight."

We were dismissed.

"Did T. Laine know FireWind had put her in for a pay raise?" I asked.

"No way," Occam said as he maneuvered his fancy car through the streets of Cookeville, driving us back toward Stella's Melody Horse Farm. "He probably wasn't supposed to announce that for weeks."

"So why did he? Announce tonight, I mean. And what's going on between Lainie and him? She was practically beating him with words. And what's up with the threat he made about separating us?"

"Two days ago, FireWind made the mistake of suggesting that Lainie might want to steer clear of Captain Gonzales."

"Ohhh." T. Laine was currently dating the leader of Knoxville SWAT, Captain Joaquin H. Gonzales, a cop she had met at our last big case. Gonzales once had the rep of a para hater, but since he and his entire team had been almost wiped out by a blood-magic user and the Blood Tarot, and since T. Laine and a bunch of paras had saved his butt, things had changed and romance had blossomed. "Why would he do that? In the church, the surest way to drive a girl into a suitor's arms is to say no to a courtship."

"Don't know, except Gonzales and FireWind are having issues. Don't know what sparked it either. JoJo tried to find a record of what happened, but nada."

"What did—How did—" I stopped.

"He walked in on Lainie talking on the phone at her cubicle and told her Gonzales was bad news and that she could do better."

"Oh. My."

"Yeah. She used some pretty colorful language telling him off. Said he had no right to dictate who she slept with."

"Oh *my*," I repeated. I had been off two days ago. I had missed the fireworks.

"And in case you might be wondering, he then dropped by my cubicle and warned me that *our* dating was against regs. I told him he could—well, he could do something anatomically impossible."

"What got into him?" I asked.

"We don't think it has anything to do with current events. Jo did some digging." Which meant hacking into governmental files, not something we would ever say aloud. "She found out FireWind was married in the late 1800s, to a witch. She was injured in a fire in 1937—the Blackwater fire in Shoshone National Forest in Wyoming. He got her out, but she was badly burned. She lived for several weeks before she died." He slanted a look my way. "Want to take a guess which date matched two days ago?"

"The date of his wife's death?"

"Yep. Worst part was, he had dreamed about fire for decades. He thought it was some kind of vision quest. He used to chase fires, looking for the vision. Turned out the dream was a premonition, not something he was supposed to chase."

"That's horrible."

"Yeah. And to keep him from knowing Jo was digging into his sealed files, we have to go on treating him like he's an ass. Which he still is, but at least we can understand some of it."

"So FireWind causing trouble and making threats was all tied up with him trying to run people's romantic lives, including ours? And him losing his wife? Grief and him having a stick up his rear end?"

"Pretty much."

"This is gonna be hard," I said.

"What? Keeping secrets?"

"No. Being nice to him whenever I want to kick that stick farther up his backside."

Occam chuffed with laughter. "You know? I dated a woman before I joined Unit Eighteen, a non-cop civilian. There was almost nothing we could talk about that wasn't off-limits on my part or considered gruesome on her part. The relationship didn't last."

"Good," I murmured.

Occam chuffed again, cat-like. "I'm glad we both work law enforcement because we can talk about anything." He extended his hand and I placed mine into it. Warmth spread from the point of contact, from the way our fingers laced together and tightened.

This. This was all the goodness I had ever wanted.

My cell rang. It was Mud. I let it go to voice mail. I was not letting my little sister spoil this moment.

It was close to midnight when we got to Stella Mae's farm and, now that the late news was over, the road out front was clear of media vans and roving reporters and cars and music fans. Except for the flowers and stuffed animals piled along the fence and the armed security guard at the end of the drive, I'd have never known a crime or a death had taken place.

Occam whirled the steering wheel and braked the sports car to show our IDs. Maybe it was the late hour, or maybe he knew our faces, but the guard let us pass through without the hassle I'd experienced earlier. Even at night the house and grounds were amazing, the buildings and plantings well lit, the security lights providing visibility of anyone approaching, if not actual protection. There were still vehicles parked out front and I recognized PsyCSI vans and the witch cars. The crime scene techs (who had their own unis) were likely at work inside, trying to collect evidence, while the witches were in the backyard at their circle trying to figure out how to rein in *death and decay*. There was crime scene tape all around the house, where there had been none before, but there was an opening that led to the side door.

We got out and Occam popped the trunk. I locked my weapon in the gun safe in the floor of the small vehicle. Occam was still armed and, in his off hand, lifted out my vampire tree, a flashlight, and the faded pink blanket I used in my readings. He had a sharp steel knife strapped at one thigh and was dressed in jeans and field boots, like me. He made a fist, working his fingers free of the stiffness he still experienced from being burned. Against the evening's chill we both wore dark wind jackets printed with *PsyLED* on the front and back, our IDs clipped near the collars.

"Something I can do for you folks?" a voice asked out of the darkness.

Occam didn't go for his weapon, so I figured he recognized the man in the dark with his cat vision or by scent. Having spent twenty years in cat form in a silver-lined cage had given him more access to his cat abilities while in human shape than most were-creatures, and his eyes were glowing with a faint gold sheen. "PsyLED business, Deputy Stanhope," Occam said. "We'd appreciate it if you could turn off the outside lights and the security lights for a bit. We need to measure the energies of the house and the grounds in the dark."

"Can do. You catch the witchy-woman who did this and I'll help you burn her at the stake."

I flinched, a motion too tiny to be noticed by anyone but Occam.

"You talking about burning women, Officer?" Occam said, both conversational and warning.

"Joke, my man. Joke."

"Uh-huh. Lights, please."

Footsteps crunched away. One by one, the lights went out. In a nearby pasture a horse snorted. I heard the sound of hooves as animals moved in the gloom. Slowly, the moon and the stars brightened in the sky and the reflected moonlight illuminated the white-painted house and the white four-board fencing, visible even to my human eyes. Plant-people didn't have better-than-human night vision.

"Ground, near the front door," I said softly.

Without turning on the flash, Occam led the way to the front, one hand on my elbow to help me. He stopped twenty feet from the door. "Here okay?" he asked. When I agreed that it was fine, he released my arm and spread the frayed pink blanket on the grass.

I sat on the blanket and he placed the vampire tree in front of me. I rubbed a few grass leaves between the fingers of both hands. Happy. Content. Well-nourished grass. Gently, I wormed my index fingers through the blades and the roots until I touched soil. "No *death* energies," I said. "Nothing that feels like *death and decay.* Nothing that feels like witch magic of any kind. Just the utter self-satisfaction of grass that isn't getting eaten, gets cut with sharp blades, and has plenty of nutrients."

"House lawn grass is self-satisfied?" Occam asked. "What about pasture grass?"

I handed him the potted plant and raised my arm for a hand up, letting him help me. "House grass is the most self-absorbed, self-centered plant on the face of the earth. Pasture grass knows its purpose is to be chomped on and it's a little less pretentious."

"Okay," he said, not disagreeing with me. And more importantly, not laughing at me. Or at grass.

"Other side of the driveway," I said, this time taking the plant and the blanket so he could keep his hands free.

We repeated the process and I found nothing there either, except more complacent, self-assured lawn. The groundskeeper was doing a great job.

We tried again at the back of the house, close to the witch circle made by Astrid and her witches today. Nothing. Nada. Standing, my blanket over one arm, I stared around the dark grounds. "Talk to me," I muttered. "Where is *death and decay*?"

The only death magics I had seen up close were the kind that resulted when salamanders from another dimension began to reproduce on earth. Wherever they walked, those energies had killed every living thing they came in contact with. Every blade of grass, every tree, everything had begun to die, a by-product of their reproduction and lives. Witch death magics were reportedly different. Witch death magics weren't a by-product, they were a weapon in the hands of a killer. *Death and decay?* I had no idea what it was, but it was killing things and I was good at figuring out about things that killed.

"Over there." I pointed. Occam led the way to the lawn nearest the barn and, when I nodded, arranged the folded blanket on the grass. I assumed the position and took the potted plant, placing it between my legs.

With one fingertip, I touched the grass. Shock and horror and fear shot through me. I jerked my hands to myself and stood up fast. Nausea rose in my throat and I shook my hand to restore the circulation.

"Nell?"

I snatched up the plant and the blanket, remembering Etain saying she could feel death through her shoes. She had been standing almost here. For a moment, I considered that Etain had known where the *death and decay* came through because she had brought them onto the property. I tucked that one into the back of my mind. Being part of PsyLED had made me suspicious of everyone.

"Nell?" Occam said again, his tone sharper.

"Oh. Sorry. Got it," I said. "Right here. They came through here."

"They?"

"The *death and decay* and the person who brought it on the property."

"Can you tell from which direction?" Occam asked.

My fingers clutched on the vampire tree's clay pot. I really, really did not want to touch the ground again. But it was my job. "I need to read twenty feet left and then twenty feet to the right of this spot."

"Okay." He took my elbow. Softly he asked, "Any roots?"

"No." I swallowed the disgusting, sour, pizza-based nausea back down. "Just death. Gimme roots in my belly any day." Which told him how bad the energies were.

"I want you to stop if you feel leafy or if you get any sensations you might have felt today before you went into the null room."

"Okay." I didn't tell him that I wasn't sure that I'd know if I got the working on me. He'd just worry. And I would be back at HQ and the null room there by midday tomorrow, so I was good. I hoped.

I felt nothing to the right. But there was a strong sensation to the left. Carrying the blanket and the pot, I rechecked two other spots and decided that the *death and decay* had entered on a direct line from the barn. We ducked between the white railings of the four-board fence and approached the white-painted barn. Thirty or so feet out, a spotlight blinked on, blinding us.

The metallic sound of a lever-action shotgun working cut through the night.

Occam shoved me to the side, out of the spotlight. Drew his weapon.

SIX

A man's voice called out. "You cops or reporters dressed to look like 'em?"

"They're the real deal," Deputy Stanhope called.

We heard the sound of the shotgun being unloaded. "Give a man a heart attack, why don't you." The light went off and I felt Occam at my side again as he holstered his weapon.

"Cat reflexes?" I asked quietly. "And shoving the little woman out of the line of fire?"

"Your hands were full, your weapon in the car. I had to protect both of us."

"I wasn't complaining. I might have a bruise, but I'm not complaining."

Occam called, "Mind us looking around?"

"Maybe ask a few questions," the voice in the dark said. "I know the drill. Some reason you folks can't do this tomorrow? It's after midnight."

"We could," Occam agreed, moving slightly toward the voice in the darkness. "But you're awake enough to aim a weapon at us. Now seems convenient."

"Yeah, well, I wasn't going to fire. Obviously I'm not sleeping tonight, since I'm here instead of home, so you may as well ask your questions." The voice was Tennessee, but there was something in the inflection that suggested other influences.

I stepped off the grass to the paddock. Without laying the blanket or sitting down, I bent and touched the earth to feel the fine dust of a well-used paddock. No *death and decay*. "That was easy," I said.

"What was?"

"Now that I know exactly what I'm looking for, I can do a

surface scan without sitting. Interesting." If I could do this with other surface reads, and save the deep reads for truly difficult scans, that might also keep me from becoming a tree again so fast, and it surely would keep the land from sending roots into my flesh. I pressed my middle with the back of a hand and didn't feel an increase in the hard, rooty stuff in my belly. This could be useful.

Occam said, "Good to know. Let's go talk with the shotgun holder."

We entered from a side door directly into a small L-shaped office. I couldn't see into the barn, but I smelled horse, warm and earthy, hay, the sweetness of apples and feed, manure. Hooves thumped in one of the stalls in the dark.

According to Credence Pacillo's social media presence, he was half Italian, half Tennessean, his photos showing a dark-haired, blue-eyed man with a narrow beard and a well-sculpted mustache. I hadn't seen him today, and so far as I could tell, no one had interviewed him yet, which was interesting for someone with such an important job on the farm. Pacillo was fully dressed in unwrinkled clothes and shoes that were clean of the paddock dust covering our field boots. Odd.

After introductions, Occam pulled out two chairs and we sat across a small table from Pacillo. He looked at the potted plant and the blanket, as if asking why they were with me. I didn't volunteer an answer and he shook his head slightly as if at the vagaries of womenfolk or cops. Or both.

"I'm Melody Horse Farm's breeder and trainer. Or I was. None of us are sure what will happen to the stock or the farm now that Stella's gone. Coffee? Tea? Beer?" He flipped a hand at the cabinets to his left. A single-cup coffee/tea maker and a microwave were on the counter, and a small fridge was below. The shotgun was nowhere in sight.

The office had a high ceiling, the rafters casting shadows, a minuscule coffee/eating area where we sat, a sagging plaid sofa against one wall, a dusty desk with a clean center, as if missing a computer or laptop, and a dilapidated desk chair, as well as a wide-screen TV hanging on the wall at a slight angle. The L of the office was created by the position of the small bathroom I had used several times today. It opened from both outside and here, but I hadn't looked into the barn until now. Occam had spent a lot of time out here today, and I was surprised he hadn't yet interviewed Pacillo, but it was clear the men hadn't met.

"We're good," Occam said. "And thank you for talking to us so late."

"At least you're more polite than that FBI agent. He was an ass."

"Mmmm," Occam said, neither agreeing nor disagreeing. "What can you tell us about today?"

"It sucked." Pacillo's face crumpled. I realized now that he had been crying, his blue eyes red rimmed. He rubbed his face with one hand, the other on the table, open and somehow help-less looking. "My friend and employer is dead, her sisters have been sniffing around the horses like they plan to sell them for dog food, and all Tondra can do is cry. And I had to suck it up all day long, dealing with the delivery of a slightly out-of-season foal on a finicky mare with a first-time pregnancy."

"How are they?" Occam asked, sounding interested.

"They ended up being transported to the vet hospital for an overnight stay, but things seemed fine when I left them."

"Walk us through the day?" Occam asked.

And tell us what you can about the sisters. I didn't say it. But anyone wanting to sell one of the amazing horses for dog food—if they even did that these days, and his comment wasn't just hyperbole—was on my personal hit list.

Pacillo walked us through his day from the moment he woke to now. He'd watered and checked on each horse for signs of lameness, injury, or illness, as he did every morning before sun-rise. He'd given the ailing two their meds in a special mash and wrapped one's leg with liniment. He had released the horses into the proper pastures, separating geldings from mares with foals. Then he had joined Stella Mae on the back deck for seven a.m. coffee. She had been tired and happy and glad to be home.

"Seven a.m. seems early for a musician who's been on the road," Occam said.

Pacillo's face softened. "Stella was a country girl at heart. Music was her livelihood and she loved it, but horses were her passion. After being on the road for weeks, all she wanted was to be with the horses, and they start early. And Stella had a gift for resetting her internal clock overnight."

"What did you talk about?" Occam asked.

"We made plans to work Adrian's Hell together that afternoon. He needs a lot of time on the trails. He's too energetic, he hates being kept in pasture, and it takes a good fifteen miles three times a week, all on new trails, to keep him interested. And he's too much for the younger riders to handle. He shies at shadows until you wear him out. We planned to take him and a mare out for fifteen and then work him in paddock."

"Adrian's Hell?" Occam asked.

"A nine-year-old Anglo-Arab stud, French registry." Seeing our blank looks he added, "A Thoroughbred Arabian cross. Stella breeds, trains, and races endurance horses—" He stopped, rubbed his face again, pressing into his temples as if he had a headache, hiding his red eyes. "Bred, trained, and raced. Because Stella's gone." He inhaled on a sob and breathed, obviously searching for control. When he dropped his hands, his face was wet and red, but he was in control. "Previously Stella and I imported semen from a stud farm in France. But she was in Bahrain for a show some years back, and from the moment she saw Adrian's Hell, she had to have him, even half-wild and untrained. She and Monica, her assistant, turned over heaven and hell to get him to the States and paid too much for a young stallion with no titles or wins.

"We had to put up a breeding shed and reinforce a stall just for a stallion, because most of them are good for nothing but eatin', breedin', destroyin' stalls, and shittin'." He looked up. "Excuse my language, ma'am." He nodded at me. "But Stella was right. Adrian's Hell settled right down and within six months became the best-behaved stallion I've ever seen. His disposition—when he gets enough exercise—is superb. Endurance horses want to move, want to run. It's their default state." He smiled as if the last words were part of happier memories. "Stella's term."

"Are the horses insured?" Occam asked.

"Of course. Seven-figure horses are often owned by multiple partners and have to be insured. Come on, I'll introduce you to Adrian's Hell."

We followed Pacillo to the closest stall, the biggest box stall I had ever seen, made from black-painted timbers with black iron bars from the top of the stall walls to the ceiling. Standing placidly inside, watching us, was the big bay stallion I had seen when I first drove up, the horse FireWind had danced with, without ever moving a muscle. The white blaze was a brilliant lightning streak starting from his black forelock, zigzagging down his face, dropping to his black nose. Adrian's Hell's ears pricked up and he accepted a carrot from Pacillo, cracking it in his big teeth. "Stella's pride and joy," Pacillo said. "He's not yet ten, but he came in second in the Tevis Cup in California, first in the Old Dominion Ride in Virginia, and he's entered in next year's European Endurance Championship.

"Good boy. That's my good boy," Pacillo murmured. "You want to go run?" The horse's ears perked again and the trainer entered the stall, leading the horse out into the central area. The stallion danced sideways, his feet lifting as if he pranced over unseen obstacles. He was solid muscle, his red coat gleaming in the dim lights. We followed farther back and watched as the breeder led the horse outside, opened a gate, and released him into a pasture. Adrian's Hell bucked, kicked, and raced into the dark, making happy horse sounds, probably calling to his mares, hooves pounding.

Pacillo indicated the barn and led the way back to the office. "Stella had a good eye. Last year, his sire, Adrian's Storm, made a huge stir in France and then in Abu Dhabi in a private race put on by the sheikh. The sheikh purchased Adrian's Storm for stud for an undisclosed sum and all Storm's issue went way up in value. By that time, we were already breeding Adrian's Hell. We are way ahead of any other endurance breeder, and even now have some interest for yearlings to train for European events." Back in the office we retook our same seats.

It sounded like an extremely expensive business if a sheikh was involved. As if he read my thoughts, Occam said, "You said something about partners. Who owns Adrian's Hell?"

"Stella has business agreements with a lot of people. You'll have to talk to her lawyer and her business manager for particulars on the silent partners." That sounded like an evasion, but he went on. "We have six yearlings and five foals by Adrian's Hell, out of Anglo-Arab mares, and if they're half as good as we think, he'll remake Stella's bloodlines—" He stopped abruptly and closed his eyes, took and released several breaths, composing himself. Tears glimmered in his lashes. "Sorry." He gave a slight, pained smile, blinking away the tears. "I get carried away talking about Adrian's Hell. He's an amazing stallion, and that's saying a lot from a man who once swore by Rocky Mountain horses and Missouri Fox Trotters for endurance." He swallowed as if his throat ached and whispered, "And now Stella's gone."

Occam gave Pacillo a moment before he asked, "Back to morning coffee?"

Pacillo shook his head as if trying to shake away his pain. "Stella seemed fine, tired of course, but happy, which always makes for good horses and good music. The take on the tour was phenomenal, the crew had gotten along well, and . . ." Pacillo seemed to run out of steam and words. He slumped back in his chair, eyes tightly shut again, as if cutting off more tears. He scratched his beard, dragging down his face, creating a grotesque expression of grief.

"I been meaning to ask," Occam said softly. "How many employees are there?"

He had already asked, because I had seen the list in the file, but asking multiple people sometimes resulted in different answers.

Pacillo pulled himself forward with one hand on the table and breathed some more. He opened his eyes. "Right. Interrogation. The band members are stable, but the backups and roadies change out often. None are technically employees. We have a full-time farm manager, Pam Gower, who is at Myrtle Beach on vacation. She handles rotating the pastures, growing hay and some grain. She checked in and talked to someone. FBI? I think."

"Good," Occam said, but I could tell by his tone he wasn't happy that Smythe had gotten to her first.

"The horses are overseen by me. I'm full-time. We currently have five part-time farmhands and always have a minimum of eight part-time riders." Pacillo paused, staring at his hand on the table. "The house was handled by Verna Upton, the housekeeper, and Stella had her assistant, Monica Belcher, both full-time.

"But we were more than employees. We were family. You never saw such dedicated and loyal people as the ones Stella gathered around her. Turnover is nonexistent among the band members and all full-time staff."

Occam opened a small spiral pad and clicked a pen. "I'd like the names and addresses of all the part-timers and full-timers."

I said quickly, "Are there other horses in the stalls right

now?" I hadn't heard any feet stomping or the restless sounds of animals.

"I turned all of them out for the night. Temperature is good, grass is as good as it will get for the season," Pacillo said. "Why do you ask?"

"I have a piece of equipment that reads magical energies," I said, patting my empty pocket as if I currently carried a psy-meter. "I'd like to read the stalls and the central area. And then behind the barn."

"Go for it. Read anything you want. Arrest the woman who did this. That's all I want."

I wanted to tell him not all witches were women. "I'll be doing my readings," I said instead, frowning.

"Ingram? Alone?" Occam asked. Because I could get in trouble with that, get all rooty again, and grow closer to becoming a tree. Not in my life plans.

I held up a single finger. "I'll be careful." The gesture indicated that I'd use only one finger.

Occam frowned. "I'll check on you in a bit. Like, ten minutes."

I gave him a professional smile—not the loving smile I wanted to give—and slipped from the room, carrying my potted plant and the faded blanket. Pacillo's eyes followed my exit with the plant. *I'm an eccentric*, I thought. In the South that was not just allowed, it was expected and accepted, a lovely thing to be. I stopped only a few feet from the office and tested the soil in the central area of the barn. Nothing. I glanced back and caught Occam watching. "It's all good!" I called out.

He gave me a jaw jut, the kind guys give each other to say they are macho and fine, and turned back to Pacillo.

All of the stalls read fine. The long central area read fine. The grooming/shower stall for horses read fine. The tack room and feed room read fine. The bathroom we had used all day read fine. The entire barn read fine, which I did not expect.

It was much faster work than any group of readings I had ever done. Midway, I realized that I had been carrying the pot-ted vampire tree at each reading—the tiny tree a part of the self-proclaimed Green Knight.

I could communicate with Soulwood over distances. The

tree had learned how to do that too, probably from observing me. The idea of being watched by the tree was a mite chilling.

I stuck my fingers into the tree's soil and whispered, "Are you'un watching over me? Making this easier on me? Or are you'un jist spyin'? 'Cause if'n you'un's doing either, I'll have to rethink about when I'll carry you around and when I'm leaving you in the car."

The potted plant didn't answer. Talking trees would be a nuisance and definitely creepy.

I called to Occam, visible through the open door, that everything was negative and that I was heading out back. He stiffened, suggesting that he didn't like me going out on my own, but after a moment he nodded, rigid, but accepting.

I walked behind the barn, away from the house, and let my eyes adjust to the total dark again. Without the security lights it was dark as the devil's armpit. There were gates in three directions, to three different pastures. Bending under one railing, I stepped into the pasture beyond, one facing the opposite direction from the one Adrian's Hell had been let free in. A night breeze, damp with a coming rain, ruffled my hair. My curls tightened and I felt a leaf unfurl. Reaching up, I found where it tickled and pinched it off. I didn't really want to drop my leaves on foreign soil, so I tucked it into my jeans pocket. I walked a short distance and turned my cell's flashlight on, studying the grass. It looked healthy and rich, and I sensed no *death and decay* back here or anywhere on the property. But my job meant verifying what I already knew.

Holding the potted tree upright, the blanket over one arm, I put away the cell, bent down, and pushed through the grass to touch the earth with one fingertip.

Death and decay grabbed my finger and slammed needles into my flesh. I jerked away, spun toward the fence. Stumbled. Whispering, "Oh no, oh no, oh no . . ." over and over. My finger burned as if I'd stuck it into hot coals. The pain was so intense I wasn't thinking, trying to see my hand in the dark, running night-blind. The stabbing crawled up my finger.

Burning. Piercing. Sharp as frozen glass.

My entire arm cramped.

Frantic, I wiped traces of dirt off my finger onto my jeans.

Lurched to the fence and fell through the bottom two rails. To the ground. I landed on top of the blanket. My back arched in agony. My lungs shut down. I closed my eyes. I saw black flames tipped with red bending, rushing toward me. Encircling me. Frozen air sliced me. I couldn't even gasp.

Something else grabbed my injured finger. Tiny rootlets feathered over it. Pulled my finger to the pot. Beneath the soil. *Soulwood soil*. Cool damp soil, the best mountain loam. I managed a breath. The relief was short-lived. The vampire tree shoved roots into my finger. And wrapped them around my hand. Climbing, following the burning invasion. My scream strangled.

Holding the pot tight for fear it would take off my entire hand if I dropped it, my body curled around the pot in a spasm, shaking. A long, pained mewl escaped my mouth. Tears and snot watered the pot's soil. Some of the soil spilled onto the barn dirt beside me. When it touched, bright lights lit inside my brain.

Against the brightness, I saw the Green Knight, sitting astride a pale green horse, the mental manifestation the vampire tree took when it communicated with me. He carried a white halberd in one hand, propped over a shoulder, trailing vines and bursting with green leaves. In the other hand he carried a lance, the long pole the dark green of fir leaves, the entire length trailing more vines, green leaves fluttering in an unseen wind. He kneed his horse forward, guiding him without reins. The horse burst into a gallop. Hooves thundered, the massive warhorse racing toward me.

The lance was centered on my chest. My body tightened in response and I caught my breath, ready to run. But there was no place to run, not here.

A thought came to me. *Hold*.

Around me death flames crackled. Black flares flickered, ice and flame tinged dully red. Roaring closer. They attacked, burning, blistering, freezing, icy. The flames were superheated icy glass, sharp and shattered, slicing along my body. Surrounding me. They were a prison that was created to consume.

The Green Knight's lance passed over my shoulder. Pierced into the blaze.

The horse rammed at me.

I felt no impact.

The knight rode through me, his leaves and bark and his

armor frozen, an arctic steel that stole my warmth. A ripping, tearing sound.

My finger stopped hurting.

Just stopped.

"Nell? Nell!" Occam cursed.

I felt his fingers at my neck, taking my pulse. I managed a gagging sort of moan and he turned me on my side. I caught a breath. I didn't throw up.

"What happened? Nell, talk to me."

"Get off the ground. *Death and decay*," I whispered, warning through a throat that felt as if I had guzzled acid. "Here."

"I don't feel it," he said. He pulled me onto his knee, off the ground, cradling me. "I shouldn't have left you alone."

I got my eyes to focus. I wasn't where I had been before. I looked around, finding my location with the house and barn as reference points. "I got away. I must have . . . run . . ." I stopped and breathed for a bit. Occam pulled me closer against him and positioned the tree's pot in the crook of my body, my hand still wrapped with roots. We were on safe ground. "I got attacked by . . . trapped in a burst of energies. They kicked my butt. The vampire tree saved me."

"The vampire tree? The potted plant that has roots stuck into your whole hand? Looks like it's claiming you rather than saving you," he growled.

"Trust me. It was saving me."

"I trust *you*, Nell, sugar." He rocked me and I leaned into him. "I don't trust that damn tree, but I trust you. You're ice-cold, Nell. Do I need to get you to a hospital?" I started shivering, and Occam unfolded the pink blanket, draping it over me. We sat there, me snuggled up to his werecat warmth, which was several degrees warmer than standard human. And he was right, I felt no *death and decay* right here. Thank goodness, because Occam was touching the dirt, holding me. And the null room was closed up for the night, nullifying the dead, and I didn't have a key anyway.

My head began to clear. "I think I'm okay," I said, my voice rough. Occam hugged me tighter. Closing my eyes, I pressed closer, feeling too cold and too hot all at once. I tried to picture the Green Knight, the shape/name/form/purpose the vampire tree had chosen when it gained sentience. I saw a field of green grass, a green horse grazing. A man wearing pale green armor stood at a fence, and though his helmet was in place and I couldn't see his eyes, I got the feeling he was looking right at me. He lifted a hand and drizzled green stuff through his green-steel fingers. It seemed to be important to him, but I had no idea what it meant.

"Ummm? Okay? And thanks," I whispered to him. He nodded his helmeted head.

Occam said, "I didn't do anything, Nell, sugar."

I smiled. "You can let go now, I think," I whispered. The knight gave a formal nod and the roots let go of my hand, pulling out of my finger. I hissed with pain and my blood ran into the potted Soulwood soil.

"You're bleedin'," Occam said.

In my vision, or whatever this was, the Green Knight reached out and held his gauntleted hand beneath mine, as if capturing my blood in his steel-covered palm. I felt my blood land in the pot and feed the root. That might be bad . . .

"I'm taking you to the hospital," Occam said, his tone grim.

"No. Not needed. I'm really okay," I said softly, opening my eyes. Even my throat was better, though I was thirsty. I pushed back from Occam and placed the plant pot on the ground. "I'd been touching dirt in the barn and paddocks, but pasture soil is different. It's alive in ways that barn dirt isn't. I was stupid. I shoulda touched grass leaves first, then the soil. I'll be fine." *Leaves then soil. Always.*

"You're not fine," he cat-growled. "Your heart was racing and you were breathing too fast and you were cold as death." His hand touched my face as if testing my temperature. "You *smelled like you were dying.*" His eyes were glowing the bright golden amber of his cat. It wasn't the full moon, but he was still close to losing control of his were-creature. Which would be very bad at a crime scene with humans all around, armed security everywhere.

I reached up with my good hand and gripped the back of his head, pulling him close and kissing him. In the dark, kneeling in the dirt, behind a barn. It was a sweet, clinging kiss, lips to lips, warm and tender and giving. When I pulled away, his eyes were human again. I smiled up at him. "I'm okay, cat-man," I said softly. "And we have a job to do."

"Woman, you scared me silly."

"Scared me too. And after this case, I have a lot of thinking to do about the vampire tree. But for now, let's get the job done."

"You sure?" When I nodded, Occam got to his feet and lifted me to mine, cat-strong, cat-graceful, and pulled me close in the night. Into my ear, he said, "How 'bout you don't scare me again tonight. Or ever. I might have nine lives, but you surely scared one outta me jist now."

"Nine lives," I said, smiling at the cat-lore comment and pointing. "We need to make sure no horses have access to that pasture. There's a lot of *death and decay* in it."

"Pacillo moved all the horses earlier. I might need to find out why he emptied that particular one."

I stood on my own. "Good idea."

"He offered to drive us across the acreage in one of the farm's golf carts, so you can read the land."

Sounding mostly normal, I said, "I think that would be lovely. A chauffeured moonlight ride in a golf cart through the countryside with my cat-man."

He hugged me and his arms betrayed the depth of his relief. "This is harder than I thought it would be," Occam murmured.

"What's harder?" I asked.

"Being in love with my partner." He chuffed in restrained anger. "Watching her get hurt."

"There's good and bad in everything," I said.

Including having a potted tree for a protector. One that did indeed have some kind of paranormal ability to talk to its other part over many miles. I remembered seeing the knight drizzle green stuff from his fingers just before he took my blood. The vampire tree was trying to tell me something important. Had the green stuff been Soulwood soil, a protection as I read the earth?

I needed to figure out what to do about the Green Knight. It protected me, but it wasn't under my control. The vampire tree had killed before. It could, probably would, kill again.

What if it decided Occam was a danger to me? Or Mud? To keep that from happening, I needed to claim the vampire tree. Or, if that wasn't possible, I might need to kill it.

SEVEN

Pacillo knew the farm, every nook and cranny, and every horse in every pasture. He would roll us up to a gate that I couldn't see and Occam would hop out, open the gate, let us roll through, and then close the gate. Even in the pitch-black dark, Pacillo could find every springhead, rocky outcrop, ditch, patch of trees, access trail, horse trail, mud hole, and salt block. At each stop, I got out holding my cell phone as if I was using it to read the land, drizzled a few grains of Soulwood soil onto the ground, and touched the grass with one fingertip, one that hadn't been harmed. The injured ones were still tender and I hadn't had the guts to look yet. I wasn't using enough soil, my power, or any of my blood that might accidentally claim the land. And I was touching only leaves, not dirt. At all.

I found nothing. Not one single trace of a *death and decay*, or any other kind of working, in the entire back fifty acres, in the orchards, or in the forested area farther back. The front pastures and the ones to the far side of the house were fine. Only the one pasture was affected. Near it, a pea-gravel parking lot was set back from the big RV shed, the lot holding eight vehicles belonging to the security crew, Stella, and some of the victims in the hospital. Or dead. Each vehicle had a small sticker with Stella's logo in the rear window. The parking lot and the cars and trucks were fine too. I took photos of each tag and sent them to HQ to be run.

I still had to narrow down the trail of *death and decay* and that meant going back to the grassland that had attacked me. I was tired. I was a little frightened. But I had a job to do. "I need to go back to the pasture where I found the energies."

I expected Occam to argue with me, but he merely said, "Okay," and instructed Pacillo back toward the barn and to the area farthest from where I'd been attacked. We were a good two hundred yards from the barn when I got out, Occam at my side. This time I carried my blanket and placed it on the ground. The night had chilled and I shivered. Or maybe that was fear.

Using extra care, as if the land was venomous, I touched the leaves. They were clean and alive and happy, so I risked a bit more and tapped the soil fast, jerking my finger away. The land beneath was fine. I blew out a breath and climbed into the golf cart. "Take me a hundred feet closer to the barn," I directed. I could feel Occam's disapproval, but he kept his mouth shut, merely fingering the clasp that secured his steel hunting knife to his thigh.

I was especially careful, reading in increments, going closer until I was near the barn. I didn't encounter *death and decay* until I was thirty-something feet out. Less than a quarter of an acre of the pasture was infected with the death energies. There was no trail from the parking area to the pasture. How had *death and decay* gotten to the pasture and the house?

We had zigzagged around the entire farm, but I couldn't figure out how the *death and decay* energies had gotten close to the barn or how they had reached the house. FireWind was going to be disappointed. *Death and decay* had seemingly popped into existence, infected a pasture, and reappeared inside the house.

It was also clear that unlike the energies inside the house, the ones in the pasture were decreasing.

Had the potted vampire tree, in its form of the Green Knight, zapped the *death and decay* out of existence in the land where I had been attacked? Was that what the lance had done when it passed me and hit the frozen glass flames behind?

Our three-person team was fast and efficient, and if Pacillo thought I was reading the land with my cell phone, which I carried each time, well, I wasn't about to disabuse him of that notion. By three a.m. we were back at the barn. I was yawning and too sleepy to continue, so we said our good nights, and Pacillo turned on the security lights.

Occam and I walked back toward the car, stopping on the way when he touched my arm. "Lemme see." When I didn't understand, he said, "Your finger. Your hand. Lemme see."

"Oh." I curled my fingers protectively into a loose fist. I didn't want to look.

"Does it still hurt?"

I nodded.

He held out his hand and I placed my hand into his. Uncurled my fingers. Occam turned on a small penlight and directed the narrow beam at my fingers. The index finger was white as bone, the skin dead. It was covered with pinholes, as if I'd stabbed it with needles. With his burn-scarred hand, Occam lifted the finger to his lips and kissed it. My heart melted. Before I could think it through, I pulled his hand to my own lips and placed a kiss on his knuckles. I felt him start in surprise, and saw a flash of his teeth in the shadows. He released my hand and wrapped his arm around my shoulders and I relaxed against him, feeling . . . cherished? Loved. Yes, that was it. Feeling loved. My entire heart melted, resting against my cat-man.

We were almost at the car when a light came on inside the house. Occam came to a stop and swiveled so I could see what he saw. "That's a mite strange, don't you think, Nell, sugar?" he said. "No cars in the yard. Officer Stanhope, you still on duty?" he asked without raising his voice.

"I'm here. The witches and the crime scene folks left while you were off working. No one has approached the house within my sight since you came through. Don't mean someone didn't get through another entrance, what with the lights off and the security system off-line for the witches and the techs. I'll check it out." Keys jangled and Stanhope appeared out of the dark. He was a tall man, wearing the uniform of Stella's security company, a gun at his belt. Stanhope was fit and carried himself like former military.

"Want backup?" Occam asked.

"Never turn down backup, my man. Never turn it down."

Stanhope opened the door and Occam followed him inside. I went on to the car and placed the potted tree in the milk carton in the passenger seat. Its roots were exposed and in need of fresh soil, but I didn't travel with a bag of Soulwood soil. That was something I might need to remedy.

While I leaned against the car, I sent JoJo a text. *Security system not show suspect entering house carrying trigger?*

She texted back, *System autostores and eventually rewrites itself. I'm trying to reconstruct old data from a saved version.*

Good thing you're our Diamond, I texted.

She didn't reply. Jo had once been known as Diamond Drill, one of the top hackers in the world. She worked for us now.

Stanhope jogged from the house. "Kid got inside. He had a key, knew how to work the security system," he called to me, irritation in his voice, "and didn't mind crossing crime scene tape. Your partner says to go on in."

Leaving the pot and the blanket, I entered the house empty-handed, to find Occam and a young man sitting at the big kitchen island. The "kid" was drinking coffee, in the middle of the night, and eating a sandwich that he had clearly just assembled from the contents of the fridge. Packages of lettuce, cheese, an open loaf of bread, condiments, and sliced turkey were on the island top.

He was older than he looked at first, a shaggy-headed blond with sad eyes, maybe midtwenties. Occam's eyes were trying to tell me something as he said, "Special Agent Ingram, this is one of Stella's roadies, Theron Workham, tech and support roadie for the band. He came in for the meeting today and apparently slept over in one of the RVs. He woke up hungry and avoided all the security guards to make a sandwich." He put a faint emphasis on "avoided all the security guards." Which should not have been so easy.

Not meeting our eyes, Theron shoved a good three inches of sandwich into his mouth and chewed. Keeping his mouth full so he couldn't talk? I tilted my head to show I understood Occam's concern.

"And he's not the only one on scene. According to him, upstairs are two of the part-time riders"—Occam referred to his notes—"Bevie Rhoden and Elisa Yhall." He spelled both names. "They're all three part of Stella's inner circle and they sleep in the bunk room upstairs, when they aren't in school. They didn't see a problem with crossing over crime scene tape either."

So, we had three people with the ability to make use of the property without getting caught. There were probably more. "Cameras?" I asked, about the security system.

Occam said, irritation in his tone, "There's a light on the door panel that shows red if the system is armed. And he knows the code."

Anyone who knew about this could get in, turn off the cameras, and come and go without being filmed. I swiveled my hand, thumb slightly up, to show I understood.

"Theron has agreed to clarify for me the names of the band members, backup singers, roadies, assorted personnel, and groupies following the band."

I gave him a half smile. Theron didn't seem the least bit willing to do that. He looked as if he'd been caught and knew it and didn't know how to get out of the breaking-and-entering mess he was in. He finished the sandwich. Put his plate in the sink. Blew a resigned breath.

Having left my tablet in the car, I just listened as Theron reluctantly went down a list of names, some of which were on my own list, some I hadn't heard until now. So many names, including Stella's band manager, Regenia Apple, her accountant, Genneille Booker, and her attorney in Nashville, Augustina Mattson. All women.

I was exhausted and half-asleep on my feet. Theron was wide awake. He poured another cup of coffee, added ice to it, and began to drink. Barely able to keep my eyes open, I heard footsteps on the hidden kitchen stairs.

"You're been very helpful," Occam said. "What can you tell me about Stella's romantic interests and lovers?"

Theron choked on his iced coffee. The footsteps stopped. Occam gave a cat smile of interest in the response, what he sometimes called a "gotcha moment." His cat ears had heard the approach, probably much sooner than I had.

When Theron stopped coughing, he said, sounding half-strangled, "Stella didn't date."

I frowned at the reply. Occam smiled wider.

Two women clattered noisily down the final stairs and into the kitchen. Both had short, shaggy, metallic-dyed hair, multiple tattoos and piercings, and the frayed jeans worn by some of the riders sitting on the fence today. The girls, looking wide awake for the hour, fell on the sandwich makings. "Bevie and Elisa," Theron said, pointing to identify the girls.

Neither girl looked up. I knew their names, but I hadn't talked to either of them today. They hadn't been on scene when Stella died, or all day long as we worked. But here they were now. Inside Stella's house.

Theron shifted his eyes to Occam and tilted his head to the

door. "I'll look at that now, if you want," he said. "I can eat and look too."

The roadie had things to say to Occam. Things he didn't want the womenfolk to hear, which brought back churchwoman memories of being outcasts and kept ignorant of important information. The men left. I pulled my cell and glanced at the time. And wished I hadn't.

The girls were busily putting together sandwiches and studiously not looking at me. And I realized they might have things they would tell me that they wouldn't tell Occam.

"So," I said, watching their movements. "Stella's love life?"

The green-haired girl, Bevie if I got the designations right, glared at me. The purple-haired girl went to the fridge and got out two beers. Popped them and passed her friend one. "Don't let it get back that we told you," Elisa said.

"Don't," Bevie said.

"It's going to come out," Elisa said. "The cops are going to figure it out and then they're going to accuse us of withholding pertinent information." That was a level of sophisticated vocabulary I hadn't expected in a local girl who rode and worked part-time on a farm. I revaluated my perceptions.

"Do. *Not*," Bevie said, her tone and her expression fierce.

"Not trying to make you uncomfortable," I pretty much lied. "You girls ride for the horse farm?"

Bevie frowned and stuffed a chunk of cheese in her mouth.

Elisa didn't look at her friend. "We go to TTU. Tennessee Tech University, College of Graduate Studies. I'm concentrating on agricultural engineering technology. Bevie is in agribusiness management. Most of the riders come from the college. Stella says older girls make less mistakes and are more dependable than high-schoolers."

"Why does a farm need so many part-time riders?" I asked. "There must be twenty on the list."

"Twenty-two," Bevie said, sounding stern and smearing mayo on bread. She swigged her beer. I didn't comment. She set the half-empty bottle on the bar top. "But most are seasonal riders. Eight of us work the horses all year."

"It takes a lot of people to care for, condition, and train long-distance horses," Elisa said. "Every endurance horse has to be worked and trained at least twice a week in off seasons, and light, but very specific, interval training leading up to a ride for competition. Stella wanted her animals worked under saddle, not so much on the walker." She nodded out the window in the general direction of the mechanical horse walker. "They get bored. Stella didn't like bored horses. Out on the trails they perk up. They get walked for long or short distances one day, they gallop short distances another, walk, trot, and canter on the other days. Hill work is especially important, and the trails go all through the hills around here."

Which meant that the riders knew every trail over the entire acreage. Getting in and out was easy to them. I didn't indicate that I found anything interesting and, because the girls were horse lovers, Elisa needed little encouragement to keep talking horse. They might not want me to know some things, or realize they were telling me things, but talking about horses fell into its own category. "I keep hearing the word *endurance*," I said. "How long is an endurance race?"

"Twenty-five, fifty, or hundred. There's even one that's one twenty-five."

"Miles?" I said, shocked.

"Absolutely, though it isn't like on a Thoroughbred track, which are one-miles and longer, where the horses run full-out for the distance. Endurance races are about the long haul, so they trot, walk, canter, and—very rarely—gallop, though sometimes it's hard to hold one back even after a hundred-mile trek. Horses are genetically wired to run," Elisa informed me. "So basically, Stella's training program means that every horse here gets lots of walking between hard work, fifteen to twenty-five miles a session. Working twenty-two-plus endurance horses—not counting training the yearlings and the horses too young to compete—means we have to be in the same kind of shape as the horses."

"How many horses are at the farm?"

"At any given time, up to seventy, but that's counting the foals, the horses under four years of age, geldings, and mares, but we concentrate on the twenty-two that compete."

That was a lot of horses, and the scope of the farm and the money involved was coming clear. I nodded encouragingly.

"And we still have to go to school and work real jobs and do papers," Elisa said, sliding her sandwich into a device that squished and grilled it. It smelled heavenly. "And most of us have families. Carmen has a kid, but she lives with her mom and she takes the kid on weekends so Carmen can study and ride."

"That makes sense," I said, wishing I had set my cell to take notes. But I had a feeling Elisa wouldn't have talked so freely had I been recording or taking notes. Or if Occam had been here. "I'm not trying to pry into anything not pertinent to the case," I said, "but we don't know what will be important, what won't, what will hide the truth, and what will reveal it. That's why my partner asked about Stella's romantic life. What we don't know could allow any potential perpetrator to get away."

Bevie made a sound that was part growl and all rage. She stabbed her friend with furious eyes. "Fine. Go ahead. Tell her. Tell her everything. My life is ruined anyway." She stomped from the room, carrying her sandwich and the beer and leaving the mess on the table.

Elisa heaved a sigh and began putting the food back in the fridge while her sandwich grilled. I could tell she was thinking things through, and I held myself still, when I really wanted to shake her and ask why Bevie's life was over. She shoveled the sandwich onto a plate with a spatula. When the bar top was clean of everything except her plate and her beer, she pulled up a stool, sat, took a bite, and considered me.

"Bevie is from a really strict farm family. Like, she couldn't date or anything until she was eighteen. Growing up, she had to work the farm, feed chickens, gather eggs, help birth cows. Like that. But she was really smart in high school, like, number one in her class, and she got a full ride at TTU. So when she went away to college she went kinda wild. Dated a lot of guys. Like, a *lot* of guys. And girls too. And then last year she met Stella and . . . well, Stella's got this public persona, a paragon of strait-laced propriety, you know? But in reality? Back before she was a star and got squeaky-clean branding? She spent five years living with several people in a pansexual relationship, and she still has, well, lots of lovers. Bevie was one of them and her family and her church will freak if they find out. And she really loved Stella. We all did. Even the ones of us who didn't spend time in her bed. Stella was this magical creature, you know?"

Elisa took a bite and chewed and swallowed. "Stella could look at you and tell exactly what you were feeling and exactly what you needed to be whole and happy. Some of her riders came from bad home lives, were really broken, and she paid for meds and counseling. Some of them were practically homeless and she let people stay here or in her RV between tours, until they got on their feet. She was a *good person*. And anyone who says different can kiss my butt." Almost viciously, she bit into the sandwich and chewed, her eyes on me. A string of cheese stretched from her mouth to the bread.

I accepted all that without a change of expression, even the butt-kissing part. Elisa turned her attention fully to her sandwich, the stringy cheese, and sipped her beer. I didn't ask her age or if she was legal to drink.

"You don't seem upset by all that sex stuff," she said.

Keeping my voice unemotional, I said, "I come from a polygamous background. My own mother is one of three wives. I was married at fifteen. I understand relationships that are different from society's norm."

"Holy shit. Fifteen? Wait. They *forced* you to get married?"

I had no idea why, but I answered. "No. I married to keep from becoming the preacher's youngest concubine. One of several, in addition to his several wives."

She chewed. Frowned. "I saw this show on TV one time. *Sister Wives*? You know it?"

"I've heard of it." Never watched it. Had no interest in it.

"So it would help to solve Stella's murder if you knew the people she slept with on a regular basis?"

I pursed my lips, thinking how I wanted to phrase my reply, because we hadn't released anything about a trigger for *death and decay*. The term *murder* was being bandied about by the press, but not by PsyLED, and my boss wouldn't be happy if I used it now. "This was a very violent way to die," I said carefully. "*If* someone set this up to kill Stella, then they wanted to not just kill her, but wipe her and her friends and her musical instruments and even unpublished songs off the face of the earth. *If* it was murder, it was personal."

"I could . . . I . . . I know a lot of names. Maybe not all."

"Anything you can do will help. And I'll try to keep Bevie's name out of any media releases. Law enforcement has no desire to bandy about anyone's personal business." The media would eventually find out everything. If this went to court they'd discover even more.

Elisa finished her sandwich. Cleaned up the crumbs and wiped down the island's surface. She stood, silent, her hands flat on the island top, and sighed. She nodded, more at her own thoughts than at me. Opening a drawer, Elisa took out a long narrow pad, the paper printed with cats at the top. She tore off four pages. At the top of one she wrote, *Commune.* At the top of the next, she wrote, *Band.* On the third she wrote, *Riders.* And on the last she wrote, *Current Regulars.* Then she began to list names on each pad with a star beside Stella's lovers. Stella Mae had been a very busy woman. And, if anyone was underage, maybe a sexual predator.

I got a bad feeling about all this.

Occam woke me with a soft kiss on my forehead. Before Occam entered my life, I had never been kissed with gentleness or tenderness. Not ever. So I knew instantly who it was that touched me in the dark. "Hey, cat-man," I murmured as cold air filled the car. My door was open and dawn was graying the sky. I had fallen asleep in the car and we were back at the hotel.

"Hey, Nell, sugar," he cat-growled. "You're tired, and I'm a big strong were-creature, so I intend to carry you to your room. You got anything negative to say about that?"

"Not a thing." I raised my arms and he lifted me out of the car, closed the car door with a knee, and carried me through the lobby, where I waved at the man behind the desk to show I wasn't being abducted. Outside my room, he kissed me again, this one far less platonic, and opened my door with my room card. I was of a mind to go with him to his room, but he pushed me inside, alone.

Moving quietly in the dark, I put the vampire tree on the table by the window, near the tiny plastic bud vase holding the slightly wilted lavender rose. I fell into bed.

When I woke, T. Laine was gone and the room smelled of coffee and donuts. It was nearly noon on Saturday. I had three texts telling me that Occam was heading back to Stella Mae's, that HQ wanted clarification on the names from the lists I had collected last night, and that FireWind was pleased with the night's

work and the lists of names. On the way home from the farm, I
had photographed the cat papers and sent them to HQ, keeping
the originals in evidence bags. I also had a voice message from
Mud that had arrived at five a.m., telling me that we needed
chickens. And that Esther made Cherry sleep on the back porch.
A second voice mail—a longer one—told me that Esther's husband formally divorced her in morning devotionals and that
Esther was now living permanently on Soulwood.

I either cussed or said a miserable prayer. Being *punished* by
Ernest "Jackie" Jackson Jr., had hurt Esther bad. I remembered
her as a happy child, but as an adult, she was neither happy nor
pleasant, seeming to want to hurt her family, the ones closest to
her. I tried to be understanding, though it had occurred to me
that she might possibly use that horrible part of her past to maneuver me to doing what she wanted. Most churchwomen were
masters of manipulation.

Esther had been a solo wife with no second wives. She was
used to getting her way. Hers had been a love match, not an arranged marriage or a negotiation for safety. She had been given
time to grow up before being subjected to Jedidiah Whisnut,
before taking care of a man, before running his household like
a good churchwoman.

She was a teenager, just eighteen. She was pregnant. Divorced. And she was growing leaves. Any of those things could
make her hard to get along with. All of those things gave her the
right to be a pain, but none of them meant I had to take it.

I started my first cup of coffee, transcribed all my notes and
thoughts from last night, texted the team that I was heading
back to HQ, and packed.

I made it to my car when FireWind appeared in the parking
lot and called, "I need a token female. Come with me."

Token female? What's a token female?

"Regional director of PsyLED, FireWind," he said, introducing
himself. "Special Agent Ingram, PsyLED. And Patrick Hooper,
attorney at law in the state of Tennessee. We'd like to speak with
Catriona Doyle."

The big boss was speaking to the woman at the front desk.
Sergeant Wherry was a grizzled veteran of the Cookeville PD.

She had the appearance of someone who had seen it all, done most of it, and lived to tell the tale. Unimpressed by FireWind's fancy title, she took our IDs, verified that we were who we said we were, signed in and locked our weapons away, and directed us to an interrogation room, where we waited for half an hour before Catriona was escorted in. She was cuffed, wearing ankle chains and jailhouse gray and an expression that said she hadn't slept. Hadn't been *allowed* to sleep.

FireWind instructed the guard to remove the chains. The guard looked FireWind in the eye long enough to prove that he had heard the request, turned, and left the room. FireWind didn't speak, but his color was heated. He bent over Catriona and unlocked the handcuffs and the ankle chains, tossing them in the corner. He pocketed his universal key, gave Catriona a bottle of water, and took his seat. She drank as if she hadn't had water since she was taken into custody. I passed her my water bottle too. She opened and drank half of that one.

"My thanks," she said in little more than a whisper. "Can you tell me? Who has ma daughter?"

"She is safe in a good social services home and will be returned to your sister as soon as possible," FireWind said softly. "PsyLED has lodged complaints with FBI and put in a good word for Etain to get the child."

Catriona burst into tears. "It's grateful I am, for that," she said, wiping her cheeks with the back of her wrist. "And for the water." She looked between us when she spoke. "Who are you?"

Far more gently than I thought him capable of, FireWind said, "We work for PsyLED, investigating paranormal crimes." Catriona's face crumpled. FireWind identified the three of us, though I don't think she heard any of it.

Patrick Hooper said, "Ms. Doyle, I'm a defense attorney. Your sister Etain Doyle retained me." He placed a business card on the table in front of her.

Catriona stared at it as if it was alive. "I didn't kill Stella."

"I know," Patrick said.

"The FBI man said since I wasna citizen I didn't have rights to a lawyer."

"Smythe?" Hooper asked.

Catriona nodded, the motion jerky, her hands tight on the bottle. The plastic crinkled.

"He lied. I'm working to get you released," Hooper said, "and knowing he deprived you of your rights is helpful."

Catriona fumbled the bottle and nearly dropped it. A fresh tear trickled down her cheek.

My boss slid a small plastic container of tissues across the table. He glanced at me and I slid her the package of pretzels he had tossed me when we left my car.

Patrick said, "With Director FireWind's assistance, I have contacted the Irish embassy and someone will be flying out to assist you. I've also notified our State Department that a foreign national has been held for a crime when there is no evidence against her and clear violations of her civil rights. I'd like to say that you will not be in here for long; however, even with your embassy's help, it's Saturday, and I think you will have to spend the weekend in jail. I'm sorry."

"I didn't kill her," she sobbed, the sound muffled in her tissue.

"We know," Hooper said. "PsyLED employs witches, and Special Agent Kent has determined that the magical energies that killed Stella Mae and the others were put in place approximately four days ago before the band came home."

I looked up at that. No one had told me and I hadn't read that report.

"You were on the road with the band at the time," he continued, "and, per the coven out of Nashville, you are not a death witch. The agents are going to record this conversation," he said, "and you will answer fully each question that I approve. Anytime I say so, you stop. After the agents are done with their questions, you and I will have some time alone to discuss the next steps and to make sure that I have a full and complete list of all the ways in which your civil rights were abused. Understood?"

Catriona nodded and blew her nose. "Thank God. I havena prayed since I was a wee lass, but I been praying so hard." She blew her nose again. "I'm such a mess."

She was, too. Makeup streaked, face chapped, hair a wild tangle. Fear and sweat had made a stink even a human could smell.

I said, "As soon as we're finished here we'll see about you getting a shower and clean clothes."

FireWind glanced at me and turned on a tiny recorder. He

gave the date, the location, and the names of everyone present. "Can you tell us what you know of the deaths at Melody Horse Farm?"

"You may answer the question, Ms. Doyle," Patrick Hooper said.

"I got to the house. They told me Stella was dead. I ran downstairs and saw the . . . the bodies," she whispered. "They were horrible and not natural. Couldna be. So I started a *seeing* working and saw these . . . these energies. I've never seen such in ma life, like black glass, broken, and on fire."

I held in my surprise. She saw the *death and decay* just like I had.

"I thought it was a *death* working, though I had never seen one before. Then the police came and the FBI agent put me in handcuffs and hauled me away." Her wrists were bruised, the skin red and irritated. Smythe hadn't been gentle with her.

"Tell me about Stella," FireWind said. "I understand she was a very special person."

"You may answer, Ms. Doyle," Patrick Hooper said.

Catriona cried through several more tissues. Drank most of my water, and then cried some more. As she cried, Catriona talked. And talked. About how wonderful Stella was, how kind, how giving. What a wonderful musician and human being.

On my tablet, I took notes of the names she mentioned and cross-referenced them with my lists, while creating a Catriona timeline. But about fifteen minutes into her monologue, I realized that Catriona was speaking to me as much as to FireWind and her lawyer, and my boss glanced a command to me, one I understood instantly. I realized that I was supposed to be asking questions and clarifying the things Catriona said. I was the *token woman* to keep Catriona from feeling afraid with male investigators? *Oh.* To FireWind, *token woman* was an important designation. There were times when I was an idiot.

I said, "Stella sounds wonderful. A true friend. We're trying to create a timeline. Can you tell us where you spent the nights prior to the bodies being found? And is there anyone who can corroborate where you were?"

Patrick Hooper nodded that Catriona should answer.

"Both nights after we got back, I slept on Etain's pull-out sofa with ma Miren. I don't have an apartment because it seemed stupid to pay rent when we'll be—we would have been—on the road two hundred days a the year." Her face crumpled. "I was finally a full-time member of the band. I was going to homeschool Miren on the road instead of leaving her with Etain. Now, I don't have a place to live. Or a job. And I'm in jail. And—" She stopped and sobbed. "And ma Miren is God knows where."

FireWind gave me another encouraging nod.

I said, "Your lawyer is working to get her back. For now, do you feel we can talk about when you first got to the farm yesterday?" Catriona nodded, wiped her chapped face again, and sipped the last of the water. "Who was there?" I asked.

A little over an hour later, the door opened and Smythe walked in. If his coloration was an indication, he was livid.

"Where are her restraints?" he spat at us. Over his shoulder he shouted, "Get her restrained and into her cell. And get them out of here."

The guard darted in.

FireWind stood. He seemed to move slowly, a gliding step, but he somehow ended up across the table and between the guard and Catriona. FireWind's black hair was down and long and flowing, an easy handle if the guard grabbed him, but FireWind's shoulders were relaxed. His hands were loose and ready. And he was smiling.

It was a chilling smile, all teeth and bright yellow eyes, a skinwalker leaking power. It was like Occam but bigger, older, and much, *much* more dangerous. Patrick Hooper stood to one side of Catriona. I took a spot on her other side. I smiled too. I wasn't a skinwalker with magical powers, but I had learned early on that an unafraid woman was a terrifying thing to some men. Smythe looked like one of those men. I stared at him, but kept an eye on the guard too.

FireWind stared at Smythe. Softly, his lips barely moving, he said, "Catriona Doyle is a foreign national, held and questioned in regards to a capital crime for which there is insufficient evidence. She asked for an attorney when she was brought in for questioning. No lawyer was provided. Yet she was questioned extensively over the last twenty-four hours, with no water, no sleep, and no food. A representative from the Irish embassy is on the way here. The assistant director of PsyLED is making extensive phone calls. The director of the FBI is being notified of your breach of conduct. The chief of police is being notified through official channels."

"I said to restrain her," Smythe snarled to the guard.

FireWind spoke directly to the guard. "I am informing you of a severe breach of this prisoner's constitutionally guaranteed civil rights. If you stay, you will take part in whatever penalties Smythe incurs. Or, you may leave this room right now."

The guard turned and left. FireWind, his power like an icy draft in the room, swiveled to Smythe. All nonhuman grace.

"You ain't human," Smythe accused.

"Turn off the recorder," FireWind said, his words soft and slow. He shifted his body a fraction of an inch. His head moved forward. One hand formed a fist. "I don't want this on record."

It sounded so much like a threat that Smythe turned and left. If he'd been a were-creature his tail woulda been stuck firmly between his legs. Under most circumstances, I didn't particularly like Ayatas FireWind, but if I was a prisoner in need of protecting, I'd surely want him in my corner, fighting for me. It occurred to me, not for the first time, that maybe FireWind was hard on his units because he saw us as the ones who were protecting others. Maybe he wanted us to be the best. Didn't make me like him any better, but I was coming to understand him.

The chief of police caught the door before it closed and stepped in. He was a big man, florid faced, clearly experienced, as he took in the room. He nodded to me, to Hooper, and to FireWind. He totally ignored the prisoner. "I understand that the FBI may have abused a prisoner in my lockup. Is that so?"

"It is," FireWind said.

"I've heard rumors about Smythe's methods. Never seen proof of it. But I made a point of sticking around today, even though it's my day off. I don't like what I just saw through the observation window." He tilted his head at the mirror behind us. "It won't happen again."

"Would you have a problem with Gerry Stapp taking over the FBI office?" FireWind asked, his body relaxing from the threat of violence to something less menacing.

The chief stuck his thumbs into his belt. "You mean because he's black and gayer than a rainbow? No. I don't care about the color of Stapp's skin. My paternal grandpappy was purported to

be half black and I was bullied about it all through elementary
school. Pissed me off. I loved that old man. Best man I ever met.

"And my baby brother died of AIDS in San Fran back in the
nineties. He was gayer than a chorus line dancer. I still miss
him. I employ two lesbians and if a male deputy is gay I don't
care. I don't care what any of my officers or employees do behind closed doors or how they live their private lives as long as
they keep their noses clean and do their jobs."

I said softly, "And yet you had heard there were problems.
That means you allowed Smythe to abuse prisoners in your in-
terrogation rooms. More importantly, you let your guards assist.
Under your watch."

The chief flushed. "Smythe's FBI. Fighting him would have
accomplished nothing without proof. I got proof now. It won't
happen again."

"We'll be finished here shortly," FireWind said. "I'll be
sending reports to my superior and to the FBI regional SAC
within the hour. It is my firm belief that Catriona Doyle will be
released soon. There will be a second press conference at six
thirty p.m. to announce the direction of the investigation into
Stella Mae Ragel's death by magical means. All official apolo-
gies will be made to Ms. Doyle, whether she has been released
by then or not. Appreciation will be offered for her cooperation.
At that time, I will personally do my best to clear her good
name. If you wish to join the lead investigator and the sheriff for
that press conference, you are welcome, provided that Ms.
Doyle has been fed, allowed to clean up, and given fresh
clothes." When the other man started to speak, FireWind spoke
over his words. "Also provided that her daughter has been allowed to speak to her on the phone, and that compelling measures have been taken to place Miren with Etain Doyle." He
gave a smile that would have done a wildcat proud.

"Might take you up on that next press conference." The chief
glanced at Catriona and back. "She'll be offered all proper and
legally available means to make her comfortable. I'll contact
social services and request a callback from the social worker on
call this weekend. Make sure your paperwork is all in order."
The chief left the room, moving fast for a big man.

EIGHT

I took Highway 62 and was back in Knoxville HQ by four thirty p.m. It had already been a long day. I updated JoJo on the interrogation in Cookeville PD, wrote up my reports, organized my files, and watered my office plants. I also went upstairs to the vacant third floor and looked around. Construction had begun in the last few days in the huge, empty, wall-less space. The studs in the outer walls were metal, not wood, with foam insulation everywhere. The floor was neatly swept concrete. Wiring extended from pipes in the walls, and plumbing pipes were roughed in. There were orange lines spray-painted all over the floor where walls might go. On the back of the building there was a shaft for a future elevator, in a space that roughly correlated with the emergency stairs.

A makeshift table stood in the middle of the room. I walked across to it and saw two sets of floor plans. One was yellowed and dusty, and showed a lab. The other was newer, and it was a plan for offices.

It was interesting. And different. If the offices went through, it meant having PsyLED brass on hand all the time. FireWind, Soul. And half of our team split up and working up here. I wasn't ready for that. I wasn't ready for change.

Which was why I hadn't gone home yet. Not being ready for change and not wanting to deal with the monsters Strife and Discord. "Time to face the monsters," I whispered. Downstairs, I gathered my gear and said good-bye to JoJo. "I'll be back in the morning."

"Watch the press conference on YouTube," she said.

"Yeah. Okay," I said, not knowing if I would be able to. I might have to catch the high points later. It was a sunny Saturday with fluffy clouds in the sky, but I was too tired to enjoy it.

Pellissippi Parkway and Oak Ridge Highway were bumper-to-bumper and I sighed with relief when I skirted Oliver Springs and turned into the hills. There were a few yellow poplars and rare orangey maples standing out against the wash of green. I rolled down the window and breathed deeply, smelling the life and the wonder of the green. Soulwood was waiting for me, and I knew the moment it felt me drive onto its lands. A rush of happiness and warmth rolled through me like the first day of spring. I was home.

Mud was in the backyard, training Cherry in the homemade obstacle course between the new greenhouse and the house. My youngest sister was wearing shorts, sneakers, and a T-shirt—not clothing she would ever have been allowed to wear were she still in the church. Mud's short hair bounced with every stride.

In a burst of defiance following her second day of public school, Mud had come in the door, gone to the kitchen, and whacked off her hair with a kitchen knife. A boy had pulled her ponytail and teased her about being a member of the "sex church." I had a feeling there had been more than that said, enough to leave Mud in tears. The ragged hair had resulted in a trip into town to the hair salon where I got my first short cut. It had also resulted in the purchase of training bras, Mud's first tube of pale lipstick, first powder compact, and first deodorant. Things I hadn't thought about for my baby sister.

Mama had nearly had kittens when she saw the short hair and the lipstick, and started a ruckus about me not getting custody. I'd been forced to pull her and the other mamas aside and tell them that the church was known by the younger townie boys as the "sex church." The mamas and I had a long, plainspoken discussion about that, and about what it meant to the church's young women in the eyes of the world. It had been a come-to-Jesus meeting for real and sure, and, while they were still speaking to me, the mamas weren't happy.

Mud hadn't noticed me drive up. She looked free and happy and adorable and gangly, just like all the other girls at middle school. I sat in the car and watched my sister run, long bare legs in the early fall sunshine. The springer spaniel, Cherry, was totally focused on her, desperate to please her master. In that moment, I knew that no matter how bad things got with Esther and no matter how badly my sisters fought, and no matter how hard and expensive it was to get full custody of Mud, it was all worth it. Having Mud here and safe and no longer in the sights of the churchmen was worth anything and everything. I was close to getting full and permanent custody. Just one more hearing. Just a few more thousand dollars in legal fees. And Mud would be free.

I got out of the car and carried my gear, the potted tree, and the bud vase up the steps to the porch and inside. The new air conditioner was purring, keeping the house at a steady seventy-six degrees. The air smelled of cleaning supplies and fresh paint from the remodeling that had only recently been completed. There was a fresh loaf of pumpkin bread on the kitchen table. I put my gear beside it. The house was spotless. No dust on the tables or my desk. No cat hair under the edge of the sofa. No dirt where an animal rubbed against a doorjamb. No dog hair on the sofa. No dirty dishes. Not a single thing out of place. It looked like . . . like Esther's place. Too clean. Too perfect.

Also, no mouser cats were in sight. And no Esther. Except for the faint squeals from outside and the AC unit, the house was silent.

Quietly, I put my things away and used the downstairs bath. It had been remodeled, with white tile everywhere, a new sink and cabinet, new flooring, and even an exhaust fan to suck the moisture out. The bath smelled of Clorox and it sparkled. My toothbrush, comb, brush, and hair dryer were lined up perfectly. There was pine cleanser in the toilet. No hair or leaves were on the floor. I sighed. Esther had clearly been in a cleaning frenzy. A common reaction to trauma.

I carried the *death and decay*–stinking clothes to the back porch to put on a load of wash. Someone had started a stew in the slow cooker that was sitting on the gardening table and it smelled fabulous.

Out back Mud and her dog were running and jumping. My twelfth year had been so very different. With a rush, I remembered the utter relief of moving here, away from the Colonel, away from danger, but also away from everyone and everything I knew. The loneliness. The homesickness. There had been no carefree moments like Mud was having. It was all different for her. Cherry raced through a succession of hoops and Mud squealed with delight.

I started the wash, lowered the machine's lid, and stepped into the day's last warmth. Mud squealed even higher in pitch and raced to me, grabbing me into a bone-crushing hug. She had gotten so tall. Gingerly, I hugged her back, not quite understanding why there were tears in my eyes.

"Come see the greenhouse!" She dragged me by one arm to the side and back of the house, as if I might try to get away. "I got all sorts of stuff growing."

We left Cherry sitting woefully outside and entered the greenhouse, which was heated from the sun and muggy from the watering system. It was all built to church standards by Daddy, our true brother Sam, and the Nicholson faction in the church. Mud and I had planted lettuce and spinach and basil and green onions in its raised beds, along with a dozen aromatic and flowering herbs she had picked out herself. All were growing faster and taller and greener than they should have. "I been telling them to grow," she said. "And they are. Look! This'un's called Thai basil. Smell," she said, breaking off a young leaf and holding it to my nose.

I sniffed. "Nice. Spicy. They're beautiful," I said, pulling her against me, my arm round her shoulders. I had told basils to grow when I was a child. Mud was a plant person like me, like Esther. I knew it. I felt it in my bones, though I had no real proof yet. I checked Mud carefully every night before she went to bed, and so far no leaves.

Mud started chattering about chickens and chicken runs in the greenhouse. Nattering about herbal vinegars and the teas she wanted to grow and sell to the townies. Happy. We walked together and talked, and then I said I had to get back inside. She hugged me once hard and raced back to Cherry and her agility training.

Back on the porch, I scooped some soil from the bucket I kept there for quick rooting and added it to the vampire tree, re-covering the roots. I also snipped off the browned end of the lavender rose's stem and tapped the cut end into a bottle of Rootone before I set the stem into a small pot of Soulwood soil. My fingers lingered a moment on the soft petals of Occam's gift, and my heart lightened, remembering the way he had brought it up from behind his leg.

About half the time, roses could be rooted from single stems, though it was better to cut one fresh off the bush after the flower had withered, and the rose hip was beginning to form, and place it into willow water. I had no willow water on hand, but I figured I might have better-than-even odds, since I used Soulwood soil. I had checked and Sterling Silver was out of patent, so I could legally root it. Legally grow it. I watered the soil, gave it a boost with my own power, and placed it where I thought it might be happy.

I hoped it rooted. I wanted a plant out of Occam's first rose to me.

Back inside, I didn't see or sense or hear Esther. I hoped Mud hadn't killed her and buried her out back.

Or worse, fed her to the land. Or chopped her up and put her in the stew.

The cats were hiding under my bed. The bedroom floor around them was spotless. They rushed out and jumped on the bedspread, all three of them staring daggers at me. I sighed again and said, "I'm sorry. I'll see what I can do."

Jezzie sniffed at me and claimed my pillow. Torquil turned her dark head away and started to clean her nether regions, in clear disapproval. Cello *mrowed*, rolled over, and showed me her belly, asking for a rub. Even knowing that the belly rub request might be a ploy to give her an excuse to scratch me, I sat on the bed and rubbed her for the comfort it brought. I wasn't a cat lover. I was a dog person. But the cats had claimed Soulwood, and that meant they had claimed me. And they had been the best of company for months, ever since the werecats had tamed them. They missed Occam in my bed. So did I. I missed his scent on my pillow, missed his cat warmth against my back in the night. But for now, the cats were my distraction and my excuse to keep from confronting Esther.

Back in the kitchen, I turned on the new electric kettle for tea and started a pot of coffee. I also put a bottle of Sister Erasmus' wine in the refrigerator. I seldom yearned for anything stronger than wine. Right now I understood the desire for a good stiff drink.

I had dithered long enough. I climbed the stairs to the upper bedrooms.

The entire upstairs had been remodeled. The four newly painted bedrooms now all opened onto the landing, and there was a full bath with divided areas: a double sink area, a dedicated shower and tub area, and a water closet, all according to the church standards, but ultramodern and sleek. Everything was white. And here again everything was lined up perfectly and everything gleamed. "Oh, Esther," I whispered.

My sister had been keeping a room here, for when she sat with Mud, on those rare evenings and weekends when I had a case that kept me away from home. I paid her a few dollars an hour, and while she was here, she had use of an empty room for her oversized quilting frame, a bedroom to call her own, and all the food she wanted to cook. It had worked out great on paper. Not so great in reality, as Esther had been more of a permanent guest for the last month.

And now Mud said that Esther was essentially living here?

I stood outside her room and debated knocking. I decided not to, because if she was asleep, I was not waking her. That made me a coward, but I could live with being a coward.

Carefully, I turned the knob and opened her door. Esther was lying on the old iron bed's mattress, on top of the quilt she had made. She lay on her side, her arms around her huge belly, her dress tucked discreetly around her knees, asleep. Her blond hair was braided but not bunned up; the tail was curled across the pillow she had pulled down from the top and green leaves and vines trailed across the white case from her hairline. Her fingertips were growing leaves as well, curling from her nail beds.

Esther's leaves were different from mine, which were very dark green with reddish petioles and veins. Esther's were like spring maple leaves, pale and beautiful. With the baby hormones, they grew fast, faster than mine ever did.

At the side of the bed were three suitcases and four oversized plastic tubs of quilting supplies and cloth. As if she had moved in over the last two days.

Esther's eyes fluttered open and she met my gaze. She had been crying, eyes red, tear-sand in the corners. We stared at each other for a while before she shoved up with her arms and let her feet fall down, until she was sitting on the bed. Her belly protruded like a huge Hubbard squash and she stuffed a pillow between her back and the iron bedstead for support. She rubbed her back the way Stella Mae's sister had when she complained about needing lumbar support.

"You'un have something to say?" she demanded.

"No." I had learned the value of silence at PsyLED.

Her reddened eyes narrowed. "'Cause a you'un, I'll never find a new husband."

The accusation cut. It wasn't true, but it hurt all the same. I wanted to yell, throw things. But . . . that was what my sister wanted. She wanted to gain control through anger and emotion and a big fight. One I would have to apologize for afterward because she would be upset and crying and it would feel as if it was my fault. Esther manipulation.

I didn't do what she wanted. "Why do you need a husband?" I asked calmly.

Esther's face twisted into pure horror. She clamped her mouth shut.

"Women don't need men to take care of us," I said. "We're fine on our own. We can protect our own land, put out our own fires, provide for ourselves. *Needing* a man to be fulfilled makes him your god, not your partner."

Her lips turned in and she bit them closed. Tears welled in her eyes and trickled down her cheeks.

I was speaking heresy according to the church. I knew how hard all this was on her. I understood. But her condition and her life were not my fault. I hadn't made Esther grow leaves. I hadn't made her what she was. Genetics had. I steeled myself against pity. "Why did Jed ask for the divorce? He knew you were growing leaves. He helped you hide them from the church up until now. What made him want out?"

Esther wiped her face with the back of one hand, the motion reminding me of Catriona, in the jail. "He's been talking to Jackie Jackson's old faction. They're making him believe lies. They say it ain't his baby. They say I laid with a demon in the woods."

I wanted to laugh, but she was deadly serious. And there was the Green Knight, who was sentient or near enough to count. And who knew what a sentient tree might do with a willing tree-woman. Then I remembered the *punishment* given to

Esther by Jackie Jackson. The thought chilled me. Terrified me, if I was honest.

"Did you have sex with a tree-man?" I asked, my voice steady, calm.

"No. Ain't no such thing as a tree-man."

Softly, gentle as a falling feather, knowing I was trespassing into deeply personal territory, I asked, "What about Jackie Jackson? Is there any chance he's the father?"

"No. Not him. I had me a menses after he . . ." She stopped, her eyes turned away. She shuddered and then continued, ". . . After he *punished* me." Punishment in church vernacular meant rape. "I know for sure and certain who the daddy is. I know the very day Jedidiah and me got me pregnant." She looked down at her belly and rubbed it with the fingers of one hand, as if her stretched skin was itching and painful. Her eyes followed her leafy hand. Softer, she said, "I remember every single moment. The very minute. It was magical and wonderful." Her face hardened. "And yet he stood up in devotions this morning and divorced me in front of the entire church, claiming I was unfaithful to him."

"Do you want to be married to him?"

Esther raised her eyes to me, and I could see thoughts running around in the back of hers, chasing each other, half-confused, half-determined. Her voice firmed. "I love him. I want him to love me. If'n he don't, well, I reckon I'd rather be alone than be an unloved wife in a house full of loved wives." She held my gaze as if the answer to her next question was the most important thing she had ever asked. "How . . . how did you'un do it?"

"Get away from the church?"

She nodded.

"One day at a time. Just like you will, if that's what you decide. You've been having trouble with Jed for a while. You've been here off and on for a month, grieving your loss of humanity and being afraid of being alone and uneducated with a child and no home. But unlike me, you're not alone. You can get education. You have people who will show you how to live independently. You don't feel strong, but you are, and so the main thing you have to do is stop grieving and stop letting him hurt you.

"You have to start making decisions and follow through.

You're cleaning the house like a madwoman, but you're being lazy about everything else."

Esther flinched. Being called lazy was the worst insult a churchwoman could be called.

I went on. "You have to be *willing* to learn how to live outside the church. Being willing means learning a new way to work, a new way to live, a new way to be."

Esther held out her hands and whispered, "If'n I stay at the church, someone will try to drive the devil outta me for growing leaves. Someone will take me and punish me again." Our mama had been punished, which was why I had a half-brother who wasn't Daddy's. Esther had suffered the same kind of punishment, which likely triggered her leaves. "Someone will kill my baby for being a devil child. The older ones will call for me and my baby to be burned at the stake."

"Like a witch," I said, "but we aren't witches."

"That's what you'un say," she said, holding up a leafy hand.

"We're genetic mutants, likely from being interbred for so many generations."

"That's disgusting," Esther said, but without the anger she had expressed the first time I explained about us.

"I've told you about trauma, especially sexual trauma, as it relates to stimulating the secondary genetic mutations of plant-people." Esther had been punished by a churchman, had been raped. We had talked about it, quietly, in the dark of night, after Mud went to bed. "The more violence, and the more we stay in contact with the earth, the more plant-people we become. It's likely that pregnancy hormones have the same effect, because that's so hard on the body."

Esther raised her eyes from her hands on her belly to me. "You'un got your'nself a plan for me?"

"I'm not telling you what to do. But I have advice."

"I'm listening."

"The next step after a man has demanded divorce? The wife can demand counseling by the elders. They don't tell us that, but it's in the church constitution."

Her chin tucked in surprise. "We'uns have a *constitution*?" She sounded incensed. "Like with rules even the menfolk has to follow?"

"Yeah. Not that anyone follows it. Sister Erasmus slid a copy into my wine delivery a month or so past and I spent a weekend reading it. It's interesting."

"Well, I'll be a dinosaur on Noah's ark."

I chuckled quietly. "To request counseling and a hiatus in divorce proceedings, we need to be willing to tell the truth about your condition." She looked confused, so I pointed at her hands. "The leaves. The real reason he's declared divorce."

"So who would I talk to? What elders will keep that kinda secret?"

I smiled, and it was my PsyLED smile. Not a sweet one at all. "An elder who had a devil dog in his lineage. Because they come from the same kind of inbreeding as plant-people."

Esther's gaze turned inward. "Oh," she said. "Them devil dogs . . . I never thought . . ." Silence stretched between us, and I waited, letting her think things through. Slowly, her shoulders went back. Her eyes dried. Her chin lifted. "I knew one. Lemme think on this a while. You'un made coffee? I smell it." When I nodded, she said, "Let's take a coffee break and eat the pumpkin bread Mama Grace baked."

A coffee break is what the mamas used to do midafternoon, after a long day in the garden, or preparing and canning vegetables, or bending over a sewing machine, a loom, a quilting frame. It wasn't a break in the work load, but more a time to do something less active in the heat of the day, like snap peas, hem a dress, sew on buttons, darn socks. It had often been a time of laughter and problem solving while the young'uns were napping. It was tradition. The good kind.

"That sounds like a good idea," I said. "Anyone planning on going to war with the church should start with a strong cup of caffeine. Or in your case, a strong cup of decaf coffee or herbal tea."

"You'un take the fun outta everything," she grumbled. But Esther followed me down the stairs, listening to my suggestions and options for her future. Before Mud came in, my elder sister and I drank our way through a pot of herbal tea and half a pot of coffee, and ate half the loaf of spicy bread, while discussing potential plans of action. Esther never lost a narrow-eyed look of deep deliberation. I had a feeling that a corner had been turned, hopefully in a positive way, though the look in her eyes was stern and calculating. Under the table, I crossed my fingers for luck, though the church said that was a sin.

Mud came in the door with Cherry at her heels, chattering about the health of the greenhouse seedlings and more mature plants in the uncovered winter garden. "We'uns is got—*we have* turnip greens and collards and varicolored baby beets and four kinds of winter squash in the outside garden. We also got bunches of little rooted rosemary in pretty shapes like one a them bonsai trees. I think I can tie 'em up with bows and sell them at Sister Erasmus' little shop during Christmas break." She told Cherry to "down" on her pallet and poured herself a cup of coffee, liberally doused with cream and sugar, talking about scheduling a round of fall canning with the Nicholson women. She joined us at the table, stopped, and looked suspiciously back and forth between us. "You'uns is mighty quiet. Why's that?"

"She's having coffee and I'm having steamed weeds," Esther said.

"We're planning on going to war with the church," I said.

"That ain't no surprise. I'm in. As long as she ain't living with us." Mud pointed to Esther.

"She'll be here a while," I said placidly, sipping my coffee.

Mud slammed her cup onto the table and said, "I don't want her living here. You and me get along jist fine. She's all, 'Do this, and do that, and it's my way or nothin'.'"

I said, "Esther?"

"I been a pain. I'm sorry."

Mud's mouth turned down in the Nicholson frown. "You're . . ." She looked at me. Sat in her chair. Brought her cup to her mouth and sipped her coffee. Set it down. "Well, that ain't fair. I hardly got to fuss at all." I wanted to laugh, but she went on. "Okay. The mamas would say you done gave me an apology. For what? And what you gonna do about it?"

I hid a smile. The church was awful about most things in life, particularly where women were concerned, but one thing they were good at teaching was problem resolution. Mud seemed to have been a stellar pupil.

"I been trying to impose order all around me," Esther said.

"According to Nell, it's 'acause I got no control over my own life or future or marriage. Or I *had* no control. That's for the apology." She took a careful breath and wrapped her arms around her baby belly. "We'uns got potential plans for my future and a solution to our fighting. So as long as I'm here, a *guest* in your'un house, I promise not to try 'n' make you'un live like I want. This is your'un house, not mine," she repeated.

"The animals?" Mud asked, wary.

"The cats and Cherry can stay in. I don't like it, but I don't hafta. But. You'un clean up after the critters every single day, including the hair on the floor in the corners, and you change the litter on the back porch."

"Are you okay with that?" I asked Mud.

"I don't know. She ain't been the reasonable type. She's a churchwoman through and through when it comes to control and manipulation. She's used to being taken care of, like a horse in a barn, told what to do and when and how. Being independent ain't easy."

Esther sucked in a sharp breath. "That right there is mean."

"Maybe," I said, "but it's the truth. The positive part is that you won't be facing the changes in your life alone. We'll be here to help you." I looked at Mud, putting steel into my gaze. "Deal?"

"Oh, all right, dagnabbit," Mud cursed in church-speak. "Deal. Besides, I been thinking. Jed will have to return your dowry, so maybe you can buy land to claim like Nell done."

"Buy land? Land of my own? Like, off the church grounds? With a house on it?"

I had been thinking along those lines and while Esther wouldn't have enough money to buy a house townie-style, there were other options open to her. "Why not?" I asked.

Esther scowled, an expression I had felt on my face. It was that Nicholson scowl, as familiar as my own hand. "Ain't no money left. Jed used the dowry to buy our'un house from the church. Maybe we'uns can . . ." A peculiar expression fell over her face.

I didn't know where Esther's thoughts went, but she got up and began setting the table for supper. "Mindy, will you'un please bring in the slow cooker?" she asked.

"Mud," my younger sister said. "Mindy is my church name."

"Humph," Esther said, severe and stern. "I done made us stew fer supper. Oh. And . . . I know it ain't my place, but I got a dozen laying hens at my house at the church, so I second the idea of *Mindy* getting chickens."

Mud hollered a woot from the kitchen. Instantly the tension vanished from the house. I kicked off my shoes and placed my socked feet flat on the floor. The old floorboards had been cut from Soulwood land and they knew me, as well as dead wood can know anything.

"Not fair. Two against one," I said, faking a sigh but feeling quietly happy. When Mud reentered carrying the slow cooker, I got up and went to the kitchen to help. "Okay. Fine on the chickens. We'll need to ask Sam about building a henhouse. Mud suggested setting chicken-wire runs through the garden and the greenhouse and letting 'em run free every day to chase pests and to keep the hens free-range." I got salad fixin's from the refrigerator. "Mud, see if the mamas will sell us six laying hens in exchange for future eggs, and let us borrow a rooster. We can have chicks inside of a month, and triple our hens." The mamas would likely just give us the hens and the chicks too, but it was always polite to offer payment and have a plan.

"Will do," Mud said, sounding like a normal twelve-year-old kid. "I'ma ask for Easter Eggers and Isbars, so we can sell 'em for more." Easter Eggers and Isbars produced varicolored eggs: white, green, blue, yellowish, speckled, rust, and a dozen shades of brown. The townies loved them. "They sell good from the get-go," Mud said, rearranging the slow cooker on the countertop and getting out bowls. "I figger we need at least twenty laying hens to make steady money selling the eggs."

My heart dropped. *Twenty hens?*

"Selling chicks is another way to make money. I'm right fond of Barred Plymouth Rocks, Red Wyandottes, and Red Orpingtons," Esther said, naming hardy kinds of chickens.

"Them's all brown and white eggs. Of course, we'uns *could* order us some fertile emu eggs," Mud said with a sly smile.

"Emus are dangerous," Esther said. "No emus."

"Fine. How 'bout some Dampierres and Deathlayers," Mud suggested, referring to totally black chickens that laid black eggs. "We could hand raise 'em, breed, and then sell fertile eggs for big bucks."

"We could call the business the Nicholson Sisters Organic Eggs and Specialty Hens," Esther said.

We? I almost asked how Esther got in on the eggs deal, but my sisters were chatting back and forth about chicken varieties, pleasant with each other for the first time in weeks. In the interests of peace and financial security, I said, "Not now for specialty chickens. Spending fifty bucks for a fertile egg or a hatched chick is a gamble for the future." I ladled stew and set the bowls on the table, thinking, *gamble for the future.* My future and my sisters' futures were major gambles. For starters, it was time for my pregnant sister to grow up. And to be protected. She would have to do the former on her own, but I could help with the latter.

After dinner, I called Daddy and put a toe into the water with a long discussion about counseling sessions for Jed and Esther, and who he should petition for the counseling. Daddy didn't like it. He was reluctant to drag Jedidiah and Esther before the church elders' court, since Jed had already demanded divorce and Esther had leaves. I didn't push it. Not yet.

Then I mentioned requesting back her dowry and Daddy went dead silent. Quietly he said, "Tradition is a strong thing in a church life. Asking for a dowry to be returned is a mighty rare occurrence. There might be . . . repercussions."

"I imagine so." I finished the call with the words, "Thank you. I just wanted to know our options, which include fighting this divorce tooth and nail. Or getting back Esther's dowry. Options are good things. 'Night, Daddy." Touching the cell's face, I ended the call.

I was thinking like a townie woman, modern and self-sufficient and sneaky. And it was about dang time.

Sunday morning meant a leaf-scaping for Esther and me, and a drive to the church for devotionals and church services under the protection of the Nicholson patriarch. It was dawn, and my legally adjudicated custody requirements meant Mud attended church on Sundays. I attended with her, except when I had a case. The Stella Mae Ragel case meant a quick escape. I dropped my sisters off at the Nicholson house and drove away fast, before Daddy could call me in and talk some more about the brewing Esther-war.

On the way from church to HQ, JoJo texted me that Catriona

had been officially charged with murder. I might have cussed just a bit, but when she sent an order to detour to the University of Tennessee Medical Center, that cut my reaction short. Her text informed me that everyone, including Tandy, was in Cookeville interviewing the dozens of people involved in Stella Mae's life. FireWind was deeply involved in trying to stop the FBI SAC's witch hunt, while simultaneously using his position to get her daughter turned over to Etain, the child's aunt. This was my solo mission. Except for Tandy, who hadn't been his best self, no one from PsyLED had been there yet.

I had been to UTMC before to interview patients and it was never fun. I wouldn't have minded had Jo sent someone else. Except there was no one else.

The University of Tennessee proper was on one side of the Tennessee River and the medical part was on the other. It was a sprawling hospital, with insufficient special parking for law enforcement, but it was Sunday, with few scheduled procedures and surgeries, and it was early enough that the church folk were still in church, so my trek to the paranormal unit wasn't too onerous. As I entered the para unit, I passed by the portable null room trailer, which was parked at a side entrance with caution cones all around. It looked empty, though with no windows, who knew?

In the paranormal unit, I showed my ID at the nurses' station and asked to talk with whichever paranormal hospitalist was on duty. The doctor was busy, so I dressed out according to instructions and meandered down the hall until I found the first patient, Stella Mae's drummer, Thomas Langer. Thomas was the man in the ambulance who had waved at me a little less than forty-eight hours ago. It seemed a lot longer. He was a heavily tattooed, bearded black man with dreadlocks. I loved dreadlocks. Normally they looked alive and vibrant, but not so much now. Thomas was on life support, a ventilator whooshing and ticking. His hands were bandaged and wrapped with sticky wrap so that I could only see the tips of his middle fingers, but they were green, and the gauze bandages were wet with greenish fluid.

I texted T. Laine, asking if null pens could be brought to the para unit of UTMC. If there was any chance to help the patients, we should take it.

She texted back, *On it. Will messenger them over.*

I tapped on the glass door and was let in by a woman dressed the way I was, in a sky blue paranormal biohazard gown, gloves, mask, and booties.

I identified myself. She said, "Robinelle Langer, Thomas' sister." Her dark eyes looked exhausted above the blue mask, her dark skin salt-cracked and rough from tears. "Have you people figured out anything? What caused this? Who did it? Any way to treat it? *Any*thing?"

"We're working as fast as we can. I promise." I looked at Thomas' bandaged hands. There was a little blood there too, and the stench was familiar from Stella's house.

"They say he's in cascading organ failure," Robinelle said. Tears leaked from her eyes and she sniffed beneath the mask. "Nothing's working. He's dying."

I had no idea what to say. There was no way to question Thomas.

"He had such a great time on the tour," Robinelle said as the ventilator punctuated the quiet. "He was on top of the world. Stella Mae was like family. We all loved her."

"How long had Thomas been with the band?" I asked carefully.

"Since the very beginning. He started out with Stella back in the commune."

I didn't know *exactly* what that meant, but I guessed, and her tone suggested that I should have understood her words. I pushed on. "Did you communicate with your brother while he was on tour? Text or phone calls?"

"Constantly. Not that he ever said anything substantive." She turned to me. "You think there's something in the texts? I can send them all to you."

"I don't want to abuse your privacy," I said while my PsyLED half was shouting to see them right now. "But if you don't mind, yes. There might be something there that would help."

"No time like the present," she said. I followed Robinelle's lead when she pulled off her gown and gloves, scrubbed her hands at the sink, and motioned me out of the room. Robinelle was pretty, in a spare, bare-boned way, with good bone structure, no makeup, and blond braids up in a big bun with loose hair sticking out all over from the hat and the elastic bands of the mask. She moved like a self-assured, accomplished woman. Nobody's victim here, even with her brother in such bad shape.

I wondered what others saw when they watched me move, victim or not-victim, confident or prey.

Standing in the hall, she pulled up several months' worth of texts between her and her brother and forwarded them to JoJo at HQ. When she was done, Robinelle handed me a business card that told me she was a tax attorney. "You'll let me know if you hear anything? Please?"

"I'll tell you anything I can," I said.

As an attorney, Robinelle seemed to understand that meant almost nothing, was more platitude than anything real. She made a face that was angry and sad and futile. The beginnings of grief. It wasn't standard operating procedure to touch people, but I couldn't help myself. I held out an arm and she moved into me, her face dropping to my shoulder, her arms going around me. We stood there, hugging, long enough that her breathing calmed. She sniffed and stepped back. "Thanks. I needed that."

"Me too," I said. And I realized that I really did.

The next patient was Connelly Darrow, who played bass guitar and had been among the first to be stricken ill, along with Langer. Just as I got to the door, an alarm went off and I was shoved out of the way as medical personnel dressed out and rushed in, and family was pushed into the hallway with me. I stood there with her weeping family as the team drew the drapes around the bed and tried to help their patient. Tried to save her. In shadows against the drapes, we watched as the medical team compressed her chest. Ventilated her. Drew blood, gave meds. As people rushed in and out. The curtain caught on the ventilator and we gathered at the corner of the glass doorway, watching.

Connelly's right big toe fell off and splatted onto the floor in a spray of greenish goo. Someone picked up the toe and closed the curtain.

From behind the curtain I heard the words, "We have a pulse."

Her family wept silently, holding on to the hope of a heartbeat. I couldn't make myself stay any longer.

I passed Robinelle Langer, standing at the closed glass door inside her brother's room, dressed in hospital blue, her eyes on the family in the hallway. There was an expression of horror in her eyes and she met mine, hers pleading.

A coward, I looked away. There would be no questioning
Connelly or her family right now, and I couldn't bring myself to
speak to the others who had been admitted. Their families were
standing like Robinelle, watching the shadows on the glass
wall. I left the paranormal unit.

Stopping a security guard in the hallway, I asked directions
to the medical university's pathology department and got into
my car, following the hastily scripted directions. I parked and
found the weekend pathologist just leaving. I identified myself
and said, "I hate to bother you, but—"

"Then don't," she said, sounding tired and taciturn. Her
name tag identified her as Dr. Gomez, her accent placed her as
a Tennessee native, and her expression said she had worked a
long shift and was mighty unhappy. She was a take-charge, no-
nonsense woman with very dark copper skin tones and a curly
Afro that sprang around her face when she released it from a
clip. "You can walk out with me. But I can't talk to you. HIPAA
laws make all patient matters confidential."

She might not have meant it to hit me the way it did, but
anger shot all through me. "Murder investigations precede
HIPAA," I said, "especially since a subpoena was delivered to
your department at seven a.m. While I appreciate you being in
a hurry and your desire to protect patients, you can talk to me
now or I can have a marked car show up at your home and bring
you in to PsyLED for a more formal discussion."

Gomez stopped and swiveled to me. "I don't like being
threatened."

I blew out a breath as the anger dissipated. I had no idea
where my attitude had come from, except from the vision of
Connelly Darrow dying and being brought back behind the curtain. "People are dying. I need information," I said. "Please. Tell
me what you know about the body."

Gomez frowned. "We received jars of sludge from a crime
scene, and I thought it was a joke. Seems it wasn't. The preliminary reports from the early samples show nothing of substance. So far nothing is growing on the plates or the broth.
Today I received four fingers from the paranormal unit from
two different patients. They dissolved before I could do more
than measure and weigh them. I sent parts of the remains to the
clinical lab for chemistries, to mycobacteriology for cultures,

and to CDC for virology and infectious disease testing, and my tech worked up what he could in histo."

"What is histo?"

"Histology. He put a few small scraps of flesh into the histology tissue processor. If the tissue survives the dehydration and paraffin processes, it'll be cut into slices of point five to point one micrometers and mounted on a slide, stained, and read under a microscope. Then I might—*might*—have an idea what's killing the patients. Your people say it's a curse, but even curses have a cause—bacterial, viral, prion-based—*something* has to cause the tissue breakdown and total organ failure. And heat, bacteria, and moisture are usually responsible for decomposition, regardless of magical energies."

I frowned. "Radiation doesn't involve those things. Magic is energy, just like radiation is energy. And we've already speculated that this could be a . . ." I tried to think of a way to say this that might be medically helpful instead of investigatively helpful. I went on. "Call it a nonwitchy time curse, speeding up death and decay rather than causing them, because death and decay happen to all of us."

Gomez crossed her arms, her scrubs swishing, her eyes narrow in thought. "Keep talking."

"You might not have anything except a magically accelerated natural progression. And because the patients were deprived of early access to a null chamber, which would halt the energies and the progression of the patients' decomp, then the energies might have taken hold and done their damage. Once the patients did get access to a null unit, it could have been too little, too late. All the affected people at the farm were put inside a null chamber and they got better. Accelerated decomposition of inanimate objects stopped. We might have . . ." My words ground to a halt. "PsyLED should have pushed use of the null room at HQ harder."

The anger on Gomez' face faded. "PsyLED has a null room in Knoxville?"

I frowned. "Yes. There is a null room at PsyLED here in Knoxville, and parked outside is a *portable* null chamber on loan to UTMC from the North Nashville coven."

I didn't have to be Tandy to know that Gomez was shocked. She hadn't known.

"Both are available," I said, softer. "PsyLED's room is a better null space because it's stable. We offered for UTMC to transport patients there for treatment. That didn't happen."

"You offered that to us? Who did you talk to, because this is the first I've heard about it," she said, redirecting her anger.

"Yes. We offered. I can find out who took the call at UTMC if necessary. We've been feeling our way through this, just like y'all."

Gomez cursed and walked toward the doctor parking area.

Feeling despondent, and knowing that communication had broken down somewhere, somehow, I moved to my vehicle and began to write up my reports. Moments later, JoJo notified me that there had been a death on the paranormal floor and for me to get back to the morgue.

NINE

I was standing at the morgue doors, waiting for the paperwork to be filled out, and for family to grieve. I had been here long enough to find vending machines and eat a package of pretzels and drink a Cheerwine, both of which were wonderful snack foods.

I finally heard a ding and the elevator doors opened. A stretcher was wheeled off toward me, preceded by the stench of *death and decay*. The body on the stretcher was zipped into a human remains pouch, a white sheet over the HRP. The transport workers were covered head to toe in blue antispelled unis, their faces hidden behind masks and goggles. I showed my ID and requested to see the body.

They stopped. One of them pulled back the sheet. The other unzipped the pouch.

It was what I had expected. Pretty awful. Sometime in the last hour, Connelly had coded again, been pronounced, and been moved off the floor. Her eyes had probably been blue; now they were clouded over. Her lips were gray, pulled back tightly from dry, crusty teeth. A greenish slime drooled from one corner of her lips around a tube that was still in place. Her brown hair was falling out. Her skin was weeping, melting from her bones like candle wax. Her hands and feet were green. I assumed I was expected to touch and read the body to verify the presence and type of the magics in it, but I couldn't bring myself to. I curled my hands into fists. The experience of fighting *death and decay* was still too fresh in my memory. My finger still ached, the skin still white and dead looking.

Before I could talk myself into it, the elevator pinged and opened. Gomez strode out, shouting, "This better be worth—"

She halted, cursed, and came on. "Worth my time to come back on my day off," she said softly. She stopped over Connelly's body. "Astounding," she said. "And damn it all to hell." She looked at me. "You get a judge's order and you can observe the PM. Otherwise get the hell out."

I got.

And I had the perfect excuse to not touch the body.

I drove to the office. My official vehicle had come to me by way of confiscation and it was "fully tricked out inside," according to Occam. It had every bell and whistle ever devised by car manufacturers—heated seats and steering wheel, autostart, Bluetooth, an onboard computer that I could link to my laptop if needed, electronic chargers, monitors to tell me when I had low tires . . . It had everything. I loved it. I'd never tell my mama, but the best reasons for entering the modern world were Krispy Kreme donuts and tech.

I parked close to HQ's door, spotting JoJo's and FireWind's cars and a dozen rusted-out vehicles I didn't recognize. The sound of music on the air made me look up to see the third-floor windows were open, the origination of the music. There were two ways onto the third floor: through the second floor and from the back of the building. Cigarette smoke and dust floated around the building from the back, along with multilingual shouting—English, Spanish, and something that sounded like Croatian or Russian, not that I'd heard those last languages except in movies. A loud thump sounded as something heavy hit the earth. I didn't have a hard hat so I didn't go around back to see.

Carrying my gear and the potted tree, I went inside, climbed the stairs, and stopped at my cubby. I set down my plant, checked its soil for moisture content, locked away my weapon, and put my lunch in the break room. I also made a fresh pot of coffee the instant I braved the main conference room, which had been taken over by JoJo Jones, Unit Eighteen's computer guru and former (mostly) hacker, who was staring at her screens. The long table was covered with printed pages, file folders, and electronic equipment. There were multiple screens of various sizes on the walls. The lights were dim, the blinds closed. JoJo was sitting in her chair, her big braided bun tilted forward, her silver earrings catching the light of the screens, her body unmoving, fingers still. She didn't seem to be breathing and I wasn't sure if she had died in that position until she blinked.

"Tell me something I don't know," she demanded without looking my way.

I nearly jumped at the sound of her voice, but took my seat and opened my tablet. "Connelly died because she didn't get to a null room," I said quietly. "No one in authority understood that they had to, that they *could*, bring patients to HQ. Communication broke down."

Jo cursed succinctly and forcefully. "I told the person who answered the desk on the paranormal wing. I've got the name here." Jo started punching keys, looking for the file she wanted. She looked tired, as if she hadn't left HQ and her computers since the case began. She was wearing heavy yoga pants, a thick black headband, an oversized sweatshirt, and no makeup. "Here it is. The woman's name was Marielle Higgins. I told her about the null room. She said she would relay the information to the doctor. I *told* her!"

"Jo. The failure to communicate was on them, not us," I said, trying to comfort.

"Not being at fault is *not* going to bring anyone back from the dead," she snarled. She looked sleep-deprived and as snarly as she sounded.

"No. It isn't," I said.

"Give me something I can use to *prove* how this crime works, something I can then track down to a practitioner, something other than a trigger, a trigger that the North Nashville coven can't figure out and never heard of *at all*." JoJo snarled the last two words.

I said, "Stella Mae lived in a commune-like place, back five years ago, before she became a star."

JoJo slowly turned her head to me and breathed out the words, "That's what you meant with that list? I thought it was people she had in common . . ." Her eyes focused on the air above my head. "I thought it was misspelled and . . . Ohhh. The missing years."

"Beg pardon?"

"There are missing years in Stella's public and personal data stream. If she was in a commune, she may have eschewed everything modern. That would make sense."

I said, "Yeah. She might have."

"Where? Who?" Jo asked.

"I got no idea. But according to the lists provided by the late-night sandwich makers, Bevie Rhoden and Elisa Yhall, one of her band members might have been part of the commune. Thomas Langer."

"Bevie Rhoden and Elisa Yhall." Jo ran a search for the photos of the lists. "Your files from the scene are well organized," she muttered, her fingers now flying over the keys. "Commune? It's a place to start. Okay. Let's find the hidden records."

I went back to work organizing the unit's case files and interrogation results. It was both interesting and mind-numbingly boring. Hours passed. I drank a lot of coffee. I prepared a lunch of salad greens from my garden and microwaved leftover stew and cut up a hunk of homemade bread for Jo and me. I put a portion for FireWind in the fridge. I took one call from Mud and Esther in which they whispered angrily at one another during church service while I listened. I hung up, midscream. They knew to text something specific if it was a real emergency. Of course, they also knew better than to call me at work over a sisters' spat.

"I got it. I got it, I got it," JoJo said, breaking the afternoon's doldrums. "I got the commune. Holy sh . . . oot. I got it. And . . ."

"And what?" I asked when she didn't continue, a small smile on my face from her revised cussing.

"No wonder Stella Mae's PR people whitewashed her background." She stopped, but her fingers were still moving and the screens overhead were flashing to life with what looked like posts from a defunct online site dedicated to . . . sex. With photos . . . I stared.

Jo said, "The typical country music fan would hate to learn that their pure Christian singing star was in bed with a bunch of people. I count six heads. No, seven. It's all out of focus, which is probably a good thing. I do not need to see what they are doing."

"Mmmm . . ." My ability to speak failed me. I dragged my eyes away, got up, and walked down the hall to the locker room. And inside. I used the facilities. Washed my hands. Several times. I fixed my hair. Pulled a tiny leaf. I dawdled. I dillydallied. I might have loitered.

I had grown up in a polygamous church where everything in life revolved around marriage, concubinage, and the punishment and abuse of women and girl-children. But sex, sex like I had seen in the photographs, was not something that was ever discussed. Not *ever*. Churchwomen were chaste by modern standards. They had a husband. The lights went out. The husband crawled into a wife's bed. There were relations. The husband went to sleep, snoring. That was it. The next night he was with a different woman, doing the same thing in her bed. What I had seen in the photographs . . .

Did modern townie men want *that*? Did *Occam* want that? From *me*?

I walked back into the hallway, let the locker room door close, and came to a stop. The big boss was standing in front of me, leaning against the wall, partially blocking the way. Not totally, not enough to activate my "trapped" instinct, my fight instinct, but more just the size of his body, his broad shoulders, his six-foot-three-plus inches of height. I caught my breath.

FireWind's arms were crossed, his long, beautiful black hair down and shimmering across one shoulder. He looked at ease. His expression blank. Or, no. It was . . . maybe faintly kind? As kind as he could manage.

"What?" I demanded.

His lips smiled ever so slightly. "I saw the images. Are you all right?" He dropped his arms and tucked his fingers into the pockets of his black pants, much like the way Rick stood. It was an odd gesture, deliberate, as if to demonstrate peaceful intents and try to get me to relax. "I understand how the photographs might affect you. Strike you."

"Yeah? How would you know anything about me?" I demanded.

"Because my wife was a woman of her time, a woman of her upbringing. Such photographs would have deeply offended her. The women of God's Cloud of Glory Church are not promiscuous, do not understand that their bodies belong to them and not to the man who owns them."

"I was not *owned*."

"Were you not?"

I closed my eyes, blocking out my boss, his probing questions, his *insults*. His . . . his *truths*. Ayatas FireWind spoke *truths*. "Yes," I whispered. "I was owned. I sold myself into sexual slavery to keep me safe from even worse things."

"And you would do it again. I understand that. And you survived." He stopped as if to give me time to speak, but I had nothing to say. "You are strong. I offer you what comfort I may as you face your memories. I honor your journey."

Tears I did not expect shot down my face like a fire hose had opened. Burning tears. I opened my mouth. Closed it. Managed a shuddering breath. *I honor your journey* . . . "Well, *damn*," I said, the curse shocking me. I opened my eyes to see FireWind watching me, his eyes gentle. I struggled with what to say and settled on, "Thank you." He gave me the barest of nods. "Your wife?" I asked.

"She was a good woman. Stronger by far than I could ever hope to be. My people did not see sexual relations as her people did. It was difficult for us at first with our differing perceptions and expectations."

I thought about Occam. About what he might want. "You miss her," I said.

"I will miss my Forever Heart until the day I die."

"Forever Heart?"

He closed his eyes for a moment and his face lit with deep, powerful emotions: joy and intense grief. "Igohidv Adonvdo," he whispered, the syllables liquid and lovely. He met my eyes. "But she was not a modern woman. She would have been offended by the photographs."

"I'm a law enforcement officer. I can adapt," I said.

He gave a stronger nod. "Yes. You will. But it may never be easy for you to view such things. I will remain in my office until such time as you are ready for me to be present."

My eyes went wide. I'd have to be in the presence of men when the photos were being viewed and dissected. "Oh dear," I whispered.

"Yes."

"Wait. Did they release Catriona?"

"No. The State Department and the EU embassy are now involved. It's becoming complicated on multiple levels." He turned and went to his new glass-walled office at the back of the second floor. He walked like a wild animal, with liquid grace, and closed the door to his office, pulling the blinds. His current office had been converted from unused space, along with the new interrogation room beside it. I felt intense relief at the knowledge that he would be moving upstairs soon.

I dropped my back to the hallway, the wall cool through my clothing. I'd have to see sex pictures in a room full of my co-workers, women and men. In front of my boss. In front of *Occam*. "Oh dear," I repeated, this time to myself. When I thought I could stand it, I went back to the conference room and the photos of the naked people doing . . . things . . . to each other.

"The commune was composed of small groups of people," JoJo said, "and if we look at this in light of the commune, then in Stella's group there were seven, counting Stella. Racine Alcock left the commune after a year and disappeared, leaving six. All six of the remaining commune members, again counting Stella, were in the band in some capacity. Stella, Connelly Darrow, Thomas Langer, Erica Lynn Quinton, Cale Nowell, Donald Murray Hampstead. Two band/commune members are dead under bizarre paranormal circumstances from the *death* working: Stella and Connelly Darrow. The other dead are Monica Belcher and Verna Upton, *not* in the band but still part of Stella's inner circle. In the commune *and* the band *and* still alive are Thomas Langer, Erica Lynn Quinton, Cale Nowell, Donald Murray Hampstead. Also, presumably alive, is Racine Alcock. So far, Nell—Ingram—cannot find records of her. If this was a TV show, Alcock would be dead at the hands of the commune members and the killer would be killing off all the witnesses."

"This is not a television show," FireWind said, amused. "Ingram, what do you have on her?" He was eating the salad from my garden with apparent relish. I was moderately gratified that he found it so tasty. An empty bowl was on the table. He had wiped the last dregs of stew from it with the last chunk of bread. He had carefully and kindly not looked at me as he ate, the photos of naked people on the screens over his head.

"Sending you my search results," I said, shifting the file to JoJo. I had begun background checks on all the band and commune members, including the missing Racine Alcock, who did not exist under that exact name, according to current databases: driver's licenses, marriage licenses, and death certificates in seven states, and current social media, within fairly broad age parameters. I didn't have access to her date of birth, social security number, or mother's maiden name. I had no physical characteristics, height, weight, current hair color. That meant that my initial search had been limited. Then I had searched under multiple spellings for Alcock: Racine, Racina, Ragine, Regina, Reagan, Raegan, Regan, Ragan, Roseann, Rosanne, Rosanna, Roxanne, Roxanna, Roxana, and Richelle Alcock. I followed that with a search for first-name-unknown Racine Alcock, first-name-unknown all the others Alcock, and a good ten other variations of Alcock. I found lots of women who might fit under broad parameters, but nothing specific. Not one mention of a female in that correct age group. Not in the military, not in the prison system, not anywhere.

Jo looked up at me. "Nice work, country hick chick. I'll make a research geek out of you yet."

I made a face at her, as if her words had a bad smell. She chuckled, knowing I hated computer stuff and wanted to be out in the open air, in nature.

FireWind gathered up the dirty dishes and glided into the doorway. Not stepped. Glided. He was grace personified, and I had met vamps who could do the grace thing better than anyone. FireWind was right up there with the vampiest. "I have some calls to make," he said. "And since I ate the last of the stew, I'll order in supper for you two. What do you want?"

JoJo said, "How about burgers from the Burgers on Sutherland Ave. They don't deliver this far, but they are the best, and you can do pickup while you talk on the phone. You can't beat their food. I'll have a Knox Burger."

"I'll have the Black and Blue," I said.

He had to know we were trying to get rid of him, but FireWind gave us a formal nod, rinsed the dishes in the break room sink, and left the building. I had to hold in a giggle as he walked past the outside security cameras. JoJo had just sent the big boss on a food run. The tension in HQ fell dramatically the moment he got in his car.

"Aren't you a vegetarian?" I asked Jo.

"Most of the time. Not tonight. Thank God he's gone. It's

hard enough looking at sex pics, but to do it with your boss in and out constantly?" JoJo said. "Your boss who is drop-dead gorgeous. And who has the best poker face on the planet. I can't read him at all. Gives me the creeps." She swiveled and stared me down in my seat in the corner. "You okay?"

I scowled at her. "Put all the sex pics back up on the big screens. And the photos of the dead bodies in Stella's basement. I gotta get used to looking at that stuff."

Without turning, JoJo tapped a single key and a dozen of the pics appeared overhead. Seven naked people. On a big mattress with lots of pillows, scrunched-up covers, and body parts. Doing things. Partially out of focus but not out of focus enough to hide all that. I closed my eyes.

"Don't worry," Jo said. "Occam doesn't want that. Well, he might think about wanting it, but he doesn't really." I stilled and she added, "He's a guy. People think things all the time. That doesn't mean they go through with them. That's why we police people for what they've done, and not for what they might do. Well, usually." She smiled slightly.

"Are you sure?" I asked, meaning the part about Occam, which she seemed to know.

"That man loves you more than anyone I've ever seen love anyone on the face of the earth." She waved a hand. "You know what I mean."

I did. Sorta. I stared at the screens, looking back and forth between sex photos and dead body photos. "Why's it harder to look at sex than to look at the dead bodies?"

"Our culture says death and violence are okay but sex isn't. And your church culture says it's worse than anything."

"Everyone on the unit knows that? About my culture? About the church?"

"Honey," she said, sounding a little sad, but not pitying, which was good because I'd get real mad at any kind of pity. "Everyone on the unit knows. Everyone wants to protect you and help you through your constraints so you can be the best special agent that ever lived."

"Oh," I said. I looked at the photos again. There were six pictures on the biggest screen, bodies everywhere doing everything. "FireWind says I'll never get used to it."

"No. You will never get used to it. But you will learn to hide your reactions and to study the photos for information. For instance, look at every photo. In every one of them, one person is right beside, or under, or over, Stella. Always close. Always right there."

"Ohhh," I said. "The missing woman? Racine Alcock?"

"Yeah. Hanging on to Stella like a lifeline."

"And then there's this." She put up a photo of seven people, all the men in tuxedoes, all the women in long gowns. Long *white* gowns, some off the shoulder, some lacy. The women carried flowers. Two of them wore veils over their faces. They all stood together in a semicircle. A man wearing a dark robe, like some preachers wore, stood in the center of them. It looked like a wedding with seven participants. Stella Mae had gotten . . . poly-married? I wasn't sure of the term. Or if there was one.

"It wasn't a legal marriage," JoJo said. "It isn't registered anywhere. But they had a ceremony. And they recorded it for posterity."

I went back through all the photos. In every one, Alcock's face was veiled or blurred or partially hidden. In every one, Cale Nowell was looking at Stella with desperate need. I checked my lists. I had done a prelim interview on Cale at the farm on Friday, but he hadn't been seen since.

"Cale Nowell went to prison for vehicular manslaughter four years ago," I said, as I dumped a French fry into a pile of mustard. "He's out on good behavior. His parole officer, A. K. Montgomery, says Cale got special permission to travel across state lines with the band, with Stella Mae swearing in court during his parole hearing that there would be no alcohol and no drugs on any of the tour buses. Cale missed his parole meeting last week, but he called, talked to Montgomery on the phone, and said he would be back for a long break and would be in to see the parole officer. He'd been a model parolee so the officer let him go this once."

JoJo and I were in the conference room eating. The big boss was in back, on the phone. The sex pics were off the main screen, thank goodness.

I punched a key and put up crime scene photos taken by Occam from the farm. Cale Nowell had taken shelter in the tents and had then spent time in the portable null room. I had talked to him through the layers of sky blue P3E unis and never seen his face so I didn't recognize him from the sex photos. He had tattoos on every visible part of his body, from knuckles to face. There were tattooed swirls over his left eye and into his carefully sculpted hairline. He was tall, buff, with chiseled musculature and beautiful bone structure. His jaw was sharp, his chin hard, his green eyes soft. His driver's license listed him as Black and Other, which meant that he was probably mixed race. In one single photo from Stella's farm, snapped by a deputy early on, his eyes were red from weeping, his expression shocked and full of horror.

I studied the photos, and then pulled up Nowell's original arrest report. At the scene of an accident that had killed a seventy-year-old woman, Cale had been arrested, pled guilty to a reduced charge, and served three years. He had been driving Stella's car and Stella had been injured. I opened the crime scene photos from the car accident. It had been awful, Stella's car half on top of the other car. There was no way that the driver in the other car had survived.

I focused on the images of the car Cale had been driving, paging through. The driver's seat was far forward. That could have happened from the impact. But there was makeup smeared on the driver's-side airbag. None on the passenger-side airbag.

In the arrest photos, Cale's face showed no traces of makeup.

I could find no mention or photos of Stella Mae, except that she had been taken to the hospital by ambulance.

I had a bad feeling that Cale, one of Stella's husbands, had taken the hit for Stella, or the arresting officer had arrested the only black man at the scene. It was unlikely to affect this case, but I ran a quick search for the family and heirs of the woman who had died in the accident, just in case vengeance was a motive. I found nothing that led me to believe there was any family revenge involved. The accident didn't look as if it pertained to this case.

Summarizing my conclusions, I sent all the information to the current case files. Almost immediately my cell rang and Occam's name appeared on the screen. A warm, slightly electric heat flashed through me. "Special Agent Ingram," I said, letting him know that I was in the presence of other unit members.

"Nell, sugar, this is good stuff. Prison record. Disappeared from the crime scene. Hasn't been seen since. I'll be contacting Cale Nowell. We finally got us a person of interest."

"I'm glad I could help."

"I miss you, sugar."

The call ended before I could reply, but JoJo snickered at my expression. Before I could figure out how to respond, the office number rang and I answered, "PsyLED. Special Agent Ingram."

"This is Sophee Anne Ragel, Stella Mae Ragel's sister. I'd like to talk to someone who can tell me about the investigation into my sister's murder."

"Ms. Ragel," I said. JoJo looked up and motioned me to put it on speaker. I did. "We're just in the opening stages of the investigation. I know this must be very difficult." JoJo gave me a thumbs-up to continue. "And I thank you for calling. Can you tell me if you have any new thoughts on your sister's state of mind in the days leading up to her death?"

"I can't think a nothing new. I can only think about the usual death threats. Are you people looking into them?"

JoJo nodded and mouthed, *Me.*

"Our very best investigator is looking into each and every one, Ms. Ragel. Was Stella Mae unusually worried or afraid of one of the threats?"

"It was always business as usual with Stella. If she was singling one out, she woulda told her security, not her family. She wouldn't ever worry us."

"Have you had any further thoughts about Stella seeing someone new romantically?" I asked, wondering if her family was really blind to Stella's lifestyle, or if I would hear the truth now. "Has Stella recently broken up with someone? Fired someone from the band? Was she having financial problems?"

"I don't know. No. And definitely not. Her band are family. This tour was a crazy good financial success, according to her manager."

I glanced at JoJo, who rolled her hand in the air in a *keep going* gesture. "Has anyone found her will?"

"Not that I know of. There've been three in the last few years. It'll turn up. Or her lawyer will come forward with the latest."

"Three? Why so many wills?"

"Stella was always adding people to her will. She'd make a few codicils or whatever you call 'em, and then her lawyer, Augustina Mattson, would tell her it was getting confusing and it was time to upgrade. This last time she created trusts and added gifts for a bunch a friends. But I haven't seen it. None of us have. We been putting together funeral arrangements, and we ain't had access to her house to look, thanks to the cops. You can check with Mattson."

I asked, "What can you tell me about the poly marriage Stella was part of at the commune?"

Sophee pulled in a noisy breath and said, "That's disgusting. We don't talk about that. Ever." She hung up.

"Sounds like you hit a nerve," JoJo said.

I stared at the wedding photo, thinking about hidden emotions and anger and jealousy and multiple-partner marriages. Thinking about secrets, church-style.

I could have, probably should have, stayed longer at HQ, but I was exhausted. I left work early, and felt my usual intense joy at driving onto Soulwood land, passing a small open space between trees, about an acre of grassland at the bottom of the hill, close to the road. A deer was standing in the center of the grass, nibbling, ignoring me as I drove past. I knew, without understanding how I knew, that Mud and Esther were not at the house, which meant that tomorrow, someone from the church would have to drive Mud to school and Esther to wherever she wanted to go. I should have listened to the messages from my sisters, but I consoled myself that they had survived the day at the church. My Honda pulled up the hill, a steady purr of sound. The car wasn't an all-wheel drive, which meant it wasn't as practical for winter driving as I might want, but the heated seats and the ability to lock my weapons in the trunk made up for not getting an SUV with better icy-road-handling for winter.

Just as I was about to turn into my drive, I spotted the trees. New trees. Trees growing where they shouldn't. I slowed, coasted to a stop on the side of the road, and stared at the trees growing among the oaks and poplars and sweet gums on the far side of the boundary between the Vaughns' farm and Soulwood. They were saplings with dark bark and very dark green leaves with red petioles and red veins. Leaves that looked a lot like the kind I grew. There were long, thin thorns on the branches. What looked like vines reached from branches to the ground. The vampire tree had taken root just beyond the boundary of my property, hiding in plain sight among the existing trees on the Vaughn farm side. The tall straight trunks were directly across the street from my dogs' gravesites, the dogs shot by the churchmen.

I stared at the graves and my eyes teared up, making the trees waver. "Stupid to grieve about the dogs now," I whispered to myself.

The trees stood in a line, a hundred feet long, at least three trees deep. As if guarding the road to the house and, perhaps, the small graves. The tree had no fruit, no others of its kind to mate with, so until it figured out how to cross to itself, it propagated via runners, rootlets that pushed through the soil. The roots had to extend far onto my land and also back, the many, *many* yards, beneath the top of the hill east of my land, to the original tree on church land.

Sneak attack. Dang tree.

I blinked the tears away, put the car in park, and walked across the dirt to the grass verge, the engine still idling. The afternoon temperatures didn't prove it, but it was technically autumn and there were a few colorful leaves on the ground, mostly maple and poplar. My three acres needed to be mowed, but it took a while to cut that much grass, even using the new small tractor and large mower attachment I had bought recently.

I walked to the graves, still easy to pick out even now. The rocks I had placed over them were mixed river rock and broken hill-stones, iron brown and deep gray, some with sharp edges. I stood between the graves, regarding the trees. They— No. *It*. It was a fast-growing hardwood, once an oak, now a meat-eating monster, despite its claim to be the Green Knight. A squirrel was speared on one of the thorns and a vine was circling around it. I had never watched to see how the tree ate. I didn't really want to know and, as if the tree knew that, it pulled the squirrel around back, out of sight.

I sank onto the ground and put my hands flat on the grass, wriggling my fingertips in through the roots into the soil. Good, rich Soulwood soil warmed me up through my hands and arms. It was like getting a hug from Mama, safe and protected.

I reached into the ground with my gift, deeper into the soil, bypassing the bones of my dogs, not encouraging the earth to digest them. I touched buried rocks and clayey soil and various layers from floods. Roots from all the nearby trees had encroached onto the land. Including the roots of the vampire tree.

They knew I was there, underground, with them. I let my eyes close and my shoulders slump. Conversation with the tree wasn't easy. It didn't have eyes or language as people understood it. However, it had absorbed mammals, probably even the man who had gone missing on the church land, a slime of blood the only trace. It had digested and taken in their sensory perceptions, perhaps even their memories. It had created for itself the human-shaped persona of the Green Knight to protect me and talk to me. Communication was possible, strangely image-based and concept-based. I envisioned the place where I sat, the house behind me, the grass beneath me, the trees in front of me.

I got back an image of a green horse, nibbling green grass.

I sent images of human shapes cutting down oak and pine and walnut and hickory trees, sawing them to make boards.

The horse raised his head and looked at me, long tufts of grass waving in his lips as he chewed.

I sent a vision of my house being built from the wood. Visions of the wood in its walls, on its floors, siding, window frames. And then I sent images of me walking on the cut boards, touching cabinets. Of me being able to commune with the land beneath simply by taking off my shoes and touching the boards that had grown on Soulwood.

The green horse was joined by the Green Knight, his hand on the horse's neck. Waiting. Interested.

I sent it images of the vampire trees being cut down, shaped into logs, some cut into boards. Of being made into a house.

The horse stomped, nostrils flared. The Green Knight fisted his hand in the mane.

The tree sent me images of bloody tree stumps and roots, of bloody leaves waving in the air. Of vines coiling around my wrists. Sticking thorns into my flesh. Pulling me beneath the ground, wrapped tightly in roots.

Defensive moves. Saying no.

I called on Soulwood. Its power rose up in me, warm, alive, and . . . mine. I gathered it into myself. And shoved. Shoved the roots away, breaking them, tearing them, crushing them. Then sending an image of the trees cut down and made into a house. Allowed to regrow in the same place. Taking and giving back. A job.

The Green Knight and the horse backed up at a synchronized pace, stepping high over the tall green grass. Aloud, I said, "You will have to find a way to survive in this world, a job to do, a purpose to fulfill, and not just as my protector. I won't have you *imposing* your will on *me*. Soulwood and I will destroy you first."

I sent an image of Soulwood rising up, a massive green predator. I had claimed leopards for my land and in my vision, the land rose as a leopard with dark green spots and emerald claws, huge green fangs like a monster. Another cat followed it, this one darker, a green so dark it might be black, but with paler green claws and serrated fangs and glowing leaf-green eyes. In my vision, I sent Soulwood after the tree.

The wild green cats attacked the Green Knight and the horse. The battle was fierce and short, and when the scarlet blood finished falling, the Green Knight and his horse were withering on the ground. Dead. The vision broke up and misted away, leaving the real Green Knight staring at me, his horse staring at me. Unmoving.

I didn't wait to see its reaction. I got up and left the tree, walking to the Honda. I had never been threatened by a tree. *The Green Knight, my pale leafy butt*, I thought. *I'll kick your'un butt before I let you'un take me.* I would not be abused by a dang tree, no matter how smart it was.

Back at my vehicle, I drove to the house, parked, and sent a text message to Sam, my brother, asking if he'd find out what the churchmen would charge to cut down and mill a bunch of trees. I didn't mention the vampire tree. My brother thought it was a murdering demon tree. And maybe he was right. I gathered my gear and stepped from the car.

Soulwood reached up and twined around my soul. Healing. Warm. Full of gentle magic, my magic. The magic of life and all living things. But life came with battle, with defending all that was mine. And if I had to fight, that might come with death.

Before I got the door unlocked, I received a three-part text from Sam that the girls were staying over with Mama tonight, that he'd take Mud to school in the morning, and that he'd check on the logging and land clearing. I had . . . I had a night to myself. A night free. Delight spread through me. And then I remembered that Occam was in Cookeville.

Dagnabbit.

I changed clothes and went to the greenhouse. Greenhouses took a lot of work, but it wasn't backbreaking work, since the beds were raised and so much was automated, like the delivery system for water and fertilizer. I worked in the garden too, which was much harder on the back. I weeded, harvested, turned over the mulch, picked off pests and wondered if chicken runs in the garden would keep most of the pests off. I'd never tried it. I worked hard, sweating, needing this, this contact with the earth. With Soulwood.

Hours later, my cell rang just as I was crawling into bed. I answered, "Ingram here. Hello, FireWind."

"Two more people who were at the house the day the T-shirts were opened have fallen ill. All of the sick are now at UTMC for paranormal medical workups. Go to the hospital in the morning and *this time*," he said sharply, "stay long enough to interview the sick and their doctors. I have done this one by cell; I want you to personally reissue the invitation for the patients to use the null room at HQ. When you get to HQ, I'd like you to spend a bit of time in it too, just to be on the safe side."

I hadn't interviewed the patients last time I visited because Connelly Darrow died. It had been the right thing to do, but I hadn't gone back yet. And FireWind was peeved. "Yes, sir," I said.

The call ended. I stared at the screen and said, "Good-bye to you too." And oddly, my brain added one silent word to that.

Butthole.

I felt dreadfully guilty.

TEN

I arrived at the University of Tennessee Medical Center, Paranormal Unit, just before dawn. I went through the usual process of showing ID at the nurses' station and gave them two more null pens to share among the patients. Following FireWind's orders, I informed and reminded them that time in a null room should be a primary component of the patients' treatment plans.

After comparing the names of the patients on the floor with a list sent to me by Tandy during the night, and dressing out in a blue gown, gloves, booties, and a mask, I eased back the patient curtain in Thomas Langer's room. Robinelle was asleep in the chair in the corner, her legs drawn up, her head at an uncomfortable angle, weighted down by the big bun.

There were purple circles under Robinelle's eyes and her skin was ashen. She was exhausted. I was careful not to wake her, and turned slowly to look at her brother. I managed to hold in my flinch. Thomas Langer was watching me.

His dark eyes were intense, and his hands, in restraints at his sides to keep him from pulling his tubes out, were balled tightly inside the bloody and green-goo-stained bandages. A pulse pounded in his throat, throbbing beneath the bluish vein. His dreadlocks had been pulled back beneath a blue cap. He was still on the ventilator.

I tilted my head. "Do you understand me?"

He tried to speak and his eyes clenched shut. It looked painful. He opened them a few heartbeats later and nodded once.

"Shall I get the nurse?"

He nodded again.

I pressed the "nurse call" button and a woman in purple scrubs stuck her head in, her eyes taking in everything. She said, "He's awake, that explains the vitals we're seeing just now. Give me a minute and I'll be right in."

She was still tying her blue gown when she entered. "Tommy, I'm your nurse, Ginny. How are you? No, don't struggle. Just listen. Are you listening?"

Thomas nodded once, slightly. Even that looked painful.

"Oh my God. Tommy!" his sister said. Robinelle flew from the chair to his side and burst into tears. So did Thomas.

Ginny said, "We just got his four a.m. labs back. His kidney function improved dramatically overnight. His liver enzymes are improving, and his gases are excellent." To Thomas, she said, "We've turned down your oxygen and your ventilator isn't doing much at the moment. The unit's hospitalist, Dr. Pench, plans to try and remove the tubes this morning. But you have been a very sick man, Mr. Langer. You aren't out of the woods yet. And if you fight the ventilator, that will slow down your progress. I need you to relax, okay?"

Thomas gave a second faint nod and his shoulders relaxed slightly.

Ginny looked back to Robinelle again. "Do you want to tell him about his hands and feet?"

Robinelle closed her eyes tightly but nodded yes. "He's going to want to see." Ginny began to unwind his bandages. Robinelle started telling her brother he had lost some fingers and toes.

I slipped out of the room. I didn't need to intrude on that painful moment, and any interview could take place later.

In the next room, I found Erica Lynn Quinton, who played lead guitar. Or, I should say, who had once played lead guitar. Her hands were heavily bandaged; blood and green goo had leaked through to the outer sticky wrap; the stench of *death and decay* was strong and Erica was on a ventilator. I started to back out, but someone wearing scrubs stopped me. It was the hospitalist from my previous visit, the one who had been—legitimately—too busy to talk to me.

"I'm Ruth Pench, the hospitalist. I'm responsible for general medical care of hospitalized patients on the paranormal unit this morning. You're with PsyLED, right?"

I gave my name and she asked, "What can you tell me about the efficacy of the null rooms?" It sounded more like a demand than a question, but she was entitled. She was a human battling a paranormal disease, one with deadly symptoms but no typical medical cause. "We put Thomas Langer in the one outside and he improved drastically overnight. We put Quinton in it and it hasn't helped."

"The one at HQ is better. Every time you move a portable one, it loses some of its—" I stopped and frowned. "Some of its nullness? And the sooner you get a patient into them the better."

"How long do they stay inside? Do they need medical personnel to stay with them?" Pench asked.

Dang FireWind for making me be here instead of a more senior member of the unit. "It's more of an art than a science. There haven't been any double-blind studies on witch energies or null energies and certainly none on whatever this is. There isn't any money for that kind of research. The Nashville coven suggested half an hour for anyone before they start showing symptoms. After symptoms, a minimum of an hour was their suggestion, and the patients need to be read by a witch after to see if the *death and decay* has been neutralized. That's what we're calling it. But frankly, longer time in a null room won't hurt them, and might help them. Medical personnel are absolutely essential." I was laying down rules to a doctor. *FireWind should not have put me in charge . . .* "You don't want investigators taking care of your patients."

"The patient who died with this magic working began to decompose immediately. The body saponified a green goo and the fingers and toes fell off before we got it moved to the morgue. I hear it decomposed so fast down there they had to scoop the body parts off the autopsy table and into plastic bags." Her eyes were hard and brittle as glass. "She was melting like wax."

I said, "Melting. Yeah. Good a term as any."

"Okay. I'm initiating a new protocol. The plan going forward is to take all stable patients from Cookeville to your headquarters before they come here. The EMTs and paramedics will have to stay with the patients. Then, I need a witch to read them. I have a few names and contact info on file somewhere."

I tilted my head to show I had heard and that I didn't disagree.

"Then we can send any patient to your office for more null

time as needed. It'll cost a fortune, and no one is gonna be happy with me."

"Except your patients and their fingers and toes and internal organs."

Pench whipped sharp eyes to me. "There is that."

"You could request a budget increase next year for a null room here on the paranormal unit."

"In-house. Yeah. Are they expensive?"

"I *think* that if you have a slab floor system and a designated place for it, it isn't too bad. Construction and then fifteen to twenty-five thousand for the working?"

"Twenty-five K?" Pench made a chuffing sound like Occam often made. "I can raise the money for that myself. And we can take over an existing patient room."

"Be careful that you get a well-regulated, full coven for the null working."

"Suggestions?"

I handed her one of T. Laine's business cards. "She isn't a coven-bound witch, but she can give you good advice on the best people to call for creating a null space."

Pench pocketed the card. "Thanks."

"One thing I've noticed," I said, "—and it might be more positional and locational than anything else—but so far we've had one male fall really badly ill. Thomas Langer. And he got better. All the dead and accelerated-decomp bodies are female. Well, so far. She needs to be in a null room. Like, right now."

"Hmmm. It's interesting but not the enlightening epiphany I was hoping for." Pench spun and left the room.

"Enlightening epiphany," I repeated to the comatose patient on the bed. "That'd come in right handy. Like a genie in an old lamp. So," I said to Erica. "Is it all right if I read you the way I read the land?"

She didn't answer, not that I expected her to. I pulled off my glove and approached the bed. I touched the bare skin above Erica's bandages. Electricity snapped at me hot-cold, scalding-freezing, and I leaped back, rubbing my fingers on my spelled gown. The feel of *death and decay* was a vile hot/icy/slimy sensation and I'd be doing no deeper read at all. Erica was dying. Fast.

I tried to interview more patients and got nowhere. No one

was physically able or willing to talk to me. FireWind would be unhappy, but there was no help for that.

Quietly, having accomplished little, I stripped off the protective gear, scrubbed my hands in hot water and vile-smelling soap, and left the paranormal wing for the pathology department.

It was Monday, so the office was open and working on a normal schedule. When I rang the bell in the outer office, a young woman came to the window. She was wearing an ID with the word *Histologist* beneath her name. I asked for Dr. Gomez; she shook her head and disappeared. Moments later, Gomez came to the window and gave me a look of distaste. It was similar to the expression I gave the cats when they deposited a hairball or dropped a headless rodent on the floor at my feet. Her uniform scrubs looked spiffy clean, but her face and hair looked as if she had been dragged through the wringer. I was guessing she was still here since I saw her last, hadn't been home, and wanted someone to blame. "You again," she accused.

"Me again," I said with equanimity. "I've been threatened with death by a bunch a churchmen pointing shotguns at me. A doctor who's pissy after being on the job for twenty-four hours is nothing." My mouth clamped shut. The word *pissy* had come out of it. *Out of my mouth.*

"Pissy?" Gomez said, blinking. She barked a laugh. "A gun, huh? Somehow I'm not surprised."

I wasn't sure if that was a sneer against churchmen or against me. Maybe both.

"Come on back." She punched a button and the door beside me opened. I followed her through a narrow space with a receptionist, offices to either side, and down a hallway that smelled of chemicals, to a back elevator. We got on, the doors closed, and the elevator descended. Gomez didn't look at me so I didn't look at her. I knew the silent treatment when I saw it. The doors opened and we were in an even stinkier place, the reek of formalin on the air and the sound of a negative-pressure exhaust fan going in the background, and the stench of *death and decay* underneath it all.

"Lemme show you something," Gomez said. She led me to

a microscope, shoved a rolling desk chair up to it, and pointed at the chair.

Feeling as if I were about to be smacked for doing wrong, I sat. I had never looked into a scope like this one, with double oculars and all sorts of magnifiers. I put my face against the oculars and figured out how to focus the fancy scope. I discovered some pretty blue and red and brownish circles and things. "What am I seeing?"

"Liver of a normal human."

"Dead?"

"Yeah. Dead." She touched my shoulder and I sat back. She removed the liver and stuck something else under the magnifier.

I returned to the microscope. There were greenish and brown things. Some were washed-out looking. "Looks like ghosts of the previous one. What's this?"

"Hepatic tissue acquired during the postmortem of the woman from Stella Mae Ragel's farm. The dead woman's liver," she clarified. "And ghost cells is as good a descriptor as any. The microscopic differences are astounding. And the slices of every single organ are similar.

"Come with me. I have more."

I followed her to a sterile-looking area where we dressed out in sky blue null unis. In the back, she opened a glass-fronted refrigerator and took out a pan full of plastic specimen jars. She opened two. One held a chunk of reddish meat that looked exactly like cow liver. The other was full of olive green goo topped by a green froth. "Normal liver and the *death and decay* liver? You need to get the body pieces into a null room," I advised. "The first body we sent here in a cooler never made it. It decomposed through the cooler, through the floor of the transport vehicle, and into the asphalt of I-40."

Gomez cursed colorfully as she put the containers back in the unit. "So that's what made my commute home to see Mama so terrible. Maybe I need to check on the recent body."

I didn't expect her to let me go with her, but when I followed, she didn't tell me no. She led the way to a separate cold room. When she opened the door, a reek rolled out, a stench like a jungle abattoir. Green rotting soup lapped out the door and into the hallway. Gomez slammed the door and jumped back all in one motion, and cursed some more.

I was instantly sick from the stink and backed away.

"The floor is rotted through," Gomez said accusingly.

"You need a full coven to deal with this. They can't fix it yet, but they can put a shield around the energies to stop them from spreading. Call T. Laine Kent. Get her to help facilitate contacting the North Nashville coven for you. It'll cost, but if you wait any longer, you'll have to replace the refrigeration unit and the floor, and you might have to dig out the ground underneath this area." With a hand over my mouth, I got out of there.

My clean clothes still held the death stink, so the first thing I did at HQ was to strip in the locker room, shower, wash my hair, and dress in fresh clothes. I didn't bother to dry my mop but twisted it into a bun before I put the stinky clothing into a sink with hot water, hand soap, and a cup of baking soda from the break room. Then I took my tablet and caught up on my files while sitting in the null room, as the chill of antimagics crept into my bones. Unfortunately, soap and null energies did nothing to stop the stench that was trapped in my sinuses and memory.

An hour later, I had a short list of questions, unanswered inconsistencies, and timeline problems. I left the null room to the paramedics and EMTs who delivered Thomas Langer, his sister Robinelle, and two other patients for a stint in the antimagic room. Thomas was free from the ventilator and waved at me, gave a thumbs-up, as we passed in the hallway. It was reminiscent of the gesture he had given me in the ambulance as he pulled away from Melody Horse Farm on day one. I was glad he still had a thumb. And someone would be taking his statement while he nulled out. Even if it was JoJo Jones herself.

The stench trailing behind the stretchers reminded me to rinse out my clothes and hang them up in the locker room. I hung them over the sink with my undies hidden behind my outer clothes. Some girlhood habits never died.

I checked on JoJo, who was multitasking and talking on the phone, and went to my desk, spending hours on files, reports, and answering the calls that got by Jo. Info came in, but it was all insignificant. I was getting good at saying nothing with a lot of words, comforting nothings to family, stilted nothings to the press. JoJo interviewed Langer when he came in to be nullified, but she learned nothing new either. I learned just how difficult it was to carry patients up narrow stairs and how badly we needed the elevator that had never been installed in the back.

I forgot lunch. Midafternoon, my stomach reminded me and I raided the break room fridge for leftovers, putting pizza into the microwave to heat, and walked into the conference room. Today Jo was wearing dozens of long clip-on braids in several shades of brown and gold, the braids woven in a complicated bun with long hanging braids and little gold beads woven into it. It looked heavy and uncomfortable and gorgeous. She was dressed in a black military-style jacket, gold braiding at the shoulders and epaulets, and silky gold frog closures. Some of the churchwomen made bespoke clothing like this, and . . .

"Mama Grace makes fabulous knotted and tied frogs like that," I said.

JoJo canted her head at me, her scarlet-painted lips stretching into a smile. "I did not go behind your back and get your church ladies to make my clothes. If I'd wanted them to do my clothes, I'd have told you first."

"Ummm. Okay?"

"Uh-huh. This came from a consignment shop." Her tone went smug and amused. "Someone in your church made it for the *previous* owner, some rich woman. Which makes me an astounding fashion-conscious-shopper-on-a-budget."

I chuckled. "You look fantastic. I wish I had half as much fashion sense as you do."

"When this case is over, we'll do a girls' day out and hit the high-end consignment shops. Then get massages. And maybe we'll charge it to His Almighty FireWind. You ever had a massage?"

"No. And I'll be honest. I'm not real comfortable at the idea of a stranger rubbing up on me."

"Put that way, me neither."

I had a feeling she was laughing at me. Jo sat back and cracked her knuckles, her scarlet fingernails flashing. "Where are you?" She meant on the investigation.

"I got thoughts and questions." I put my list of curiosities up on the screen. "What can you tell me about the timeline of the T-shirts? Some of the sick never touched the shirts. So far as I know were never in the room with the shirts. Yet they're sick or dead."

"T-shirt timeline, I have. The band manager handled ordering swag for the tour and the screen-printing company shipped them in boxes. The roadies opened the boxes and packed them in heavy-duty plastic bins, according to size, for easy transporting back and forth. They took forty T-shirt bins, unpacked from forty-eight T-shirt boxes, with them on the tour. They ordered additional batches of forty-eight boxes while on tour, drop-shipped to various hotels. I have records that all were delivered and are accounted for in the manager's accounting database, along with the original twelve boxes. When they got home there was one box in the studio, unaccounted for, no shipping label.

"Things get lost or misplaced on a tour. Even expensive musical instruments and electronic equipment. But there is never extra stuff just appearing; the manager insists it was not present when they left on this leg of the tour. I've tracked every single sale and accounted for all the shirts, including two full bins on the RV. And then there's the mystery box."

She looked up. "I've verified that the shirts are official tour shirts, not a knockoff. Some unknown person put that box in the swag room, at some point during a twelve-week tour, while people were all over the property. Dozens of people. Not one of them was a death witch or an evil magic practitioner. Not that death witches advertise, since the U.S. military complex and a dozen foreign enemy combatant states would want them, find them, take them, and they would end up dead or disappeared."

"How would anyone get to a death witch?" I asked.

"They'd set off a sleeping-gas bomb—assuming anyone was still alive—after she went to bed, and walk out with the witch wearing null cuffs."

"Oh."

"Yeah. You know, for a child raised in God's Cloud of Glory, you are the epitome of innocence."

I made a face at her. "So we are nowhere?"

"We are nowhere."

"Well, dang."

The microwave dinged and I brought in plates and slices and sat. I pulled up research on death magics. There wasn't much. All magics worked differently for each witch, depending on the individual, her element (earth, air, water, etc.), her power level, her training, and any previous coven affiliation. Death-magic witches didn't associate with covens because a coven would stick her in a null room and leave her there until she rotted. Death-magic users were not blood-magic users. Blood witches used the usual methods of working energies, but powered with blood sacrifice. Death-magic users were a group all their own. Death was raw black magic—not worked with math and focals, and always a curse. It was a direct interaction with life forces and earth forces and something darker, more predatory.

This . . . this *death and decay* . . .

My mind went still, remembering it under my fingers, in the land at Stella's farm, in the body of Erica. I made a fist, my fingers still not completely healed, thinking. The Green Knight had recognized the magics and attacked instantly.

Death and decay was oddly familiar. To the Green Knight and to me. Where had I encountered it before? When a demon had been summoned and tried to rise to Earth? When the salamanders bred?

Minutes had passed. JoJo was scanning multiple files and photos and her hands were clicking and clacking all over multiple keyboards. I said, "Jo?" She grunted; I took that as permission to continue. "I wondered what I would feel if I tried to read Erica. In the hospital."

Her hands went still. "You didn't."

"I did. That was part of the reason I spent so long in the null room. I didn't get much from the read." I described the awful, burning cold sensation when I touched Erica's bare flesh. "I'm wondering what I'd get on a deep read on Erica's body. And now I'm wondering what I'd get on a deep read on a dead body."

"No. You will not do that, girl. You get me? *No*. People are *dying*," she added, as if I hadn't noticed.

"I'm not planning on trying it. But what if I *could* read who the culprit is. I've never read that deeply into a magical working on a human body, but I've followed magic through the land. What if I could track a magical working back to the originator? What if I could do it through the air, so I didn't grow roots? What would that do to law enforcement? To a case?"

JoJo had never been able to resist a puzzle. She pulled on her left earrings, five gold hoops that dangled up the curve of the ear. "Under current law it couldn't be used in court, and it's possible that it could be ruled as a form of magical attack. It might also be contested as a loss of civil rights if you did that to a suspect. There would be no way to use illegally obtained evidence as part of a case."

"But people are dying. Isn't stopping that magical attack more important than gathering evidence for a case? If it's a witch, the local witches would take the death witch into custody under witch law anyway, and we'd never hear from her again. Nothing we do in a death-witch case would be used for the courts. And if it isn't a death witch, the person responsible will still never see a courtroom. Not with that kind of power at their fingertips. The person who did this will be destroyed by other means long before that can happen."

We both fell silent. The air conditioner came on, a soft, nearly noiseless whir. Into the hush a mechanical voice said, "CLMT2207. Please provide appropriate file heading for the previous discussion."

JoJo cursed and said, "Clementine, Jones. Preserve previous conversation under heading 'Death Magics, Ingram, Temp File.' Then go off-line."

The voice-recognition program repeated the orders and went off-line.

We stared at each other. "Sometimes I hate computers," JoJo said.

Which was a terrible lie. Even with Clementine listening in, she loved that the program had the ability to do all the cool stuff.

Jo said, "Seriously. Do not read a person until you have this convo with FireWind. I'm sending you back to the Ragel horse farm. You need to reread the land around the house to see if it's less contaminated. FireWind left for Cookeville while you were in the null room, and we'll have people and equipment and probably body parts in and out of here all day and night now that the null room has proven so necessary to the survival of the victims."

"FireWind wanted two people here in HQ at all times." I frowned at her. "You're trying to keep me from reading the hospital patients."

"You can thank me later."

I frowned harder and pulled off a twisted leaf trying to open at my hairline. I stole a gesture from Mud and gave a teenager's *whatever* shrug, gathered up my gobags, my vampire tree, and extra magazines, and left. On the way, I alerted my mama where

I'd be, possibly overnight, and arranged with Sam to drive my sisters wherever they needed to go. I also added teaching Esther to drive to my mental Esther To-Do list, along with opening a bank account and discussions of getting a job. My list was getting quite long.

I left for Cookeville in the very late afternoon, fighting traffic, listening to my onboard computer reading the other unit members' case notes. I learned nothing new and gained no new insights. Having learned the probie's lessons about showing up at a crime scene without bearing gifts, I stopped at a sandwich shop and bought a half dozen varieties. I didn't stop at the hotel to drop off my gear. Occam was at the farm, and that was where I wanted to be.

Clouds were moving in and it got dark before the sun set. I switched on my lights as the farm's fencing came into view. Dusk pooled in deep shadows, murky darkness, lightless gloom, profound enough to hide the monsters and demons used by church folk to scare their children into obedience. Today there were very few cars blocking the road. I took the turn past the wilted flowers and showed my ID to the bored guard before continuing up to the house.

As I took the first turn, I spotted something in the tall, fall pasture grass and hit the brakes. The thing scuttled away. No. Not something. Someone, crouched, skulking. A white head dropped below the tops of the grasses and then darted off. Soul and Rick had white hair. No. They were nowhere near here; Soul was off doing director-ish things and Rick LaFleur was on a case in Chattanooga.

Pulling over, I gathered up my flashlight and my weapon, wishing for a null pen, but I had none. I sent out a group text giving my exact location and saying that I was checking out something. I slipped from the car and maneuvered between the boards of the fence, into the grass, my torso higher than the grass near the road. I moved slowly through the pasture, the leaves *shushing* against my pants.

The acreage had been planted at some point in a perennial natural mix of tall fescue, Kentucky bluegrass, big bluestem, and a dozen other native grasses for natural grazing. As I moved deeper into the pasture, the grass grew higher, the shadows deeper around me. For the grass to be so high, few horses had grazed it, maybe since early summer. The night breeze blew, the grass whispering. Owls called in the distance. Bats darted overhead. I had left the driveway behind.

I found an open place where a deer herd had slept at some point, the grass pressed down in circular areas as big as their bodies, like dimples of safety. I stepped around and over old horse droppings and fresh deer pellets. I startled a bird off her nest. But nothing unexpected was there. No white-headed person. There were no footprints in the soil, no hairs caught in the grass, no indication that a human had raced through here. Had the white thing I saw been the rump of a white-tailed deer? Feeling foolish, I moved in a semicircle around and back toward my car, a sudden gust at my back.

Just ahead, I spotted a sleeping horse. Not wanting to get trampled, I stamped on the ground. But the horse didn't leap or climb to its feet. It didn't move at all. I edged closer, parting the grass, scanning with my flashlight. The beam fell on the horse. It was dead and decomposing. Melting like wax. Its coat looked reddish brown beneath the green froth. I shined my flash all across the horse and settled the beam on its face. Beneath the green goo, the lightning blaze shone white. It was Adrian's Hell, Stella's stallion. I whispered an anguished, "Nooo. Oh no."

My flash fell on its lips and tongue. They were green.

The horse wasn't female, but it was decomposing like one.

I stood there for too long, uncertain, grieving, before I marked my location and turned away, tracing my way back to the car. I debated calling Occam, who, according to the group text reply, was interrogating riders in the barn with T. Laine. Calling him felt like a girl asking her boyfriend for help. If I wasn't dating him, I would call my boss, so I sent a group text that I was okay, then called FireWind.

"FireWind. Ingram, is there a problem?" he answered. I realized how softly, how quietly he spoke. Much like Jane Yellowrock spoke. Maybe a Cherokee thing?

"Dead horse near my twenty," I said, meaning near my current location. "Same symptoms as the humans. And I saw something or someone moving in the grasses, but it's gone. Who do you want me to notify for a search?" I could almost feel him assessing my request.

"Stay put. I'm on my way."

FireWind was coming. I remembered the sight of him standing, arms out at his sides, as Adrian's Hell pranced and danced and challenged. And then slowly accepted the man. His arms around the horse's neck as they embraced. I needed to tell him first. Not let him recognize the stallion, dead.

Moments later, FireWind appeared at my side and placed his gobag on my car hood. I holstered my weapon and stood in the dark, silent.

"Ingram?"

I cleared my throat quietly. "Something you need to know. This horse is decomposing like the female humans at UTMC and here. But he's a he. *Was* a he."

"I understand," he said. But he didn't. Not yet. The vision of FireWind with the horse, his stillness like part of a dance.

"He's Stella Mae's stallion."

It was too dark to see my boss' face, but his body went preternaturally still. His voice held no emotion when he spoke, but his words were too soft, too crisp. "I see."

When he said nothing else, I turned into the grass. Together, we walked, our feet and bodies rustling the tall leaves, my flash lighting the way to the dead horse. The animal's black mane and tail were tangled and damp. His eyes were whited over and weeping the familiar green froth. Again, my heart clenched in despair. I wasn't sure why a dead animal was such a tragic thing when a dead human should surely have been more important. But I hadn't responded to the dead people the way I was reacting to Adrian's Hell, Stella Mae's beautiful stallion. Not at all. And neither was FireWind.

He said something softly, in that language I didn't know, the words sounding formal, grief in his tone. In English, he said, "I saw him the first day I arrived here. He was a beautiful animal."

"Do you . . . do you want me to read Adrian's Hell like I read the land?"

"Is that what you thought I would want? No. You are not to touch the *death and decay*. How do you know the name of this animal?"

I explained about Stella's breeding plans and her hopes that this stallion would take her bloodline to major championships. I paused. "You don't think this horse was the *real* target, do you?"

"I don't know what to think. Days in and we still know little." FireWind touched my shoulder and we backed away, my flash falling for a moment on his face. He was as distraught as I was, but in the moment the light fell on him, there was something more there too. Vengeance.

We reached my car. I turned off the flash and placed the gear on the hood. I let the big boss have a moment of introspection, his eyes closed, his face lifted as if he was smelling the slow breeze. I thought it smelled like rain and autumn. And then the wind shifted and all I smelled was the stench of *death and decay*. His face was grieving and reluctant and oddly full of recognition, as if he had been searching for answers and had found them. I said, "You've seen something like this before, haven't you."

He took his time to answer, lowered his head, and seemed to focus on me in the dark. "Perhaps. In a little town near the Mexican border," he murmured.

I shifted to show I was listening.

"The town was supposedly cursed by a witch, though not a witch in the white man's meaning." I waited and eventually he went on, his cadence and cant dropping into that of a storyteller, slow and painstaking. "It began when four white prospectors came into town for a night of carousing and drinking. While there, they saw a girl from a local tribe, who was bringing jewelry to sell to a white store owner. They took her. Raped and beat her.

"Her name was Sonsee-array. She died several days later." His voice was without inflection, yet carried weight and power in the soft syllables.

"The girl's mother was a woman of power among her people, wise in the ancient ways, but willing to trust the white man's law to deal with this murder. She went to the sheriff."

I didn't know what all this had to do with *death and decay* or a dead stallion, but I had no desire to interrupt. The quiet words drew me in.

"The sheriff laughed at her."

I flinched at the stark words.

"The grieving mother fell into the trap of pain and grief and anger. She called to the spirits for vengeance. The spirits did not answer as she intended. They counseled peace and forgiveness. The grieving mother turned to the dark spirits instead. They answered her, whispering dark knowledge.

"At dawn three days after Sonsee-array died, the town woke to find the witch sitting inside a circle drawn with white chalk, in the middle of the town crossroads, beating a small drum. Her hair had turned stark white in the days since her tortured and dead daughter had been returned to her. Her eyes had gone white. Her hands had become lined and wrinkled as if she had aged into a crone.

"The townspeople gathered around her chalk circle. The mother, now a witch according to her tribal ways, stopped beating the drum and put her hands flat on the earth. She spoke in her native language, a chant that was bleak and despairing. Then she took her hands off the earth and began to beat on the drum again, while she spoke words the white man did not understand. She beat the drum and chanted those words all day, without stopping, over and over, beneath the hot sun, until sunset, when she stood and stepped over the circle. She walked away.

"In the circle where she had sat was a bone-handled knife with an obsidian blade. The sheriff stepped over the chalk circle and took the knife. Put it into his belt. The next morning, the sheriff fell off his horse, dead. The people of the town began to fall ill. The animals began to fall ill. Chickens, a pig and piglets, a milk cow, all died. The townspeople died. Within a week they were all dead, even the ones who tried to run away."

I was watching FireWind's face as he talked, his expression stark and barren.

"I found a dying man on the road to the town and from him heard of the witch and the curse she called down. I left my horse in safety and I walked into the town on the tenth day. The bodies were pools of filth and bones. Even the rats who came to eat the bodies had died."

"Were the bodies green?"

"No. They were white, bubbling, like—" He paused, thinking of something I might relate to. "Like vinegar and baking soda."

"So. Similar symptoms, but not exact."

He gave a single nod and his black hair slid forward with a quiet swish. "Not exact, which is why I have not mentioned it until now."

"When was this?"

After a too-long pause, he said, "Nineteen oh two."

"I saw something white running in the pasture before I found Adrian's Hell dead. At first I thought it was a white-headed human. Then I decided it was a white-tailed deer."

"But now you question that conclusion?"

"Yes. Now I don't know what to think."

"I will shift to a St. Bernard and see if I can catch the scent of a human."

"Why a St. Bernard? A bloodhound would have a better sense of smell."

My eyes had fully adjusted to the night and I saw the flash of teeth as FireWind smiled. Amusement lightened his voice when he said, "Because of Einstein."

"What?" I asked, startled.

"The equation E equals mc squared was suggested by that scientist. It is an equation that suggests energy and mass are interchangeable with each other, and it seems to explain skin-walker magic. The most I have ever weighed in my long life is two hundred and fifteen pounds. Therefore, I need an animal that is two hundred pounds and more in weight to shift into, but not greatly more or greatly less." He opened several packs of stinky commercial jerky and dropped them on the ground. "Keep watch for a few minutes while I shift and then go into the house while I work."

FireWind, my skinwalker boss, took off his shirt, folded it, and placed it on the car hood. He slipped off his shoes. Belatedly I realized he was stripping in order to change shape. There wasn't time to drive away, so I quickly turned my back and closed my eyes. I heard the soft *shush* of cloth on skin and the swishing of grasses, but I didn't open my eyes until long after I heard FireWind walk into the pasture. I glanced at the pile of clothes and FireWind's shoes on the hood of my car. *Oh yes. Naked.*

I might be in love with a were-creature, and he and the other local weres might strip and change shape on my land three nights a month, but I had never watched. Naked human bodies were not something I ever watched.

"Yes," I whispered to myself. "I am a prude, through and through."

I texted the others that FireWind was shifting to search for a possible intruder and that we were both safe. From the grass came odd sounds, cracking and snapping, and then silence that went on too long. About ten minutes later, a St. Bernard dog trotted out of the pasture, a bone in his teeth. He rose up on his hind legs, dropped the bone, and nosed an empty one-day gobag near his clothes and shoes. He looked me, at the bag and clothes, and back at me.

"You want me to pack the bone and your clothes into the bag?"

The big dog gave a slow nod and dropped to all fours, gobbling up the jerky without chewing.

"You coulda put your clothes in it yourself, you know." He didn't respond, just kept eating jerky. I tucked the shoes into an expandable pouch on the side. Careful not to touch his undies, and feeling silly about my reactions, I packed the clothes into the bag, on top of a collection of bones, teeth, and what looked like animal claws inside, each with a drilled hole inserted with a steel ring for hanging on a necklace. *The big boss carries around a stack of animal bones in his gobag.*

Of course he does. He's a skinwalker. Right. I put the bone he had carried in his teeth on top of the clothes.

FireWind looked at the house and back to me. He clearly expected me to follow his orders and go to the house.

I held up the bag. "Leave this here or at the house?"

He looked at the passenger seat of my car. And back to me. I placed the bag on the seat. "I'll leave the door unlocked," I said. The big dog nodded at me, trotted into the pasture with a swish of grasses, and vanished.

Shaking my head at all the strange things that were stomping around in my brain, I got in the car and drove to the house. As ordered, I left the car unlocked and the gobag on the passenger seat. Occam was standing at the side door of the barn, haloed in the security light, watching me, a grindylow on his shoulder. I hadn't seen any of the cute neon green killers since we arrived and I had put the absence down to the were-creature judges and executioners being with Rick LaFleur and Margot Racer in Chattanooga. The black wereleopards were young weres and the ones most likely to make a mistake and spread the were-taint. And need to be killed. I had to wonder why one had re-turned here, but Occam didn't seem upset by its presence, one hand stroking along its back and tail as if it were a cat.

As I walked toward Occam, he smiled. A sense of utter well-being fluttered through me as if a thousand butterflies had just taken flight. I followed him inside and slid into his arms, my head on his chest.

"Nell, sugar. I've missed you like a fish misses water." He breathed in my scent and I scrubbed my fist along his jaw.

"I've missed you too, cat-man."

The grindylow leaped away and up, into the rafters of the barn. There was a cat up there already, a gray-striped, green-eyed cat. Behind it were more cats. I tilted my head, my face scraping against Occam's work shirt, and counted four. I sighed happily. I hadn't seen cats until now and I had wondered why. Except that cats had a strong sense of self-preservation. It was likely they had smelled *death and decay* and taken off. It was the same reason there had been few flies. The smell had been evil mixed with rot. Not good to eat; not a good place to lay eggs. But I wondered why the cats weren't melting. Perhaps the same reason Occam couldn't feel the *death and decay*?

The cats accepted the grindy, or perhaps ignored it was the better term. Cats were always welcome at a barn, even the most feral. Most barn owners set traps, got the cats spayed or neutered, gave them shots, and put out dry food in return for the cats keeping pests out of the grain and feed.

Occam propped his chin on my head. "You gonna tell me what happened between you and FireWind out there in the dark?"

I smiled against his shirt, the buttons pressing into my cheek. "You ain't jealous, are you?"

"Jealous of tall, dark, and deadly? Not any more than I am of anyone who gets to spend time with you. Heck, woman, I'm jealous of your cats, your sister, and your family. I'm jealous of every moment that takes you away from me. And if that sounds a little too much possessive and old-school toxic masculinity, well, I do apologize for saying it."

"But not for feeling it?"

"A man can't help what he feels. He can only help what he

does about those feelings. And I'll never hurt you, Nell, sugar. Not ever, in any way, not even by my natural jealousy. I'll cut off my hand before I let myself harm you. I'll cut out my tongue before I let myself speak words that hurt you."

Tears gathered in my eyes as he spoke. "I love you, cat-man."

"I love you too, plant-woman."

"You two finished saying hello and rubbing noses?" T. Laine called from the back door of the house. "I need to update Nell."

"We're mostly done," Occam drawled. "Though that might be speciesist, suggesting we rub noses just because I'm a were-leopard."

"Yeah, yeah, whatever. Write me up. Turn me in to HR." T. Laine backed into the kitchen. "I'm making fresh coffee," she called. "Did you bring anything to eat, Nell? I'm starving."

Occam and I separated. I said, "There's a bag in the trunk with sandwiches. I forgot to bring it in. And Occam will have to go get it." At Occam's odd look, I said, "FireWind's clothes are in the passenger seat. He turned into a St. Bernard and is chasing scents in the front pasture."

"You do realize how weird that sounds," T. Laine said from the house.

"Yes. I do. And when he's done, he'll have to shift back to human and he'll be naked as a jaybird. I already had to see too many coworkers naked. I don't particularly want to add FireWind to that list of people I've seen in their naked glory."

There was a chuff of amusement, quickly silenced. "Back in a sec," Occam said and vanished out the door. I moved across the open space to the house.

"Naked glory," T. Laine said. "Yeah. I'll bet he is glorious naked."

"I thought you were dating Mr. SWAT-Wonderful."

"I'm not dead," she said. "I can still dream."

I decided that was not something I needed to discuss. "The house smells odd," I said, "dank, like a damp basement. Less like *death and decay*."

"Yeah. We cut out the carpets and put them into the portable null room, which is why the trailer isn't at the hospital anymore. But the North Nashville coven got a shield around the slab of the house, and around I-40 where the transport unit died, so the energies aren't spreading down."

"Someone might be calling you soon about how to get a null room installed in the para unit at UTMC."

"'Bout time. We got PsyCSI and a specialized military para hazmat team on the way from Maine. FireWind is worried and wants another set of trained eyes here in case CSI is missing things."

Occam reentered, his gait cat-smooth, the bag of sandwiches under his arm. "Food. Let's eat."

As we demolished the sandwiches, I told them about FireWind and the very expensive dead horse and that we needed to get the paranormal hazmat team to take care of Adrian's Hell as soon as they got here.

"Can't wait. We'll have to handle this ourselves," T. Laine said, "and put a shield around the energies to contain them. I don't want the *death and decay* to reach the groundwater."

A fresh shaft of horror lanced through my chest. "You know for *sure* that the energies are moving down into the water tables?"

"The shields we set up seem to be holding, but with magical energies like this? I don't know. Too bad you can't burn a melting body. We could set it on fire in situ instead of shoveling it into containers and carting it into the null room." T. Laine stopped with a meat-filled bun halfway to her mouth. "Wait. That might put the working into the air. Never mind. Astrid and I will put something together." She took a bite ravenous enough to qualify as a werecat bite. Through the food she added, "We'll put a shield around the death site until we figure out how to kill it. Because right now, I can't do jack."

After that bit of frightening news, we ate and filled each other in on case notes and info we hadn't had time to read. After we ate, I said I was going to read the houseplants. No one argued, no one suggested the probie should do something else. It was, maybe, the first time I felt like an equal member of the team, exerting power over my own investigative techniques—exciting and a little dangerous.

ELEVEN

There were lots of houseplants on every level, all in the south-facing windows to give them the best sunlight. Someone knew their plants. After a trek through the house to get an overview, I started by reading the plants on the upper level, flipping lights on and off as I moved. The attic library was full of paperbacks, mostly romance and fantasy, with a few thrillers, all by people I had never heard of. There were comfy chairs and two recliners, cozy furniture you could put your feet on. The plants here were flourishing in little blue clay pots in the south dormers, alive and healthy. They were happy plants, the soil the right composition and drainage for species, moisture, and nutrients. I felt like I was getting what might be called a baseline of what the houseplants had been like before the *death and decay* energies.

Stella had been gone for weeks, but the plants were fine. Someone else took care of them. I assumed it was the housekeeper, but she was dead too so there was no confirming my guess.

Thinking about that, I went down the stairs. Reading plants, touching the soil, occasionally sticking my fingers deeper, invading the root-space. On the bedroom level the plants were less healthy. They drooped even though they didn't need water. They looked sadder. They felt sadder too, when I touched their soil. I gave each one a little boost, hoping it would be enough. On the main level, all the plants were dying. When I touched the soil, it felt dry and . . . weak wasn't exactly the word, but they needed nutrients and water.

As I touched the plants off the kitchen area, I began to feel nauseated. My head started to ache. As I neared the basement stairs, my fingers started to tingle and felt cold to the touch. But

I forced myself to dress out in a spelled uni and gloves, requested a null pen from T. Laine, and went downstairs.

The plants near the basement's French doors, close to where the bodies had been found, were brown and dead. I thought back. For once I hadn't noticed the houseplants consciously, my attention on the bodies, but in my memory, they had been green when I was here last. I didn't touch them, curling my arms around myself in a hug.

For safety's sake, I returned to the stairs, holding my middle, looking around at the rotted guitars, the cracked plastic casings of electronic equipment, the pile of dust and rusted wire where the piano used to stand. The metal chairs were piles of rust. The wall colors were faded and brittle. The carpet was gone and the slab cracked, as if I looked at a long-abandoned house.

At the top of the stairs I heard a thump and shout. I stripped off the uni and other protective gear and raced down the hallway, into the kitchen, my heart in my throat, breath fast. No one was in the kitchen. And then I heard a faint panting. On the other side of the island, Occam was kneeling beside FireWind, who was still in St. Bernard form. He was panting in distress, his tail down, head hanging. FireWind's legs quivered, his knees unable to hold his weight. He dropped to the floor in a doggy heap.

"Nell," Occam said. "T. Laine!" he shouted.

I was by FireWind in an instant. I touched him and jerked back fast, shaking my hand. "He's covered in the *death and decay*."

"I don't feel anything," Occam growled.

T. Laine raced in from outside and dropped to the floor, her hands tracing over the dog in a professional manner, checking for fever against her own skin, checking pulse and respirations, shining a light into FireWind's eyes. T. Laine had been to vet school and was the unit's were-creature medic in the few times when shifting wasn't enough to heal them. But what did she know about skinwalkers? Had FireWind told her about his species' health? I told her what I thought had happened and T. Laine wove a null pen deep into FireWind's silky coat. Nothing seemed to happen, so she wove in several more. "Don't lose these," she whispered to the dog. "My boss says they're expensive and he might kill me." She was talking to said boss and it might have been funny if FireWind wasn't having trouble breathing. "Why aren't you shifting?" she asked him.

Occam sat back on his heels and watched. "What do we do?" he asked.

"I don't know," the witch said. "The null pens don't seem to be making a difference. I don't know how to help a skinwalker shift. Can you?"

"Methodology is totally different. Magics are different. If it's the *death and decay* keeping him from his human form," Occam asked, "do we put him in the null room or would that mess up his skinwalker energies?"

I envisioned FireWind stuck in some broken shape of mismatched parts forever.

"I don't know," she said. "We need a manual. 'How to Skinwalk for Dummies.' Nell? You healed LaFleur and Occam. What do you think?"

I studied the panting dog. He had never hunted on Soulwood. He wasn't mine. Still, I reached out a hand again. The *death and decay* grabbed my fingertips as if it recognized me. I jerked back. "I need my plant from the car."

Occam moved out the door werecat-fast and was back in a moment with the potted tree. I scattered a little of the soil over FireWind and stuck my fingers into the pot, shoving them deep. "You try to stick your roots into me or my boss and I'll let the *death and decay* take you," I warned the tree.

Occam raised his uneven eyebrows, a gesture that was both cat and human and would have made me smile if FireWind wasn't in such distress, his panting growing faster. I drew on Soulwood through the soil, and my land welcomed me, warm and safe and full of joy. Through that connection, I could tell that Esther and Mud were in the house and were fighting. Cherry was inside with them, miserable at the anger in their words, her tail thumping softly on the floorboards. The cats were in the garden chasing mice in the dark. When I focused on them, the cats jerked midleap/step/crouch, and raised their noses. Cherry stopped the rhythmic thumping of her tail. I realized that the animals knew I was paying attention to them and the land and I soothed them. "It's all good. You'uns go on about your business." The cats tore back after the family of mice. Cherry huffed a breath and put her head down, relaxing.

"Nell?" Occam.

FireWind was hurt. I remembered.

I reached for the skinwalker. And wrenched away. Yanked my hand from the pot. Found myself standing, my entire body tingling. Breathing hard. The leaves on the tree shivered. I felt some of my own leaves uncurl in my hairline. "No." I shook my head. I'd have to bleed my blood and his onto the land to possibly heal him, and that would claim the land and my boss for me. At the thought, my bloodlust, which had been quiescent for days, raised its predatory head. *So much strong blood in FireWind*, . . . It *wanted* . . . "I can't help him," I whispered. "I'd have to claim him and the land and I doubt he'd like that."

"Better than being dead," said Occam.

"Maybe not," I said, thinking about the vampire tree and the bloodlust of my land. "He might be dead before it was done."

T. Laine said, "His pulse is fast and irregular at nearly one fifty and his respirations are too fast, about twenty-seven a minute. I don't know why he isn't shifting." She looked at me. "We need to talk to another skinwalker."

She was asking if I would call Jane Yellowrock for advice.

I didn't argue. I pulled my phone and scanned through the address book for Jane Yellowrock, FireWind's sister and my sorta-friend. I dialed and it went to voice mail, not that I had really expected her to answer. Jane was busy being the Dark Queen of vampires and trying to stop a worldwide vampire war, or so one of Rick LaFleur's confidential sources had said. Jane might not even be in the country. We hadn't been able to confirm or deny any of the rumors surrounding her. When the mechanical voice finished leaving instructions, I left a message. Then I called the council house of vampires in New Orleans and spoke to a man who identified himself as Wrassler, which was a strange name. I told him about FireWind's condition. Wrassler said he would try to get a message to Jane but that we shouldn't hold our breath. "She's underground," he said. Which made no sense at all, not that I'd come to expect sense when talking to or about Jane.

I hung up and shook my head.

"We might have to try the null room," T. Laine said, "but we've never tried it on a skinwalker in crisis."

"Better than being dead," Occam repeated.

"I'm not so sure of that," T. Laine said, echoing me.

Occam got his feet under him in a squat and lifted FireWind by his front legs and upper body, up over his shoulder. "Get the door."

I got the door. Occam stood, easily lifting FireWind's two-hundred-plus pounds and carrying him outside. Wereleopard strength. T. Laine raced ahead, pulling on special null gloves. She opened the back ramp to the portable null room and shoved out a roll of soggy, stinking carpet. She pointed to a folding table and I helped her carry it into the middle of the null room cargo trailer. Occam dropped FireWind onto its surface with a thump-rattle that shook the trailer.

T. Laine walked down the ramp and closed it up, leaving us shut inside, in the silence and the dim light. I opened some folding chairs and sat, though the stench still in the trailer was so bad I was nearly ready to lose my dinner. Occam repeated his exam of his boss.

"When the *death and decay* is neutralized, can you make him shift back?" I asked.

"I don't know. I was able to help LaFleur some, early on. But shifting won't be the same with skinwalkers. They aren't moon-called. They aren't forced into their beasts. With them it's an effort of will. They can and do shift anytime, anywhere, into anything if they have sufficient DNA for the form they want. The only similarity FireWind has mentioned is the mass-to-mass ratio and he hinted at the possibility that it might be easier to shift during the full moon."

Occam dialed Rick, but the call went to voice mail.

FireWind opened one doggy eye, looked at Occam, and whined softly.

"Don't change shape," Occam warned, "even when you start to feel better. We're in the null room. I don't know what skin-walker magics, *death and decay*, and a null working might result in. You could end up with three legs and a wing."

FireWind closed his eyes and shivered with what looked like pain.

Occam shifted his eyes to me. They were glowing softly yellow, which I found odd since we were in a null room. "What's wrong with your tree?" he asked.

I looked down at the potted plant, which I was still holding, and said, "It didn't like the *death and decay* energies."

"Join the club." Occam pulled his chair closer to mine and sat. He put the pot on the floor, took my hands, and absentmindedly massaged my cold fingers as we watched FireWind. "I really shoulda brought in that bag of sandwiches."

"How can you stand the stench enough to want to eat?"

He shrugged. "Cat."

Nearly an hour later FireWind's breathing had evened out and slowed to what looked like normal for a big dog. Occam was satisfied with FireWind's pupils and his heart rate, and he was awake and no longer whining in pain, so that seemed good. But he looked exhausted and his limbs were quivering as if he'd been hit with an electric current.

"You ready to change shape, boss man?" Occam asked him. FireWind looked at the door. Occam tapped and T. Laine opened it, one hand moving unconsciously in a *seeing* working.

"Clear," she said.

Occam carried the St. Bernard outside, into the shadows, where he laid the big dog on the grass. Curious, not knowing what to expect, I followed. FireWind closed his eyes, and . . . things happened. A cloud of glowing grayish mist seemed to lift from his furry coat and swirled slowly around him. The mist was shot through with darker bits of something, but it was hard to see, impossible to focus on. It had to be some kind of magical energies. I stuck my fingers into the Soulwood soil, but that didn't help me any. Occam had no trouble seeing the magics, however, his eyes roving over FireWind and inspecting the air around him.

I heard a sharp snap that echoed off the nearby house. FireWind, draped in shadows and hidden by the silver mist, panted again. He began to re-form out of the St. Bernard. His bones cracked and snapped and he whined and grunted, breathing faster, though, despite the snapping bones, the sounds didn't sound like agony, more like hard exertion. However, it looked excruciating. FireWind had been a skinwalker for around a hundred seventy years, and he had shifted shape all that time. I wanted to turn away because it was too horrible to watch. But it was a teaching and a learning and something I needed to see, even though it hurt.

Eventually, after a good ten minutes, FireWind was human, on the ground in the fetal position, naked, his black hair like a veil over him. He looked skinnier than he had before, the muscles clearly defined, his cheeks and jaw and prominent nose sharp in a spare face. *Naked glory.*

"Food," he whispered.

Occam said, "Nell brought sandwiches. Roast beef okay?"

"Not as good as bison roasted over a fire at night, but I'll take it," FireWind said, beginning to uncurl. I left for the house, feeling as if I had just witnessed something spiritual and wonderful and terrifying and maybe even holy—though it was a very different form of holy from that preached by the church.

Back inside, I told T. Laine the boss was human, opened the foot-long roast beef sandwich, and spread the paper wrapping on the island countertop. I poured a glass of water, which I placed by the sandwich. It was busywork while I considered what I'd seen. When FireWind and Occam entered, FireWind was dressed, down to the polished leather dress shoes I had put in the expandable pouch. His hair was loose and fell down to his hips, a lustrous wash of black, darker than the night. I wondered what would happen if he cut his hair. Would he shift back with cut hair? If it was all DNA, how did his body know? Why didn't he come back with fingernails two feet long or hair that was no more than a buzz of black roots? Still caught up in the thing I had witnessed, I didn't ask.

Moments later, my boss had inhaled the sandwich much like his dog had inhaled the jerky. When he still looked hungry, I opened a turkey sandwich and placed it in front of him. He ate that too. When it was gone, he drained the water and went to the sink, washed his hands and dried them, turned, and leaned his backside against the counter, facing us. He began to braid his hair into a single plait. The movements were economical and smooth and much less shaky.

"You're not moon-called. So you pay for all of your shape-shifting energy use with calories, don't you," I said.

As his fingers flew among the three strands, FireWind lifted his eyes to me, sharing the minuscule smile that had to be a tribal thing. "Yes. Were-creatures take some energy from the moon when they shift. Skinwalkers must eat or we die."

I hadn't realized that, but it made sense now that I saw it in person. "That's why you liked my bars. What do you need most? Fats? Protein? Jerky?"

"Commercial jerky has too little oils and fats"—his smile widened—"and it stinks when I have an animal nose. But it's convenient and has a long shelf life. When I'm human, the commercial bars and jerky are too sweet or too dry or they taste like clay." He bent his head, like a small bow. "I am hopeful you will create the perfect protein bar for the weres and that you will share some with me. If I hunt a bear this fall in my cat form, I'll bring the bear fat to you to add to your homemade protein bars. And I can hunt deer for jerky."

I didn't know what I'd do with bear fat, which I thought had to be rendered to be used in food, but his statements felt formal, like a pact. Carefully, I said, "Whatever I make for the weres you are welcome to share. For now, I have some more energy bars in my vehicle. Homemade fish-flake and nut, a dried milk and peanut butter bar, and some commercial salmon jerky."

"That would be kind," FireWind said.

I wondered for a moment why I normally disliked him.

He stood straight and said to all of us—T. Laine, Occam, and me—"There is a body at the barn. It will need the null room, and it's likely too late to obtain any clues beyond a scent I recognized from the pasture where Nell sent me."

I had done no such thing, but I didn't contradict him.

"I think it's possible that I have the scent of the magic user—not a witch in the traditional sense," he said to T. Laine, "—who cursed the T-shirts. And . . ." He paused, thinking, finishing up his hair and hunting in a pocket for a tie. "It isn't truly the human scent of the practitioner, but the scent of foul magic. Yes, that is what I was smelling," he mused. "I will shift again as soon as I've recovered and search the house for more of the scent, hoping to identify the practitioner."

"The death magic is still active, stronger in the basement than it was before," I said.

"That's not possible," T. Laine said. "The North Nashville coven put a shield around and under the energies. They're stable."

"Not now," FireWind said. "I believe the murderer returned. Perhaps the practitioner got back inside with some sort of focal attuned to the original energies. Nell thought she saw someone in the field. I believe I have the scent. The body in the barn has only been dead a few hours. The horse in the pasture has been dead several hours longer."

"Can you tell if the practitioner is female?"

"I believe so, though the scent of the energies makes it difficult to be certain. Do we have a list of everyone who was allowed onto the property today?"

T. Laine frowned, thinking. "Yes. Kept by the deputies," she said, sounding distracted. "I've been here all day. If someone got in, right under all our noses, then she's very, very good."

"That specific magical scent is all over the pasture where the stallion died and around the barn and the house. If it is also inside the house, then, yes, you are correct. We are dealing with someone quite controlled and powerful." His lips turned down in an expression I had seen on Jane's face. "Perhaps she is controlled enough to pull an obfuscation glamour? Or to carry an amulet that provides one? I believe that I can recognize the scent of the practitioner even in my human form now. It was potent, smelling like a whiff of raw, rotten beef, a stronger mix of decaying trees, and even more strong, the scent of blood and . . ." He shook his head slowly, thinking. "Perhaps graveyard dirt?" His face cleared. "Are there old graveyards near here? Or better still, battlegrounds?"

"Except for Virginia, Tennessee saw the worst fighting in the Civil War," Occam said, pulling his phone to verify and identify any sites. "There are dozens of them listed, and that doesn't count smaller skirmishes. The Battle of Stones River, near Murfreesboro; the battle near Gallatin; a battle near Hendersonville; and the Battle of Nashville were all close by. Sherman spent a lot of time in the state. And back a century ago, people buried their kin on their farms as often as they buried them in church graveyards. There are battlegrounds and unmarked graves everywhere. And before that, tribes fought each other for land and resources."

T. Laine said, "You think the practitioner took dirt from a grave and dirt from a battleground and used it as part of the *death and decay* working?"

"The plants in the basement," I said softly. "The soil felt . . .
odd. I need to read it again." I dashed to the stairs and down.
There was a window at the landing and a dead plant on the high
window ledge. I grabbed the ceramic pot and carried it back to
the kitchen, placing it beside the potted vampire tree. Before I
could change my mind, I stuck my left fingers into the dead plant's
dirt, and my right fingers into the tree's pot. I expected it to hurt.
A lot. It didn't.

Thoughtfully, I inspected the dead soil, the dead roots. The
oddity I had noted but paid no mind came clear. There were two
kinds of soil in the pot. Most of it had come from here, from the
horse farm. That part was rotted hay, dried manure, commercial
vermiculite, crushed eggshells, the rotted detritus of green
plants. The other was different. The different stuff rested on top
of the pot. It was foreign. And dangerous. That small bit was
electric, biting at my fingers like tiny spiders.

I drew on Soulwood.

My land raised its metaphorical head and pricked its ears, so
much like a cat in my mind. It searched slowly out from the hills
that were my home, out and out until it reached me and surrounded me in its embrace. Soulwood stretched like a lazy cat,
wanting me back. It warmed me, pressing into me, much like a
cat would roll over begging for attention. I thought to my land,
*This soil has been mixed with death. Where did this dirt come
from, this dirt of death?*

Holding me, or holding on to me, it swept out and back, from
the hills to me, back and forth, as if tying itself to my location.
It settled for a moment, then began to reach out, circling farther,
hunting, tracking, shadowing, prowling. Searching out earth
that was battlefield and gravesite . . . They were everywhere.
Hundreds of cemeteries and family plots. Dozens of battlefields.
A half dozen locations within a hundred miles where war and
violence had taken place, where blood had been spilled. One
was close by, within a few miles. It was a small, ancient plot of
ground where a skirmish had been fought, a battle, and men had
died, bleeding their life into the land. *There . . . Yes. Right there.
All the soil from all the pots in the studio were contaminated
from there. But I couldn't seem to locate it on the surface. It
was just farmland, shaped by man for hundreds, if not thou-*

sands, of years. I could find nothing that would lead me to that land, nothing that showed me how to find it aboveground.

I marked the place in my mind and pulled back. Closer to the house was a bright spot of grass, the place where FireWind had shifted shape. The grass and roots and the dirt itself were glowing and dazzling. Beautiful. Soulwood wanted to know it, so I reached out to it, sank my mind into the earth there, and sighed with delight.

"Nell!" Occam shouted. He wrenched my hand out of the vampire tree. "Nell, stop. Stop now."

I tried to speak. Tried to lick my lips. A faint croak came out. I looked at my hands. The skin of my fingertips was white again. Tiny pinpricks covered them. I looked at the vampire tree. It was putting out new leaves. It was growing.

The room telescoped down. I tried to warn Occam, but no words came. I dropped the pot.

I fell forward.

In the dark of semiconsciousness, I knew I had been placed on the grass out front. Oddly enough I was close to the place where Occam had laid FireWind. I slid my hand across the lawn to the warmth of the happy grass. My fingers ached and I was cold all over, but the ground where FireWind had shifted eased some of that.

Occam dropped to his knees beside me.

"Good, you're awake," he said. "That dang blasted tree put in roots through the floor. I yanked it up by the roots and it *stuck me*," he said, irritation in his voice. I smiled. It stuck me too sometimes, when I did stuff it didn't like. "T. Laine says that in the short time it was rooted in the house, it already sucked up and digested some of the *death and decay*. Did you know it could do that?"

No, I mouthed, but no sound came out. I had a feeling that the vampire tree would be happy to clean the earth of the *death and decay*, but it would claim a patch of land in return. A big patch. And probably the house and all the horses and any people nearby. And it would fight to keep control of the land it had claimed.

I was managing to plant vampire tree forests all over and that would never do. Eventually the tree would be seen killing a human and humans would try again to kill it. I would have to use Soulwood to destroy the tree, just as I had threatened. And if I was unsuccessful, the military or combined law enforcement would bomb it, burn it, and destroy it. Eventually the military and the government would figure out the tree was connected to me and they might kill me too, and probably Soulwood and my sisters. The tree might be sentient, but it wasn't mature nor did it understand human problems or human judgments. It killed things and people for nourishment. I couldn't let it be free.

"Is it back in the pot?" I whispered.

"Yeah," Occam groused. "Looking no worse for being dropped, rooted, uprooted, shaken, and replanted. But it probably ain't happy."

"It ain't never *happy*," I said.

Occam made a cat sound. "FireWind wants us in the barn manager's office. I'm figuring the manager is dead. T. Laine's pulling the trailer around and backing it in close. And I have a feeling this case is never gonna end." He stood and held down a hand. "Nell, sugar, I'd offer my hand to any linebacker who got tackled. And you got tackled by a tree *and* a *death and decay* working."

I managed a smile and looked at my white, waxy fingers in the meager darkness. They ached. The damage looked similar to frostbite. "Where'd you put the tree?"

"In your car."

I wanted to smile at his tone, but I thought he might think I was laughing at him instead of commiserating. "It's jist a tree, cat-man." I put my hand into his and he clasped it gently, pulling me to my feet.

When I wavered, he put an arm around me and steadied me. "It ain't jist a tree, Nell, sugar, and you and me both know it."

I sighed and stood on my own. He was right. I did know it. "Come on. Let's check out the barn."

"Don't get in FireWind's way. He's back to being a dog and he's in nose-suck."

"Squirrelly and all over the place? Tail wagging?"

Occam snorted. "More like a two-hundred-pound wrecking ball. On a mission to knock down all his coworkers."

I leaned into Occam again. Pressed into his warmth. Knew I was safe, just for this moment. His longer-than-normal hair was soft under my cheek and he rubbed his jaw into my hair, cat-scent-marking me. I rubbed a fist along his jaw the way his cat liked and gave him a final hug, pushed away, and walked to the barn door under my own power. The stench hit me before I opened the door, the foul, sweet-sick reek of the *death* working. The lights were on and, though it wasn't glaring, it was bright enough to see that the stalls were all empty, the tack room door was open, and so was the manager's office door. The body was lying in the wide central area between stalls.

I had expected to see Credence Pacillo, the breeder and trainer, or perhaps the farm manager, Pam Gower, who had been away on vacation when Stella died, and who I hadn't met, but who had been interviewed over the phone by Occam. I'd seen her bio and photograph, and Pam was a bulldog of a woman, midforties with prematurely gray hair. This body was female, but it wasn't Pam. Instead it was a short, slender, young white woman with cropped blond hair, a girl I had seen on the first day; I had taken her preliminary statement. Ingrid Wayns, a twenty-one-year-old college student, had been ready to graduate, a part-time rider looking to find work in the agribusiness industry. She was stretched out, facedown much like Stella had been, her arms under her as if she fell forward. She was still human looking, still had skin, hair, and her flesh was nearly normal, not oozing green bubbles. Yet.

Ingrid had not been inside the house and there was no reason for anyone in the barn to be dead.

I touched Occam's elbow to get his attention. Softly, I said, "I need to reread the earth here and around the barn to see if the energies have changed or worsened or spread."

"I don't like it, Nell," he said.

My instant response was less than nice, because it was clear he was talking like a boyfriend and not like my coworker. I held in my reaction and said instead, "I'm not too fond of the idea either, Special Agent Occam, but I wasn't asking your permission."

A strange look crossed his face, to be replaced with a dawning comprehension. "Oh." He stepped back. "It's hard to let someone I love do things that might hurt 'em."

"I get that. But that's the way life is, cat-man. Difficult, dangerous, and disturbing."

Occam laughed, a single odd, pained note. "You got a point, Ingram. Otherwise you'd be boring. And I reckon I never signed on for boring, not with you, woman. Fine. I'll accept it. Jist remember. I'm here if you need me." He flipped me a companionable wave and vanished into the night.

As Occam, the security guys, and T. Laine maneuvered the null room trailer into the barn and scooped up the dead girl, I took a fortifying breath and leaned down to touch the ground with an uninjured pinkie. The death sensation was present but not nearly as strong as the sensation at the house. I stepped into a stall and tested the earth beneath the deep wood shavings. Less strong. I moved into each stall, testing, and most were without the *death* working. Then I checked the manager's office. The sensation there was much more powerful, but not on the floor. More as if someone had walked in, touched things, and then left. The coffeemaker was particularly strong, the plastic cracking, and I left a note in the grounds bin that the appliance was contaminated.

Satisfied that the barn was not inherently dangerous in the short term, I sat and opened my laptop, signed on, and started work, but my fingers, still looking frostbitten, ached and my typing was slow. I looked longingly at the coffeemaker and reached slowly back over the chair, stretching my spine.

High in the corner, in the rafters, I spotted a small camera. I managed not to flinch or shout or do anything else, and went back to my business, thinking, wondering why I hadn't noticed it before. I pulled up the schematics of the house and barn's security system. There was no camera listed in the manager's office. Had someone else put a camera here? A spy camera? If so, what was so interesting about this table and the manager's desk?

I got up, stretched again as if I hadn't noticed anything, and walked to the spot where I had sat when Occam and I talked to Credence Pacillo. The camera was placed behind a rafter and looked directly down over the desk and the one spot at the table. The angle seemed perfect to watch the laptop that sat there. Someone had been spying on the office. Pacillo? Or maybe Pam Gower? Stella herself?

Out of sight of the camera, I texted the information to HQ and pretty quickly got back a comment from Tandy. *Interesting. Overall security feed is not kept in storage but is overwritten every week. Camera is not part of security grid. Will search more on this end. Does camera have memory card?*

I texted back, *Beats me. 12 ft overhead?*

Careful to make sure the camera couldn't view what I wrote now, but concerned that it might have already captured my password entry, I retook my seat, adjusted the laptop so the camera couldn't capture the screen, and continued with my work. But working, or trying to work, under the eye of a camera was challenging, an exercise in thorny memories. It was like being under the watchful eye of the churchmen. There was no, *absolutely no* privacy.

I got up and moved away from the chair, out of sight of the camera. I was breathing too fast and anxiety skittered up my spine, which was stupid. Except it wasn't stupid. It made total sense. I thought about the churchmen. I thought about the ones who tried the hardest to hurt me. I had fed them to the earth. I had won. I had defeated them and I had survived. *I* had survived.

I had PTSD of a sort, I knew that. But I had survived. I was still surviving.

My breathing steadied. Okay. *So what do I do with the camera?* I asked myself, thinking like a PsyLED officer, not a victim. I propped myself against the doorway, considering.

A red-brindle and white St. Bernard rammed inside the office, shoving me against the wall. I nearly fell and I whacked FireWind's shoulder with the flat of my hand. "I ain't never in my life smacked a dog, but you'uns know better," I said, shaking my finger at him. "Shame on you," I said, louder. Just like the mamas might. I clamped my mouth shut on the church words.

The St. Bernard went still, turned his head in a totally not-dog manner, and glared at me.

I could apologize. Or not. "Yeah, I know I slapped you. You knock me over and I'll do it again. *Pay attention.* Oh. And jist so you'uns—*you*—know, *death* energies are more powerful in this office than anywhere else in the barn. You know who the death witch is yet?"

FireWind dropped the glare and shook his head no, then yes.

"Is that a maybe?"

FireWind chuffed a happy sound, let his tongue loll out one side of his mouth. He gave me a doggy yes and began to snuffle all around the office, up on the cabinet, under the table, shoving my chair around.

"There's a camera." I pointed up. "You agreeable with me climbing up there and getting it down?"

He chuffed again and whirled from the office, back into the barn.

I interpreted that as a yes, but to cover myself, I made photos of the camera and texted Tandy what I was planning to do. While I waited for a reply from HQ, I hunted for a ladder and found one leading up into the loft. I brought it into the office, propped it against the rafters, and braced the rubber-coated feet. If the ladder somehow slipped, I'd take a nasty fall, but that wasn't likely. I climbed the ladder to get a good look at the metal frame holding the camera in place, and determined that I'd need a screwdriver. I climbed back down and rummaged through the tack room until I found a toolbox, which I brought back to the office. I stuck two sizes of Phillips head screwdrivers into a pocket, pulled off my work gloves, and unfolded a medium-sized evidence collection bag from my pocket. I checked my cell for permission to remove the camera.

Tandy's response was, *This is covered under current search warrants. If MC is present, call and I'll walk you through downloading it.*

"MC? Memory card. Excellent," I said, setting the cell phone down, "because I'm way better with a screwdriver than I am with computer stuff." I pulled on nitrile gloves, climbed the ladder, reached for the camera, and got a jolt of *death and decay*. I nearly did fall, and that woulda proved to Occam that I couldn't do my job. "Dagnabbit," I cursed.

I shook my death-cursed fingertips, which were hidden inside blue nitrile gloves. The magics on the camera were much stronger than the other ones in the barn, and even stronger than the ones in the coffeemaker. Had the death witch put this up? If so, why wasn't it disintegrating? There were cobwebs all over one side of it, so it had been here a while. "Death energies are really strange," I muttered. And then I realized that the clean side was cracked, just a bit. The *death and decay* was only on one side. And there were smudges on the clean side, like fingerprints.

Carefully, not touching anything I could avoid, I disconnected the camera from its supports, traced the electrical line to the lighting fixture, and yanked it loose. I carried my prize back down. All without proving Occam right, that I needed a minder. "Stupid cat," I whispered.

I was talking to myself. I remembered my mama talking to herself, under her breath, when I was a young'un. Looking back, I recognized it as a stress reaction. I took a deep breath and forced my shoulders to relax.

Back in the office, I studied the matte brown camera boxing. It had been spray-painted to look just like the barn rafters. And wasn't that all kinds a sneaky. Finding and removing the memory card was easier than I expected, and the *death and decay* was less powerful now for some reason. Maybe because I had unplugged it? Could it run on electricity? Had an old affected memory card been removed and replaced with a new one recently, like when the woman had been killed? Had she been killed because she had walked in on the practitioner working on the camera?

Will it ruin my tablet? I asked Tandy.

Probably. But if tablet dies as direct result of case, you can turn it in and requisition new one. Brand-new one. With more functionality.

I sighed. Thought about it. And typed, *OK. You tell FireWind. Deal.*

With Tandy's help, I figured out how to attach the memory card to my tablet, which came equipped with multiple ports. I began downloading and sending the contents of the camera to HQ. There were a lot of photos, all using unencrypted standard digital photo software, according to Tandy. The memory card hadn't been replaced recently, and it was going to take a long time to transfer all the files. I sent a text with my thanks and a cute dancing-tree emoji to Tandy. *Easy as pie,* I informed the office.

On my laptop, I sent in my thoughts about the death of the woman found in the barn, and the timing with the reappearance of the *death and decay* in the basement and finding it here.

I closed the laptop, left my tablet working for me, and carried my paper and pen into the night. Once again, I wondered how law enforcement had ever managed to investigate anything without computers.

Beyond the barn lights, all around the barn, I touched the earth in dozens of places, paying careful attention to the locations I had read on the first night. Unexpectedly, things had changed and not in a way I might have thought. Within an hour, my arm was aching with the cold of death magics and I was longing for a stint in the null room. However, while I was moving ladders and breaking into cameras, T. Laine had moved Ingrid's body into the portable null room and then pulled the trailer into the pasture. She and Occam were shoveling Adrian's Hell and the ground under him inside it too. There wouldn't be room for me anytime soon.

Back in the barn manager's office, I checked myself for ticks, which I hadn't thought to do before now, and sat at the table to write up reports. The memory card was still delivering up its secrets, and the barn was quiet, peaceful. As I sat, three horses raced into the barn, tore through the main area, whirled around several times, and raced back out, leaving the whole place in a choking dust. Waving the dust away, I got up and discovered that someone had left one gate in an odd configuration, allowing the geldings into another pasture. "Stupid horses. You should be asleep."

I looked up at the rafters and couldn't spot any cats. Maybe because of the remaining stench. Back at the table, I drew out a rough sketch of the house and grounds and marked the places I had touched, giving them numbers between one and ten, with one being the least strong *death and decay* reading and ten being the strongest. It was clear that the magics had been somehow reinforced and were bleeding out from multiple places.

Not sure what I was seeing, I walked into the pasture, toward Occam and T. Laine, lighting my way with my flashlight, reading the earth here and there with a fingertip. I determined that the *death and decay* magics were not particularly strong this far away from the house and barn. I assumed at that point that Adrian's Hell had spent time in the barn and been contaminated there. Or spent time with the death-magic user there. But then, horses are mobile. He could have come into contact with the energies most any time. That was the problem with death. The energies got out of control when they were used and spread to the ones the user loved, like my bloodlust could do if I wasn't very, very careful. If the maker of the *death and decay* had hidden her power from the world, controlled her magics all her life, and then suddenly started using them, they might now be impossible to restrain. It was like letting the djinn out of the bottle—impossible to get the evil thing back in.

Back at the barn, all the photos had been downloaded to my tablet and sent to HQ. And my tablet had died deader than a doornail. I sat again, thinking. Calm settled in the air. A slow rain began to fall, whispering down, which was going to make moving the dead horse more difficult. Tree frogs began calling, a raucous concert of mating. A horse neighed in the distance. My chair creaked softly.

I might be in a griping mood, but the quiet night was bringing back calming, soothing memories of my youth: the wind moving over grasses, the stamp of hooves, the rare horsey snort, the smell of hay and feed, the bark of dogs and clucking of chickens, the sound and wet feel of rain. Happy memories of time in the Nicholson greenhouse, feeding the basils, making them grow. Not everything about the church was a bad memory and it was good when I could overlay the bad with something wonderful. I rebooted the laptop and amended reports.

By the time midnight approached, I desperately needed sleep. And I heard footsteps approaching. The cadence didn't belong to Occam or FireWind. My breath hitched.

TWELVE

Moving slowly, I eased my weapon from its shoulder holster and slid it to my lap, pointing above my thighs and at the door.

"Hey! Who lef' da ligh'sss on?" a voice slurred. "Who's here?"

I knew that voice. Credence Pacillo had reentered the barn.

Silently, I got up and moved to where I could see him but he wasn't likely to see me, my weapon hidden at my thigh. Pacillo stumbled slightly in the open central area, unsteady on his feet, as he walked through the barn. When I didn't answer, he stopped and looked down at the ground, but not where Ingrid's body had lain, which I thought was telling. Instead, he stared at the prints of horse and humans, overlaid with the deep ruts of a vehicle in the barn dust. "Wha' da fu . . ."

"I'm here," I said.

He whirled and nearly fell. I stepped into the light, gave a *come here* finger wave, and backed into the office. He followed. I took his former seat again. He stood in the doorway, wavering slowly, breathing the sour scent of old liquor into the office. I closed my laptop, reseated my weapon in its holster, and sat back in the chair, my arms out to the sides, my hands on the chair arms, making myself look bigger. Internet Spook School class, Interrogation 201—Body Mechanics. More importantly, the mamas had always said to start out as you intend to go forward. And I wanted to appear accusational. "You looking for Ingrid? You two were having an affair, right?"

"What? Ingrid? No. Why you askin' 'bout Ing?"

I focused intently on his face. "She's dead."

Pacillo sat down hard, landing on the office floor with an ungainly thump. "Why would Ing be dead?"

Not "why would anyone be dead." Of course, he was drunk,

so I didn't know what importance to assign to that. "Did you kill Ing?"

He didn't answer right at first and when he did it was a peculiar, distraught whining sound. He raised his head and I was shocked to see he was crying. "No. Why would I kill *Ing*?"

"Did you kill Stella?"

He shook his head, his confusion growing. "No."

I leaned forward. "Did you kill Monica?" Head shake. "Did you kill Connelly?"

"No," he breathed.

"Did you kill Racine?"

"Who?" Head shake. "I didn't kill them."

Not "I didn't kill anyone." But "I didn't kill them."

"Were you having an affair with Ingrid?"

"No. Not with Ingrid. I'd never touch Ing." He closed his eyes and slid to the floor. Out cold.

FireWind leaped out of the darkness and over Pacillo's body. I nearly jumped out of my skin. My shriek echoed through the night. My boss' dog form skidded under the table, ramming into my knees. He grabbed my hand in his massive teeth and pulled me out of my chair. My boss was no gentle service dog.

"Bite me and I'll kick you," I warned. He let go and raced into the barn. I followed.

At the bottom of the ladder, which I had replaced at the entrance to the loft, he turned, looked at me, and made one of those soft chuff-barks dogs do when they're excited. At the bottom of the ladder, he bounced on all fours and looked up at the big square hole in the ceiling/flooring above, the kind built for access to hay and feed. I had spotted another such opening outside, at the back of the barn, with a lift for carrying up the hay and feed. FireWind bounded up the ladder and disappeared. It was a comical view from below, but I didn't laugh. I had likely pushed my improving relationship with the big boss as far as I could. I retrieved my flashlight and followed him into the barn loft.

Hay in rectangular bales was stacked here and there. The light was dim, and what light there was shone up from small holes in the floor, situated over each feeding trough. Dust hung in the unmoving air, caught in my flashlight beam. Support beams ran from the foundation below to the rafters overhead, and hammocks were strung between them, all empty except for cats, which raised their heads and peered over the hammocks at us. "So that's where you've been," I said.

One gray-striped cat jumped down and sauntered closer, curious or thinking I might have food for it. Then it spotted FireWind and arched its back, hissing. FireWind growled and the cat leaped straight up to land on a joist. The mouser peered down, its tail tip twitching in annoyance.

"Be nice to the kitties," I ordered my boss as I looked around. He snorted.

There were old saddles on supports, and a line of bridles hanging from hooks, all dust covered. There were rectangular bales of hay and fifty-five-gallon plastic barrels with heavy-duty lids. I peered into several to see different kinds of feed. There were buckets and scoops and brooms and shovels and openings into each stall for hay and feed to be dropped.

There were cardboard boxes and an old trunk along one wall. A cat was sleeping in a plastic laundry hamper that was full of folded clothing. Other than that, the loft was amazingly clean and free of the kind of old, rusted equipment I was used to seeing in church barns. The only surprise was a long, narrow bench holding a candlestick and several puddles of melted dark red wax. FireWind trotted to the bench and sniffed. His body went stiff and quivering, his hair standing on end. A snarl curled his muzzle into something fearsome. St. Bernards had seriously big fangs.

"FireWind?"

He whirled to me and growled. There was nothing human left in his eyes. It occurred to me that I should be angry, frightened, something. Instead I recalled Occam's words describing the boss: nose-suck. Dogs' brains were hardwired for tracking from back in the day of being wolves, and scents could take over that part of their brains, just latch on and not let go.

FireWind whirled back and buried his nose in the candle wax, huffing and puffing in the scent. Yeah. Nose-suck. I moved up beside him in the dark and touched the wax with a pinkie. I jerked away. Mega death magics. I looked closer and I realized that there was blood mixed into the wax, giving it the strange reddish color. Black magic? Death-magic practitioners didn't usually practice blood magic. One was raw power, the other was ritualistic and required a blood sacrifice. And *death and decay* was actually neither, so why the focals? And then I remembered the intruder. We had been wondering how the energies had been restored and repowered. Someone had been up here.

FireWind breathed deep, his nose touching the wax.

I needed something to knock my boss free. Like a hosepipe attached to an icy water source, turned on full blast. A rolled-up newspaper to the snout. But both of those might just make him mad. I went back down the ladder and found the potted tree, which I carried up. I shook some of the tree's surface soil out on the floor, in a trail back toward the ladder. Then I walked to my boss, who was still transfixed by the wax, and carefully dumped a bit of the soil onto his snout.

FireWind jumped as if I'd hit him with that rolled-up paper, spun, and snarled at me again. Firmly, I said, "*No*. You. Come with me." I backed steadily to the ladder. FireWind looked back to the wax. "No!" I commanded. "Come!" The big dog dropped his head and padded to me. "There's something wrong with your brain. Shift. Right now. As soon as you start, I'll go find clothes. You need to be in human form."

I started down the ladder and paused with my head above the opening. FireWind padded the rest of the way to me and leaned in until we were nose to nose. He breathed in my scent. I breathed in his. "If you snort right now? I'll be ticked."

FireWind's eyes sparkled with mischievous delight, but he didn't snort, and he was clearly back under control. He lay down atop the trail of Soulwood soil and breathed out slowly. The now-familiar silver mist rose from his fur and I went down to the barn proper. Luckily, his clothes were again in my car, in his gobag. I carried the bag and his shoes back to the barn and up the ladder. I could feel the magic tingling on my skin as I reached a hand up over my head and deposited the shoes, and then the bag, before going back down.

In the office, Pacillo was still passed out half under the table. I really, *really* needed a cup of coffee. Which I was not going to get from the contaminated coffeemaker.

FireWind was fully clothed and his hair rebraided when he climbed down the ladder and entered the office. He looked at me, at the camera parts, which I had placed into evidence bags, the used gloves, the laptop, my paper chart, my gobag, a half-completed chain of custody, and the potted tree. "Why are you carrying the plant?"

"To eat bad guys."

FireWind shoved Pacillo all the way over and made sure he was on his side in case the man threw up. With a breath that sounded like a tired sigh, he sat across from me and dug through his gobag for his snacks. I figured that meant he was done with the plant Q and A.

I pulled the last of my homemade protein bars out of my bag and placed them on the table between us. I wasn't sure why, but FireWind smiled when he accepted the last fish-flake bar and the last salmon jerky strip. In return he handed me the null pens that T. Laine had woven into his dog fur. I took them all into my hands and the pain of my fingers eased a little. He glanced at the coffeemaker, reading the sign. "Contaminated?"

"The coffeemaker, a few other things in here, the camera that was mounted directly below the dark wax that sucked you in, and the hay and water in that stall." I pointed to the stud stall. "It's closest to the bench upstairs."

"Someone put the *death and decay* into his feed?" FireWind asked, too softly.

"I think so."

He looked away, though I had a feeling he wasn't really seeing anything. When he looked back to me he said, "Your hands look bad."

"My hands *are* bad. Sitting in the null room with you helped, but I need time sitting with my hands and feet in Soulwood soil."

"Will you heal?"

"Probably." If I don't become a tree first, but I didn't say that. Half of becoming an adult, for me, had been learning when to keep my mouth shut. The other half had been learning how to shoot a gun, defend against my attackers, and say what was on my mind. I was aware of the contradictions. "The null room should be available again at dawn. I don't really want to go in with a dead woman and a decomposing horse."

FireWind smiled again, leaned over, and lightly pinched my thumb, lifting my hand from the table with his index and thumb, as if inspecting something dead. "I think we can't wait." He dropped my hand. "Come."

I said, "Are you ordering me around like a dog because I ordered you around like a dog?" FireWind's rare laughter echoed through the barn. He stood, picked up Pacillo and tossed him over a shoulder as if the man weighed nothing, and walked away. It was . . . impressive. I gathered up my things and followed. "Hey, FireWind. Do you have the scent of the creator of the *death and decay*?"

"I'm not certain," he said over Pacillo's rump. "I have the scent of the person who placed all the *death and decay*–contaminated things in the barn loft. I have the scent of the person who *is death and decay*. I am not convinced the creator and the delivery person are one and the same."

I caught up with FireWind and handed him my laptop to carry. "So we have a conspiracy? Or a *death and decay* coven?"

"Either one would be very bad."

The stench was not to be believed, so bad I coughed or gagged with every other breath. And that was after Ing's body had been zipped into a cadaver pouch for quick transport to UTMC for a para postmortem, and Adrian's Hell's chopped-up body, which had been rolled onto a heavy-duty tarp in the pasture, was pulled out of the trailer. The decomping bodies were gone, but the air was still poisonously rank. For an hour, I sat in the enclosed space with the big boss, the bench from the loft, the puddles of dark red wax, and an unconscious Pacillo, who had a snore that rattled the null room. And the stench.

FireWind occupied the chair beside me, his face serene, not coughing, not reacting to the stench in any way, looking through the downloaded photos on my laptop. I didn't know how he did it, but it was annoying. And he expected me to keep working while I asphyxiated on the stench. Protective tears gathered in my eyes. My nose filled with mucus.

"What is the time stamp on this one?" He pointed to a photo. "And who is it?"

"Today, make that yesterday, at three a.m. Nearly twenty-four hours ago. His name is Cale Nowell, and he's one of the band members who was also in the commune. He spent several years in jail for an accident that I believe was Stella's fault." I stopped and breathed through a mentholated handkerchief. It didn't help. I checked the timeline and said, "He was present the day Stella died, but he hasn't been seen or heard from since except here. Due to the jail time he likely spent for Stella, Occam marked him as a person of interest and sent the local deputies by his place. JoJo pinged his cell, but they can't find him or it. No one admits to seeing or hearing from him."

"Cale Nowell, Donald Murray Hampstead, and Racine Alcock are the last remaining members of the original poly marriage. I'd like you and Jones to concentrate on Hampstead and Alcock. They didn't just fall through a hole into a pocket universe. They have to be somewhere. And based on the appearance of Cale's fingertips in these photographs"—he expanded a photo from the day of the murders—"he didn't spend enough time in a null room. He has been affected by the *death and decay*." FireWind pulled his cell and dialed HQ. To whomever answered, he said, "Issue an all-points bulletin for Cale Nowell. He is to be brought to the local law enforcement center in whatever county or city he is found, and held for questioning until I arrive."

A knock echoed from the door, concluding our null time. FireWind ended his call, I grabbed my gear, and the moment the big door opened, I raced outside, fell on the ground, and nearly lost the long-ago remains of my sandwich.

FireWind walked down the ramp to the ground looking like a fashion model, his clothes unwrinkled, his hair glinting in the security lights. It was beyond unfair for a man to be so composed and unruffled. As he passed me by, he said, "You did a good job in the loft, Ingram. Thank you for not swatting me on the nose." He disappeared into the night like something from a fantasy movie, all magic wands and smoke and mirrors.

Occam appeared from the darkness and held out a steel mug. My heart melted. I accepted the cup, finding it contained warm lemon ginger tea. "Thank you," I whispered to him.

"Anything and everything for you, Nell, sugar." Occam left me sitting on the ground in the dark, because that was my happy place. Not something any other woman would want or any other man would know. I sipped my tea from the metal mug and let the night wind and the earth beneath my body ease my discomfort. I also scooped a little soil out of the pot and called on Soulwood to help me heal. Occam hauled Pacillo back to the barn and the remains of horse and human back into the trailer. Again.

I sipped. My innards found their places. My nausea faded. As I sat and drank, the warmth of Melody Horse Farm rose in me, rich and content. Alive. So very alive. I could come to love this land.

Softly, something else rose in me. A yearning. A quiet craving, something like desire. Desire to claim the earth beneath me. All I would need was blood. I opened my eyes, not even aware that I had closed them until now. There was a small vine tendril curled around my ankle. This land wanted to be claimed. Wanted to be fed. A battle had been fought near here in the war, blood spilled in violence and fear and hatred. The bodies had been buried in an unmarked grave. The land had accepted the sacrifice, but no one had claimed it. And that was so long ago. And now *death* threatened to wipe the land clean of all life. The land *wanted* . . .

I peeled the vine off my ankle. I couldn't feed this place and clearly the *death and decay* bodies had not been acceptable sacrifices. This wasn't my land. I couldn't take it. I couldn't care for it. "I'm sorry," I whispered.

When I could stand, I pulled my PsyLED persona back around me like a cloak, shook my clothes in the faint wind to remove some of the stink trapped in the fibers, yanked five leaves out of my hairline and tucked them into a pocket. Satisfied that I was at least partially presentable, I went looking for Pacillo. The breeder/trainer was awake and drinking coffee from the contaminated coffeemaker. I didn't bother to tell him he was being stupid. He had removed my note about the contamination and made coffee anyway. Occam often said, "You can't fix stupid," and in this case, I figured he was right. Pacillo stank of liquor, sweat, and coffee, and his hair stood up at odd angles like a punk rocker I had seen on TV. I had a feeling he didn't even remember being in the null room.

I sat across from him and pulled up a pic of Cale on my laptop. I asked, "You know him?"

He blinked several times, as if trying to focus on the screen.

"Cale Nowell. One of Stella's old friends. She made him part of the roadie crew and then a backup guitarist. Haven't seen him around much."

"Really? He's been on the property."

Pacillo looked at up me, bleary-eyed. "Okay. So?"

I shook my head and left the barn office. Sitting in my car, I left a message for Nowell's probation officer, A. K. Montgomery, but it was the middle of the night and I didn't expect him or her to get back to me right away. Shortly after that, FireWind called it a night. I found my car and followed the other cars back to Cookeville and the hotel there. We needed sleep.

As I drove, I kept myself awake thinking about the case. For lots of reasons—mostly because it was likely he had done prison time for Stella—I had a feeling Cale Nowell might be involved, but feelings weren't evidence and guesswork wasn't a case. And my feelings didn't address why a man who had given years of his life to save a lover would hire a witch to make a trigger to kill that same woman.

And then.

A single thought lit up my brain like a torch.

Unless that same man came back from prison expecting that woman to be waiting for him. And she had moved on. Taken other lovers. And left him behind. Killing her by dissolving her entire body was the kind of thing a churchman might do to a wife who strayed.

If, and that was a huge if, that man also had some kind of previously unknown magical power, would he use his power to kill that betraying woman and all her friends and lovers to get back at her?

Oh yes. He surely might.

Except there were two bad guys working together. And I had no idea how that fit into any scenario.

The hotel room phone rang at five a.m., waking T. Laine and me. *"Gaaah,"* she moaned, arms flinging until she woke up enough to answer it. She said, "What. Okay. We'll be ready in five." She hung up the phone and said, "Get up, plant-woman, and pluck your leaves. We got a body."

"Of course we have a body," I grumbled. "We always have a

body." But I rolled out of my hotel bed and stumbled to the bathroom. It took seven minutes, not five, before we were downstairs and I was still not awake. Because I was so sleepy, I rode with Occam, trying to wake up but not able to get my brain in gear. He pulled through a fast-food drive-through and I frowned at the arches, not sure what was happening until he placed a McDonald's muffin sandwich and a cup of mocha in my hands. As I stared at the food, a peculiar warmth spread slowly through me and turned into a blush when he took the sandwich back and unwrapped it for me. It wasn't a cat mating ritual. It wasn't a churchman act of courting. It was simple kindness, a kindness so foreign to me that tears gathered in my eyes. "Thank you," I whispered.

"Eat. Drink the coffee," he said as he pulled back onto the street. I ate. I drank the large coffee. By the time we turned off the Nashville highway, I was moderately awake.

"Who's dead?" I asked as Occam pulled onto a gravel road.

"Cale Nowell's car was found. FireWind said he's dead but decomping slowly. Not fast like Stella Mae and the others."

"He's male. It seems to be the females who are melting." I frowned. "Except for the stallion."

"Gender-specific *death* working. I read your report. It's an interesting theory."

"Except the stallion," I repeated. "He was decomposing like the females. His feed and water trough were affected by *death and decay*, dropped from the loft. The horse was deliberately killed. Stella and her most expensive horse? Dead by the same means?"

"We got no motive, and a suspect pool that's going nowhere fast." A moment later he said, "Up ahead."

Blue lights were flashing. Lots of blue lights. I counted five sheriff's deputies' cars from two counties, two city cop cars, a fire truck, and an ambulance. "Why an ambulance? He's dead, right?" I asked.

"That's what I heard."

We weaponed up and grabbed a bin of blue spelled unis from behind the seats. No one approached us, but that was because FireWind and T. Laine pulled in front of Occam's car and went straight to the gathering of law enforcement. We went the other way and approached the side of the road.

A deputy was guarding the vehicle, twenty feet away, standing hipshot on the uneven ground, lit by the blue flashes. He touched his hat brim as we approached, recognizing us. "It ain't pretty," he said.

"Seldom is," Occam agreed.

The car in question was off the road, down a slight embankment, resting against trees, the front driver's-side panel and door dented in. I flicked on my flash and shined it in through the dirty window. Cale Nowell's face was resting against the glass, one hand trapped in the steering wheel. His lips and fingertips were green, and he was covered in a fine, glistening green froth. "He's decomposing," I said. My theory about it hitting women harder might be disproven.

"One vic," Occam said, walking around the car, inspecting it with his flash. "No sign of other vehicle damage. Tires look okay. Deputy," he called. "Any skid marks or debris?"

"No. Nothing. We're treating it as a single-vehicle accident, but it'll be worked up as a murder-by-paranormal-means investigation as soon as all your people get here. All paras should be gathered up and shot."

"Ummm," Occam said. He returned to me, where I stood on the street by his car, and said softly. "Charmin' fella."

"I reckon being shot is marginally better than being burned at the stake?"

Occam chuckled, the tone harsh, and began removing P3Es from their small bin.

"When will the para hazmat team be here?" I asked, my eyes on Cale Nowell.

"PsyCSI and the military PHMT will arrive here by seven a.m. Soon," Occam said, placing our protective gear in the seat of his car. "The local LEOs brought in a drug- and bomb-sniffing dog and got no hits. We need to get our workup started."

I had no answer to that. I accepted the sky blue P3E and dressed out.

Clad in one-piece P3E null unis and thick gloves, masks, and goggles, we took Geiger counter readings; performed quick tests on the air and the ground beneath the car for on-scene chemical residue; took soil and air samples; photographed the street, the ground, the trees, and the victim inside the car; sketched the scene; and started to take fingerprints from the vehicle body and door handles to send to IAFIS, the Integrated Automated Fingerprint Identification System, but there was a problem. Green goo was slimed all over the outside of the driver's door handle. Green goo started toward the end of the dying process and after respiration was affected.

I shined my light into the car and studied Cale's hands, where he gripped the steering wheel. Several fingers were missing. They weren't in his lap. I borrowed a small step stool from the fire truck. Firefighters had everything. Positioning it at the car door, I got a better angle. The fingers weren't on the floor of the car. I felt a chill that had nothing to do with autumn's weather change.

"Occam?" He raised his head from the back bumper and looked back at me. "I think he got into the car after he lost fingers."

Occam walked to me and shined his light into the car, looking for fingers, as I had. Cale's face was sludged against the window, sliding down as gravity exerted its power. "HPD got here within minutes of the crash. The officer sent me photos." Occam paged through his cell. "Cale's eyes were already whited over." He studied the goo on the outside of the car door. "This don't make sense."

"Unless he was driving after he died," I said, too softly to be overheard.

Occam's scarred eyebrow went up. "Like a zombie? Ain't no such thing as a true zombie, Nell. Just fangheads rising too early, or revenants. And Cale ain't neither."

"We know humans and witches can be demon ridden. Is it possible that this body was . . . being ridden? After he was dead?"

"Like a necromancer? Necromancers have never been proven to exist either." Occam looked back at the man in the vehicle. "But it's possible, I reckon. Until Marilyn Monroe was staked in the Oval Office trying to turn President Kennedy, vamps hid in the closet for near two thousand years, so yeah. Zombies and necros might be real and not sci-fi, but don't tell that to the powers that be just yet. We'd need proof."

"Necromancer," I said, trying the word on my tongue. That subject hadn't been covered in Spook School. "So that's what we call magic users who kill and then control dead bodies?"

"That and dangerous, Nell, sugar. Dangerous as hell. But a

better question would be, if the magic user *was* riding Cale Nowell, why?"

Laine and the North Nashville coven leader waved us over to take readings on the psy-meter 2.0. By the time the government para hazmat team arrived, we had done everything we could without opening the vehicle doors and had peeled off our P3Es. We were waiting in the gray light of dawn, sipping coffee from paper cups poured from an insulated gallon container brought by a day-shift deputy. The PHMT team leader who got out and approached us was midfifties with brightly dyed hair in shades of green, purple, and dark burgundy, clearly a civilian, not a soldier. I had a wig in similar shades as part of an identity created by JoJo, for my one and only—so far—stint undercover.

"Jamie Lee Frost," she said, shaking first with me and then with Occam as we identified ourselves. "I've read your CBRNEP workup of the Ragel farm site." CBRNEP covered chemical, biological, radiological/nuclear, explosive, and paranormal materials as causative agents. "Your team did good work."

"We're not crime scene techs or hazmat," Occam said, "but we try to not mess up our scenes too much."

Frost gave a half smile. "Update me on this one?"

"Since the vic is tied to the Melody Horse Farm," Occam said, "we think we can eliminate everything except paranormal as COD," he said, referring to the cause of death. "There and here, we've given it a prelim classification as a type of death curse, which we're calling *death and decay*, because it seems to be normal death and decomp process, but vastly speeded up. Nothing reads like witch magics, but we also have nothing to prove it isn't being perpetrated by a death witch."

"If it's a *death* working, that'll be hard to close," she said, while pulling on a uni. "I've worked up exactly one *death* working and it's still open."

"How long ago?" I asked.

"Four years, twenty-seven days, and counting. And I still can't get the memory of the withered and desiccated body out of my mind and the smell out of my head. I smell it in my dreams. I had to burn my clothes. Thank God for the better unis. They keep the worst of the stench out. Excuse me," she said, spotting FireWind.

"Withered and desiccated," Occam murmured to me. "Not what we have here."

It appeared that Jamie Lee Frost and FireWind were old acquaintances, if not friends. They fell into instant discussion, and the boss pulled T. Laine in. He left Occam and me out of the discussion. "He'll be sending us back," Occam said, "bringing Tandy from HQ again to deal with any interrogations. I'll be glad when LaFleur and Racer get in from Chattanooga. And I'll be glad to sleep a few nights in my own bed."

I got a text from Mud, who should be on the way to school. I called her back. "Morning, Mud. Is it spurting blood, roaring flames, or dead bodies?"

"None a them. It's worse. Esther's gone home to her and Jed's place. She's got a gun."

After a night with only a couple of hours sleep sandwiched between too many hours on my feet, I drove past the armed guards and onto the church compound. As I drove onto the property, the church guards watched me with scowling faces that told me exactly how unwelcome I was. I ignored them, if not their shotguns.

The fencing was being pressed outward by the vines and trunks of the vampire tree I had foolishly set to grow and guard the church, back when the tree was amenable to suggestions, and before I realized that it was truly intelligent and not just a plant I could push around like all the others I encouraged to grow.

I was learning the hard way what I was, what I could do by act of will, what my blood did all on its own, and I had made mistakes. I hoped the tree was a mistake I could control. I hoped the mess I had set in play with Esther staying at the farm was something I could control. Or fix. Or run away from. I'd take any of the options that didn't end up with me or one of my sisters killing someone we loved or ending up dead at the hands of the church folk.

I motored down the road to Esther and Jedidiah's place, aware of the scowls and anger on the faces of the church folk I passed. Mostly. It wasn't easy, as the worst offenders were from the faction that had once wanted to see me burned at the stake. Still did. A big batch of armed menfolk were standing outside of Jedidiah and Esther's house. As I eased into the short drive, they turned to face me, silent, accusatory. I parked, checked my weapon and holstered it, took a deep breath. Got out of the car. Wearing pants, a wrinkled store-bought shirt, and a man's-style blazer. With a gun peeking past the lapel, under my left armpit, a weapon I didn't try to hide. And carrying a stench that had in no way dissipated on the drive back.

I walked toward the men who barred the way, standing in a line, shoulder to shoulder. Nine of them, a Lambert and a Vaughn standing with two McCormicks, and five more I didn't recognize right off, all of them a little older than I was, all looking mean, staring at my legs and my chest, the way weak men did when they wanted to intimidate and remind a woman that she was a thing to be used. I smiled. I let the spark of whatever I was shine through my eyes, malevolent and violent and willing to feed the land with their blood. "Afternoon, boys," I whispered. Two of the men flinched. *Weak links.* They'd run if things got bad. That was good to know. "Move aside. I need to speak with Jedidiah and his wife."

"Jed done divorced her," a man said.

"You'un caused this," another said. "You'un created discord and discontent and brought anger unto this holy land." The speakers were from the Jackson faction.

"Move. Aside," I said. I felt leaves curling from my hairline, beneath the wild curls, a tickling, insistent sensation as my body reacted to the unspoken threat.

"Let her through," Jedidiah called out. He was standing on the front porch.

"She's a law enforcement officer," a familiar voice said from behind me. Sam, my brother. Backup. And I knew he'd be armed. I caught a breath, dropped my shoulders, and unclenched my hand, which had been lifting for my weapon.

"She was called to deal with this," another voice said from my other side. Ben Aden. The man who had wanted to marry me, who my entire family wanted to marry me, and who was engaged to one of my sisters. And whose brother, Larry, had wanted me and then kidnapped Mud, and who had—I stopped the thought, but it was the truth. I knew that. Larry had been eaten by the vampire tree. Mixed bag, but I'd take the backup.

The men forming a line in front of me moved aside, just

enough to let me through if I shoved hard enough. They'd make it a point to force me to touch them. To be touched by them. I nearly froze at that thought and my leaves rustled against my nape; I wondered if I had leaves growing from the front too. I strode toward the small opening. Two arms, wearing different shades of plaid, reached out from either side of me and shoved the men in front out of my way. Sam and Ben. They shoved them hard, tandem strength, sending the two men closest and the ones next to them stumbling, opening up a clear line for me. I didn't even have to slow down. As if my backup had planned it.

My heart beating too fast, I walked toward Jed, who was standing on his porch with a shotgun. I stopped at the base of the short stairs and took in the house with its newly painted green front door and shutters, the rocking chair to the side of the door, the windows open, and what looked like the barrel of a rifle in the front corner. Daddy had taught all his womenfolk how to shoot. I had a feeling I had gotten here just in time to stop a bloodbath. And blood on the land in my sister's condition might be a very bad thing. "Jed," I said, no emotion in the word.

"Nellie," he said back.

"You planning to use that shotgun on Esther?"

His eyes narrowed and his mouth firmed. "You'un know better. I been protecting her from her own damn foolishness."

I raised my eyebrows in a noncommittal *you don't say* gesture and waited. When a woman in pants, with a gun, didn't talk to a churchman, it could be more effective in making him speak than when she cajoled.

"She's refusing to leave," he said. "She thinks she owns this house."

I pursed my lips, thinking, remembering the moment that Esther had stopped talking when she and Mud and I had been discussing her future. Suddenly I wanted to laugh. "Esther," I said, louder than necessary. "How much was your dowry?"

"Twenty thousand dollars," she shouted back through the open window.

"What did he do with it?"

"Jed used most of it when he paid for the house."

My laughter broke through, a single soft chuckle. Most houses passed through family lines. When a new house was needed, it had to be "purchased" from the church in a financial sleight of hand that worked out to a lifetime rental. Twenty thousand dollars was enough to purchase use of a house from the church. "Jed. You accused my sister of infidelity. You got proof? You see her with any other man? You catch her out? And don't you lie to me. I'm an officer of the law and if I think you're lying I'll cart your sorry ass to jail."

Jed flinched at my use of the word *ass*. He looked at the small cluster of men standing behind me. His tongue flicked out and touched his lips, top and bottom, in what looked like a nervous tic. Quietly, for my ears only, he said, "Esther's growing leaves."

Just as quietly, I said, "Yeah. This church has practiced inbreeding for two hundred years. Things from the old country, from the distant past, are beginning to break through, like the devil dogs. Like the leaves. That your kid in her belly?"

Jed looked out again and then down. "Yeah."

Sam cursed. Ben spat.

"Say that part loud enough that the men can hear," I said. "Restore my sister's reputation or I'll let my brother rip your guts out."

Jed's eyes whipped to Sam and away. Such lies were time-honored reasons for church families to go to war.

"Say it," Sam ground out.

"Esther's baby is mine," he said loudly. "But I'm still divorcing her. She . . . she *displeases* me."

"Did she request marital counseling by a church elder?" I asked, just as loud.

"I ain't spilling my guts to nobody."

"I ain't leaving," Esther shouted. "And if them men try to make me go, I'll burn the house to the ground."

Without looking away from Jed, I said, "Sam, you get that information about a portable sawmill?"

"The Adens got one, Nellie," Ben answered. "What you need cut?"

"Wood for Esther's new house on my land. As soon as Jed repays her dowry."

Jed's eyes went wide. Esther gasped.

"See, Jed," I said, speaking loudly again. "God's Cloud of Glory has a church constitution, one that could be used by men to support polygamy in spite of scripture. It was effectively buried about a hundred years ago, because it also gave the churchwomen specific rights and protections. It hasn't been studied much in the generations since, but I've read it. And that constitution has wording suggesting that a man can't divorce a wife married before the church and in the sight of God without scriptural reasons. Unless she wants to go. Which Esther doesn't. Without cause, and without her consent, if you make her leave, you have to repay her dowry." Technically the money went back to the girl's father, but I didn't bring that up. I had a really good feeling that Jed had never read the constitution. At the moment, he looked like a fish on the line, all googly-eyed, his mouth opening and closing on things he wanted to say but was thinking better of fast.

"Esther," I said. "If you get your dowry back will you allow the divorce, and leave the church?"

"I want the money, all my furniture, all the dishes, the cook-stove, and my chickens. And the henhouse."

"That ain't right. I won't h-h-have nothin'," Jed stuttered.

"You'un came into this marriage with nothing and you bought what you have with the dowry. Esther's dowry," Sam said. "Nellie's right. The money she brought in goes with the unfairly divorced wife. You'll have to move in with the bachelors or back in with your'un daddy." Sam sounded mighty happy about that.

"But . . . but . . ." Jed went silent, looking like he'd been mule-kicked.

"You haven't been married long enough to provide sweat equity equivalent to the dowry," I said.

"You can keep your truck and guns and personal things," Esther said through the screen. "That should equal the sweat equity. And the dogs, you can keep them mangy things too."

"We'll talk to my daddy," Ben said, talking about Brother Aden. "I'll go with you. The church will reimburse you for the house from the church coffers and return the money to Esther."

"You got an hour to make that happen," I said to Jed. Actually, he had four weeks, according to the church constitution, but again, Jed didn't know that.

Sam's expression told me he knew, but I just gave him my most innocent little-sister look. Sam exhaled hard. Ben handed Jed's shotgun to Sam and took the newly divorced man by the arm as he led him away, leaving Sam to back me up.

It all felt familiar and yet alien, a part of me and yet removed from me. Odd to be part of a family and have things happen around me, without my input, after so many years of being alone. Odd to step back into it all and know what to say and how to say it and to . . . and to not fall apart or have to draw my weapon. Odd to have a brother at my back, supporting me. I sent him a look full of love and thanks. He returned one filled with wry disbelief more than affection, but I'd take that too. And I was also proud, so proud, of Esther for taking a stand. "You can put that rifle away, Esther," I said.

"Nope. Not till them menfolk disperse."

"You men heard her," I said. "Go on about your business."

Shooting me looks filled with murderous hate, which was infinitely better than shooting me with their weapons, the men shuffled away. When they were gone, I said, "Esther, I'll sit a while on your porch and keep an eye on things. But I missed breakfast. You got anything I could eat?"

"I'll scramble you'un up some eggs. Make you'un some flapjacks. I got some Vaughn butter and church honey. And some coffee that ain't been on the hob too long."

"I'd be much appreciative," I said.

"I'd love me some coffee, sister mine," Sam said.

"Comin' up," Esther said. I heard the pregger-shuffle as she moved toward the kitchen. She was getting big fast.

"Who's watching the back?" I asked quietly, because I knew he'd have someone covering the house there too.

"Amos and Rufus," he said, referring to our older half brothers. "Heavily armed and well hidden." My brother rested his backside on the edge of the porch, his feet between the leafy fronds of bulbs my sister had planted when she first married. Totally without church inflections, Sam said, "I took Mud to school today. I took a yard of cut wood to your house yesterday. I did maintenance on your windmill while I was there."

I smiled. "Thank you, brother mine. Looking after the widder-woman?"

"Until she marries a werecat, yes."

I felt as if I'd been gut punched. In the church, when brothers talked about their sister's marriage, it was usually with an interest to control said sister. "Ummm."

Sam grinned and said, "You are mighty welcome, sister mine. Your fella says it's up to you to propose or to ask him to be your concubine. A man as a concubine is a little modern, to my way of thinking, but I'll support you if you decide to go the concubinage route. Though Mama might have kittens. She wants to see you in a wedding gown."

Sam's words said he, too, was leaving this decision in my hands. That was . . . unexpected? Shocking? "Ummm."

Sam laughed, the tone kind, as if he was letting me off the hook, and tilted his head back to view me from the corner of his eye.

I snapped my mouth closed, made a face at him, and said, "You'un's teasing me."

"Only a little. Occam loves you. Don't keep him waiting too long."

I made a harrumphing sound, a lot like Mama made, and scowled at him. "I have a feeling we'll be here a while. Mind if I get my laptop and do a little work?"

"I'm fine with a little peace and quiet." He hesitated a breath and then asked, "You know you stink, right?"

"I know." I went to my car, retrieved my laptop, and took the rocking chair Sam had left me. He was sitting on the porch, his back against the porch wall, legs outstretched. I discovered an update on the single-vehicle accident, posted by Occam an hour past. It was official to the case file, so it was coached in official-ese, but it boiled down to: The para hazmat team had vacuumed and collected trace evidence from Cale Nowell's car and finger-printed everything inside. The vacuum cleaner had been placed into two interlocking null bags for hazardous waste and null magic transportation and messengered back to the military's new joint armed forces crime lab. It would be at least forty-eight hours before the evidence was analyzed. The military crime scene techs were in the process of sealing the entire car in over-sized hazmat drop cloths and pulling it onto a trailer to be taken to the same location. Evidence in this case was moving out of PsyLED's hands. This case was getting away from us, just like the Blood Tarot case had. The body count had been unaccept-ably high then and the discussions to include military interven-tion at certain paranormal crimes had gone into high gear. The military was entirely too involved. They had to be interested in how *death and decay* worked. An attempt to weaponize such energies couldn't be far behind.

A second update had been posted while I was facing off with the churchmen. When Cale Nowell's trunk was opened, it revealed a pile of junk two feet deep. Among it, the CSI hazmat team discovered duct tape, a shovel, heavy-duty plastic bags, lye, and rope.

That was all stuff used by serial killers to kidnap, transport, and bury bodies. Or maybe to cart graveyard dirt for making a *death and decay* working. It wasn't likely happenstance. Once is chance, twice is coincidence, third time is enemy action. That was military canon.

JoJo had been tracking the car and the team had pulled an address out of the car's GPS system. Cale Nowell had spent a lot of time in a trailer at the back of a farm halfway between Knoxville and Cookeville. Cale could be a suspect, or he could be a victim. Or both, if he'd messed up and magicked himself in some way, especially if my thoughts about a necromancer had any merit. My cell dinged with a GPS location and address. They wanted me there. ASAP.

I sat, staring at the request, the address, and the small map that popped up beside it. I was so tired I could hardly move. I wouldn't be safe on the road.

The door to my side opened and Esther exited, backing onto the porch. She was dressed like a proper churchwoman, in a calf-length blue gingham dress with a white apron, her hair bunned up. She was wearing a pretty, purple scarf around her crown, adornment approved by the church, but I knew it was really worn to hide leaves. She was also wearing bright purple sneakers with lime green ties, which was not church approved, though I had seen other Nicholson women wearing brightly colored shoes and I approved. Esther turned around, revealing a wood tray with two coffee cups, a white porcelain coffee carafe, and an entire breakfast on a heavy white plate. She placed the tray in front of me, across the arms of the rocking chair. The smell of morning-fresh eggs and bacon and coffee woke me up fast.

"Holy moly, that smells good," I breathed.

Esther smacked me on the shoulder. "You'un don't be cussing at my house, and you'un best say a proper thanks."

"Ow." I rubbed my shoulder, saying, "Lord, I thank you for this amazing meal and my wonderful sister. And brother," I amended. "Amen." I dove in.

"Good enough," Esther said and returned to her house. For all her recalcitrant ways, my sister could cook a mean breakfast and her coffee was strong enough to stand a fork up in it. I wolfed the meal down as I reread the reports and studied the map. The street view I wanted was nonexistent, the road too unimportant for Google to have driven down it, but from the satellite view, I spotted the address. It was an old farmhouse surrounded by oak trees, with a dirt drive and two trucks parked out front. Behind the house a good ways, maybe half a mile along that same dirt drive, was a trailer, and around a curving hill, an outbuilding smothered in kudzu. Back on the road in front of the address, I finger-leaped along the road back to Highway 62, spotting cleared fields, a postharvest view of farmland, farmland, and more farmland, with houses perched here and there, silos, barns, mobile homes. Near 62 I saw what looked like long, narrow foundation systems, probably the remains of an old chicken farm, with ancient farm vehicles and a house that was caving in. I knew where to turn in now, and I plugged the route into my phone system, wondering how I'd stay awake to reach the address.

As I was reading, a third update appeared on-screen with a soft notification ding. Sam looked over his shoulder at me. "Everything okay, Nellie?"

I grinned tiredly at him. "Except for exhaustion, I'm good. I got me a job, brother mine. The dings are case stuff."

Sam shook his head and stretched out his legs, crossing his feet at the ankles. "That incessant dinging would drive me right into the loony bin."

"Roosters crowing all night would drive me there."

My brother grinned. "Different strokes."

"For different folks," I finished. And opened the new report.

As the wrecked vehicle was leaving under the auspices of the military, FBI Senior Special Agent Macauley Smythe and his partner Gerry Stapp had shown up and Smythe had demanded to know why FBI wasn't called to the scene. FireWind and Smythe had words, most of them not particularly polite, but I managed not to laugh out loud at the record of FireWind's formal and heavily applied politeness. Especially when he noticed that

Macauley Smythe's fingertips were green. The FBI chief had somehow come into contact with *death and decay*. The hazmat team had immediately placed him in quarantine, suited him up, and taken him with them when they left, transporting him to a null room. He'd been screaming about witches and evil magic users being burned at the stake as he was driven away in the back of the military van.

Gerry Stapp was currently on the way to FBI headquarters to begin paperwork to set Catriona free and to dismiss all the trumped-up charges his senior agent had brought against her.

I was sorry I had missed out on that confrontation. It sounded like fun, way more fun than an armed showdown with church-men. Or maybe not. I had won, with a little help from my brother and his friend. And I hadn't developed bloodlust. That was . . . that was pretty wonderful.

The caffeine was waking me up. The food was filling me with fats and protein and carbs. The flapjacks were fluffy bites of heaven. When I was done, I looked from the plate and the reports to see Sam grinning at me. "What?" I asked, suspicious. It was the same look he had given me when I was a kid and he was planning something mean, like putting a frog down my dress or a blacksnake in my bed.

"I like you, Nellie. I mean, I love you like a brother, but I like you too."

I picked up the last scrap of honeyed pancake, wiped it across the greasy, eggy plate, and popped it into my mouth. Chewed and swallowed, grinning at him the whole time.

"Your manners need some working on, but other than *that* I like you," he said.

I chuckled. "I like you too, Sammie." I hadn't called him that in years and a peculiar warmth filled his eyes. Brother-love. All in all, it was a great way to end breakfast. "I gotta go." I set the tray on the rocker, called out my thanks to Esther, and went to my car. I popped the portable beacon light on the roof and pulled out of the church grounds before I turned on the lights and siren. I drove with the windows down to decrease the stench clinging to me.

The drive to the address was fast. T. Laine would have said I was jacked up on caffeine. She would have been right.

THIRTEEN

I took 62, the old Nashville highway, through Wartburg and Lancing, through rolling hills, farmland, and woods, thinking about Cale Nowell and whether he was a victim or a murderer or both. My gut insisted he was innocent, but my gut was mostly emotion and no evidence.

My cell told me to slow when I passed a turnoff tertiary road I had marked as a landmark. I spotted the remains of the dilapidated chicken farm. A couple miles later, my cell told me I had arrived. I was the first member of Unit Eighteen on-site, but two Morgan County deputy cars were parked in the dirt drive out front and two uniformed officers were talking to a man in his thirties, all three standing at the side of the farmhouse I had noted on the satellite map. The man was wearing beat-up jeans, rubber farm boots, and a stained T-shirt, his arms bare to the growing chill. Three hunting dogs were sitting at his feet, tongues lolling, tails thumping with excitement.

I turned off the siren, popped the beacon back inside, raised the windows, and walked to the deputies, flipping open my ID and badge. "Special Agent Ingram, PsyLED," I said. Two of the dogs leaped to their feet, but the civilian snapped his fingers and they both stayed.

"Sergeant Gunter," the woman said and pointed at the other deputy. "Prince." Both officers had the well-trained, fit, muscular look of young law enforcement, both were African-American, and both were clearly curious.

I put away my ID and nodded to the civilian. "Special Agent Ingram," I repeated. "Your name, sir?"

"Holcomb Beresford. This is my land. I need to know what's happening. Where's Cale? Is he in more trouble?"

"Nothing I can say right now, sir. Can you tell me how long Cale Nowell has been living here?"

"I rented to him the day he got out of prison. Where is he? Is he in trouble again for the singer woman?"

Singer. Stella Mae . . . "Why would you think that, sir?"

He spat a stream of tobacco juice to the side. "She ain't been nothing but trouble all his life."

"Can you tell me if he has family?" I asked.

"He has a mama. I got her number, but I ain't tellin' you nothing until I know where Cale is."

"Thank you, sir," I said.

I tilted my head to my vehicle, silently asking the two deputies to meet me there. They followed and we formed a tight group at my driver's door. I said, softly, "Sorry to not divulge more, but Nowell was involved in a single-vehicle accident last night. That's all I can say. The county sheriff has been contacted by my up-line boss and I imagine we'll be inundated with the brass any moment now."

"I went to school with Cale. Holcomb Beresford too," Gunter said, nodding her head toward the farmer. She smiled and there was an edge to it I didn't understand. "Holy Bear ain't bad, but he's not exactly an evolved thinking man either."

"Holy Bear?" I asked, thinking of a stuffed bear with a halo.

"Holy's mama called him that in kiddy-garden and it stuck. Anyway, I knew Cale's mama's address from ten years ago, but I don't know where she lives now. He was all-star in double A basketball the year we nearly won the state. Cale was a hero in high school."

"He's dead, isn't he?" Prince stated, watching my face.

I looked at him, giving him the law enforcement stare that told him all he needed to know about the condition of Cale Nowell.

"Son of a bitch," he said, the tone grieving.

"You got a reason we were told to secure the drive but not let anyone down to the trailer?" Gunter asked.

"I got lots of ideas," I said. "None of them good."

"Cale didn't do whatever he's been accused of doing," Prince said. "He's a good guy. One of the truly good guys I know. He was railroaded and did time he didn't deserve. Everyone around here knows it. If anything, he's a victim, not murderer."

"I read the accident report," I said.

"Then you know he took the rap for his girlfriend."

My mouth tightened and I tried to find the right words. "That's . . . not an unexpected conclusion."

Sirens approached, soft on the morning air, the sound rising over the low hill to the west, growing louder, preceding the appearance of law enforcement. We three leaned against my car, the deputies at either side of me, and watched the excitement begin to build. The sun was fall-cool, the breeze soft, carrying the smells of manure, freshly turned earth, dog poo, man-sweat, and exhaust. Black flies swarmed, buzzing around our heads, the deputies and I waving them away. I hated those flies. They bit and hurt.

The cars appeared over the rolling hilly horizon. FireWind's vehicle was in front, with Occam's car just behind, and they were all but flying down the country road. They braked, turned in, came to a stop, and thankfully turned off lights and sirens. The sheriff pulled in just behind them. More cars and trucks from multiple law enforcement agencies came from both directions. The noise was incredible.

FireWind gave Occam orders I couldn't hear, one arm making a circle that seemed to encompass the entire property. The PsyCSI van appeared on the horizon and followed them in, the techs sitting in their vehicle, drinking from metal travel mugs, looking as tired as I felt. More official vehicles pulled in and parked on Holcomb Beresford's land. The landowner spat tobacco juice, took pics of the excitement on his cell phone, cussed a lot, shook hands, and stuck his nose into everything he could. In the distance, Occam was stringing crime scene tape, wrapping it around trees, an old tractor with flat tires, and blocking off the dirt drive. I just waited. I figured I would need to read the land and I was saving my meager strength.

FireWind spoke privately to the local sheriff and Sergeant Gunter for several minutes before he waved me over. Occam jogged to us, breathing steadily, his eyes glowing a gold so pale and dim no one else would notice. He glanced at me, his gaze far warmer than the autumn sun.

FireWind said, "I'd like you"—he indicated the sheriff and Gunter—"to keep everyone back except PsyLED and our CSI team until we ascertain the hazard level. The three of us will

proceed to the trailer and read the land with our instruments."
FireWind glanced at me and his look said clearly that I was to
read the earth with my hands.

I gave him a truncated nod of understanding and got my
blanket and my potted vampire tree out of the car. The sheriff
did a double take, but no one asked why I had a tree. I really
needed to come up with a good story for it, one that didn't include a people-eating tree or me being part plant. I wasn't good
at lies, so maybe I'd ask JoJo and T. Laine to craft one worthy
of an undercover alias.

"We'll take my vehicle to the tape," FireWind continued,
pointing to Occam's flimsy barrier, "which is a hundred yards
out from the trailer, and work our way in. As soon as we've assured safety protocols"—he looked at the sheriff—"you and
your sergeant are welcome to join us. We'll send in CSI at that
point and, lastly, allow others in. This working has cost too
many people their lives, so we are not taking chances with it."

Gunter pursed her lips. I could almost see her thinking that
there was no way Cale had killed anyone, but she kept her
mouth shut on the words. One thing law enforcement taught us
early was that people could and would do most anything under
the proper—or improper—circumstances. And we had no idea
if Cale was victim, perpetrator, partner in crime, or some combination of all three.

I got in FireWind's car, backseat big enough to stretch out in.
At some point he had returned the tiny Fit rental and begun to
drive his own, much larger Chevy. Occam took the passenger
seat and we waited in the sun-heated car as FireWind and the
sheriff talked to the assembled law enforcement officers and
personnel. Without turning his head, Occam said, "You okay,
Nell?"

"I'm still on a caffeine high so I'm good for now. But I'm'a
crash soon, jist so you know."

"I got your back," Occam said. "And I picked up a gallon of
coffee on the way. It's in my car."

"If I didn't love you before? That right there would make me
fall head over heels."

"Coffee is better than roses?"

"I can't grow or root coffee, cat-man."

He was chuckling when FireWind got in, punched the start

button, and drove us up to the crime scene tape. Occam got out, held the tape high as we rolled slowly by him, and threaded the tape over the car. I tucked my fingers into the soil of the potted tree and waited as we rolled ahead and around a bushy tree and stopped, mostly out of sight of the gathered cars behind us.

"Ingram?" FireWind said, his yellow-eyed gaze meeting my eyes in the rearview mirror. His expression was piercing, and I had a feeling he was trying to tell me something, but I had no idea what it might be. "Do not get lost in the earth."

"Ummm. Okay?"

He opened his door and I opened mine and placed my field boots onto the ground. Occam and FireWind filled a gobag with equipment, including cameras, the psy-meter 2.0, small pyramid-shaped plastic markers—yellow for mundane evidence, blue for magical—evidence bags, yellow flags on stakes for marking dangerous places, and P3Es. We dressed out.

"Ambient magic background checks," FireWind said. He pulled a spiral notebook from a pocket and drew a tiny map of the property. Occam began to test the psy-meter, pointing it at the four cardinal points, at the house behind us, at FireWind for skinwalker readings, at himself for were-creature readings, and at me for plant-people readings, though I was officially classified as nonhuman, paranormal, undifferentiated, plant-people not being a recognized para except among Unit Eighteen and my family.

I reached down and touched a leaf of grass. "Something here," I whispered. "Something bad." I stood upright, cradled the potted tree, and put my still-damaged fingers into Soulwood dirt. The tree shivered slightly, its leaves moving. It could have been the wind. But I knew better. The vampire tree was reacting to the strange energies in the land and on my fingertips.

Occam said, "Same odd readings on all four levels of magical energies. I think we got our suspect."

"If he's our suspect then why is he dead? He spent years in gen pop in prison," I said, drawing on the thoughts and deductions I had made while driving. Gen pop referred to general population prisons where humans went, as opposed to being policed by the individual paranormal communities for harming or potentially being harmful to others. Witches policed witches. Vamps policed vamps. And the ones who slipped by were tracked and killed by monster hunters. Few of them ever made it to a human-populated prison system. "They scan everyone for magical energies these days to keep the mundanes safe from the *big, bad dangerous paras*," I said, sarcasm in my tone. "If he's a death-magic user, then how did he get by that?"

FireWind didn't answer, but pointed to the right. "Widdershins twenty feet and read again." Widdershins meant keeping the item being circled to the left-hand side, so walking counterclockwise.

Occam and I followed orders, me touching a grass leaf blade while he read with the psy-meter. And then read again in another twenty feet. And so on for a hundred feet in one direction before we retraced our steps and read the land in increments sunwise or clockwise. The earth read the same everywhere. Death energies of some strange kind were in this land. All the trees and the grass were affected, most dying.

I had been part of two previous cases of dark death arts—blood-magic curses and salamander death energies. They were supposed to be rare and maybe for the average law enforcement officer they were. Maybe if I was a deputy I'd never see one, but this was my third. And not a one of them matched the typical death magics theorized and taught in PsyLED Spook School. Not a one.

"Do you smell it?" FireWind had stopped, his face lifted. Sniffing the air.

Occam and I followed suit. "Nothing except country and turned earth and harvest," I said.

"I smell what Nell does. Nothing. Why?"

FireWind frowned slightly, his eyes flowing over the landscape. "I am getting whiffs of the *death and decay*. Faint on the wind. That and chemicals I can't identify. Something other than pesticides and herbicides and fertilizer."

Occam and I glanced at each other. His brows rose. I shook my head.

"Let's move in beside the drive and read at ten-foot increments," FireWind said. Which we did. An hour later, my fingers were aching, my back was stiff, I was sweating, and my coffee high was long gone. But the trailer finally came into view, something made in the sixties or seventies, with tiny windows placed up high, a rickety front porch and cinder-block steps, and a couple dozen wild privets that had grown a good twenty feet high and nearly obscured the metal structure. We kept moving in, ten feet at a time. After the umpteenth reading we were nearly at the front door and the energies in the grass hadn't changed.

I pressed against my lower back, stretching hard, trying to stay alert. To my boss I said, "This don't make a lick a sense. If Cale was a magic practitioner, we shoulda gotten higher readings everywhere, and shoulda been getting higher and higher *death and decay* readings as we got to the place he laid his head. In fact, if he was creating *death and decay*, those readings should be off the chart right now. And his car, at the accident, shoulda been red-hot with them. Ain't nothing any stronger here than back there where we started." I thumbed at the drive and the farmer's house.

"I agree," FireWind said, staring across the property.

"How about down there?" Occam asked, pointing.

The drive we had been following curved past the trailer, down a low hill. About half a mile later a small building appeared. On the sat map, I had seen a small vine-covered roof, what I had assumed was a shed. As we moved toward it, the slight breeze died and the day's humidity began to rise. I was sweating in long wet trails beneath my clothes.

As we rounded the curve, a barbed-wire fence came into view and a farm gate blocked the way. On the other side, halfway down a low rolling hill, perhaps another half mile away, was the shed.

I mentally compared the shed on the satellite photos to the building in front of us. The tin-roofed outbuilding had never seen a coat of paint. There was a single closed door but no windows on the two sides I could see and the far side had a small porch. A power line ran to the building. More telling, the kudzu was dead. Kudzu didn't die until frost set in. Yet every single leaf within a ten-foot radius of the near walls was dead, dry, broken off the spiraling vines. The plants at a much longer distance were also dead, in a long trail.

I got a bad feeling in the pit of my stomach and in my hand, which been aching for too long now. I tucked those fingers beneath the other armpit to warm them. I wasn't going to be worth much if I didn't get a break and a lot of Soulwood time. And sleep. I surely needed two days of sleep.

We came to a stop, and FireWind was watching me. "Yeah," I breathed. "There."

"Approach slowly," FireWind said. "I want a reading every five feet."

"No. Nell needs to stop," Occam said. He pulled my hand from beneath the warmth. My fingers were blanched white and the little pin-sized holes in it had grown larger, exposing dead flesh beneath. I should have bled, but I never had. Because dead flesh doesn't bleed.

"Ingram," FireWind said softly, his tone full of reproach. "You were supposed to say something."

"I can give it another few readings," I said.

"Nell—" Occam started.

"I know my limits. Five more fast readings, and one deeper one. Then I need to get to Soulwood."

Occam didn't like it, but this was one of those job things where he had no right to protect me any more than he would another unit member. Here he was not my boyfriend. Here he was a partner. The near snarl he sent me and then sent our boss told us both how much he didn't like it, but he stepped back and aimed the wand of the psy-meter at the shed. He walked five short steps and took a reading, walked five more, took a reading, leaving us behind, the stiffness of his spine communicating how unhappy he was, but he didn't persist in his disagreement.

FireWind and I followed up to and through the gate. A hundred yards beyond the gate, I bent to the ground and touched a blade of a weed. I yanked my hand away. "*Death and decay* energies," I said to my boss. "A little stronger." Yeah. This was the place.

It took another half hour of careful approach, with readings to both sides, before we reached the shed. By then I was shaking and cold and miserable and wanted to throw up from the stress and the *death and decay* on my fingers and crawling up my arm.

The shed door was latched with a simple padlock-style hatch, the kind with a metal loop you could hook a lock through, but this one was secured with a leather thong. It was drawn tight, knotted in a Spanish bowline, a knot taught by churchmen to their sons.

FireWind glanced at Occam, who gave a quick nod. Occam put the psy-meter 2.0 on the ground and drew his weapon, holding it down beside his leg as he moved in a crab step around the building. FireWind inspected the door, and the wood to either side, then bent to shine a light around the threshold. He was looking for traps, which did nothing to improve my shakes, and made me realize that I was in no condition to help should this be a ruse or an ambush. I pulled the potted plant closer into my abdomen, feeling the pot's edge grind against my rooty belly. Stuck my burned fingers into the soil. I didn't feel it when they touched the soil, which seemed very bad.

Occam reappeared on the other side and gave a stiff, sharp nod.

FireWind lifted a pants leg, exposing a leather sheath strapped there. From it, he pulled a knife, which shocked me. I was pretty sure that eight-inch blades were against regs. Occam joined him at the door. FireWind jutted his chin to Occam, who leaned close to the doorjamb, out of the way but close enough to provide cover. With a swift downward motion, FireWind sliced the leather latch and kicked open the door. Occam ducked inside and called, "Clear," before stepping back out.

FireWind pulled sky blue P3Es from his gobag and we put on booties, gloves, and masks before we went in. Electric lights came on, illuminating the interior. I followed last, the over-heated air still escaping with a chemical stench, the place feeling like an oven and stinking like a commercial soap maker.

The inside of the shed was in little better shape than the outside, with a deeply stained concrete floor, a dilapidated sofa, electric lights, and two large steel cylinders, standing upright, reflecting light from the overhead bulbs and the open doorway. One of the round contraptions was a good four and a half feet high and that much around; the other was a third that size; and both were older than I had thought at first glance, corroded and spotted with filth around the seals.

"What are they?" FireWind asked of the steel devices. It sounded like a rhetorical question, but I knew the answer.

I frowned, not liking the fact that I was about to pull on information I knew from my church background. Not that this had anything to do with the church. I hoped. "They're commercial-sized cookers. Well, technically they're called fully jacketed stationary kettles." I pulled up the info on my cell to refresh my memory. "You can poach, boil, sauté, or steam for canning, making soups, barbecue sauce, whatever, in large batches. The whole thing is on a mechanism that allows it to tilt for easy pouring." I patted the large one and bent over to see the gas burner, which was off. The stench in the room was making my eyes water. "The big one is still hot," I said, "and the goop at the seal says that whatever was cooking is still inside. This one holds a hundred gallons."

"Are they expensive?" Occam asked, a strange look on his face.

"The big one sells new for between sixteen and thirty thousand, depending on the extras."

"Dollars?" FireWind said, startled.

"Dollars. The little one holds six gallons and sells for closer to five." I patted it too, but it was ambient temp in the overheated shed. I stepped back to the door and breathed in fresh air. Occam followed.

"No way an ex-con has the money for this," Occam said.

"So does the canning equipment, and this shed, belong to Holy Bear or has it been repurposed from elsewhere?" I said, thinking.

"Holy Bear?" FireWind asked.

"The farmer. It's his nickname. His mama gave it to him when he was a baby," I said.

Occam shook his head, sucked in a deep breath from near the door, and walked over to the bigger cooker. "Namin' a kid that was jist mean."

"Maybe not Holy Bear," I said. "We mighta crossed a property line at the gate. Someone else may own this land."

"Yes," FireWind said. "But it's convenient and too coincidental for the *death and decay* energies to be here unless planted by someone to kill Cale Nowell, or planted here *by* Cale Nowell."

"Is there a cannery around here where used equipment might come available every so often?" I asked. "Or maybe Holy Bear puts up commercial vegetables? Maybe to sell canned produce or soups at a local farmer's market?"

FireWind, who seemed unaffected by the smell, toed a pile of bags in the corner and said, "Several pounds of lye: both sodium hydroxide and potassium hydroxide."

"Maybe making soap?" I asked. "That's what I thought when I first walked in and smelled it, but I don't see tins for pouring soap bars. And I don't see canning facilities, no table, no jars, no spoons, strainers. No . . ." I stopped, my eyes on the bags of lye. A memory struggled up from the darks of my mind. "Strong bases can . . ." I tilted my head, making sure I remembered what I thought I did. The memory rose through me slowly and solidified. ". . . Can dissolve bodies."

FireWind looked at me, waiting, so I went on. "At three hundred degrees, a pressurized lye solution can turn a human body into a liquid in three hours." I studied the kettle and more slowly I said, "This kettle isn't pressurized. It won't heat much above the boiling point of water, two hundred twelve degrees or so. It might take an additional hour or two to complete the process."

"Nell, sugar. That don't sound much like Spook School teaching. That sounds like, well, like something else," Occam said, trying not to bring up the church, but then, where else would I have learned what I was talking about?

I frowned hard at the oversized stainless-steel kettle.

FireWind asked, "Are you saying that you think this is part of the recipe for the *death and decay* energies?"

Recipe . . . That word brought up more memories. "We used to make bone broth with the bones of beef cattle, pigs, eggshells, chicken bones." I stopped, dredging through my memory for more. "Vinegar. Some apples, if I remember right. Once, just before I left with the Ingrams, some of the men were dumping in the bones for the broth and talking. One of them said that about the lye. About dissolving bodies. They laughed. They said a full-grown man would come out pure liquid with the consistency of mineral oil."

A tan liquid, they had said, thick and almost creamy. The men had known all that for certain, which meant they had dissolved a body to get rid of it. And they had been laughing until they saw me standing behind the door, listening. My head had been painful, my scalp aching because my hair had been bunned up for the first time. I had just started my first period and . . . and the man talking had been the Colonel. The man who had come for me, demanding that I become his wife or concubine. Had he come because he hoped to keep me from talking about what they had said? "Ohhh," I breathed, too many thoughts and memories dumping into the forefront of my brain.

"Nell. Why would they know that?" Occam asked gently.

"What? Oh. Um. I could guess, but I don't know the answer to that."

"Are you okay?" he asked me.

"No. Not really. But I'll hold for a bit longer." I glanced at my boss. "I don't have any idea what this has to do with the recipe for *death and decay*."

"But it is conceivable that there is a body inside," FireWind said, looking from the lye bags to the big kettle.

My mouth had gone dry and I tried to wet my lips, but my tongue dragged along, tearing them. "I think we're gonna have to open it and see. And if it's lye, it'll be caustic."

"Do we need breathing equipment?" Occam asked.

"I don't know," I said.

FireWind unlatched a lever on the kettle's side. The kettle moved a little on its horizontal axis. "The spout points that way." He indicated the back wall.

Occam holstered his weapon, ran his hands along the wall to one side, and shoved upward, making something click. He moved to the wall's other side and shoved up, making a similar-sounding click. The exterior wall groaned a little and light poured in from one side as the entire wall cracked opened several inches.

As Occam worked, FireWind adjusted the psy-meter 2.0 and took a reading, with the small wand pointed at the kettle. "I'm not certain what's going on here," he said, "but the psy-meter is reading *death and decay* magics stronger here than outside. Let's get CSI in here for a full CBRNEP workup, and make sure the portable null room is on-site."

Occam and he moved to the front door and started pulling off their P3Es for collection by the PsyCSI team. I didn't move. "Nell?" Occam asked.

I stepped around them to the back wall and placed my gloved hand on the old wood. There was no *death and decay*. I shoved the wall-door fully open. On the other side of the shed was a twelve-foot area, round on the shed side, draining down to a dry creek on the far side. Everything beyond the shed was dead, down to the ground, the dirt itself looking thick and hard and almost roasted. Lifeless. Dead plants everywhere. I clutched my potted tree close to my chest. I didn't even have to touch the earth to know the earth was dead. Didn't have to. But. I gripped a fingertip and pulled off one glove, the blue nitrile dangling. I stepped out there and bent, placing a bare fingertip to the bare branch of a sapling.

In an instant, a fraction of a heartbeat, *death* and *death* and *death* swarmed from my fingertip to my palm, around my wrist, up my arm. Holding me in place like burning icy chains. A scorching wreath coiled from a vine of fiery frozen thorns.

A cage of arctic agony.

Superheated broken black glass.

Death stole my breath. Blistered my flesh. I staggered. Breaking the contact with the dead tree.

Dropped the potted tree. Tried to catch it.

Death stabbed into my chest like a red-hot poker. Stopped my heart.

I fell. The pot hit the ground with a distinct *crack*. Clay shattered, spilling Soulwood soil in a tiny avalanche. My hand landed in the soil. I fell, Soulwood soil cupped in my hand.

The Green Knight thundered toward me, his massive pale green horse in a full gallop, lance aimed at me. I knew what would happen this time. I braced myself anyway. The lance pierced my chest and the Green Knight raced through me. Rammed into the fiery, raging death land.

The *death and decay* rose up, blacker than tar, blacker than a night with no stars, yet red as steel in a forge, heated, glistening like glass. Rising up, amorphous yet cutting, dense as a sizzling fog. *Death and decay* and the Green Knight met on a field, green on one side, burning coals on the other.

Death parted.

The Green Knight galloped into the blackness and disappeared.

FOURTEEN

I came to sitting on the seat of the car, my body leaning forward, sweating and shivering, the sun through the windows nowhere near warm enough. I made a faint hand motion, heaved, and Occam turned my body to the side, supporting me. I didn't vomit, but it was a near thing, and the sick, gaggy feeling left me gasping. The P3Es were gone, a faint memory of someone cutting mine off me. A blanket appeared from somewhere and went around me, warm as the car, a loomed geometric pattern in bright reds and blues on an undyed wool background.

It was soft and smelled vaguely of horse and hay and tobacco. It was sweater-soft.

"Ingram," FireWind said. "Did you break protocol?"

"No. I touched a branch with one fingertip. Just like I'm supposed to." My fingers ached. I was afraid to look at them. "You know how I told you the land has a mind of its own and it sometimes . . . does things?"

"I recall our debriefing after the incident with the demon you trapped and the forest growing overnight." His tone told me that he knew then and knew now that I had still not told him everything.

I sat up, eyes closed as the world spun about me. When the earth settled, I glanced down and saw dead brown leaves at my fingertips. Occam's body was between the big boss and me, and I watched as he plucked withered leaves out of my hairline and off my fingertips. He didn't look me in the eyes. He was mad that I had done something stupid, mad enough that his eyes were glowing the gold of his cat. But he didn't say anything. He just finished grooming me and put a bottle of tepid water in my hand. I drank. I could feel more dried leaves in the toes of my field boots. They'd be crinkled and squished. I drank some more. "Well, there's the tree I made."

"The one you call the vampire tree," FireWind stated. "I have observed the tree on your property line eating, or perhaps digesting would be the better term, a field mouse. I assumed that was why you called it a vampire tree. However, there has been no discussion of you *making* the tree. What do you mean by this?"

"I was on church land. I was shot. I fell on an oak tree. I called on Soulwood to heal me. Soulwood used the oak, shoved its roots into me. They grew into me and healed me."

"The tree near your land, eating the mouse, was not an oak."

"Right. Well. What I didn't know when I was trying to stay alive, was that when my blood and the tree mixed, and Soulwood was healing me—" I stopped and breathed, forcing down nausea. The words felt odd in my mouth, on my tongue. "The tree mutated. Into a tree that eats meat. And . . . it's sentient."

"Sentient. You created a sentient plant." There was disbelief in his tone.

I wasn't looking at him, didn't want to look at him, didn't want to see derision on his face. "Yep," I said softly. "Not that I knew right away it was sentient, and a separate sentience from Soulwood itself. But I figured it out. It calls itself the Green Knight. It fights for me."

"Did you know of this?" he said accusingly to Occam.

"No," I said, before Occam could answer. "I mean yes. Sorta." Occam knew. So did Tandy and Rick. But we hadn't put that into a report. And I was now aware that I probably should have. "I can't prove it. It might not even be true. My body's changing, so my brain is probably changing too. I might be learning to think in a different way, with my evolving, mutating brain. Or I might jist be insane. Or hallucinating."

"When were you going to report this?"

Never? I thought. "I pretty much only figured all this stuff out in the last few days." A few weeks ago, maybe a few months ago, but I wasn't offering that unless he cornered me.

"The little tree you have carried around is more than simply a container of Soulwood soil that allows you to commune with your land?" he asked, his tone colder. "Have you endangered the unit and the integrity of the mission with a *stunt* that uses wild magic?"

I got my eyes open again to see the big boss towering over me, one hand on the car door, the other on the car roof. Something heated and pure flared in me, some part of me that had survived the church, its menfolk, its followers, its traditions. "You want to tell us *how*," I said, dragging out the last word. I slid away from the warm blanket. Swung my legs over and got to my feet. FireWind didn't move so I straight-armed him away from me. He didn't stumble back, but his braid flew, so it had been a good shove. I lowered my voice into a growl that might have come from Occam and started over. "You gonna tell us all about being a skinwalker dog and how you get stuck in nose-suck? How you get lost in the tracking and the chase? Is that in *your* personnel files? Might that cause problems with *this case*?"

The flesh at the corners of FireWind's yellow eyes tightened.

"Yeah. I figured not," I said, taking a step closer to him, feeling fresh green leaves twitch at the back of my hairline. "Tell you what, boss. You report how being in the skin and the brain of an animal affects your brain and I'll do the same with my tree being self-aware. Until then, this is need-to-know and that means you and me and Occam. Now get outta my way before I feed you to the land."

"Feed me to—"

I interrupted him because if he thought about that sentence he might figure out that I had just threatened his life. "I dropped the damn tree and I need to see what it's doing." Steady on my feet, the spike of adrenaline giving me energy I hadn't had a moment past, I walked away.

"She cursed," FireWind said softly, shock in his tone.

"I heard." There was laughter in Occam's voice and he jogged after me.

Someone had moved the car up to the shed when they put me into it, which was a good thing because my legs were not going to make it far. I reached the shed and the adrenaline gave out. I grabbed the wood corner of the shed as I rounded the back and I stopped, breathing hard, though how much was fury and how much was fatigue I didn't know. I stared at the scene behind the outbuilding.

"Well, dagnabbit," I cursed more appropriately.

The vampire tree was a good two feet high, but all the leaves on the lower branches were turning brown. The *death and decay* was stronger than the small bit of Soulwood soil that had spilled from the pot to the dead land. Or . . . Or the *death and decay* was enough to kill the tree. Maybe all the tree, everywhere, even on church land. If I could reproduce the dark magics.

Shock went through me that I would even think of using *death and decay*.

"Nell?" Occam asked.

"The *death and decay* is killing it. Which I've never seen happen before. And which is probably a good thing because otherwise it might take over the property and then we'd never learn—" I stopped abruptly and said instead, "Did you open the kettle?"

"Yes. Nothing in it but a thick, foul-smelling, tan liquid. Not soap, which is what FireWind was expecting, by the smell."

I breathed out slowly, thinking about the *death and decay* that had grabbed me and tried to pull me under. I took up where I'd left off. "If the vampire tree took over, we might never learn how many people were killed, dissolved, and dumped out here. Because there's a body in that kettle, or there was originally."

"Are you sure?"

"Yes, but I can't prove it. That military paranormal woman might be able to, though."

"She and her team will be here shortly. Do you want me to cut down the tree?"

I crossed my arms over my middle and closed my eyes. "You'un better," I said, fatigue driving the church-speak into my words. "You'un know what it can do and you'un'll stay far enough away from it to keep from getting hurt." I chuckled, the sound and the words sour and rough. "It might eat them crime scene techs, jist to stay alive." I opened my eyes to see Occam studying me to see if I was serious. "It wasn't a joke. The tree might really do that," I whispered.

"I got an ax in my car. Hang on." He trotted away. I leaned against the shed and watched leaves flutter to the ground as the little tree fought to stay alive and failed and continued to grow and die. A butterfly fluttered near and landed on the top of the tree. A vine whipped out and snared it, the yellow wings broken and quaking.

We were a mile from Holy Bear's house, but Occam was were-creature-fast. He reappeared, an ax over his shoulder. He approached the small, hungry tree. Car and van engines sounded from out front as the rest of the law enforcement personnel arrived. We didn't have much time.

"Be careful. It's hungry," I said, "and so is the *death and decay* under the ground."

Occam made a cat chuff and ground his work boots into the dead earth for a firm stance. He took a two-handed grip and reared back with the ax. He swung. The blade bit deep into the narrow trunk and Occam wrenched it out. In the deeps of my mind I heard the beginnings of a scream. Occam swung again, and again. The trunk separated. The top two feet of the tree fell onto the dead earth. Its leaves shriveled and turned brown. Occam stepped away from it, the ax over his shoulder. With the top gone, the small roots that had tried to find life in the dead earth shriveled and died. The faint scream grew feeble and vanished.

"Your shoes?" I asked.

Occam came close and lifted a foot to me.

I touched the shoe and felt only leather, no *death and decay*. "Nothing," I whispered. "I got a feeling that were-creatures can't get it."

"You know why?"

"I got no clue, cat-man. But the cats in the barn were fine too, so maybe it's a species thing? Tell the big boss that this location is part of the *death and decay* recipe. It's too strong here to be anything else."

He touched my shoulder and walked away. I studied the scene before me.

The *death and decay* and an ax had killed a small vampire tree. I honestly wouldn't have thought it possible. Did the Green Knight know? Did it know it had lost part of itself? Did it know I had a part in its death? Would it retaliate?

Three witches from the North Nashville coven walked around the side of the shed. They were here to contain and shield the *death and decay* energies. They had to be getting tired of all this. But they were probably making a huge amount of money each time they had to do magic, so I didn't worry about them being tired.

I walked after Occam, to the staging area where someone had already set up a field stove and put a metal percolator on for coffee. I took a paper cup and poured a cup of weak coffee.

Trudging back to the parking area at Holy Bear's farmhouse, I sat in my car and drank down the coffee and tried to read updates and reports.

I got as far as reading a report from JoJo stating that the box of sabotaged tour T-shirts had been hand delivered after Stella Mae's band had left for the tour. They had what they thought was the delivery on security cameras, though the suspect was wearing a hoodie and loose pants and they were speculating it was a man, simply because Cale was so clearly involved in the *death and decay*. Visual inspection and chemical testing showed that the shirts were from the same company, the same dye lots, and the silk screen ink was the same lot number as all the other shirts.

That seemed really important, but my brain had done all it could. I fell asleep with the laptop open on my lap and the empty coffee cup in my hand.

"We'll see that my car is taken back to Knoxville HQ," FireWind said.

I jerked awake, some inexplicable dream ripping to shreds. The big boss was standing near my car, talking to me; he had been talking for a while, probably, as the dream had been about cars that could fly and FireWind had been flying them. "Huh?"

His face expressionless, he said again, "You are too tired to drive. Move over to the passenger seat. Occam will drive you back to Knoxville HQ in your car while I follow in his car. He'll see that you get home." A faint smile lit his face. "I've been informed that you haven't slept sufficiently and that I'm endangering this case by allowing my agents to work forty-eight-hour shifts."

"Yeah?" I said. "Who told you that?"

"Jones."

"Mmm."

"And Kent."

I squinted at him.

"And Occam." His smile was wide enough now to be a smile without qualifiers. "You have become an excellent team."

I made the same noncommittal noise, crawled across the seats, and strapped myself in. And promptly fell asleep. I didn't wake until Occam pulled onto the mountain and Soulwood welcomed me home.

Occam had stopped for a few groceries at some point, a stop I had slept through. While Occam unloaded the car, I dragged my body to my new shower and turned on the water as hot as I could stand it, letting it beat the filth of Cale Nowell's shed off me while the scent of maple-syrup-cured bacon, scrambled eggs, toast, and tea filled the house. Bacon. Occam was fixing maple-syrup-cured bacon on the new hot plate. My mouth watered and my belly clenched at the aroma of heaven in my house.

I pulled on sweatpants and a roomy sweatshirt and tied my hair back in an elastic. It grew so fast, and the curls were like spirals of vines, bushy, heavy, and springy. In the mirror, my eyes looked more emerald than they had a week past, my skin darker bark brown. My fingernails were more woody and leaves curled out here and there. I plucked three, but there were too many and food smelled too good.

I made it to the table and we ate in silence, me picking at leaves in my hairline, snapping off the tiny budding ones from my nail beds.

Occam finished eating faster than I did and started wash water in the sink. I scraped my plate and sopped up the grease and the last of the eggs with toast. I must have dozed off in my chair because Occam was suddenly kneeling at my side. "Here. Lemme." He wiped my hands with a warm damp cloth to get all the breakfast foods off them. I watched as he cleaned my hands, the towel warm, his nails clean, neatly pared, his hands tanned and strong, yet pale next to my wood-toned skin.

I had a flash memory of John's hands, calloused and rough from a lifetime of hard work. His nails had always been clipped short but not smoothed, snagging on everything, a line of dirt under the nails that he never got clean. I hadn't minded then, that John had farmer's hands. We had worked hard all our lives. It was the church way, and my nails often looked just as grimy. But that was my past and Occam . . . Occam was my future.

His beautiful hands lifted to my hair and he gently groomed me, finding more leaves deeper in my hairline, breaking the thin petioles, piling the leaves on the table. Tears gathered in my eyes and he placed a soft kiss on the corner of my mouth, gentle and sweet and kind.

This. This right here. This was the romance I had read about in books. This was the beginning of heat and passion and . . . and it was the foundation of love. Tenderness and kindness that had nothing to do with hot sweaty sheets and the moans of passion and orgasm. Not that I didn't love that too. But this. Just this. This was love.

I raised my hand and rubbed my fist along his jaw the way he liked, his beard scratchy. I realized he must have used the shower upstairs at some point in his cooking spree. He smelled like my lavender soap. I hoped his cat nose wasn't offended at the scent. I needed to make him something special that a cat-man would like to shower with. I rubbed harder and twined my fingers into his hair, rubbing his healing ears, his scalp, and the back of his neck in a cat caress. He tilted into my hands, rolling his head.

"I love you, Occam." Was I saying that too much? Too often?

"I love you, Nell, sugar." He pulled back slightly, smiling, one hand twisting a curl in my hair around his fingers. Our hands were close, both cradling each other's faces. "Come on," he said. "I'll carry you to bed. I have the late shift at HQ, so if you don't mind, we'll get some sleep, curled up like cats. Mud won't be home from school for a few hours so it won't be inappropriate."

Inappropriate in a polygamous household was a totally different thing from inappropriate in a two-spouse home, but I nodded without comment and raised my arms. Occam slid his arms around my shoulders and under my knees. As he carted me to the bed, I caught a glimpse of my gobags on the table. I needed to restock them, but not now. I was asleep before I hit the pillow.

When I woke it was to the feel of footsteps on the parking area out front. Soulwood told me who it was, and I patted the bed beside me to wake Occam. But the sheets were cold except for three cats all snuggled in where his body had lain. Occam had left for his place or had been called into work early. I was betting on the latter. I rose up on my elbows. Where his head had lain was a brand-new tablet to replace the one that had been killed from the *death and decay*–contaminated photo memory card. I nearly squealed with delight, grabbed it up, and rolled out of bed.

I heard the sound of a key turning in the lock and Mud shouted, "We're home! Are you home?" Mud's "we" included Mud, Cherry the springer, and Esther, who was waddling like she was gonna bust open at any moment, but she was humming a church song and smiling as if . . . as if she was happy. Which was really strange. I hadn't seen Esther smile in ages.

"What are you grinning about?" I asked, walking barefoot into the main room.

Esther said, "I got me a check for twenty thousand dollars written on the church account. I also got the churchmen to agree to build me a house on the land you'un promised, labor free and clear." She laughed and said, "Close your'un mouth afore flies fly in."

"How did you do that?"

"I done thought about what you'un said and I used them words. I got a contract and everything. They're starting the septic, the plumbing, and the well tomorrow, and the church is gonna store my furniture and woodstove until the house is built. I'm divorced. A free woman. And Jed has to pay me child support of two hunnert dollars a month."

That was nothing in terms of the money she would need to support a child, but so far as I knew, the church had never demanded child support from a man. This was a first.

Mud, who was pulling off a lightweight jacket, said, "Sam said she was badass. That was his word. *Badass*. He said so when he picked me up at school and then brung us for shooting lessons."

"Took us for shooting lessons," I corrected, checking the time. Nearly five p.m. Late for a school night. "And that is not a good word to use for your sister."

"Whatever. I'm a crack shot. Esther's pretty good too." Mud opened the fridge and got out some homemade jelly we had bought from Old Lady Stevens' vegetable stand. All my life I had canned my own fruit and vegetables, but since joining PsyLED either there hadn't been time or I'd been a tree and trees don't can. Mud pulled a jar of Nicholson homemade peanut butter from a tote and unwrapped a loaf of Mama's fresh bread. Clearly Mama had loaded them down.

I returned to the subject of the check in Esther's hand. She had dropped into a rocking chair and was waving the check around, laughing softly in victory. "Money, money, money, money. And no husband to take it away from me." She looked at me, the glee sliding away from her eyes. "I got a favor to ask." When I nodded far too cautiously, she said, "I want to talk about my life and my plans." She stopped abruptly and breathed slowly, steadily.

I knew those signs. I might have been only twelve when I left Mama's house, but I knew the signs of a woman in labor. And this was way too soon. "How far apart are they?"

"I've only had a few and Mama says they're most likely Braxton Hicks, seeing as I'm not due yet."

"Human gestation is forty weeks," I said slowly. "You're the first plant-woman to give birth so it might be shorter." When my sister didn't reply, I continued, still cautious. "Sister mine, it'll take at least six weeks to build a house. You might have a baby by then." And it might be a plant, but I didn't say that. Church-women didn't get ultrasounds or a doctor's care unless there were problems. "You'll need help with a baby. That's what you want to talk about, isn't it?"

"I asked Daddy to build my house fast. I want to give birth in my own home. Until then . . ." She took a breath and her tone changed, taking on a stronger timbre, a bargaining pitch, firm and persuasive, one I was familiar with from growing up in the church. I held in a smile. "Until then I want to buy that plot of land you mentioned and build a house on it. I plan to be back and forth from the Nicholsons' and here if you'un'll have me. I can look after Mindy and I'll do my share of housecleaning and cooking and suchlike. Sam said he'd put my chicken coop here temporary like. I'll take care of the hens and your'un—*your*—chicks 'cause I got me a way with 'em. I'll contribute my own eggs to our living if you'll have me." She glanced at me to see if I was in agreement. I didn't change my expression, waiting her out. "I promise not to be such a whiny-pants," she said. "I promise to help and not complain. And I'll find a way to pay rent."

A smile of delight pulled at my mouth, but I held it. Our

bargain wasn't done yet. "You'll not pay me a penny for rent or for the land. It's a gift. We're family. But you can do laundry and cook. Your cooking is wonderful."

"To die for," Mud said.

"I ain't never kilt nobody with my cooking. Mighta thought about it some with my hus—my ex-husband. But I never did it." I chuckled and Esther shot her eyes to my face. "Is that a yes?"

"You can stay here until the baby is born," I said, "or until your house is finished if that happens sooner and you need privacy."

Esther frowned and pulled at the leaves trailing through her hairline, smoothing them in her fingers. "I don't rightly know what privacy is. But I reckon I better get good at it." She sounded pensive, uncertain. Taking a deep breath, she said, "I put a chicken on at Mama's. It's stewed and sitting on the front porch. Mindy, go get it and let's us eat."

Working together, a team for the very first time, we set the table. I knew it wouldn't last, but while it did, I was more than content, and Soulwood warmed its way all through me, my land as happy as I was at so many plant-people in my house.

Dinner, eating and sharing our days, laughing at Cherry's antics as she licked crumbs from the floor, was wonderful, just the three of us girls, seven counting the dog and the cats. I felt an unexpected and welcome sense of peace. It was family. I had always planned to save my sisters, to offer them a better way. I had done the right thing taking Esther in, getting custody of Mud, I knew that. But I also knew that my time with Occam would be different and I wondered how he'd feel about spending time here with three plant-women. And maybe a plant-baby. And I wondered how my sister would feel about having were-leopards wandering the grounds and hunting at the three days of the full moon.

A mental image leaped from the deeps of my brain. Occam in spotted wereleopard form, curled around a plant-baby, green with leaves. I couldn't help the smile that softened me, from my heart out to my face.

This was an experiment. I hoped Occam and I would survive it. Did he like babies? Maybe our babies? Did he want one? More than one? Did I? If we managed to have babies would they be leopard plants? All these were questions I couldn't answer.

* * *

I slept again until five a.m. and woke with that heart-dropping fear of falling in a dream. I got up to find Esther walking the floors in the dark, rubbing her back, breakfast laid out to cook. It was fast, oatmeal with brown sugar and cinnamon and dried cranberries. While I ate, I dressed, repacked my gobags, and made a trip to the garden. Apologizing, I left Esther my nasty dirty clothes to clean, the ones that still stank of *death and decay* and that I had forgotten to wash. Without complaint, she threw herself into cleaning.

Someone must have picked up Occam, because my car was in my drive, so I loaded up my gobags and gear and a new plant and bag of soil. The sky was graying when I drove out of the drive and down the mountain.

I parked my car next to Occam's in the parking lot, happy to see it there, and gathered my things, including the small purple cabbage I had dug up from the garden and potted to carry around. I wouldn't be carting the vampire tree again. In hindsight it hadn't been the smartest thing I could do, and I had begun to wonder if the Green Knight had influenced me to carry it around as a way to keep tabs on me. Was the tree that smart? This was a question and a worry to add to the worries about Esther and her future, both short term and long term, worries about Mud living with me, worries about whether I'd be a good mother figure, worries about money.

Once upon a time I had worried only about myself. Now I had people to care for. There was a big part of me that missed living off the grid and in isolation.

I loaded up. Besides the cabbage plant's pot pressed against my belly, I was carrying coffee in my metal travel mug and had a sealed plastic bowl full of leftover chicken stew and a half loaf of Mama's bread in a carryall, dangling from an elbow, with a passel of fresh greens on top. I had my one-day gobag on one shoulder and my four-day gobag over the other. I was holding my ID in two fingers; I would use the same fingers to punch in the code as I made my way through the two entrance doors.

Except that Occam met me partway down the stairs and took my gobags. "Hey there, Nell, sugar," he said softly. "You look pretty as a picture."

"A still life with plants? Maybe a skull? Giovanni Francesco Barbieri did a painting with flowers and a skull sitting on top of a book. I sorta feel like that. Still half-dead."

Occam chuckled and looked up at the camera in the ceiling corner. I had a feeling that if it hadn't been there we might have kissed. My face warmed at the expression on his—just a little frustrated. Just a little needing. Just the way I felt.

My cat-man carried my bags to my cubby. Cubby was office-speak for cubicle. I kinda liked all the modern words and slang I had learned. It made me feel included, part of the team instead of the backcountry consultant I had been at first. The country hick chick I had truly been. I locked away my weapon in my desk, put the plant in the windowsill with the herbs and lettuces I grew in the office, and stashed my four-day gobag in the locker room and the food in the break room. I rejoined Occam at his desk and we drank our coffees, chatting about the weather and the cool air that was blowing in. Everything was quiet. I liked this time of day in HQ.

Half an hour later, we joined both day and night shifts in the conference room. Everyone looked more perky than I expected, even T. Laine, who had been working day and night. She had bruised-looking circles beneath her dark eyes and her shoulders were slumped, but her clothes were fresh and her hair was clean and combed. I got the feeling that she too had slept last night. Null pens were lined up on the conference table in front of her.

JoJo was dressed in bright reds, a silky skirt and blouse, with her braids up in a massive bun, full of beads and sparkly things, and a half dozen gold earrings in each ear. Tandy, who I hadn't seen for what felt like weeks but was really less than one, looked dapper in khaki pants and a white shirt with a dark jacket. His reddish hair had been cut short and the Lichtenberg lines that traced across his skin, from the lightning strikes that gave him his empath gifts, were bright against his pale skin. He was sitting next to Jo, looking over her shoulder at the screens as they loaded up the files for the EOB/SOB (end-of-business/start-of-business) debrief.

Rick and Margot were still on the case in Chattanooga. They would be back by the full moon, to shift and run on Soulwood in safety and privacy. I'd have to talk with Esther about that, and soon, if she was going to be living at the base of the hill. She might see them at night and I didn't want her shooting my were-cats.

Occam and I took our seats and opened our laptops and tablets.

Coffee gurgled in the coffeemaker, a full pot brewing, the red bag from Rick's place of choice, Community Coffee, on the counter. The scent was . . . was home. My second home. HQ. With friends. As if he caught that feeling, or perhaps that scent on me, Occam slid a look my way and smiled, his blonder hair catching the pale light from the windows. I remembered the texture of it in my hands from yesterday, more silky than it had been, as he continued to heal from being dead.

FireWind entered last, from his back office. As usual, he looked as if he had stepped out of a fashion magazine: crisp white shirt, charcoal pants, black jacket, black shoes. I was pretty sure he owned nothing that wasn't some shade of black or white. "Good morning," he said. "Clementine. FireWind. Mark current date and time and open file for SOB meeting." He dipped his head in a gesture that told us to ID ourselves and, one at a time, we stated our names. He took Rick's seat at the far head of the table, which I didn't like, but I kept my mouth shut. Like my sister, I'd pick my battles.

"We have an update on the names of the deceased," FireWind said. "Stella Mae Ragel, Monica Belcher, Verna Upton, Connelly Darrow, Ingrid Wayns, Cale Nowell, Erica Lynn Quinton, and one very expensive horse. Other bodies may have been liquefied at the shed behind the residence of Cale Nowell, though T. Laine has stated categorically that there are no death magics nor any *death and decay* inside Cale Nowell's home, which in her mind is proof that Nowell is not our suspect."

T. Laine pursed her lips at the words "in her mind," but she didn't argue. I wanted to know who else but the suspect would have been making people-soap in the shed behind his house, but I kept my mouth shut because the boss was still talking.

"Infected but recuperating in hospital are Thomas Langer and four others. The rest have been released from hospital. The doctors agree that time in the null rooms is the reason there are survivors at all.

"We have a mountain of trace evidence being worked up at PsyCSI in Richmond and at the military's PHMT. I have directed that we be updated straightaway on anything they find, even basic preliminary reports. But it will be days before we have final reports, and there is a great deal of pressure from up-line to discover something actionable. So far, we are treating as evidence: the box of T-shirts, the witch trigger that set off the working, the *death and decay*–treated soil of the plants in the basement studio, the liquid goo in the kettle at the shed behind Nowell's trailer, the melted remains of the victims—" FireWind stopped abruptly and added, more slowly, "And not much else. Talk to me, people. Brainstorm. Guess."

"I'm looking at the poly marriage," T. Laine said. "Out of the original seven that lived together at the commune, four are dead. Connelly Darrow, Stella, Erica Lynn Quinton, Cale Nowell. All four were also in the band. Surviving the commune is Donald Murray Hampstead, who moved to New York City, and who, when interviewed, was able to offer nothing substantive. Also Thomas Langer and Racine Alcock. Per all surviving members of the poly marriage, Alcock left the commune early, for reasons no one knew, and was not in the band. I haven't been able to find her and neither has Jones."

I looked at JoJo, who didn't glance up at me. If JoJo couldn't find someone, they didn't exist.

"She has no social media presence," T. Laine said. "For all intents and legal purposes, she vanished."

"What if Racine Alcock wasn't her real name at all?" I said.

"I thought about that and we asked Hampstead about that possibility several times. He has no idea where she is or if she was using her real name in the marriage. He has not been part of Stella's life since he left the commune."

"Bad feelings?" FireWind asked.

"He says no," Tandy said. "I was listening on the call and I believe he was speaking the truth as he knows it."

"What about the photo albums FireWind and I collected from Stella Mae's closet?" I asked. "They were old. Did anyone go through them?"

"The albums." FireWind stood fast and left the room, returning in minutes with a cardboard box, sealed with evidence tape. He filled out the COC—chain-of-custody—paper with today's date, time, location, and his name, and slit open the evidence tape. "I brought them back and entered them into evidence, but

I've been here so seldom I never got around to going through them." He passed around the albums, three of them fancy decorated leather books, the pages adorned with cutouts made from colored paper and cut pieces of metal. There were also loose photos in the bottom of the cardboard box, which FireWind handed to me.

"I didn't know people printed out photos anymore," Occam said, "let alone made albums of them."

"It's a thing," T. Laine said. "There's an entire craft market devoted to people creating albums like this one." The album she was paging through was devoted to Stella's school years, with photos of her family. "We got Christmases and Thanksgivings and teenaged parties Stella attended. There are a lot of photos from Stella's youth, from middle school through high school, but nothing that looks as if it might help us."

"I have the early years of the band," Occam said. "Lots of faces. Nothing jumps out as incriminating or worthy of a *death and decay.*"

"I have the commune years," Tandy said. "And we may have photos here of the missing woman, Racine Alcock." He turned through the book, eyes flicking up and down each page. "Unfortunately, her name has been removed from every single photo so I can't prove it."

JoJo said, "Hang on. I'll put it on the screen." She pushed a small stand over the album, a thin metal candy cane–sized and –shaped thing rising in the middle. On its tip was a tiny camera and the album appeared overhead on the main screen.

As she worked, I said, "In all the photos from the online commune site and the marriage, her face was missing or blurred or partially hidden." I flipped the loose photos front and back. Some had names. Most didn't.

Tandy said, "We have Racine Alcock's face in focus . . ." He flipped back through the album. "Once." He tapped a photo. "With age-progression software we can get an idea what she might look like. Change her hair color, hair length, style, weight gain or loss. We can get several versions of what she might look like now."

FireWind said, "Go through all of these with a fine-toothed comb."

"Wait," I said. I flipped an old photo back and forth. It was a school photo, like ones used for middle school yearbooks, with a name on back. "Her name was Elizabeth Racine Alcock."

"Gimme," JoJo demanded. I slid the photo to her and she went to work, keys clacking.

"One thing I find curious," I said, "though I think you all already know it."

FireWind looked mildly interested.

"No one on this unit believes in coincidences. But you used the term *liquid goo* to describe the victims here at the house and in Cale's car. We've been using the word *melted*. There was melted wax in the barn loft. And the kettles contained liquefied—melted or gooey—human remains. And we have the graveyards."

T. Laine said, "Some of my contacts have speculated that *death and decay* might use liquefied bodies and graveyard dirt as part of the curse, energies, whatever it really is. I'll contact them and get an update."

Occam said, "Nell hasn't updated her files yet, but she made a good speculation yesterday."

I blinked. *I made a good speculation? What was it?* I looked the question at Occam, but it popped into my consciousness. "Oh. Right. We have at least one man who was driving a car when he was likely already dead or so close to dead his body was falling apart before he started driving. There may be no records of such creatures as necromancers, but this practitioner has some skill sets that fall into that category."

FireWind made a sound that might have been a Cherokee grunt of interest. Jo's eyes gleamed. T. Laine's face pulled into a hard frown. "That would be bad," she said.

JoJo said, "To make that speculation something stronger, I have traffic cam footage of Cale Nowell's car running a red light and nearly hitting another vehicle. The other car's headlights gave us a good view inside Cale's car." A photo appeared on a screen, showing blurry Cale Nowell behind the wheel of a car. His eyes were already starting to whiten out, which was a symptom we had noted only after a *death and decay* body was dead.

"Necromancer," FireWind said, as if testing the word on his tongue, his eyes going unfocused in thought.

The meeting broke up soon after and Occam pressed my hand as he left the room. It left me with a warm feeling and helped to settle the worries I had about the future and the living arrangements over the next few weeks.

My workday was office stuff: updating files, rereading Clementine's dictation and making corrections, calling to schedule witness and suspect interviews, which would be conducted by T. Laine and Tandy in Cookeville, not me. I did a lot of sitting at my desk or in the conference room, and not a lot of moving around, which left me tired and a little achy, after all the exposure to death, so at three p.m. in the warmest part of the day, I told JoJo I was taking a break. She grunted that she heard.

With a thunderstorm blowing along the horizon, I pulled running shoes, running clothes, and a thin hoodie out of my locker, decided they didn't smell too sweaty-stinky, and dressed for exercise. My weapon covered, ID and badge in a pocket, I grabbed my cell, hooked it to my comms headset, and left the building. I had learned the hard way to check the parking lot really carefully, to watch for cars pulling out when I left, to spot a tail. Or an attacker. Which was why after two blocks, I noticed the blue short-bed truck pull out of a parking spot and follow my route. It turned to the left when I turned right, but I kept an eye out for it.

Five minutes later, I spotted it again one block over. I was being tailed.

It could be the church, but it wasn't likely. The truck was an older Chevy, but it was tricked out, to use Occam's term for a vehicle that had been restored with lots of aftermarket parts. It could be related to the case. Someone wanting to share information off the record? Or a drive-by. I wasn't taking chances.

FIFTEEN

I pressed my cell to autocall HQ.

JoJo answered with my last name, telling me that FireWind was close by. "Ingram."

"Yeah. I'm possibly being tailed. A blue short-bed Chevy pickup, older model, the kind with the wheel wells outside the bed. It's been restored or well cared for. High shine, new paint. Fancy chrome wheels. Nothing too splashy, and in this town, not particularly noticeable." I gave her the street names of the crossroads I was approaching.

FireWind said, "Keep your pace slow. Save energy for a sprint."

"Right." I slowed, not letting panic push me, realizing only then that I was breathing too fast. I slowed my breathing, deeper, the cadence steady. "The truck's been traveling to my left. Aaaaaand yep, there it is, crossing one street over and just behind me."

A wry note in his voice, FireWind asked, "Jones. Can you follow her real-time?"

He was asking Jo if she could hack into security and traffic cams. She hesitated only a moment before she said, "I have programs for some camera systems. Others not so much. Are you authorizing their use?"

"Yes."

"Accessing traffic cameras," JoJo said, her voice toneless.

"I'm on my way, Ingram," he said. "Are you armed?"

"Yes. Affirmative," I corrected. "But there're civilians everywhere."

I heard doors opening and closing way faster than humans could do it. Over the earbuds, I heard nothing after that, no feet running, but FireWind moved silent as the wind, so I didn't really expect to. "Ingram, can you see the driver?" he asked.

"Negative. Haven't been able to see the license plate either."

"Jones?"

"Negative. Not yet." The sound of tapping was rapid-fire over the comms.

At the next crossing I said, "The Chevy isn't there. Oh. Wait. I think it's in front of me, stopped at the light." The light changed green. "I think—" I remembered my earlier thought. *Drive-by . . .*

I was in danger. Not passive hazard like on the case, but being *chased*. As I had been all my life. I was under attack. Instinctively, I knew there was no greenery anywhere, no bare earth for me to stand my ground. My heart sped. Something stirred deep inside me. *Soulwood . . .*

My magic was rising. My leaves sprouted. Rustled.

"I have you on camera," JoJo said.

"I see you ahead," FireWind said, his words without strain, his breathing even.

"There's a coffee shop half a block to your right, Ingram. It has a back door," Jo said. "See it?"

"Yes."

Ahead of me, the blue truck revved its engine. Sped forward.

There were people on the streets. I had a weapon, but if the driver shot at me, there could be collateral damage. A mother and child *there*. An old lady *there*.

No ground. No earth.

"Run!" FireWind commanded. "Get into the building."

I dashed into a sprint and threw open the door of the coffee shop. Glanced back.

The truck turned sharply across traffic. Accelerating.

Heading directly at me. Fast.

It wasn't trailing me for a drive-by. It was trying to ram me. I had nowhere else to go.

I screamed, "Car! Get back!"

Grabbed people at the table nearest the door. Shoved hard.

"Get back get back get back!" Racing. Jumping over the bar, sliding across it.

I dropped behind the bar, slamming into three baristas ahead of me. "Go!"

The truck crashed through the glass front. Engine roaring.

Glass panes shattered, shooting inward like rounded pellets and small slivered knives. Skimming across my arm, back, neck.

My blood splattered on the wall, a thin trace. Everything slowed. In an instant, my bloodlust rose. Soulwood reached out to me. *Need* flooded through my body as if a dam had broken, jagged *want* tearing through me like a flood. *Hunger* . . . Soulwood knew my blood had been spilled. It wanted to be fed with the blood of my enemies.

The truck hit the bar. Shattering wood, plastic, glass. Coffee exploded from bags everywhere. I shoved off the bar top. Dived along the narrow bar alley. The bar and the truck hit the back wall. Missed me by inches. Bottles of flavorings crashed down.

The truck came to a stop, the engine still racing, shoving at the debris and the narrow space where I had landed on top of the baristas. One was bleeding.

Need. Want. I reached out to touch the blood, the woman.

"Ingram!" FireWind shouted.

I jerked back. Swallowed the saliva pooling in my mouth. Curled my fists and hugged myself. *No*, I thought, shoving down the bloodlust. No. *No*. The need receded. "I'm okay!" I shouted to my boss, breathless. "Three women and I are on the far end of the bar. No one is crushed against the wall."

The bodies beneath me began to move, struggling to free themselves from the pile. I reached up and caught the bar, lifting myself so they could crawl from beneath me. So that I wasn't touching them.

"Clear the site!" FireWind said, suddenly inside, his long black hair wild and windblown. "We have a melter."

A melter. A dead person inside the truck who was melting. Contaminated by the *death and decay*. Yet who had been driving a truck. Like Cale Nowell.

"It was a 1967 Chevy short-bed," JoJo said to the gathered members of Unit Eighteen. "One owner, bought new. Brett Hudgins, sixty-nine years of age, five-seven, two-forty, retired farmer, widowed in 2010. No relation to Stella Mae Ragel, to the poly marriage, or to the band. No relation to the church. No relation to anyone. The owner was a deacon in his church, tithed regularly, didn't drink or smoke. According to his son, he went into town this morning to look over a new saddle for his granddaughter's birthday. He didn't show up for lunch and didn't answer his phone. His son activated tracking on his cell and discovered it on the side street half a block from HQ. He had just called police to check it out when he saw it start to move on his cell. He tracked the chase virtually." Jo looked up at me. "He says there's no way his dad was responsible for the attack. He says someone did something to his father to make it happen."

"I believe that," I said.

T. Laine nodded. "Agreed."

"Yet he attacked Ingram," FireWind said. "When did the truck park there? How did a dead man know she was in the building? How did he see with dead eyes?"

"He arrived and parked at eleven-oh-two," Jo said, "according to nearby cameras. Nell was the first person to leave the building after that."

"It may have been opportunity and not a specific target," FireWind said.

I wasn't sure if that made any difference to me. I was still picking pebbled safety glass and sharp shards of bottle glass out of my hair, clothes, and shoes. I had myriad cuts (none requiring stitches) and a few bruises. I was bloody and sticky. Horribly sticky. I smelled like sugar and caramel and hazelnut, splattered by the crashing flavoring bottles. But my bloodlust had gone silent at the sight of the dead melting man behind the truck windows.

I realized that my bloodlust had not risen at all on this case until now, when I was exposed to the blood of a healthy human. Soulwood didn't want *death and decay* bodies. Soulwood knew they were . . . unclean. That was a religious-sounding word, a church word, but it felt right here. They were fundamentally unclean. They didn't belong here or anywhere. They were *wrong*.

"There were four injured, including Nell, one seriously," Jo said. "If Nell hadn't shoved people out of the way it could have been much worse."

"Yes. You did well to get so many patrons away from the door," FireWind said.

"I'd have done even better if there had been time to find a good place to hide. One without a storefront, glass, or civilians," I said, bitter guilt in the words for the woman with the broken leg and no insurance. "He was targeting me, whether by opportunity or personal intent. I led him straight to them." Not that I had had other options. I hadn't known until too late that he was going to crash into the store. I had thought he just intended to shoot me, not take out others too. None of us had been thinking worst-case scenario. None of us had thought that far ahead.

FireWind said, "You did as you were instructed. You followed orders."

I scowled at him. "Following orders without thinking is stupid."

JoJo grinned. T. Laine gave a quiet snort. The hallway door blew open.

Occam, who had been on the road for the last ninety minutes trying to get here, practically flew down the hallway and into the conference room, cat-smooth, cat-fast, his eyes glowing yellow. He dropped beside my chair and ran his hands over me, barely touching. It was too fast, too much like a churchman claiming, and I tensed. Fought off a flinch. Slammed down on fear. Knowing he was searching for wounds, for broken bones, for blood. Knowing it wasn't sexual or demanding but his own worry in tactile form. Knowing that but still reacting.

Suddenly he stopped. Eased his hands back. Occam's eyes met mine and he swallowed hard, breathed, fighting his own battle, as I fought mine. "I'm sorry, Nell. Sorry I wasn't there for you, to protect you. You okay?"

I saw FireWind from the corner of my eye, watching the public display. He was frowning. I caught my breath, needing to remind Occam where we were, and calm his cat. "Special Agent Occam, I'm fine. Unit Eighteen gave me exceptional backup and kept me safe." I pushed him away with one finger and pointed to the chair beside me. "Have a seat and you can watch."

Occam blinked once, slow, and when he opened his eyes, the cat-gold was less bright. He swiveled to the chair and sat. "Occam present," he said, and gave the time.

"Jones," FireWind said in a long-suffering tone, "put up the first footage." Above us, in the conference room, the security camera footage appeared. "This is the moment you saw the vehicle was headed toward you. Note his increase in speed. Note the woman with the baby in a sling just in front of you. Note the elderly woman with the cane behind you. Had you stopped, tried to run in any other direction, these three people would likely have been in the path of the truck. You entered the building under orders because none of us expected him to use the truck as a weapon, not until he corrected his angle for your position and attempted to ram you. Next footage, please," he said.

The angle of the view of the street changed, this camera showing only shades of gray, a grainy, indistinct view of the street, taking us back to before I entered the coffee shop. I was on the sidewalk. Running. A hand was visible at the lower corner, as if someone was reaching for me. I saw the woman with the baby.

Occam was breathing harder, faster, as if he ran with me. He reached over and took my hand and I didn't pull away. We were getting close to the full moon. He needed contact. JoJo must have realized that too because the music created by an air witch to control or ease were-creature shape changes began to play softly through the speakers.

"Next," FireWind said.

The next footage showed me dashing into the coffee shop. On the street, twenty feet ahead of me were the mother and child. Behind me hobbled the woman with a cane. Before me and after me were more people who would have been killed had I not turned in to the store. The final footage was inside the coffee shop. I saw me grabbing people in each hand and yanking them out of their chairs, my mouth open, shouting, my face furious, urgent, screaming. Me sliding across the bar, shoving the baristas farther along the way.

Well, kicking one woman with both feet, which I did not remember doing. But she ended up on the floor and so had been safe.

There were several still shots of me with my face contorted. I knew when I saw them that I had been in the midst of fighting bloodlust. I had won that battle and kept my magic at bay, which should have made me happy. Except that it was more likely that the presence of *death and decay* had more effect than my own will. The footage played again, slower.

The woman with the broken leg had been on the way to the restroom and when I ran through the door shouting for people to get out of the way, she had stopped and looked around for the problem. Typical civilian. Once upon a time I might have done the same thing. Instead I followed orders and kept people alive. I blew out a breath that puffed my cheeks.

I met FireWind's eyes. "Thank you. And thank you, Jo, for picking a place."

"My pleasure, Ingram," and "Anytime, country hick chick," were spoken at the same moment, overlapping. FireWind said, "Let's continue with Nell and me clearing the coffee shop and the arrival of the local police, ambulances, and later, the arrival of the local witches."

The footage showed us clearing the coffee shop, FireWind lifting the woman with the broken leg and carrying her out back. Me making calls. Local PD and medic units arriving. A fire truck, in case the revving truck caught on fire.

T. Laine said, "Since no local coven leaders have been answering or returning my calls, and with the North Nashville coven so busy shielding multiple sites, I did an end run. I contacted Wendy Cornwall, one of the local witches who helped close the hellmouth. She got Theresa Anderson-Kentner, Suzanne Richardson-White, and Barbara Traywick Hasebe to help her, which gave us four witches. With the long-distance advice of Astrid Grainger, they managed, barely, to contain and shield the *death and decay* in the truck and not let it spread."

FireWind said, "This why we need more covens on a consultation basis. You are wearing yourself too thin." When Lainie stiffened, FireWind said, calm lacing his words, "It was not a complaint, Kent. It was an observation. I do not want you to fall apart. You are too important to PsyLED, to this unit, and to me."

T. Laine blinked several times as if it took time for her to process his words. As if to cover her reaction, she said, "I headed back as fast as lights and sirens let me, but I was still ninety minutes getting to the coffee shop. Astrid talked Wendy through a new working that Astrid and her coven have been testing the last few days. It was moderately successful." On the screen, I saw the local witches we had worked with in the past. The local covens had been resistant to working with PsyLED for a long time, but the recent misfortunes had driven some of them closer to T. Laine, close enough for them to trust her and work with her even when the coven leaders were recalcitrant.

"The circle they set up in the debris and the working that followed was enough to shield the decay of the man in the truck, and the truck itself," FireWind said. "His body is now undergoing a postmortem examination inside the portable null room purchased yesterday from the North Nashville coven by UTMC."

"They bought it?" T. Laine said, startled.

"Yes," FireWind said. "It will be outfitted for first responders and can be transported off-site for emergency use at scenes."

He shifted to me. "Nell, Dr. Gomez asked after you. The forensic pathologist with a minor in paranormal medicine?" he said, reminding me who she was. "I have the impression she wants to examine you."

"Yeah. Probably looking forward to *examining* me on her autopsy table someday."

Occam, still too close to his cat, went all catty-still and I realized I shouldn't have said that. I patted his hand where it gripped the chair arm hard enough to stretch the fake leather.

FireWind tilted his head for me to continue, but I shook my head. I had been a patient at UTMC a few times before I stopped letting Unit Eighteen take me there when injured. The paranormal doctors became way too interested in me when they realized I wasn't human and wasn't anything they had seen before. I figured that patient confidentiality only went so far when a doctor was feeling nosy, and that Gomez had gotten into my records despite HIPAA.

"I got something," JoJo said, interrupting us. "I got a name change," she said, excitement in her voice. "Elizabeth Racine Alcock changed her name legally after she left the commune. She took the name Cadence Blue Thompkins. I show a new birth certificate, new IDs, new everything. She married four years ago and took her husband's name, which changed it yet again. No wonder it's been so hard to track her.

"She's now Cadence Blue Thompkins Merriweather. She lives in Kingston, halfway between Knoxville and Cookeville. Her husband is a conservative businessman." Her fingers flew, her lips pursed, and Unit Eighteen looked suddenly revived. "A CEO of a large, politically active, financially successful company that makes . . ." Jo leaned in and read, "Ball bearings, sleeves, flanges, and thrust bearings, whatever they are, in bronze, copper, brass, iron, sintered products—again with the 'whatever they are'—self-lubricated bushings and wearplate. I have no idea what most of that stuff is, but it makes them a lot of money. The couple are movers and shakers."

"Dollars to donuts says her new husband doesn't know about the commune years," Occam said, sounding more his human self.

"If she changed her name there might be real good reasons why," T. Laine said. "Privacy reasons."

Jo said, "I've tracked the name change paperwork . . ." Tapping on the keyboard increased in speed. "She was born in Florida, Union County. And that leads me to check the Florida system aaaand . . . Yes! She has a juvie record under the name Elizabeth R. Alcock. Sealed. Hang on." Her fingers flew. Files appeared on the screen and were just as quickly removed. "Yeah. Got you. She came from the middle of bumfu—fart nowhere. Family on welfare and food stamps." She typed furiously, files flashing onto the screens.

"About six months before she was remanded into the system, there was a death in the area. A schoolteacher was shot and killed. Aaaaand yes, she was in his classes. Looks like someone tried to hush up reports that some of the kids had been abused."

JoJo looked at FireWind. "There were complaints from social services that she should never have been charged, and should certainly never have been remanded into the juvie system." JoJo leaned away from her electronics and pushed a loose braid back from her eyes. "She got a bad deal in court and even worse in juvie. There are reports . . ." Jo stopped and started under a different tack. "When she changed her name, she did it right. She's probably still running from something. Privacy protocols should be followed. Sir."

"We'll approach her carefully, Jones. Quietly," FireWind said. "When will Margot Racer and LaFleur be back from Chattanooga?"

"They're halfway back now," JoJo said. "They wrapped this morning."

"Mmmm," FireWind mused. "Divert them to Racine's address. Ingram and I will meet them in Kingston."

"Sending her address and the husband's business address to your cells," Jo said. "I'll forward her contact info and cell as soon as I have it."

I went to gather my things, knowing that FireWind had chosen me because of my background. Because I'd be the one to bond with a woman who killed her abuser, if that was possible at all.

As FireWind drove I studied up on Kingston, which was close enough to Knoxville to qualify as a bedroom community of the larger city. Tennessee was a long narrow state, and most of it was rich with water resources, with rivers and reservoirs created by dams and hydroelectric plants. Yet large swaths of the state were powered by coal. The Clinch River and the Emory River met in Roane County, practically in downtown Kingston, the water resources managed by dams. The farmland was lush, the mean income was somewhere in the midrange of the state, and the area's power was provided by a huge coal power plant built in 1955. When I told that to FireWind he asked mildly, "And all this is important why?"

"None of it would matter to the case at all, except Racine Alcock, aka Cadence Blue Thompkins Merriweather—and that's a mouthful—her husband's family benefited from the Tennessee Valley Authority and the coal-fired power plants from the outset. He has a trust fund that makes my eyes bug out of my head. He has access to fully ten times the county's annual mean income each year. His family contributes to local politics and gives heavily to charity."

"And?" he asked with exquisite patience.

"We can't just bulldoze our way in there and expect no pushback. Local law enforcement will side with the Merriweathers, who likely support both sides of any campaign."

"You and the other members of Unit Eighteen seem to feel that I am unfamiliar with social graces and appropriate methods to approach a wary witness or possible suspect." His lips lifted slightly. "I assume that is because when I accepted the position over the eastern seaboard, I was less than elegant upon my approach to the unit."

"Less than elegant?" I let my question settle on the air as I thought about my answer. "You've been rude more than once and bossy more than once, and you've stuck your nose where it doesn't belong more than once, but I don't necessarily think you're obnoxious by nature, stupid, or trying to tick us off."

FireWind's eyebrows rose, black as raven's wings. Amused, still patient, he asked, "No?"

I frowned, putting things together, things he had said, things that had been going on and that I hadn't paid much attention to. "I think . . . I think you've been trying to integrate us into PsyLED, the first mostly nonhuman unit. I think we were an experiment started by Soul, and that you wanted a hand in what we were becoming. I think there might have been a lot of push-back about that, about letting paranormals into the department at all, starting with Rick and Paka, the first were-creatures in PsyLED. I think the pushback got worse after the Blood Tarot case. I think you've been trying to keep us safe and to make us better at our job, and better as a team. I think you've pushed to make Knoxville PsyLED the regional HQ because you want to protect us." I glanced to see if I'd made the big boss mad before I added, "I think you want to protect Rick especially, maybe because he was involved with Jane Yellowrock, and Jane is your sister."

"Interesting." He glanced at me as he drove. "You would be correct. You have a gift for complicated relationships and for figuring out motives. Even mine." He was silent, but I had a feeling he wasn't finished. "Yes. This has been an experiment for all of us, even me. I am accustomed to certain protocols, and they are not always suitable to the unit or the circumstances. I have never worked with other paranormals." He glanced at me from the corner of his eye and a faint smile touched the corner of his lips. "Yet even someone as old as I can learn. We'll tread carefully with our witness."

"Good." I went back to my study, but nothing else jumped out at me.

JoJo sent more info to our cells and, faster than I expected, we were in Kingston, our GPS directing us to the Merriweather home. I expected a mansion, but the house was modest sized for the trust fund and the business' coffers, but it backed up to a water view, the roof was new, the trim had been recently painted, and the landscaping was clearly professional, using all the latest chemicals and fertilizers and planted with the fanciest of nonnative, imported flora. There were two new cars parked beside the house and, as we pulled down the street, one backed out and passed us at a sedate speed. The driver looked like a rich businessman. I checked the business' website and identified the driver as Luther Merriweather.

We parked in front of the house and took the walkway to the front porch, rang the bell, and stood there. Two minutes passed. I rang the bell again, and this time held my ID in front of the doorbell alarm.

"Mrs. Merriweather. Your car is in the drive. We know you are home," I said, speaking in a normal tone of voice, assuming she was listening and watching us through the security cameras. "I'm Special Agent Nell Ingram. With me is Senior Special Agent Ayatas FireWind." I folded my ID and put it away. "We'd like to talk to you about Stella Mae Ragel. We'd like to do so in the privacy of your home, but if you wish to come to Knoxville PsyLED headquarters that can be arranged. However, it will be much more public. And you may not want that."

Over the doorbell speaker an elegant female voice said, "My lawyer will arrive in fifteen minutes. I've been instructed to tell you to wait outside unless you have a subpoena. Do you?"

"No, ma'am," I said. "No one in PsyLED wanted to make this public."

There was a silence, as if she was digesting my meaning, then she said, "My lawyer will come to the front door shortly. After she arrives, you will be invited in. Until then, please leave my property."

I turned and went back to the car. More slowly, FireWind followed. On the way, I not-so-accidentally dropped my cell phone onto the grass. I used the excuse to touch the grass and then push through to the ground beneath. No *death and decay*, just snobby grass that had started out as snobby sod.

We got in the car and FireWind touched the starter button. The air conditioner blasted in, though the day wasn't hot enough to need it. We waited for several silent minutes until my boss said, "What did you detect when you picked up your cell phone?"

"Not a thing. No *death and decay* there at all."

He made a little *hmmming* sound and tapped his fingers on

the steering wheel as he stared out the windshield, thinking. "I misspoke. I'm not certain I'll ever fit into this electronic world. I know about doorbell cameras and security systems, but I am still occasionally flummoxed by the swift pattern of changes and developments."

"Me too, and not because I've lived too long but because I lived off the grid for so long. Technology is confusing."

We exchanged wry smiles and drank water from bottles offered by FireWind. The water wasn't cold, but it wasn't hot either.

"You got any idea how the man drove the truck? The man who tried to kill me? That's magic, not electronics. And I still don't understand."

"No. T. Laine is working on discovering how it was accomplished. The four members of the local coven who helped on scene are joining her. They are all quite curious. One of them used the term *homunculus*."

I looked that up to discover that it was a small, artificially produced human sometimes grown in a flask. A manikin. Which made no sense at all, when looking at two dead men driving trucks.

"Of course, they also used the term *zombie*. They were brainstorming."

A black Lexus passed us, pulled into the Merriweathers' drive, and parked. A long, lean woman in a pencil-thin black suit got out and adjusted her sunglasses, staring at us. The stare went on a little too long before she strode to the house and entered.

"Interesting," FireWind said. And I had a feeling his *interesting* was of a sexual nature rather than an intellectual nature. FireWind liked strong women. And *that* was interesting to me. In a strictly intellectual capacity, of course. FireWind put a tiny device behind his ear and pressed an even smaller earpiece inside his ear canal. He said, "Testing. Do you copy? Excellent." He looked at me. "We have intel backup with Jones at HQ. If anything needs to be verified or researched on the fly, she will be able to do so."

More minutes passed. As we sat, a car pulled up behind us and parked. I had thought Occam was hyperaware, but my cat-man had nothing on FireWind, who went from relaxed to holding a weapon in about a quarter second. His eyes were on his rearview and the weapon vanished just as fast. I blinked, uncertain what I had just seen. "LaFleur," he said to me, casually, as if he hadn't just done a magician's parlor trick. He glanced at me and that almost-smile lit his face again and was gone as he turned off the car and reached for the door handle.

"You're playing games with me, ain'tcha?"

My boss halted his motion and turned his yellow eyes on me, an odd expression on his face. "Yes. I suppose I am. Oddly, I feel quite comfortable with you. I know that if I overstep my bounds you will tell me to my face." He breathed out through his nose, a short, sharp sound. "You remind me of my wife that way. She was a straight-speaking, strong woman too. So few people speak their minds, men or women. In another time and place, you and I might have been good friends."

"Ain't no reason we can't be friends now," I said, opening my door. "As long as we both remember there are specific boundaries on that friendship. Meaning that you can and will fire me if I mess up, and that I can't speak my mind in front of other people." I stopped, my legs and feet swiveled around to the grass where we had parked, my back to him. "Frankly I find that one sorta hard."

I had the pleasure of hearing FireWind's laughter as I stood and closed my door. Rick and Margot were already standing in the street and the looks they sent me, at the sound of FireWind's laughter, were priceless. I just shrugged, but I was sorta proud of making the big boss laugh. I had a feeling he didn't do that often.

Rick looked good, better than I had seen him in a long time, since I had helped to heal him of supernatural bindings. He stood tall and straight, and had put on weight that he sorely needed, in his shoulders and back and thighs. He had been working out. His white hair blew in the afternoon breeze, too long for regs, nearly at his collar. He looked older than before his trauma, but he had the perfect skin of a were-creature. Rick LaFleur was chick candy. Or maybe it was a chick magnet? One of those words. And he and Margot looked good together. Not romantic or as if they were in a relationship, but comfortable, which was good, since they were still dealing with the results of Margot becoming a black wereleopard in a freak shooting accident.

"Boss," I said softly.

"Nell," he said with a half smile. "I hear you've been doing good work."

A flush warmed my face, any color change hidden behind my tree-bark-toned skin. To cover my self-conscious reaction, I said, "Thanks. Full moon's coming in a few days. You two planning to hunt on my land?"

"If you and Soulwood permit. There's no finer hunting ground in the world."

I ducked my head in pleasure.

Rick turned his attention to our up-line boss.

"FireWind."

"LaFleur. You wrapped that case up quickly. No bloodshed, no collateral damage."

The four of us stood in the sun while the two male senior agents talked about the Chattanooga case, their backs to the Merriweather house. Margot and I were facing the house, standing side by side, listening, and I took the opportunity to study the probationary special agent. Margot Racer, formerly a special agent in the FBI, exuded self-assurance, a confidence I had never seen in women, especially not in any churchwomen. Her shoulders were back, her chin up, her eyes narrowed. Her dark skin glistened in the sunlight as if it was dusted with gold dust, and her buzzed short hair looked elegant and tough at once. She looked *badass*, a word I never associated with females but that certainly fit her. And fit Esther, though in a very different way. I would never be badass.

As I had hoped, some time spent with Rick, also a were-leopard, had helped Margot adjust to the loss of her humanity and the acquisition of a furry body during the full moon. When she and Rick had left for the case in Chattanooga, she had been grieving, often staring out the window, one arm hugging across herself, the other hanging to her side, too limp, her posture desultory. Grieving.

Grief was like living inside a weighted net, pulling you down. You could see out but not get away, not breathe freely, not . . . not live the life you once lived. I had grieved like that when Leah died, Leah who had been John's first wife and my friend. And then John had died. And though there had been no romantic love between us, I had grieved his loss as well. And I had been alone. I hadn't known how to help Margot, how to untangle the threads that trapped her, how to set her free, but the time spent with Rick had gone a long way to healing.

It made me want to cheer to see her back to her old self. Margot might be a probationary agent in PsyLED, but she would never be viewed by her coworkers as a probationary *anything*. Watching Margot, I stood straighter, as if a chain hauled the top of my head up several inches. I tilted my chin high. Narrowed my eyes. The posture changes made me feel more in control.

We were a strange grouping, confident Margot Racer with her glowing dark skin and elegant business suit, Rick LaFleur with his navy jacket and pants, black eyes, and startling white hair, and FireWind with his yellow eyes, black clothing, and long black braid. And ordinary-looking me with my fading red hair, greenish eyes, and clothes from Target. Even with my shoulders back I knew I looked dowdy standing next to the others. It wasn't a feeling I particularly liked.

I wondered if the churchwomen could make me some elegant suits. The thought was shocking. An almost violent collision between my two worlds.

At the house, the black-suited woman opened the door and stared us down. She didn't motion us forward so much as simply stand there and study us. I figured it was a power play of some sort. My stride long and sure, I walked around the jabbering men and up the walkway. I didn't look back, but I could feel them start after me. As I moved up the walk, I studied the lawyer, because that was surely what I faced. She was lean and muscular and exuded the same kind of power that Margot did.

I smiled a churchwoman smile as I walked up the three short steps, flipped open my ID, and turned on just a smidge of my church accent, along with a big smile. "Hey. I'm Special Agent Nell Ingram. I thank you for coming to protect the identity and juvenile record of your client. She'll need you."

The lawyer blinked in surprise. Point to me. She didn't know her client had once had another name and a juvenile criminal record.

I felt the others step onto the small porch behind me, and the lawyer, who regrouped quickly, said, "I'm Dominique Goode, Mrs. Merriweather's attorney. I understand that you do not have a warrant?"

"No, ma'am," I said, still churchy. "We'd rather not intrude too much on Mrs. Merriweather's life, and acquiring a warrant would make this public record instead of a nice private chat. She has a new name and a new reputation to uphold, after all."

The lawyer's expression didn't change at all this time, but I knew, just *knew*, that she hadn't known, still didn't know, about her client's past. I resisted looking at Margot to see if she had picked up on anything.

Goode said, "I advised my client against this interview, but you may come in. You may have half an hour of her time. You may ask questions. She may or may not respond. In most circumstances, I will be speaking for my client. There may be questions she does not wish to answer, and she will not do so. Is all this understood?"

"Pretty much," I said, stepping over the threshold. The client was standing in the hallway in a dim corner, a curvy, more mature version of the out-of-focus girl from the poly wedding and the photos of group sex. Her face looked fierce and tense and . . . guilty. No one had said I was lead on this interview, but I continued anyway. "But honestly, how can you answer any questions when you got no earthly idea about her name change and her juvenile criminal record?"

Racine/Cadence Merriweather went pale at my words and backed into the far room before she turned and ran down a hallway.

Ms. Goode stared me down. I smiled sweetly back at her. She pointed down the wide foyer hallway and said, "Sit. Do not roam." She followed her client.

I went down the hallway and into the main room. While the three other special agents gathered together and spoke in low voices, I looked around. The main room had ten-foot-tall ceilings with crisscrossed moldings all over, what they called coffered ceilings. The ceilings, moldings, and walls were painted in three warm neutral tones that were reflected in the couches and the chairs. There were hardwood floors everywhere I could see and fancy rugs. The décor was kept from being boring by a threadbare Persian-type rug that was probably ancient and expensive. To me it just looked as if it needed to be replaced. Despite its age, it was a pretty shade of faded fuchsia pink with mint green and pale blue, the deep pink tint picked up by throw pillows and two small chairs.

There were family photographs on the walls in groupings, a big painting of sunflowers, wild roses, and honeysuckle on the wall over a fireplace, and antique vases on the shelves of built-ins. The neutral couches were darker than the trim, and the back of the room was mostly windows that looked out on the water and a pool, which had to be new because it hadn't been in the satellite photos. Instead of sitting, as the lawyer instructed, I walked around the main room, taking in everything that could be taken in without touching anything. Taking surreptitious photos of the art and vases, the antique ones in particular. One of those voice-activated security systems was sitting on a table, so I didn't say anything aloud. There were no visible cameras, but security could be monitoring our every move, so no one overstepped a legal code of behavior and I kept my back to the security device while taking pictures of everything on the shelves and on the walls, thinking—knowing—they were important but unable to tell the others.

Sotto voce, FireWind said, "Ingram." When I got to the group he said, "Jones informs me that Mrs. Merriweather's personal checking account shows she wrote a ten-thousand-dollar check to a private security firm, the kind that does background checks and divorce investigations. On the same day, she wrote a similar check to Ms. Goode. This took place eight weeks past."

Before he could continue, Merriweather and Goode reappeared; they sat on the sofa that faced the room, and the lawyer pointed again at the sofa she wanted us to stuff ourselves on. It was too short, so I sat on a small pink chair, running my hand over the fancy upholstery. It was amazingly soft. I wondered how much it would cost to get my sofa covered in fabric like this, and then I wondered how hard it would be to keep clean of cat and dog hair. I sighed sadly.

My bosses and the probie took the sofa that had been pointed out to them, which left them facing the windows, squinting in the brightness. Ms. Goode was holding her mouth a little tighter than she had at the door, likely because her client had just revealed crucial info and the lawyer realized she was flying half-blind.

The special agents introduced themselves, all fancy-sounding titles, which did not seem to impress the lawyer at all.

When it came my turn, I said, "I really like this fabric."

The lawyer closed her eyes, either trying to keep from cussing me out, or praying for patience. I was betting on the cussing option. Rick LaFleur raised his brows, fighting a smile, Racer shook her head, and FireWind's eyes twinkled. "Special Agent Ingram, you have questions for Mrs. Merriweather?" he asked.

"A couple," I said. I wasn't a cat like Occam, but I had learned a lot about ambush hunting in Spook School and from my cat-man. I crossed my legs and my arms, elbows on my thighs, making myself look small, like a wereleopard on a limb. I leaned forward, staring at Merriweather. She was dressed in a bright shade of pink, almost matching the color of the rug. Her shoes were aqua, with pink bows on them. She'd never be able to walk very far or, say, work in her garden in the shoes, but they were pretty. "Can you tell us why you left the poly marriage with Connelly Darrow, Thomas Langer, Erica Lynn Quinton, Cale Nowell, Donald Murray Hampstead, and Stella Mae Ragel? You seemed happy in the photographs at the wedding ceremony. And now most of the poly marriage members are dead."

Merriweather closed her eyes and dropped her head.

Goode went dead quiet for a half beat too long. More gently than I might have expected, she said, "Cadence, does Luther . . . ?" She stopped and began again. "We can postpone this. I think we need to talk more thoroughly, just you and me, before you talk to the special agents."

"Why?" the CEO's wife asked. "They know. All these years, all the money to get away from it all, and it's out again. It's come back to haunt me." Eyes still closed, she leaned back against the sofa. Racine/Cadence looked as if she might cry, and I should have felt guilty, but I didn't, because there was something about her demeanor that was off somehow, and also familiar. Almost as if . . . as if she was manipulating, like a churchwoman who kept secrets and engineered situations and controlled people from the background, a back-stage conductor or puppeteer, pulling strings. I couldn't exactly put my finger on why I thought that, but it was there all the same.

"I was born Elizabeth Racine Alcock," she said. She sat up and her eyes found mine before dropping to her hands, folded in her lap. There was a huge, multidiamond set of rings on the left one and they glittered with white fire. As if the rings gave her strength, her tone altered, going from quiet to pedantic and unemotional in a single heartbeat. "I killed my high school assistant principal for attacking me. I was fourteen. No one wanted to believe he was a pedophile, even after more girls came forward. They blamed me and . . ." She took a breath as if it hurt to speak. "They sent me away. I served my time." Her tone said she had gone through hell doing that, but her words had hardened and she raised her eyes, looking from one to the other of us, staring us down.

"They sealed my records when I got out. I was eighteen and fresh out of juvie, back home and trying to find myself after all that had happened. A county councilman decided I was used goods and acceptable prey." She took an unsteady breath. "He accosted me in a parking lot. I knew I had to leave. I'd never be safe in Florida. So I stole Mama's cigarette and liquor money and got on a bus. I rode the bus until my money ran out in Tennessee. At a local diner, I ran into Stella and her friends. They bought me a burger. They took me in, no questions asked."

Cadence Merriweather's eyes were fierce and I understood how she had survived all that had happened to her. "There was an acceptance in Stella's group that I had never experienced before. It was recognition, approval, and tolerance. It was this amazing . . . joy." The fierceness faded and she smiled, but the happiness of the memory didn't last. "But things didn't stay the same after the ceremony. Or maybe I grew past the need for what they offered, I don't know. Things got messy. People started pairing off more. Jealousy started to be a problem. There was this one big argument, I don't even remember what it was about now. But I packed up and left the group. Then Donnie left too, heading north. I went east, to Knoxville."

It must have been a pretty big argument and very traumatic, I thought. Stella Mae had erased her name and most of her images from the photo album. That suggested strong feelings.

"I worked two jobs. I changed my name legally to Cadence Blue Thompkins because I thought it sounded artsy and I wanted to be an artist." She glanced at the sunflower, rose, and honeysuckle panting on the wall.

"I took online classes and when I graduated, I went to work

for a small shop in town. They let me hang my paintings on the walls. I met my husband, who had just graduated from Duke. He was this big, brawny, earnest, energetic man who said all the right things and pushed all the right buttons. I fell in love, we married, and I became Cadence Blue Thompkins Merriweather." She took a breath. "I haven't seen or talked to Stella or any of the others in years. But I knew when I heard about the deaths that you might find me." She looked at Goode, her expression a little guilty. "Sorry I didn't tell you."

Margot said, "Do you want to reconsider part of that? Everything you told us was mostly the truth until the last part." Margot smiled and leaned in. Margot knew truth or lie, a gift from the witch blood that ran in her family. She couldn't do magic for nothing, but she could sure 'nuff sniff out falsehood. "The part that said you hadn't seen or talked to Stella or the others. That wasn't the truth." Margot looked at her tablet as if checking notes, and back up, focusing on the lawyer. "Ms. Dominique Goode, of Goode Law Firm. You specialize in divorce. So, let's start back at the part about not talking to Stella and move to the part about the divorce."

Goode stood up. "That will be all for today. I know you have questions and we will provide answers. Perhaps it would be best to provide them in writing, rather than stress my client. She isn't well. I'll be talking to my client and be in touch." She pointed at the door.

I got up and left the room, back out into the cool bright sun of autumn. After a while the others followed. Back at the cars, FireWind spoke, his voice far too soft to be anything but a threat. "Perhaps we should have discussed who was lead in this interview."

I pulled my phone. "Remember in Stella Mae's room, when you told me about the tea set you got for your wife in St. Louis?"

"San Francisco."

"Okay." I'd never been to either place and where he'd bought the tea set didn't matter. "You recognized the vase in Stella's bedroom because of that trip, right?"

"Yes," he said, his voice sounding more normal and curious. "It was a Roseville piece. Sunflower pattern."

I held out my cell, with the photos I had taken of the objects on the shelves. Centered in the rows of shelves were three vases, two short, one tall. All three were sunflower pattern vases; one was an exact match for the one in Stella's room. The one with the small card that said "I love you," with a date only a few months past. "The painting had her name on it and the sunflower on it is an exact match for the vases."

"LaFleur, will you please read the house with the psymeter?" FireWind asked. "Racer, schedule an appointment with Ms. Goode and Mrs. Merriweather at HQ for this evening. Or we will get a paper and pick up her lying client. In handcuffs for all the neighbors to see."

"Yes, sir," she said. Walking briskly, Racer went to the front door. Rick went to his car and opened the trunk. That left FireWind and me alone.

He said, "Good work, Ingram. Is that why you took lead?"

"No. Ms. Goode had her walls up against professional questions, and especially against good-looking men, but she didn't have them up against a little country hick chick like me." I grinned.

"Country hick chick?"

"That's what JoJo calls me sometimes. I kinda like it. And just so you know, Mrs. Merriweather wears the exact same shade of pink of all the clothes I saw on the floor of Stella Mae's bedroom before someone cleaned it up."

Only minutes later Rick returned and said, "No indication of death magics, but I could hear Margot talking to Goode. By her tone of voice, that woman is not happy with her client or with us."

Margot, who walked up on his heels, said, "You got that right. But we have an appointment in two hours with Goode and Merriweather at HQ."

Rick frowned. "Two hours? That's awfully fast. Why not wait until morning? Get a chance to put together her story. Prep her client."

"Because she bargained with us. We've agreed to not obtain warrants for her home and her husband's business, or a subpoena for her client," Margot said. She looked at FireWind and her full lips widened. She looked a little wicked. "She suggested that she wanted only you at the interview. Not me, because I must be some kind of paranormal, and not Nell because she is, and I quote, 'an obnoxious child.'"

FireWind laughed softly. "Let's get back to HQ and prep. I

hate to throw you two directly from an out-of-town case and into a new one, but I need you."

"You couldn't care less about throwing us into another case," Margot said. She tapped her nose. "Truth-senser, here."

"True. I was trying for polite," FireWind said, his tone droll. "We'll meet you at HQ."

SIXTEEN

I didn't much like being called an obnoxious child by a powerful woman. My method had worked, but I needed to alter the way I approached females like the lawyer Goode. That would take some cogitating that I didn't have time for just now.

FireWind and Margot sat across the table from Goode and her client. Racine/Cadence had changed clothes and was wearing black jeans and a white T-shirt, with sneakers. Her dress and her body language were very different from the cowed woman we had met at the Merriweather home. Either that woman had been a fake or she had metamorphosed like a phoenix from the ashes in just a couple of hours.

Rick, Occam, Tandy, and I were crowded into the small cubicle behind the new observation mirror. I glanced side-eyed at Rick and Occam and they seemed fine together, no cat disharmonies, which I figured was a good thing. Unit Eighteen hadn't had a standard interview room until recently. Previously we had just used the cameras in the null room, but that room was being saved for UTMC patients and to decontaminate evidence from death energies, so the new interrogation room was getting its first workout.

"I specified only Special Agent FireWind for this interview," Goode said, in an opening salvo.

"If Special Agent Racer leaves, this interview is ended. We then proceed with a warrant for Mrs. Merriweather's home, and this becomes much more invasive," FireWind said, his voice without inflection. "Luther Merriweather would likely discover just how close to separation and divorce he is. And why." It was a baiting technique. None of us knew for certain Racine/Cadence was looking to leave her husband, but hiring a PI and a divorce lawyer was a good indicator.

Goode narrowed her eyes at him.

Margot said, "This interview is being video recorded." She gave everyone's name and the date and time. "Now. Mrs. Merriweather. When did you resume the affair with Stella Mae Ragel?" She pushed the small card from Stella's bedside across the table to the suspect.

Racine/Cadence stared at the card, emotions rushing across her face too quickly to read. She looked at her lawyer and Goode nodded permission.

"I ran into Stella Mae in an antiques shop in Nashville, in December," Cadence said. She leaned in and put her folded hands on the tabletop. She was no longer wearing the glittering diamond rings. There was an indention and a white line where they had rested for so long. "My marriage was disintegrating. My life was falling apart. Seeing Stella was like a lifeline." She smiled sadly. "Things went fast after that."

"True," Tandy murmured.

Racine/Cadence admitted that she and Stella Mae had been involved. Meaning they had been having an affair when Stella was not on the road. Things had been getting serious. Racine/Cadence had decided to leave her big-money, deep-pockets CEO husband and had begun divorce arrangements. She had him followed by a private detective for the weeks when the tour took place. There was significant photographic evidence that the CEO was cheating on his not-so-devoted but much-more-discreet wife with three mistresses in three cities. There was an evidence trail for dinners, hotels, gifts, and flowers, none of which had been given to his wife.

Ms. Goode said, "Let me make it clear to you all. Mrs. Merriweather stood to make millions off a very nasty divorce and had no reason to kill Stella Mae Ragel. My client is not a witch or a magic user, or a paranormal of any kind. Her intent was to divorce, take her share of the proceeds, and move in with Stella Mae. They were in love and planning a future together."

"True, not true," Tandy said. "Things hidden and things not said."

I remembered four pages of Stella's lovers, given to Occam and me at Stella's kitchen bar, and figured Racine/Cadence had no idea that Stella had been seeing other people. And Cadence's name hadn't been on the cat-paper lists. Secrets all around. I watched as FireWind tilted his head, his long braid sliding across his back, letting the silence build in the room. His tone ever so slightly disbelieving, he said, "Mrs. Merriweather. Considering your shared history, I find it highly unlikely that you were unaware Stella Mae Ragel was sharing her bed and body with others in her band, including Catriona Doyle and members of the original poly marriage, Thomas Langer and Cale Nowell specifically. Possibly even Erica Lynn Quinton and Connelly Darrow, among others."

"No," she whispered. "No. Stella said . . ." Cadence fell silent and her face paled. She blinked several times and looked down, staring at her naked finger, her breath shallow and too fast. Tears gathered in her eyes. Her lawyer glared at FireWind, who stared back at her unperturbed.

"She didn't know," Tandy said. "She is . . . pained."

I crossed my arms over my middle, trying to put it all together and also grieving with Cadence. She had been through so much in her life, had lost so much. Since Stella Mae died, she had been grieving the loss of her lover, added to the loss of her current life and husband, and now she was grieving the betrayal of Stella sleeping with others. Again.

But life had given Cadence Merriweather a backbone of steel and her tears dried quickly. She said, "Stella sleeping with other people was what drove the wedge between us back in the commune. Even then, I wanted a monogamous relationship. I wanted Stella all to myself and Stella . . ." She took a steadying breath. "Stella wasn't interested in monogamy. I guess she wasn't interested now either."

Tandy murmured, "Truth."

Something about the sequence of events and the intertwined relationships seemed . . . incomplete. My thoughts wandering, I watched the woman in the interview room. While she was holding herself together, Racine/Cadence was also floundering. It made me want to offer the peace of Soulwood to her, but I was afraid the vampire tree might take her instead.

"My client also has been blackmailed by a former commune member," Goode said, "threatening to go to her husband with details about Cadence's previous life unless payments continued

under the table. His name is Hugo Ames." She slid a folded
piece of paper across the table to FireWind. "His contact information."

FireWind opened the paper and nodded, passing it to Margot. "Will your client be bringing charges against Ames?"

"Yes, as soon as the separation from her husband is legally
formalized. My only purpose in giving you the information is
candor and transparency. And the slight possibility that if he
was blackmailing Cadence, he was also involved with the murders." Her tone was hopeful and the glint in her eyes suggested
she wanted to see him stretched on the rack for punishment if
possible.

Cadence told her interviewers everything, monitored by
Margot in the interrogation room and by Tandy, Rick, and Occam in the equipment room with me, watching. As part of not
pursuing an investigation into Cadence Merriweather (though
the bargain hadn't been stated so bluntly) PsyLED was provided
full financial records, including a list of businesses owned all or
in part by the CEO husband, who was now a person of interest,
if not an outright suspect, because he had stood to lose millions
if his wife had divorced him for the murder victim. If he knew
about Cadence's affair or thought that she knew about his, that
would give him more motives to commit crimes. FireWind was
also informed that any further harassment of Goode's client
would result in legal consequences.

Rick and Tandy slipped out of the observation room during
the game of 3D legal chess, the main participants claiming territory and threatening each other. I was still thinking. "Occam?
Was Stella trying to put the original poly marriage back together?"

He slid his eyes to me. They looked greenish in the odd
lighting. "Not just the original version. FireWind thinks she
wanted a houseful of partners, some new, some old. Check this
morning's summation."

I frowned and pulled up the summation, scanning it fast.
Then I skimmed through the pics of all the injured and dead.
They all fell into a similar age range and they were all attrac-
tive, single people. "Was she having an affair with Monica
Belcher too? And what about Verna Upton, the housekeeper?"

Occam gave a half smile, watching the people on the other side of the window wrap up the interview. "Yes, she was, Nell, sugar. Does that creep you out?"

"Creep me—" I tapped on his shoulder.

He didn't turn to me, but his smile did widen.

"Occam. Let me be perfectly clear. I am not offended or emotionally distressed about the lifestyle of these people. I may not like looking at photographs of a bed full of naked people, but I am not a prude."

He laughed. "Oh, Nell, sugar." Occam's eyes captured mine, and he put his hands on my shoulders, massaging them with his fingers. The stiff ones felt weaker than the others, but they were warm and my tension slid away. "I don't think you're a prude. In fact, I know from very pleasurable personal experience that you are not a prude. But in a lot of ways you are god-awful innocent. You're still kind and compassionate and virtuous and—" He stopped, as if trying to decide to say the next part. I scowled at him. "And a little naïve," he finished.

I huffed at him. "I am not naïve."

"Not about humans, no. But about sex, yes. You are. If this had been a man having sex with all the females, you'd have understood it perfectly. But it's a woman having sex with all the men and all the women, and that fights against your upbringing." He leaned and kissed me on the forehead, like he might a child. Without another word, Occam left me alone in the observation room. Which was probably a good thing, because I was irked. Very irked. Maybe even riled. Because I thought I had hidden it so well.

Goode and the grieving Mrs. Merriweather left HQ and I left the observation room.

Back in my cubicle I opened the files Jo had scanned and downloaded to us from the Merriweather financial records and began comparing information. And I found something that inserted a lot of questions into Cadence Merriweather's sworn interview. But . . . did my discovery mean that Cadence had successfully lied, perhaps by omission, to Margot Racer?

I stood from my office chair and carried my tablet to the conference room, where FireWind, Rick, Margot, and JoJo were discussing the case. FireWind was standing in the doorway, a cup of coffee in his hand, his crisp shirt blinding white in the bright lights. As I walked up the hallway, he stopped in midsentence and turned to me. "Ingram. You have something?"

"Some of the companies that the Merriweathers own are listed solely in Cadence's name," I said.

"Of course," FireWind said. "There can be tax benefits to putting some businesses under one name."

I said, "Cadence Merriweather owns forty-nine percent of the silk-screen-printing business that handles Stella Mae's promotional merchandise. Merry Promotions, and by extension, Cadence, made the T-shirts in the box at Melody Horse Farm. She said she ran into Stella Mae at an antiques store. But she's had a business connection to her for over two years. And the person who owns fifty-one percent? Is a man named Hugo Ames."

Rick whispered a soft curse. JoJo started pounding on her keyboards.

I said, "Hugo knows Cadence and is blackmailing her. And Hugo knew Stella Mae. But Cadence might not know Hugo was doing business with Stella."

FireWind asked, "Why didn't she tell us that? Did she lie by omission?"

Margot said, "No. No way. There was not one single hint of a lie in that woman."

FireWind started to speak and Margot interrupted. "Not one hint."

FireWind held up a hand as if to stop a possible tirade. Margot glared at him. "I am not saying you were wrong, Racer. We can't assume that Cadence knew Merry Promotions' connection to Stella Mae Ragel's death, because we haven't released that information to the press. If her husband set up the business arrangements, she might not even have known she owned the business. It happens. We need a subpoena for Merry Promotions. We need to work this by the book."

"Or," I said, "Hugo was blackmailing Cadence about her past life in return for money poured into the business, money Hugo took out. Like money laundering."

"Hugo is our linchpin," Rick said, dropping to a chair and pulling his laptop to him. "He knew everyone."

JoJo muttered, "We told Goode there would be no interference in her client's life. We signed papers drawn up by a very expensive, very astute, very unhappy lawyer."

"But if Luther Merriweather had figured out that his devoted wife was in the process of a legal separation and wanted to point a finger at his bride, what better way than to use her business. I'll contact Goode," FireWind said, "and find out if Mrs. Merriweather knew she owned the business that provided promotional merchandise for her lover. And I'll ask if the blackmail against her client involved money poured into the business. Jones, facilitate subpoenas into the company's financial records and Hugo's financial records. The rest of you, gear up. We need to raid Merry Promotions before anyone can destroy any evidence."

As we changed clothes, and checked weapons, ammo, null pens, comms equipment, psy-meters, and vests, JoJo created a timeline on Luther Merriweather's travel, based on his business credit card expenses. Luther was in Nashville the week the T-shirt box was delivered to the horse farm owned by Stella Mae, and Nashville was only a short drive away. But Luther was a big guy, six feet, two inches, two hundred forty pounds. We had video of the delivery and the person was shorter, stout, and the body mechanics looked female. Luther Merriweather did not deliver anything to Stella Mae's farm.

However, Hugo Ames, the blackmailer, was smaller, knew about Cadence's and Stella's past lives, and he lived close enough to Stella's to have made the delivery.

Jo also checked into Cadence's whereabouts that week. Mrs. Merriweather was in Atlanta with two friends from her church, attending a play and a concert and shopping. She flew both ways and spent a fortune. It was possible for her to drive to Tennessee and make a delivery, but it was extremely unlikely.

T. Laine initiated a background check on witches in the Merriweather family history and, according to all publicly listed (and some private) witch bloodline sites, there was nothing. As she put it, on paper Luther was a plain old vanilla human and so was his wife, Cadence.

JoJo worked like a fiend while we geared up and found proof that Hugo had been part of the commune, though not part of the poly marriage. And Hugo's mom was a single mother. He took her last name. The Ames family had produced a line of witch blood, until the 1850s when it died out. Had it come back in some strange manner in Hugo?

When I was as ready as I could be, I stopped by the conference room and Jo handed me a burner cell. "Turn on your church-speak, country hick chick, call Merry Promotions, and ask to speak to Hugo. See if you can find where he is today."

I turned the small flip phone over in my hands and thought how I would handle this call. Why did it have to be in church-speak? Was church-speak becoming a crutch for me? Would Margot or Goode use a crutch when there might be another way? I had been undercover once for a few minutes. I was more than a churchwoman.

JoJo slid a scrap of paper across the conference desk to me. On it was a phone number and the words *Merry Promotions*.

I dialed the number. A woman answered with the words, "Merry Promotions, how can I help you?"

I remembered how the lawyer Goode had spoken and took a slow breath, lowered my voice, and said, "This is Maggie Jones, Loretta Hopkins' business manager. Put Hugo on."

"I'm sorry. Mr. Ames isn't in today," the woman on the other end said cautiously.

"What? Where's Hugo?" I demanded. "He was supposed to meet me an hour ago. He isn't answering his cell, texts, or e-mail. I don't have time to keep sitting around waiting on him. Does Merry Promotions want the swag contract on Loretta's next three tours or not?"

"Loretta Hopkins . . . Oh my God. He was supposed to meet you?"

"He *was*," I said stiffly. "Where is he?"

"We don't . . . I'm sorry. We don't know. He left early yesterday, not feeling well. We can't get in touch with him either."

"Oh." I hesitated and let my voice fall into worried tones. "Have you called the police? The local hospitals?"

"No, I—"

"Never mind." I hung up.

"Who are you and how did you get into Nell's head?" JoJo asked, her eyebrows trying to meet in the middle and a fist on her hip.

I grinned, my shoulders back, my head held high. "That was fun. He isn't at the shop. Went home sick yesterday."

Occam was standing at the door, his eyes on me, warm and full of approval. "That was amazing, Nell, sugar. Come on. We're raiding Hugo Ames' home and business at the same time. Rick and Margot are leading a team on Merry Promotions. We'll be at his house with T. Laine. We need to hit the road first because we have an RVAC to launch and look over the house. FireWind will be staged at the Campbell County Sheriff's Department, halfway between the two locations, running the show with local LEOs."

I handed the small cell back to JoJo, picked up my gear, weapon, and the potted cabbage at my cubby. As I followed Occam down the stairs, I called Esther to let her know I'd be late. Everything I could control was in place and managed, and I could turn my attention to the coming raid, which was in Crossville, on the I-40 corridor between Knoxville and Cookeville. All the crime scenes seemed to be along the interstate, no outlying towns. That made Merry Promotions close enough to deliver, but not expensive to ship to Stella's studio. Merry Promotions could easily have delivered a late box of tour T-shirts, though who then set up the trigger was still an unknown.

According to the sat photos and files Jo had sent to everyone's tablets, Crossville was in Cumberland County, which meant integrating into this case even more people we hadn't worked with before, but at least it wasn't so far away.

Like a lot of homes in the area, Ames' rental house was isolated, at the end of a quarter-mile-long, two-rut gravel drive. We planned to approach from the north, along the next street over, from an overgrown lot with a vacant trailer, but when we arrived, we found the front half of the lot had been cleared and planted with a garden. The lack of rain hadn't done the garden much good, and the plants looked stressed and ragged. The trailer home looked worse as we pulled around behind it. It had to be sixty years old, the metal a faded blue, windows busted. Household furniture was in a pile out back and critters were using it as a home. When I opened my door, the air stank of garbage and dead animals, but with the cars behind the trailer, we couldn't be seen from the road, giving us privacy to work.

A sheriff's deputy car pulled in behind us, but the deputy

didn't get out, leaving his engine running, which contributed to the miasma of stinks, so I ignored him.

We had done this sort of prep work for a raid often and there was little need for instructions or chitchat between us. FireWind, however, was full of suggestions to both teams and was in communication with the locals too. While we worked, I turned off the main comms channel and concentrated on the para freq, the frequency used by PsyLED.

Occam got the remote-viewing aircraft checked out in record time and the deputy assigned to us finally got out of his vehicle. He joined us at the laptop to view the aerial footage. Deputy Robb was male, about my height, slender, muscular, didn't talk much, and asked no questions about the equipment or the proceedings. I went back to the general frequency when the RVAC took off, its multiple little rotors spinning too fast to see. The laptop screen showed the trees and nearby houses as it gained altitude. Occam adjusted its direction, his hands maneuvering the small craft with multiple trackballs and levers on a handheld device. "Okay," Occam said softly. "Let's see what's happening at Hugo Ames' place."

Less than five hundred feet away, the view of Hugo's home wasn't what we had been hoping for. The RVAC camera sent back a steady camera footage of dead trees, dead bushes, dead grass, and a dog lying in the backyard. Occam guided the RVAC closer to see that the dog was dead and oozing green goo. The deputy swore softly, leaning in to get a better vantage.

T. Laine said, "Increase altitude. We don't know how high the *death and decay* reaches. You don't want to damage the RVAC."

Occam maneuvered the RVAC higher and circled the house from a good hundred feet up.

Over our earbuds, FireWind, who was viewing the video in real time too, said, "Bring the RVAC home. Move to the Ames' house. Dress out in P3Es. Approach the house. Read it on the psy-meter 2.0. We'll adjust our strategy after we know more. We are moving in now on Merry Promotions. Hold." We heard a click, a silence that lasted for ten seconds or so, and another click as Occam guided the RVAC back to us. "The portable null is on the way from UTMC with two paramedics, but it is a good hour behind you if traffic is good. Turn on vest cams. Stay alert."

We drove to Ames' house, easing down his bumpy, potholed gravel drive until the house came into sight. I pulled in behind Occam and T. Laine, all of us parking far from the house, in an area still green and alive. When I got out, there was no noise, no birdsong, no dogs barking in the distance. Occam's nose wrinkled at the faint stink of death hanging on the still air. The house might have been pretty once, cedar siding, painted shutters, cedar shake roof; now it was falling apart, the siding brittle gray, shakes falling off, paint curling from the trim. The trees and shrubs all around the house were dead. Three dead male cardinals lay in the front yard, their bright red plumage the only spots of color. Even without reading the property with the psymeter, it was clear that we had found *death and decay* in an advanced state. The deputy's car backed away and disappeared. I didn't blame him.

"Levels?" FireWind asked over the para freq.

Occam read the property with the psy-meter 2.0 and said, "Off the charts. Redlined. This is a stronger *death and decay* or it's been going longer than at Stella Mae's farm."

"Merry Promotions said Hugo was at work yesterday," I said. "And if he killed Stella, why is his place falling apart? And . . ." I fell silent. There were too many variables and nothing made sense.

"Kent. How do you want to handle it?" FireWind asked.

"Want?" T. Laine asked, sounding bitter. "I want to sit the grand pooh-bahs of the Witch Council of the United States of America down and compel them to design and fabricate a major-class *nullification* working to defeat this—this stuff." I had a feeling she wanted to use stronger words but had managed not to. "A major *nullification* working needs to be a priority. But that isn't gonna happen, ever, because, one, they don't like me, and two, no witch is going to create a true antimagic working for fear it will be used against them. And three, they aren't going to listen to anyone in law enforcement anyway, not with the antiwitch bent of most law enforcement types for, say, the last two millennia. Other than that? I want us to go in, in case there are people in there who happen to be alive."

"Copy," FireWind said, his tone unchanged.

We stepped forward, onto the crunchy grass, and stopped. The sound of field boots on the lawn was odd, unfamiliar. I leaned down and touched a pinkie to a single blade of grass. The cold of *death and decay* cut through my finger. I rose up quickly and took a step back. The grass leaf crumpled. The lawn beneath us was still green, but it was dead, as if the leaves hadn't yet figured out they had been killed.

"Move the cars back fifty feet," T. Laine said, her voice tight. As the unit's witch, she had been going almost nonstop, burning her candle from both ends, and not getting anywhere. This had to feel as if she needed to cut her candle in two and burn it at four ends just to keep up with the bodies and the spread of the *death and decay.* As we all reentered our cars and pulled them to safety, T. Laine spoke into her mic. "FireWind. We won't be wearing vest cams or electronics. I don't think they'll hold up to the energies here."

"Copy that," he said back. "Limited exposure. An hour in the portable null room after."

"Copy," T. Laine said.

T. Laine called the North Nashville coven to come deactivate the working. Knoxville was closer, but the local covens would take a lot of hand-holding to be able to shield the energies and that was if the coven leader bothered to answer when we called her. The four witches who had helped out at the coffee shop were disinclined to work on *death and decay* again.

T. Laine slammed her ID, badge, and vest cam into the trunk of her car, where they clattered. She raised her arms and gripped the trunk lid over her head, her face hidden by her arms. Her clothes were fresh and clean, but her skin was sallow and tired; exhaustion molded every line of her body. I could hear her breathing, anger in each breath until they slowed into a controlled pattern. She dropped her arms and went back to work. To us, she said, "Put all electronics aside, no jackets, badges, or IDs. Dress out in spelled unis, goggles, masks, gloves, no comms equipment. Vests are our only protective gear. And, God help me, no weapons."

Over comms FireWind asked, "Why no weapons?"

"Accidental discharge," she snarled, "as they and the ammo fall apart. Our suspect was at work yesterday. Alive. I didn't think about it at the horse farm, but weapons might be affected by the energies. And the chance of there being anyone alive enough to shoot at us is nil so we don't need weapons anyway."

Occam said, "I'm carrying a knife, but it won't do jack against a dead body guided by a necromancer."

There was an odd silence over the earbuds. "Copy," our boss said. "Keep me advised."

Moments later, every bit of our skin was covered; null pens were in our pockets. Eyes visible above the masks but behind goggles, we exchanged fast, silent looks of . . . that odd expression law enforcement and military exchange before potential trouble. It was part determination, part mental preparedness, part encouragement, saying things without speech, the way a good team could. Warnings, reminders, and promises to make it out okay.

T. Laine said, "This will be a deliberate clearing, victim rescue but no retrieval, non-suspect-based only. Touch nothing. Get in and get out. Fast."

Occam and I nodded and followed our witch to the door to raid the house, though it was more like a slow, steady advance, up several brick stairs that shifted with our weight. The mortar was dusty and crumbling. T. Laine knocked. Called out, "PsyLED! Open—"

The door dropped. Toward us.

We jumped back. The door landed with a clatter and splintered into a pile.

A blast of fetid air swept out.

Moving slowly, stepping over the busted door, we entered. Staggered positions. Careful to keep a safe distance between us for two reasons: so our weight didn't bring down the floor, and so an ambush shooter would be unlikely to hit us all at once. My breath came fast, my fingers tingling. I had no weapon. No weapon except the earth, and I couldn't touch it even if I had wanted to, not with *death and decay* everywhere.

It was hot, stuffy, and dark. Shadows wavered through the goggles like the tattered remains of ghosts. The ceiling had partially caved in. Wallboard was sifting down, onto the carpet, which was dusting away. Everything was disintegrating.

Hugo Ames, or so I assumed, was sitting in a recliner in the front room, facing a TV that had fallen off the wall. He was a slimy bubbling decaying thing, left fingers on the floor near his chair, right fingers in his lap, all detached from his hands. His eyes were slimed, his mouth open, jaw tilted to the side, rotten teeth visible. His ears were drooping, the lobes hanging like so much melted wax. As I watched, a green bubble extended from his mouth as if he were breathing. It popped. Another expanded in the cavity behind it. My stomach heaved.

As my daddy often said, he was *dead* dead, as if certain kinds of death made people more dead than others. Hugo was *very* dead and appeared to have been dead for a while, though the curse would keep us from establishing an estimated time of death.

"Get out as fast as you can," T. Laine reminded, her voice tight.

Moving carefully to keep from crashing through the floor, which was dissolving as fast as Hugo, we cleared the house in record time, Occam taking photographs on a cheap disposable camera that no one would miss if it was destroyed by the death energies. There were no more bodies, either alive to rescue, or dead to not retrieve. We eased out, staggered egress to prevent us falling through, and rushed back to our cars. "Clear," T. Laine said, her voice too loud and stressed. "Accessing comms."

The stench clung to my uni, to my mask, and even when I yanked off the P3E, the reek was still a part of me. I felt as if I'd never be clean again. I put in my earbud and heard FireWind speaking over the freq channel. "—have just spoken to the newly elected leader of the Witch Council of the United States of America. She has agreed that this *death and decay*, though not a witch working, is a type of spell against humans, and therefore falls under the category of workings which they do and will police. They have agreed to assist in capturing and punishing the magic practitioner who set *death and decay* in motion. They have null room prisons in New Orleans that are better equipped to handle such a magic user than anything we have here."

"How did you get them to cooperate?" T. Laine asked.

"That is a story for another time," he said. "For now, I want you all away from the house until we determine the next course of action. Come back to the city PD and sit in the portable null room."

"Copy," T. Laine said. "But we need to get a coven to sit a circle around Hugo Ames' house pronto and put a shield around the *death and decay*. It's already spread and it's working faster than the others. I can't promise that it can be contained. If it reaches bedrock or a water table, we're screwed."

"Noted," FireWind said. "I'll make some calls."

The null room was boring, but there was a box of donuts and three sandwiches on the table inside and the chairs were more comfortable than my previous experience. We also had Wi-Fi and chargers for our electronics so we could write our reports, work, eat, and get nullified all at once. Nullify. A good word for the process.

While we were in the portable null room trailer, Rick sent us a group text. I had missed my boss, or at least missed his input to cases. He didn't go around with a stick up his backside like some bosses. His text said, *County records: Hugo's landlady lives near his house. When you get nullified, go talk to her.*

"No rest for the wicked," T. Laine said. She stretched her shoulders as if she wanted her shoulder blades to touch. She looked more and more tired. Yet there was a softness there that I hadn't noticed while we were facing danger. And she was wearing a thin gold bracelet that was new. "Pretty bracelet," I said.

T. Laine blushed and, attempting to sound offhand and casual, said, "Gonzales got it for me." She held it out and I saw the five small green stones.

"Emeralds?" Emeralds were expensive.

"Yeah," she said, her voice and expression going soft. "The card said, 'Emeralds are called the Stones of Successful Love.'" She looked from the bracelet to me. "And flowers. Every week, he sends me flowers. I never had a man send me flowers before. He sent me a gift certificate for a massage. Can you believe it? A massage! What kind of guy thinks about that?"

A second text came through, this one from FireWind. *La-Fleur and Racer's raid on Merry Promotions discovered that all boxes of T-shirts ordered for the tour were shipped before the tour. No one knows about a box delivered later, though one employee thinks there were overruns, none of which can be*

*found. It is still feasible that Hugo applied magical energies to
a box of shirts, delivered them after the start of the music tour,
and set up the trigger when he positioned them in the swag
room, then accidentally contaminated himself. However, all
records indicate he never displayed the faintest hint of magic,
and the figure delivering the shirts appears much smaller than
Hugo's records indicate.*

All of which meant that Hugo, despite blackmailing one of
Stella Mae's lovers, was looking less likely to be Stella's killer.
We were back to square one.

An hour, a lot of paperwork, and a delicious sandwich later, we
met briefly with FireWind and Racer, who had taken off her
business jacket. Without the extra padding, she looked as if she
had lost weight. She was razor-thin, a long, lean, muscular
woman. I knew I didn't need to join a gym to work out, but seeing her made me want to plow the garden or cut some wood. It
was a quick meeting and we headed out to Hugo's landlady's
house.

I strapped into my vehicle and reached for the start button.
Occam, his long legs in tight black denim, got in beside me and
placed the potted cabbage on his lap. "You okay, Nell, sugar?"

I tapped the car on and fiddled with the mirrors, thinking. "I
know we've talked about this, but how did you adapt to becoming and being a wereleopard? Emotionally."

Occam shrugged. "Children are adaptable. I was a rowdy
boy one day and then I was a cat in a cage in a traveling carni-
val. I didn't shift back, so I didn't have a human brain or human
grief patterns for twenty years or so. I know you're still worried
about Margot, but she smells fine. She's adjusting to the effects
the moon has on were-creature minds and bodies and spirits.
And she isn't alone." He didn't add, "Like I was." He wouldn't
appreciate my pity, any more than Margot would.

"Have you three adapted to being a . . . a mini leap of
leopards?"

Occam chuffed, much like his cat might. "We drew a little
less blood last full moon. Our cats will work it out." He glanced
at me and said, "Don't you worry your purdy li'l head about all
that."

"Worry my—*humph*. Put on your seat belt, cat-man," I said, my voice a little too gruff. "I know you could survive a car crash by shifting into your leopard form, but there would still be blood all over my new upholstery."

Giving me a scar-twisted grin, Occam strapped in. I started the car and pulled in behind T. Laine, following her to a house near Hugo's place, a cute stone cottage that, from the outside, looked like four rooms, a front porch with stone arches, and a screened porch on one side.

A woman came out on the front porch and watched as we parked and walked to her. She was smoking, a cigarette in the corner of her mouth. "I reckon you folks are here about the roadblock. What's ol' Hugo done now? Pissed off the sheriff? Run his mouth to the judge about paying alimony? Shouldn'ta been banging that li'l college girl, her and them dang horses."

College girl? Horses?

The old woman laughed, her little belly bouncing. She looked to be in her mideighties, with skinny legs and ankles, a neck that was all tendons pulling up her chest and shoulders as she breathed. She was wearing a cotton dress in a tiny green plaid and a red wig that looked as if rats had nested in it. White curls stuck out at the back of the wig as if trying to escape. Her skin had a yellowed look, as did the whites of her eyes, and she had a belly shape that I thought might come from drinking. The reek of cigarettes and strong liquor wafted to us on the air. "Man can't keep it in his pants, he deserves to pay alimony for a couple years. Right?"

We didn't answer, just slowed our steps as we reached the porch.

"Honest to God," she went on, "that man can be sweet as pie, but when he gets something in his teeth it's either dangerous or stupid. And boinking that girl was stupid."

T. Laine said, "I'm Special Agent T. Laine Kent, PsyLED. These are Special Agents Ingram and Occam. Are you Ethel Myer, landlady to Hugo Ames?"

"No foreplay? Yeah. I'm Ethel. And before you ask, no, you can't come in unless you got a paper. So talk."

"Fine," T. Laine said. "What can you tell us about Hugo?"

"Only what the whole county knows. Everything he says is a lie. His wife kicked his ass out four months ago for diddling

around. He rents month by month. He likes sports twenty-four/
seven and Bud Lite by the case. Whole city knows he'll screw
anything that walks on two legs, but I wouldn't limit it to that
criteria. He owns that business that makes bowling trophies. He
was born and raised in the county." She smiled widely, showing
surprisingly healthy teeth. "His mother is Tina Ames."

The way she said *Ames* suggested something different and
derogatory. T. Laine's body tightened, almost imperceptibly.
"We've heard things about the family," she said.

"Shoulda. Most folks around here is good God-fearing
Christians. The Ameseses," she said, adding syllables, "are different." She hesitated and dug in a pocket. Occam and T. Laine
nearly drew their weapons before Ethel pulled out a pack of
cigarettes. She had trouble getting a cigarette out of the pack
and took her time lighting it from the smoking butt of the other
one, squinting at the smoke curling up to one eye and tangling
in the strands of her red wig.

She puffed several times, coughed hard, a wet, racking
sound, and seemed to enjoy making us wait, standing in the
sun. Her voice went bitter. "Witches is what everyone figgers.
The Ameses had money back in the day, before the Great Depression. The Ames women had *stones* in the backyard." She
leaned in and whispered, "In a circle." She grinned at whatever
she saw on T. Laine's face. "Ask anyone. The old Ames farm."
Ethel turned and went back inside, the screen door banging behind her.

"And why didn't the sheriff tell us that?" T. Laine asked
softly.

From inside the house Ethel shouted, "He's young. And he's
a *man*." The last word was caustic and bitter. "The young don't
know nothing and men stick together when it comes to banging
a woman. Men and their secrets."

We trudged back to our cars and motored down the street,
driving slowly as JoJo worked back at HQ, widening her search
into the Ames witch family, tracking down the family line
through county land records and birth and death records for the
last hundred years, and giving us the address of the old Ames
farm, which had passed from Ames to Ames, mother to daughter. JoJo was brilliant.

"Check it out," FireWind instructed needlessly.

* * *

The property was an abandoned, heavily overgrown fifty-acre farm, the closest neighbors out of sight in the trees, the house itself long gone in a fire that had left two soot-blackened chimneys standing in hip-high brown weeds and twenty-year-old saplings. Away from the house the trees were older, larger, as if they hadn't been cut in seventy years. Maybe longer. We got out and T. Laine and Occam waded in where the house once stood, searching among the trees. I carried my gear away from the chimneys, until I found a small open space between the trees. I placed my faded blanket on the ground, sat with the cabbage in my lap, and touched the earth.

The grass wasn't a lawn. It didn't have that snooty feel of cultivators or sod. The land had been fallow for decades and the plants had begun to breathe in wildness and freedom and to spread their roots, making communities. Instead of reading down, I stretched out across the land in a widening circle around me, the earth sparking with life. In the first few inches of soil, there were the roots of dozens of species of grasses and wildflowers and fungi; there were seedlings just getting started. The larvae of bugs. Colonies of ants. There was a large rabbit community living on the property, bird nests in the grass and trees, and snakes basking in the sun. Feral cats. Homeless dogs in a small den. Opossums and foxes and raccoons. A dry streambed flowed through the property, underground water following similar contours. No graveyards. No battlegrounds. As I read broader and deeper, I found the older deep roots of mature trees. A true forest in the making, some hardwoods over a hundred years old, far older than those found on most farms, which were cut every forty years for wood.

I could take this land and make it thrive, could bring the water back to the surface, encourage the trees to full forest and health.

If I was willing to kill and spill blood and claim it.

But it was doing well enough without me and neither it nor my bloodlust called to me.

And . . . there had to be another way. There had to be a way to heal the earth—and the Earth—without death and bloodshed.

I read deeper and found a layer of limestone containing a

water table with clean happy water. To the east was broken
granite and a near-vertical shelf of marble, hard and jutting, that
had once reached the surface. To the north was an ancient dump
and several buried foundations, the remains of a small community. Miles away, but still close enough to feel it, was Soulwood, basking under the fall sun, soaking up energy and
sunlight. I didn't call on it, and eased away, back toward my
body.

Closer to me were foundations of outbuildings, animal bones
from where farmers had slaughtered their meat. Three small
dumps were filled with broken glass and pottery and rusting tin
cans, a coil of rusting barbed wire, rusting chicken wire, cor-
roding farm implements. I pulled into myself and pushed out
again, concentrating on the house and the young woods.

I found the stone circle and wrapped around it, staying outside, tasting and testing the ancient magics within. The circle
was composed of rough-shaped oval stones standing upright,
each about two feet above the surface and one below. Twelve of
them had been set in place, in a nearly perfect circle but not
equidistant apart, not clock-like. Four stones were at the primal
compass points; others were in odd positions, maybe to match
the stars or the moon or the equinoxes. Something witchy. All
the stones were the same marble that I had felt below the
ground, as if part of the jutting slab had once been exposed and
chiseled out and used by the landowners. I marked the location
of T. Laine and Occam, who were pacing widdershins outside
the stones. There was something within the circle, something
warm and sleeping but not dangerous. I would come back to it.

I eased away from the stone circle and found more of the
marble. The buried foundations of the burned house were made
of the stone, along with the buried hearthstones, cracked and
hidden in the tall grass. The long-gone barn had stood on marble stones at the four corners, now buried beneath the ground.
The beautiful stone had been removed from the earth and then
been reclaimed by it. It seemed fitting. I found more marble
near the dry creek, a single large rounded stone that had fallen
over.

Near the boundary of the property, I found another circle.
This one was newer, perhaps only ten years old, located near a
narrow gravel road. Like the others, the circle was overgrown.

Or it had been. Now it was laced with *death and decay*. A thin trail of the energies led off beneath the ground.

I pulled back to my body, wrapped a tendril of Soulwood around my wrist, and followed the trail. It didn't lead far. The connection circled back to the land near Crossville, where Cale Nowell had lived, where the kettles had been kept, and where the dissolved bodies had been poured. There was a third circle there, buried beneath almost two feet of . . . graveyard dirt and lye chemicals, stones I hadn't been able to discern when reading from the site itself, due to the intensity of *death and decay* there. I'd nearly died, trying to read there. Now I was coming from underground, and the circle near Cale's was obvious, two feet beyond the shed.

Someone had dug out the soil within the circle and filled it in with graveyard dirt. Liquefied bodies had been poured into it, several of them. Three? Five? More? The liquefied bodies and magic had created a strange, dark place. A place of shadows and sparking power, black and deep and murky. I studied it and realized that the place where the potted vampire tree had died was a place to store power. Power that felt a lot like *death and decay*. A lot like, but not exact. Not quite. The energies had been gathered there, stored there, for years. Perhaps as long as a decade.

I circled around the . . . power sink was as good a term as any. A place where unused power had been sent to . . . what? Do nothing? And then it hit me.

This was more than storage for dark energies. It was a battery for power that could be used to kill.

A vibration thrummed through my connection to Soulwood, and I allowed it to draw me back and back to the small circle on the far edge of the Ames property and then farther, back to my body near the house. I took a breath. Another. Before I allowed myself to stop, I reached out and felt the warm magics inside the stone circle that was so close. I circled the twelve stones. Placed my awareness against the stone at the north point, and pressed. Nothing hit me, nothing grabbed me.

A stone witch had lived here. Considering the placement of the stones, also maybe a moon witch. I slipped inside the circle.

Shock spiraled through me. Whatever I had expected, it wasn't this. In the center of the circle were bones. Buried. Wrapped in roots from long-dead trees. Or . . . No. Not exactly.

Her bones held old magic. Old energies. I reached for them. They tasted faintly of *death and decay*, or something very like it. Something very like the power in the energy sink I had just left behind.

And also, something very like my own energies. Familiar.

A frisson of shock quivered through me.

I studied the bones wrapped in wood roots and buried in the circle. The roots looked odd. And I realized the bones were not wrapped in the roots. The bones *were* roots.

Like me, she had put down roots and become part tree. She had died, a long time ago. Seventy-five years? Longer ago than that? I had no way to tell.

I didn't want to understand what I was seeing. But I did.

One of the Ames witches had been an earth sprite, a *yinehi*. Like me.

Within her belly, the fragile bones of a baby lay. The *yinehi* had been pregnant.

My whole soul stilled, my spirit shaking and withering. *The yinehi had been pregnant.*

Her blood had been spilled here.

I sank into the ground, all of what I was and all of what I might become centered on this curled ball of bone-wood. I circled her, my power reaching out. Touching the fragile remains.

Buried with her, beneath her left hip, was the rusted knife that had killed her.

She had been sacrificed.

Or murdered.

Or . . . Or she had killed herself here. A *yinehi* was buried here, in a witch circle. Her bones had turned fully to wood, to roots. She had become a tree.

Had she lost control of her bloodlust? Had she been put down like a rabid animal?

I trailed the trunk up toward the surface and saw where the tree had been cut down, ages ago, the stump splintered and broken by an ax blade. Tears gathered and I watered the earth here, crying, my grief trickling down as I understood. As I accepted what I was seeing.

The magic of *death and decay*. It was *my* magic, but turned and taught to destroy. That was why my bloodlust had been so quiescent. That was why it was taking so long for my fingertips to heal. Unlike the Green Knight, Soulwood hadn't recognized the energies as a danger.

The power of the dead *yinehi* in the circle, the *death and decay*, had reappeared now, in the modern world. There was another bloodline similar to mine.

I felt sick and agitated and eager all at once. We were trailing a type of *yinehi*.

Whoever this current *yinehi* was, she was of this line, part of this woman's lineage, a great-niece or second cousin. The *current yinehi* had been using the darkness of her power, killing and storing those dark energies in a power sink. And she knew Hugo Ames and Cale and Stella. Somehow, she was tied into the commune or tied to one of the commune members.

I backed out of the ground and placed my hands in my lap, thinking, eyes closed. Quivering and shocky, I took several long breaths, seeking to calm myself. Tears dried on my face.

Hugo Ames had come from witch roots. Hugo was not a witch.

Hugo Ames had been married and having an affair with a college girl. Hugo was dead.

We were still searching for the killer. And that person came from a bloodline like mine.

I knew it was time to tell my friends all about me. Because this burial was . . . was what might need to be done to me if I lost control of my bloodlust. Fear and horror shivered through me.

I forced my eyes open to see Occam in front of me, on one knee, elbow propped on the other knee, his chin in his hand. I had the feeling he had been there for a while, watching over me. His eyes were warm and full of tenderness. "Hey there, Nell, sugar."

I caught my breath. "Hey there, cat-man."

"No vines and thorns around you this time. I'm thinking you're learning better control."

I reached up and touched my hairline. "No leaves."

"Just the one." He reached over and plucked a miniature leaf from near my temple. He slipped it into his pocket over his heart. My heart melted and he twined his fingers with mine. "But you been crying. You smell like fear, Nell, sugar. Not prey fear, but violence fear."

"There's a difference?"

"There is. And you're cold. Cold as a grave." He took my

other hand and warmed them in his. When I didn't go on, he said, "We got a circle of standing stones."

"I saw. Black marble. Stone witch and moon witch?"

"That's what Lainie thinks. We've got a lot of thoughts about suspects, but we ain't narrowed it down much."

"Question. Hugo Ames' wife. Is she from a witch family?"

Occam frowned, a thin line forming between his sandy brown brows. "Revenge is a good motivator. Hugo's dead. His ex-wife isn't. Don't know about his lady friend. Lainie's trying to narrow down who Hugo was sleeping with. Maybe Hugo was sleeping with Ingrid Wayns? She's dead. Or maybe it was another one of Stella's riders? You think his wife mighta tried to kill her rival and him and missed on the woman? Mighta got Stella instead? Hugo ain't on her list a lovers and he ain't Stella's usual type." He shook his head. "None of the riders read as a witch on the psy-meter, but we ain't read the wife yet, because we didn't know she was a factor." He frowned around his fist, thinking. "What if he was sleeping with Stella's housekeeper?" he asked. "Or Monica. They're dead too."

"Ethel Myer said the woman Hugo was sleeping with was a college girl and rode horses. All the riders fit that description," I said, pulling my tablet and checking my files. "And everyone at the farm had access to horses if they felt like riding."

Occam's brow smoothed. "You mentioned early on about the possibility of the target not being Stella. But Stella . . ."

"Stella is a focal," I said softly. "The big important person, the victim that drew our eyes. But betrayal and revenge? They cross over all the socioeconomic lines. Those feelings don't care about stardom or wealth, just getting back, getting even, and killing."

"Monica didn't travel the entire tour with the band. She was back and forth to the farm. Plenty of time and opportunity to still be seeing Hugo. The housekeeper, Verna Upton, was young and she didn't travel at all." Occam pulled out his tablet and sat on my blanket with me, our sides barely touching. "We don't have a signal, but I have most of the files here." I leaned against him, thinking about what I needed to say, as he hunted through the files. "I don't see a full job description," he said, annoyed. "All I got is, Verna was taking online college classes. Like half the employees, she fits in with the information we got from the old woman, Hugo's landlady."

"If there's any evidence at his house, it's decomposed by now," I said. "And Monica was a recent college grad. She could fit the parameters too."

"We need to know whose job it was to unpack the swag. Maybe Monica was supposed to have all the deliveries unpacked already. Maybe she was too busy sleeping with Hugo to do her job, and that's why she dove in when Stella's body was found."

Brainstorming was usually one of my favorite parts of this job, but not this time. I was silent. Still processing the bone-wood.

Occam said, "They said Monica was high-strung and had to be doing things all the time. They said she was frenzied, putting swag away, and they couldn't stop her. They thought she was both grieving and in shock and doing her job."

I nodded because Occam expected it of me.

"But maybe she saw the box of T-shirts and they were her married boyfriend's production," Occam said. "Maybe all sorts of emotions erupted in her, making her unpack the shirts. Could be." Occam stood and pulled me up with him, my hand in his. He tossed the blanket into the crook of his elbow and took my potted plant in his other hand. I hadn't explained about the root-wrapped bones.

We wandered through the grass to T. Laine, who was sitting in the center of the old circle, eyes closed, a smile on her face. She was in a yoga position, her legs bent, ankles crossed, hands on her knees. It looked an awful lot like me communing with Soulwood. When she opened her eyes, it took a while to focus on us. When she did, Occam explained our speculation on the latest suspect.

T. Laine pursed her lips, staring around the stones, seeming peaceful. "JoJo's already started on a family background search of the Ameses."

"Afore we do that," I said, my voice still soft, my feet standing above the bones wrapped in old roots, "I got things to tell you'uns. And you might need to arrest me."

"Nell, sugar?"

He reached for me, but I sidestepped away and took the blanket, unfolding it to its full size. No way could I let him be loving to me when I had a confession to make. I sat.

Occam's eyes were on me, his body still as a hunting cat, focused with his whole being. Moving like a cat, he folded down, a nearly boneless motion, and sat beside me. T. Laine scooted closer, until she was on the blanket too, the three of us all but touching, in our own small, paranormal, three-person circle. This grouping, the three of us, together—witch, were, and *yinehi*—felt important, like a pact, a promise of some kind. Though I knew it meant nothing. Not really.

"The *death and decay*," I said. "I thought early on that it was familiar somehow. And now I know why." I leaned out and touched the ground, both palms flat. "Under the earth, exactly here, are the bones of a plant-woman. She was part tree when she was murdered. Or sacrificed. Or maybe when she killed herself."

I looked at my friends. They were silent. Watching me.

"A plant-woman," I said again. "A *yinehi*. Like me." Still they said nothing. "I have killed two men in my life. The first . . ." I touched the ground again, aware of the bones below me. Had she been attacked? Was she pregnant from the attack? "I never saw his face. I have no idea who he was. He attacked me on my farm. In our struggle, I scratched him. His blood landed on the dirt. It was unknowing instinct. Self-defense. I fed him to the land."

"Where's the body?" T. Laine asked.

"There is no body. When I feed the land, there's nothing left. Not a hair, not a fingernail, not a leg bone. Not a sole from a shoe. Not a belt buckle. The land dissolves and absorbs it all. Soulwood even takes the soul. That life energy makes the trees grow. And it gives me my power."

"I see," T. Laine said, no emotion in her voice, none in her eyes.

"The second man I fed to the earth was Brother Ephraim, not long after I met Rick and Paka." Paka had been Rick's wereleopard mate before she tried to kill him. "Ephraim and two other churchmen attacked me and my home. Paka, in were-cat form, defended me and nearly killed Ephraim. He was dying."

"She bit him?" Occam asked. Biting a human was an automatic death sentence. "And the grindylow didn't kill her?" His tone was confused, disbelieving.

"Before the grindylows got to him, I fed him to the land. And though Paka had bitten him, and may have deserved to die according to were-creature law, she didn't. The grindy let her go free."

"No grindylow woulda let a were-creature go free after biting a human," Occam said.

"Rick knew about this?" T. Laine asked.

"Yes."

"And there are no bodies?"

"When I feed the land," I repeated, "there's nothing left. Nothing at all."

"No evidence," she persisted.

"Not a lick. Except my word."

Occam got a strange look in his eyes. Softly, as if turning the thoughts over in his mind even as he spoke the words, he said, "If Ephraim was *human*, then you, a *para*, killing him, a *human*," he emphasized, "*might* be a crime, especially if it could be argued that it wasn't self-defense. But the grindylow didn't kill Paka, therefore Ephraim was not a human being. He couldn't get or spread were-taint. What if he was a *gwyllgi*? *Gwyllgi*, attacking you? It's a clear self-defense, para on para."

I nodded. It was possible. And if Ephraim was a *gwyllgi*, then I had killed a violent nonhuman. And human law didn't apply to me. It was an out, a paranormal defense, a justification I had never thought others might consider. Fresh tears gathered in my eyes. My breath came in jerks and heaves. Ephraim had raped my mother. My half brother Zebulun was his son. Was Zeb a *gwyllgi* too?

T. Laine nodded deliberately, still not meeting my eyes. "You just now figured out this stuff about a *yinehi*?" She tapped the ground beside the blanket.

I wiped my eyes, the sudden relief that I, maybe, hadn't killed a human, at least the second time, filling me the way wind filled a grassland. "Most of it, yes. I traced the body buried here to another circle on the edge of this farm, and then to a third circle. It is in the same place as the kettle of dead humans. There's a stone circle there too, buried about a foot underground. Not so sophisticated. Not nearly so old. The dead bodies

from the kettle were dumped and spilled there, giving the circle
power. It's a power sink, a place to store death energies, probably so the death practitioner didn't kill someone by accident.
But something happened and the power was used. That use
turned the energies even darker. Into *death and decay*." I looked
at my teammates. "I gotta wonder who lived there before Cale
Nowell moved in. It was rental property. We need to ask the
landlord, the farmer, whose name I've forgotten."

"Holcomb Beresford," Occam supplied. "Holy Bear."

"I have always thought my magic is a mutation from witch
genetics. And those mutations may also include *gwyllgi*."

"Did you know all this?" T. Laine asked Occam.

"No."

"When were you going to tell us you killed people?" she
asked me.

"When I had to."

"I see," T. Laine said. "So, from the church inbreeding, three
paranormal creatures have emerged: witches, *yinehi*, and
gwyllgi. And you think we're chasing another para here, similar
to *yinehi*."

"The builders of God's Cloud of Glory Church came from
all over Europe and settled here," I said. "Cousins married
cousins. People left the church. Married out. Others married in.
Powerful witches were killed or ran away. Weak witches who
had a gift for finding water or making plants grow or helping
livestock to birth safely were able to hide their gifts. They
stayed and married in. Recessive genes that went back to common ancestors began to appear. Began to mutate. Same thing
happened here and a *yinehi* was born. And died. But the genetics were still there, in that family. And that same line produced
a creature with the magics of *death and decay*."

I looked at T. Laine. My friend. Her face was closed and
hard and she didn't look back at me but kept her eyes on the
trees around us. She asked, "Could you create *death and decay*
magics?"

"At first, I worried about that possibility," I said. "But I think
it's a separate path. Like earth witches can't use moon magics.
Your magic is familiar to each other, but it's also very different.
Death and decay is like mine but very different." I hoped. I
truly hoped.

T. Laine met my eyes. Hers carried something in them, something that made me acutely uncomfortable. "Is this the magic that helped me win the fight at the house with the Blood Tarot and the vampires in cages and blood-magic attacking? The magic that killed the blood witches, Lorianne and Jason?"

My mouth went dry as dust. *She knew.* Knew I had taken them as sacrifice for the land and to power my magic. "Yes," I whispered.

T. Laine Kent rose to her feet. "I have some thinking to do. Y'all head on back. I'll be along in a bit."

Following orders, I stood, shaking. Occam stood with me. I gathered my blanket and my potted cabbage and trudged to my car. Got into the passenger seat. Occam got into the driver's seat. He didn't start the car. Instead he took my hand, his warm and strong. I clasped it back. "I'm hungry. Want a steak?" he asked.

I turned to face him. He was watching me, a small smile on his face. "You'uns not mad at me?" I asked.

"Nell, sugar, I'll love you forever. Someday I'll tell you about the time I killed and ate a man." He turned on the car. Smiled a satisfied cat smile. "For the record, humans do not taste like chicken." He turned the car and drove back to the law enforcement center, sharing a silence that felt . . . amazing. And terrifying.

SEVENTEEN

On the way back to HQ, we stopped at Tina Ames' house. Tina was Hugo's mom, and the sheriff himself was standing with her on the front stoop, one arm around her shoulders.

"Looks like they just told her about Hugo," Occam said. "Gimme a minute and let me read her for *death and decay* and witch magics. Unless you can tell just from looking at her?"

I shook my head, making a negative sound, and he left me to my thoughts, thoughts pulling me deep inside myself. They were thoughts about Soulwood and about the bone-wood that we had just left. Thoughts about the feel of the *death and decay* at Stella's farm, that stark absence of life.

"All of earth is magic," I whispered. "All of the land, everywhere. Even the land tainted by death. The magic of the land is *still there*. It's just been changed somehow."

Maybe, just maybe, I could help the land to heal the *death and decay*. Maybe I could help the witches to neutralize the energies that they had currently shielded, but which were also leaking into the earth. Maybe I could do that without claiming the land or sacrificing a human. Or dying for the land.

The bone-wood in the circle of stones . . .

Had she lost control of the land? Had she begun to become a tree, like I had? Occam said I had been learning control. Had I learned enough control to try to heal without spilling the blood of an enemy? Without needing to harm myself? Without my friends needing to call in a military strike to take out the dark *yinehi* that I could become?

Occam got back in the car. "Nada," he said. "Not a single blip. Hugo's mama's as human as they come. She's the last of her female line. The Ames witch blood dried up."

"But, maybe like with Margot, there were some genetics

leading to a gift of some sort," I said. "We need to find Hugo's wife. And we need to know who stayed before at the rental trailer where Cale lived."

We walked into the local county law enforcement center, which was bustling and overcrowded. We were just in time to hear JoJo on the para freq channel, saying, "LaFleur, FireWind. I got something."

Both bosses waved us all into a small conference room, we shut the door, and Rick called HQ on his cell. He put it on speaker and said, "LaFleur here, with FireWind, Ingram, Occam, Kent, and Racer. What do you have?"

"Hugo Ames' estranged wife is one Carollette Myer Ames. Until two weeks ago, when she quit, she worked part-time at Merry Promotions as needed. With her husband. She worked there while Stella was on tour. I tracked her phone for the day the T-shirts were delivered to the horse farm. Guess who made the trip from her own home to the horse farm that day?" Everyone in the little room perked up until JoJo added, "Only problem is, there is no record of Carollette being a witch."

I turned her name over in my mind. "Did we read the woman . . . What was her name? The one with the cigarettes and the liquor?"

"Ethel Myer," T. Laine said. "Hugo's landlady." Her eyes lit up with more life than I had seen for days. "Myer! Ethel *Myer* and Carollette *Myer* Ames, Hugo's wife. I'm betting good money Ethel and Carollette are related."

"She knew an awful lot about the families and the affair." I looked up at Occam. "When we got to Ethel's house, not a one of us opened her file. Not a one of us read her. Why didn't you read her with the psy-meter?" My face scrunched up. "Why didn't I read the land when we got close to the house?"

"Daaaaang," T. Laine said. "I bet good money it's because there was a suggestion, a compulsion to listen, believe, and get out of there." The light left her eyes. "I didn't catch it."

"And if she's a paranormal death practitioner?" FireWind asked softly.

"We had our chance to take her out," Occam said. "She won't be surprised again."

"She'll hit us with *death and decay* if we go back there, or she'll just be gone," T. Laine said. "JoJo, does she have a cell? Can you track it?"

"Already on it," Jo said through the cell phone speaker. "Already looking up DL, voter registration, social media presence. And one thing to know. Our country hick chick had me research who rented the property before Cale Nowell moved in. That mobile home is where Carollette Myer Ames grew up with her mother, Reba Myer, single parent, deceased. No father was listed on Carollette's birth certificate."

"So it's just coincidence that Cale moved into that same trailer? No way. They have to be connected some way," T. Laine said, pulling up her tablet. "Checking witch family ancestry sites for Myers."

"Cale was in the commune," I said, pulling myself out of my mental mire. "Hugo was in the commune. They likely knew one another there. It's also likely that Hugo would have known where his wife grew up. Maybe Cale and Hugo talked? Maybe they were still friends? Maybe that's how Hugo found Racine/Cadence Merriweather and started blackmailing her, through Cale? That makes sense. Everyone liked Cale. People were trying to help him after he got out of jail. Hugo was probably one of those people and helped Cale rent the trailer, where he also ended up contaminated by *death and decay*. All because he knew Hugo. But how did he end up dead and being ridden by the necromancer, Hugo's wife, Carollette? Unless the power sink and the kettle full of people-soap was still there because Carollette needed to use her power or store it when it got to be too much, and she needed the power sink to do that."

JoJo said, "I've got the GPS on Hugo's car somewhere here. Hang on." We heard keys tapping.

"Timeline fits," Occam said. "Commune, to Stella, to Cale, to Hugo, to Carollette, who was betrayed by Hugo sleeping with one of the people at Melody Horse Farm, which leads us back to the commune. A nice, convoluted, but circular trail."

Her voice vibrating with excitement, Jo said, "Got it. Hugo Ames' car made the trip to Cale's trailer four times since Cale got out of jail. We have our connection point."

"Good work," FireWind said. For him that was high praise.

"If we can find Carollette before she sees us, we could deliver null pens all around her," T. Laine said.

"How old is Ethel Myer?" I asked, my fingers having found their way into the soil of my potted plant. I hadn't realized that I was carrying it around.

"She's forty-two," JoJo said. "Hang on for DL pic."

T. Laine cursed softly and said, "Jo, she looks eighty. We *had* her! And we didn't take her."

I placed the pot on the table beside me, my hands around it, my eyes on it so I didn't have to look at them. "Ethel is a witch. Maybe even a death witch, because her magics are slowly killing her, that and the cigarettes and the liquor. But *death and decay* kills faster than what we saw at her place. And *death and decay* is not witch magic," I said, "although it could have come from the same source, back far in the past, mutated genetics that resulted in witches, in *yinehi*, maybe other creatures, maybe recessive genes that pair up when certain people breed too close." I felt T. Laine's eyes on me and I took a steadying breath. "Anyway. What I'm trying to say is that *death and decay* is old earth magic, ancient magic like mine, but turned on its head and perverted, fueled by sacrifice."

I could feel my bosses' eyes on me. I had told FireWind, Soul, and Rick a lot about my magics. Rick knew even more from the time Paka had nearly killed Ephraim. It had been kept off my record. So far. I didn't look up or meet anyone's eyes. I was staring at my potted cabbage, my fingers touching Soulwood soil. I was growing tiny green leaves on the tips of my fingernails. One unfurled, dark green with red veining.

"When was this determined?" FireWind asked.

"Today," I said. "That's what I'm here to report. I recognized the origination of the *death and decay* on the old Ames farm. The family were normal witches. One of them married . . . I don't know, maybe a second cousin. Or even a boy from the church. Stranger things have happened. And then, probably due to intermarriage, recessive genes began to pop up. Around seventy-five to a hundred years ago, a *yinehi*, a nature creature like me, was born, grew up, and was killed and buried on the Ames farm. *Yinehi* magics appear most strongly when the woman is attacked and has to defend herself. Something about the adrenaline spike of self-defense brings them to full power. The bones I discovered under the ground were mostly tree."

I had been attacked. My sister Esther had been attacked. We grow leaves. My sister Mud had not been attacked and it was my goal to make sure she never was. She could still use her earth gifts to make things grow, but hopefully she would never—

"Ingram?" FireWind said.

I realized I had fallen silent.

"The second time the recessive genes appeared is more recent, about ten or maybe fifteen years ago, if the power sink I discovered is any indication, probably at puberty. The energies there are just a little different from mine, but recognizable. As if they come from common stock."

My mind went all sorts of places, remembering T. Laine's fear that the magic would get into the water table. Would infect the earth itself.

Would Soulwood be enough to defeat that kind of magic? Even with the Green Knight to help? The magics had killed the potted vampire tree, at least enough for Occam to cut it down.

His body still as stone in my peripheral vision, FireWind said, "Oral tales speak of such a creature. The Tsalagi might call it *ajasgili*."

I lifted my head to him. His face was both expressionless and full of emotion at once. Grieving and angry, stoic and firm.

He said, "The *ajasgili* will be very different from the white man's witches, and I fear this dark magic user will be different from what I might have known once upon a time. Find the *ajasgili*, the magic practitioner of *death and decay*. I will seek authorization for extreme measures to shut her down."

Extreme measures was a PsyLED code word for military. The top brass in PsyLED and in Homeland Security were creating—probably had been for a long time—protocols for every magical eventuality. Worst-case scenarios included intervention by fighter jets, special units with high-tech gear, maybe bombs. Margot was standing still as a marble statue in the corner, reading us all for truth, for lies, for things left unsaid. Her face was sheened with strain, as she followed our words and FireWind's judgment.

Her voice tense, T. Laine said, "I have a Myer witch family, last recorded in 1902. Either they died out or went underground."

"Ethel Myer isn't a *yinehi* or an *ajasgili*," I said. "Ethel didn't look like me, no wood fingernails, no leaves." I had a feeling that Ethel would read exactly like a witch, not like *death and decay*. The trigger in the T-shirts had been created by a witch. "Ethel probably made the trigger. And that means she knows who the *ajasgili* is. She sent us to the Ames farm." I stopped, thoughts whirling. "What if Ethel recognized what I was? What if she knew what I was and she sent me to the farm?"

"Why would she do that?" T. Laine asked.

Tilting up a thumb in uncertainty, I said, "Maybe Ethel understood how badly the entire thing had gone wrong. Maybe she thinks her *ajasgili* is growing very dangerous."

And they would bomb the *ajasgili*. For certain, unless—

"What if extreme measures don't work?" I asked. "*Death and decay* works on everything except null energies. What if our *ajasgili* shuts down high-tech weaponry before it's fired? The power sink I found was the place where she stored her magics when they got to be too much to carry safely. That means that the *ajasgili* knows how to store, use, and direct *death and decay*."

Unit Eighteen were all staring at me. I could feel the weight of their attention, their worries, their fear. I went on, speaking into the silence. "If there was a chance that ambient *death and decay* magics would cause our semiautomatics to malfunction, why not something bigger." It was technically a question, but I stated it as a fact.

I could almost hear the frown in her voice as T. Laine said, "Someone sent that man chasing Ingram in his truck. Someone killed a kind old man and forced his body to drive his truck to PsyLED, wait there, and then chase down the first person who exited."

Occam said, "Someone sent Cale Nowell on a drive in the countryside until he crashed his car. How close was he to his trailer? Could Carollette have been at the power sink, maybe planning to use her kettles, when he came home? Killed him accidentally and made him drive himself away?"

FireWind said, "That makes sense. If the *ajasgili* is losing control of her magics, then anything is possible."

I shook my head and lifted a bit of Soulwood soil in my fingers, letting it dribble back into the cabbage pot, my finger leaves rustling. I looked at FireWind. "You were there too, when the truck charged across traffic to kill me." I sifted Soulwood soil through my fingers. "You knew what I was when you first saw me. When you first took my scent. At Melody Horse Farm, you said you smelled the *ajasgili*. You had her scent. What if she knew that? What if she heard us talking the night she killed Ingrid Wayns? Or before she killed the stallion? She had access to a witch who might have provided obfuscation charms that let her be there with us." I looked up from the soil. "Whoever sent the man to HQ may have wanted any of us."

The rest of the team were silent, watching. FireWind jutted his chin in agreement. "Your scent is like all living things. The scent of the *ajasgili* was like the earth of graves. Like the absence of life."

I thought about Soulwood. About the vampire tree. About its image of killing me. What if I had misunderstood what it was saying? What if it wanted a sacrifice? Was asking permission. Or what if it was simply asking me to give it permission to live, knowing I could, and might someday, kill it? "Oh," I breathed, my thoughts whirling as too many possibilities tried to find places inside me at once. I looked back at the potted cabbage and kept my eyes there. Without lifting them to LaFleur or FireWind, I said, "May I speak to you both privately?"

Somehow, they knew who I was talking about because the others left the room, Occam's gaze on me in case I needed him. I shook my head, the tiniest shake, and he went on out. The door closed.

I raised my eyes and looked from Rick to FireWind. Rick's once-black hair was a glacial white now. With the new age lines, he looked older than FireWind, though FireWind had decades more years. There was compassion in Rick's near-black eyes, a kindness I hadn't expected. I had missed him, a man I had detested at first. I had actually *missed* him. My eyes filled with tears.

"Nell?" Rick asked.

I realized they had been waiting for a while. I had forgotten to breathe while I thought. I inhaled hard. Blew out. Took another breath. "I might be able to stop her," I said. "The *ajasgili*."

Over the cell, which was still on, JoJo said, "Lainie's searching for a familial connection between Carollette's parents, something that might create an abnormal witch-type gene."

I said, "It should be within just a few generations, based on the body buried on the old Ames farm, which was abandoned in the early to mid 1900s. Maybe after 1902 when the Myer witch family went underground." I remembered the trees on the land. Some had seemed larger, older than I expected. The *yinehi* buried there had been like me, like my sisters, not an *ajasgili*.

The *ajasgili* was similar, except her magics drew life from the land and left it barren, and stored death in the land, opposite to the way that I gave life *to* the land. This *ajasgili* was feeding death to the land, storing and using that power. Feeding death to her enemies.

Was that similar to the way I had killed Brother Ephraim? Had I come close to becoming an *ajasgili*? Was it intent or was it all genetics? And if genetics, had Ephraim been *gwyllgi*? The grindylow, Pea, had confirmed that he wasn't human. His life force had contaminated the earth.

What if Ephraim was ajasgili*?*

Leaves budded and curled from my hairline at the thought.

I'd found a way to block off that life force, to fence it in, just like T. Laine and the Nashville coven had blocked off the *death and decay* and captured it in shields to keep it from spreading.

"Ethel Myer and Carollette Myer Ames are related back four generations," JoJo said, "when two first cousins married, so that gives us a recessive at that time. And their grandparents, two generations back, were second cousins. According to the witch-family lineages T. Laine sent me, there was an Ames witch family in Tennessee prior to the very late 1800s but nothing recent—" Her words broke off. "Hang on. Hugo and Carollette come from a common ancestor. The Ameses and the Myers all came from a common Ames witch line."

Three generations back my parents had a common ancestor or two. All church families did. Keeping the family lines straight was paramount in polygamous churches. Did inbreeding in families with latent or recessive witch genes stimulate abnormal magical abilities and create unusual magic users? Like me? Like the *gwyllgi*? Like the *ajasgili*?

I had neutralized Brother Ephraim's evil from the land. I had reclaimed the land from the death magic of the salamanders. I had used my magic to fight a demon. In each case there had been sacrifice, of myself and of blood. It nearly killed me. I had given myself to the land to heal it and had become a tree in the process, one time for six months. I almost didn't make it back.

I had noted early on that this *death and decay* was similar to natural processes.

I could try.

I looked to my bosses. "I'd like to try to neutralize the *death and decay*. Now that I know what it is, my magic is enough like it to, I don't know, maybe nullify it?" Or maybe send it into magma and let the crust of Earth neutralize it. I had done that before.

"Ingram," FireWind said. "Reading the land, especially this *death and decay*, has been dangerous to you. You may understand it better, but that will not make it less hazardous."

I had claimed Soulwood long before I killed a man and fed his body and soul to the woods. I had claimed it with a few drops of my blood on the roots of the married trees behind my home.

If I was careful, if I used my magic—mine, not the vampire tree's, not Soulwood's, *mine*—and didn't let it use me, I might be able to fix this without feeding it a blood sacrifice, without killing someone. Without becoming a tree. "I'll be careful. I'll go slow. And I'll pull away at the first sign of trouble."

"For the record," Rick said, his white hair swinging forward as he leaned to make a point, "I'm against this. Totally and unequivocally." He made eye contact with FireWind and the expression was all wild leopard, vicious and untamed, a challenge even I could see. FireWind lifted an eyebrow in unconcern. Rick finished, "Nell is too important to this unit, too important as . . . as my *friend* for this."

Friend. Friend wasn't a law enforcement word. Or a boss word. It stood on its own. I warmed.

"Noted. Do you see another option?"

Rick snarled, his cat breaking through.

"Neither do I. We are not far from Hugo Ames' house," FireWind said. "You can try there."

I had admitted to Unit Eighteen how I had claimed land in several locations, with a blood sacrifice, mine or another's, and now the entire unit, except for Occam and T. Laine, was gathered on the street a safe distance away, watching. I sat on my faded pink blanket on the edge of Hugo Ames' rental property, the potted cabbage on the blanket between my folded knees. Occam, Lainie, and the plant were closer, in case I needed rescuing, in case my magic wasn't enough and I needed help, needed to call on my land to enter the fight. I had tried to tell them what might happen, but mostly, I had no idea.

Occam was immediately behind me, his knees touching my back, standing with a steel blade drawn, ready to cut me free from roots and vines if the land tried to claim me. He was quietly furious and desperately afraid, but we had agreed that my life was mine, to do with as I saw fit. Afraid or not, he was backing me up, proving his promise to let me choose in all things. He also carried a small plastic bag of healthy farm dirt that I had dug from the side of the road on the way over.

I looked at him and said, "I love you, cat-man."

"I'll keep you safe or die trying," he said.

"You'un jist cut me loose like you always do." But it might not be same and we all knew that.

Lainie was kneeling beside me, having insisted that she be close with null pens primed and ready, in case anything went wrong. She had also prepared incantations for special workings and had brought a sterile steel lancet for a blood draw. Lainie thought her incantations and workings might allow her to strengthen my magic, like a battery powering a motor. One of the incantations was a scripture verse we had chosen on the way over. I didn't think any of that would help, but I wasn't going to naysay her.

The unit had walked through the steps I'd take to try and neutralize *death and decay* using a different sort of sacrifice. Not a bunch of salamanders or the blood of invading vampires, but a sacrifice of life. However, to get the attention of the *death and decay* energies, I needed bait. Bait meant me.

I studied the remains of the house. No coven had shielded the energies yet and they had spread. We had left only a few hours past, and now the roof had caved in, the side wall had fallen inward. Two dead pine trees had dropped limbs and bark and one of the trees had broken off at the roots and fallen. The birds had disintegrated. The stench coming from the remains of the house was worse, if that was possible.

"I'm ready," I said. "Occam, I need the two piles of soil, here and here." I pointed in front of my knees to the ground just outside of the *death and decay* infecting Hugo Ames' house.

He tipped the bag and shook it to make two small piles of local farm soil. Beside me, T. Laine tore an alcohol pad open and, to make her happy, I cleaned my finger with it. She opened the lancet and held it out to me.

I stabbed my fingertip and inhaled a gasp. "Dag*nab*bit!" It *hurt*. It hurt worse than when a plant stabbed me with a thorn. Maybe, like a plant, I was becoming sensitive to steel. And dagnabbit was an exceptionally unsatisfactory word for the pain.

My blood ran down my finger as I steadied my breath. Curling my fingers over my palm, I caught the blood-trail and the drops. I placed my other palm flat on one pile of dirt and said, "Okay. Step two."

From the King James Bible, T. Laine said, "For, behold, the Lord cometh out of his place to punish the inhabitants of the earth for their iniquity: the earth also shall disclose her blood, and shall no more cover her slain." She had assured me that this was not a sacrilege or a blasphemy, to use scripture to cleanse the earth, though I knew most members of my church would see it that way.

I shook off my uneasiness and sank my consciousness into the earth. I hadn't read deeply in weeks, hadn't searched for the sleeping sentience, the soul of the hills. It hadn't occurred to me to search here at all, so far from the mountains, so far from home. But I dove deep, just beyond the *death and decay*, reaching through loam and clay and shattered rock, through limestone riddled with holes and full of water, through ancient riverbeds with rounded stones and curved boulders, farther, deeper, into the dark. I touched the sleeping sentience, the presence of the Earth, or one of them.

When I was certain that it was deeply somnolent, I placed my blood-filled palm onto the other small pile of farm dirt.

T. Laine was saying the biblical quote over and over, her words rushing like water across dry ground. My blood soaked through and touched the land beneath. Lights crackled and sparked and the energies of the land below me came alive. It was a three-dimensional palette of spinning bright green, churning dark red, and the almost painful deep purple of bruises.

The *death and decay* spun like a top, swirling like a fire devil. It rose up, hot as liquid glass, yet glacier cold. Alert, but not attacking. Not sentient, not self-aware. It was blind and seeking, sizzling and fiery, frozen and shattered. But not alive.

It was death. Emptiness.

But so very powerful. A burning frozen black hole where no life was, or could ever be.

The energies of death rolled closer.

It was like watching opposites attract, the positive light and joy of fecund life and the brittle burning/icy opposite, the negative darkness and emptiness of *death and decay*. My own power, the power of *yinehi*, of nature and earth, reached out toward the death energies, the *wrong* energies.

Carefully, I held my magic back. Not letting the energies touch.

When the conflicting energies were stable, only inches separating them, I sank into the earth. Deeper. Getting a feel for the parameters of *death and decay*, how wide its reach, how deep into the soil.

Slowly I wrapped and wove my magics into threads and then skeins, the soft spring green of leaves, the dark burgundy red of summer flowers, the deep purple of grapes and berries. I pulled in the browns of soil and the sparkling reflections of falling water, the powerful black of local marble and the charcoal of local granite, the greens and grays of limestone.

I twisted and knotted my energies together, weaving a basket of life, vines and roots and thorns and rocks and soil, strong, alive, and healthy. The power of the Earth. Though there was no light so far beneath the surface, colors glimmered and flashed, the cool green, green, *green* wrapping like roots, circling around the burning emptiness that was death. I slid the weaving through the ground, pulling and shifting it until it surrounded *death and decay*, fencing it in. But not touching it. Not letting it touch me, though the emptiness searched, my blood calling to it as it flowed.

Time passed. And I thought I had won.

I held it there. All of it, cupped and wrapped and twined in my magics.

But . . . something was wrong. There was a pain. I slitted my eyes open to see Occam, kneeling beside me, his blade flashing and cutting, slicing and sawing through icy blackness coiling around my fingers. "How . . . ?" I tried, but no sound came. The *death and decay* had found me. I sank back into the earth and scanned the energies trapped there. And I saw the tiny hole, a spot of blackness against the vibrant colors.

It was no bigger than the tip of my pinkie finger. The tendril of the blackness had found it, had pushed through the hole and slid along the outside of my magics. Up to the lines of energies that flowed from me to my basket. And into me.

Pain flared, branding hot and cold as space. It swept up my arm and into my chest. I heard a moan. Felt a weight, heavy, pressing.

Realized that on the surface, I wasn't breathing. Knew that moan had breathed out my last bit of air. I fought back into myself. Up along the pathway of energies.

Death and decay crawled and oozed, a sickly green now, as it digested my life force.

My magics weren't enough. Not against this.

I forced my body to take a breath. And I screamed. And screamed. Until the screaming stopped.

I reopened my eyes. Cat-Occam was face-to-face with me, so close I could feel his cat whiskers on my cheeks. His fangs were bared, only inches from my face. His leopard was snarling.

EIGHTEEN

"Occam," I whispered, my voice hoarse from screaming, my mouth dry as drought-parched dirt. But my cat-man heard. He pulled back enough for me to focus on his amber cat eyes and on the people around me. FireWind and Rick were slashing and sawing at the vines of death. T. Laine was stabbing null pens into the ground around me, still repeating her scripture.

"The cabbage. Now," I whispered.

Lainie said, "Done that, Nell. It withered and died. You got anything else to suggest?"

I licked my lips. "Soulwood. Blood. Bindings."

"Son of a witch," she said. She drew a silver blade. "LaFleur. Gimme your fingers."

He didn't ask why. He just held out his hand. T. Laine sliced along all four tips. Blood spurted and flowed. "Bend across Nell and bleed on her. Occam. I'm going to cut your ear. You bite me and I'll be pissed."

I missed the movement of the cut, but felt warm wetness on my face as Occam smeared his blood onto me. Growling. Panic in the sound.

"Nell," T. Laine said. "Draw on Soulwood. Draw!"

I reached into the earth through their cat blood. Reached for my land through the bindings that had tied them to Soulwood when I healed them. The land answered. Soulwood flared high, bright and singing like a bell. It formed a spear of might. The same kind of spear that I had used to kill Brother Ephraim. The spear flew through the darkness of the earth and landed in my blood-filled palm. I gripped the spear of life and power and might.

I stabbed through the webbed basket of my own energies and into the heart of *death and decay*.

It screamed. Darkness flashed, heated molten knives.

I felt more blood on me. More. More. And the land took it all.

The somnolent presence deep and deep rolled over. And over again. Struggling to awaken, struggling against the energies above it. The earth shook.

"Earthquake!" someone shouted. Occam shoved me down and lay across my torso, his cat blood slathering my face and neck. Dripping onto the blanket and beneath me and the ground beneath it.

"LaFleur," FireWind said, demand in his tone. "You have to shift. You've given too much blood. Shift! *Now!*"

I couldn't help Rick. I couldn't help Occam. Not until I healed the Earth and sent the presence back to sleep. And that meant I had to put this spell into the magma in the center of the Earth. Now. Right now. Lessons from the last time I fought death, that the Earth was all healing.

I reshaped the spear of Soulwood, the light and life of all that was good in the universe, re-formed it into a net, but one much stronger than the basket I had tried to weave all alone. I tied the magic net and the life of Soulwood around *death and decay* and cinched it tight. Soulwood flared, bright as the sun, and encircled the energies that were so opposite to its own. It sent love and willingness into me.

I shoved the net deep and deep, into the magma that rolled and roiled and pressed upward, seeking outlet to relieve its own terrible pressure. Surging into the cracks of the earth, in search of the surface, filling every vacant weakness—the cracks I had inadvertenly made not so long ago.

Soulwood and I pressed the energies deep. Into the heat. The earth trembled and shook. *Death and decay* resisted for one awful moment, clawing at my chest. Cutting into Rick and Occam.

The presence in the Earth rolled over. The heat and energies of the Earth accepted *death and decay*, pulling it into itself.

As if a far stronger magnet had attracted the energies, *death and decay* turned from me and latched onto the power of the active core of the planet and . . . slipped into a crack. Into the magma. It was sucked down in a long spiral. And it was gone. Absorbed totally.

Or, this part of it was. There was more in other places. In the power sink. In Stella Mae's house, her pasture, and so many other locations. But I had done all I could for now.

I heard shouting and sirens. Pain like nothing I had ever felt before stabbed me, electric and icy all at once, profound and all-encompassing, a cold tearing claws into me, as if they scooped out everything inside me and tossed it on a trash heap.

Soulwood saw it. Felt it. Wrapped around me. It sent vines and roots and tendrils plunging up from the earth to wrap around me, into me. Healing. Healing. *Healing* as only it could. The pain eased. Time passed. My pain vanished.

I took a breath, still intent on the earth beneath me as Soulwood worked, as life crept back to the land beneath me. That life reached up to the surface, reached for sunlight and rain and air. Soulwood searched through the roots of grass and trees on the periphery of the property, the ones with the faintest spark of life, and fed them. It drew water from the limestone beneath the ground and pulled it toward the sun. Acting on its own. Its sentience giving it full choice and full control over its own power.

When it was satisfied, it found others that belonged to it and healed them. Occam. Rick. Beings Soulwood had claimed. Energies poured into them, merging with their were-energies and creating the wholeness of a full moon shift.

A sound, a crash that shook the ground, almost pulled me back to the surface, a vibration that rocked the land. But I heard T. Laine repeating the scripture, and I reached back deep, to the sleeping energies of the spirit of the Earth, the sleeping power of the hills. I soothed it, petting it with Soulwood's power. It quivered and it slept.

Breathe. I needed to *breathe.* Air rustled through my leaves. Filled my lungs.

I blew out in a long soft sigh.

Once again, I opened my eyes. Blue sky was overhead, streaked with golden and orange clouds. *Sunset.* The day was gone. I was cold, shivering.

I raised my head to find I was trapped beneath vines and roots, a cage of greenery like a basket over me, as if my land had done to me what I had tried to do with *death and decay.* But there were no roots growing through me. No vines or thorns growing into me or piercing me. I was still flesh and blood.

A tree grew near the soles of my feet, massive. It was leafed out, golden in the autumn chill. Near me on the edge of the tattered pink blanket, Occam lay, also under a leafy cage, human shaped and naked, having changed from his cat back to human.

I turned my head to see Rick, in his black wereleopard form, sleeping under his own viny cage. A neon green grindylow was perched on his shoulder, chittering at me accusingly, as if I was responsible for the vine cage that enclosed her. This one's steel claws were out, her cat lips pulled back to expose long pointed canines. She hissed.

"I totally agree," I said to her.

"Ingram. You're awake." I turned my head to see FireWind, sitting on the ground on the far side of a fire. He had dug a shallow pit and lined it with rocks. His fire burned merrily in it.

"I think so."

"You are growing leaves."

I reached up and touched my hair. It was, once again, wildly curly, red, and full of leaves, not just at my hairline but all through it. I touched my face, which still felt like skin, thank goodness, and held up a hand to see my fingernails were woody and leaves had sprouted all along the cuticles. I didn't sigh in dismay, but I wanted to. "Yeah. It happens."

"A bird just landed in the yard. It didn't die. You were successful." It was a statement, not a question.

I focused on the big boss. He had removed his jacket and unbraided his hair. It flowed in a braid-kinked veil across his shoulder and down across his still-crisp white shirt. He was sitting on the ground in his black dress slacks, his knees crossed, his shoes off and feet bare. I smelled charred herbs, the smoke of ritual, and knew that he had participated in the healing of the earth in his own way, with a ceremony of healing.

"Is she okay?" a voice croaked.

"She is. Drink some water, Kent," FireWind said mildly, "or I'll get up and pour it down your throat."

"You can try," T. Laine said, her voice rasping.

"Have you been repeating that scripture for . . ." I looked up at the sunset. "All these hours?"

"Yeah. I seriously need to bone up on my Bible verses if I

have to keep saving your ass," She plopped down beside my viny cage and opened a bottle of water, uncapped it, and drained it in long gulps. She was sweat stained, pale, and shivering.

I smiled, my lips dry and cracking. "Save me, huh?"

FireWind said, "Ingram. The *death and decay* energies are gone, though I have no idea how you did it. You did, of course, cave the house into a pile of splinters."

"FireWind, sweet as always," I said.

"I have never in my life been called sweet," he said.

"That was sarcasm," I whispered. "Like a townie woman."

"Ah. Well. When she's back to normal, drive her home," he instructed T. Laine. FireWind pulled on socks and shoes and upended a gallon bottle of water over his fire. It hissed, spat, and smoked, and he stood, kicking dirt over it and rolling the heated firepit stones into it. "Ingram. The scent here is both like and unlike the scent of the magic user from Stella's horse farm. There *are* two of them, working together. You still have work to do."

I caught a glimpse of his face as he left, smiling, peaceful. I wasn't sure any of us had known he could look so at ease. I laughed, though it was little more than a breath. I pressed my hand against my viny cage and the vines and roots parted, slithering to the sides. I rolled over and sat up, pressing a hand onto the vines encasing Occam. The setting sun cast golden light and soft shadows over him, and . . . he was such a beautiful man. Soulwood had healed the last of his burn scars. His hair was long and platinum gold. A five-day beard softened his cheeks and chin.

And then it hit me. I shouted, "FireWind! We need to go back to Ethel Myer's house. Right now!"

Occam, dressed in gym sweats taken from his gobag and eating his second sandwich, drove me to Ethel Myer's home and parked next to FireWind's vehicle. He was standing with T. Laine, who was studying the house, reading the property with the psy-meter 2.0. The stone house had been perfect only hours past. Now it was a pile of rubble. Occam turned off my car, his gaze on the grouping of our coworkers. From their body language it was clear *death and decay* was contaminating the land. "If FireWind asks you to heal this land, you gonna do it?"

I shook my head. "I'm wore slap out, Occam. Maybe in a few days."

"Good. You ain't grown roots yet, but that won't last. Not with you using your gifts so deep." He leaned to me and tucked a strand of vine-hair into the curly mass behind my ear. He grabbed the back of my head and pulled us close, forehead to forehead, much like his cat had. "Good God, woman. I love you to the full moon and back. You know that. And you always got the right to do what you think is best. But you scared me half to death."

"Is that what made you shift?"

"Fear is a powerful motivator, Nell, sugar. Love is a better one. Don't do that to me again, you hear?"

Instead of agreeing, I said, "I love you too, cat-man, to the deeps of the roots and the heights of the trees."

Our foreheads crushed together, Occam's now-white eyelashes closed for a moment. Without a reply, he exited the car, leaving me there. Too tired to walk over and join my unit, I lowered the passenger window as Occam reached the small group.

Rick was there, looking pale and shaky, having shifted in the car on the way over, but human shaped, dressed in sweatpants and a shirt against the chill, like Occam. He glanced to me in the dim light cast by the houses closest. He lifted a hand in what looked to be more than simply *hello*. Maybe that friendship he had claimed, more so than boss-to-employee. I raised a hand back. He smiled. It was wan, but it was a smile, and it lit his black eyes.

FireWind said, "The scents here are mixed, but one is a scent I smelled all over the farm and in the basement at Stella Mae Ragel's home. This is the scent of the *ajasgili*."

"It's an odd scent," Rick said, "hard to detect with a human nose. A little like muskrat and old cat urine? And something three days dead?"

"Exactly," FireWind said, sounding a little surprised.

"I scent better right after I've been my cat," Rick said.

Occam said, "I smelled it before, but thought it was just part of the smell of *death and decay* and critters at the farm. And like Rick said, it's too weak to notice until you brought it to my attention."

"LaFleur," FireWind corrected.

"He's my friend as well as my boss," Occam said, his tone calm but unyielding.

"You boys work that out later. I got nothing," T. Laine said. "Here." She handed them null pens as protection. I sniffed the air. I detected nothing, and that included no dead body stench. I had a feeling that Ethel Myer was not decomposing beneath the stone of her house. She had vacated the premises.

"There's another scent." Occam tilted his head. "I smelled this at the horse farm, near Adrian's Hell, where he was murdered in the field."

I called to FireWind. "The person who brought *death and decay* into the land managed to kill Hugo, his girlfriend, and the horse? We know it was Hugo's soon-to-be-ex-wife. But I postulate there have to be additional reasons for the murders than simple revenge." I stole a line from one of the others. "Dollars to donuts there was a big insurance policy on Hugo that would expire when the divorce was final. And maybe it was even more than that. Stella's estate is huge; and add in the value of the horses, it gets even bigger. JoJo and I have been working on who benefits, but we've barely made a dent in the estate. Maybe Carollette had an insurance reason to kill the horse. The man in the barn, Pacillo, said there was a lot of insurance on the horses. Her mother said Stella had made sure her family were taken care of. Maybe that included the commune family. Maybe Stella allowed all her former commune members to invest in her stallion and put them on that insurance policy. Has anyone checked?"

FireWind said into his headset, which I hadn't noticed, "Jones? Yes. Thank you." He looked at me. "The insurance policy on Adrian's Hell listed a Richard H. Ames. DOB and social match Hugo's. As his heir, his wife stood to receive a hundred thousand dollars on a mid-seven-figure insurance settlement in addition to his life insurance policy."

"Daaaaamn," T. Laine said. "Vengeance for infidelity *and* money. Those are good motives."

Too tired to think, I closed my eyes, but FireWind had understood. He said, "Insurance monies on the horse would have gone directly to the beneficiaries without going through probate. Stella dies, the horse dies, then Hugo dies, in that order, and any potential monies, including his portion of the insurance monies for Adrian's Hell, would go to his not-yet-ex-wife. If he has not yet changed his will."

"We're living in Dick Francis' world," T. Laine said, "if Dick was a para and wrote magic death stories."

"Yes," I whispered.

I wondered how many people would still be alive if we had looked at the other victims of the initial attack as carefully as we did Stella. Stardom had an allure all its own, dangerous for law enforcement.

In a line of cars, PsyLED Unit Eighteen drove toward Carollette Myer Ames' house in Crossville. A couple blocks off of Lantana Road, we turned off all car lights and eased into the drive of a vacant house, a weathered For Sale sign in the overgrown front yard. We were a hundred feet from Carollette Myer Ames' small single-family home where she had lived with her husband. Occam handed me a pair of binoculars from his gobag and I adjusted them. He had cat eyes, and didn't need them.

The red brick house was surrounded by dead oak trees and a dead flower garden. The death of the land was leaching out from the front porch where Ethel Myer sprawled in a rotting rocking chair, illuminated by the porch light. She was recognizable only by the holey, rotting green plaid housedress and the pile of rotting cigarette butts in a dish on the concrete beside her. Ethel was leaking green goo, her body falling apart as *death and decay* took her. Dust filtered over her as the front porch ceiling gave way and a board clattered down.

Carollette was sitting across from Ethel in a rusted metal rocker. She was pretty in a hard sort of way, her face seeming composed of angles made by frowning, her form stiff and projecting caged fury, even while just sitting, staring at her dead aunt. She was dressed in frayed jeans and ragged layered T-shirts. Leather shoes were curled and disintegrating on the floor beside her bare feet. She was the burnished platinum of some brunettes who go white-headed early, the same shade of white I had seen in the pasture where Adrian's Hell died.

"She don't look like much," Occam said of the necromancer, "until you realize how many people she's killed." I didn't reply and he added, "They want her alive."

"Who?"

"FireWind didn't say, but he was ticked off."

Etain and Catriona pulled up beside us in an old dented Subaru. They got out and headed for Unit Eighteen, who were talking quietly nearby. Etain tossed us—or maybe just Occam—a wave as she moved around my car.

"T. Laine called for backup?" I asked.

Occam said, "FireWind took the warnings to heart about bombing the necromancer. We're taking her down the old-fashioned way, magic-against-magic and low-tech human weapons."

Margot parked on the other side and joined the unit, not noticing us in the darkened car.

"I got all the energy of a dead possum," I said, so tired that church-speak came out. "I got no way to help here, not to capture a necromancer." I held up my raw fingers. They looked worse in the dim light—white dead skin. Exhausted tears dribbled down my face, heated and stinging. *Embarrassing.* I turned my head away.

"Nell, sugar. Why you crying, darlin'?"

"This is jist me feeling useless." I dragged my sleeve across my cheeks, pulling on my tear-rough skin. I faced him, and his eyes were glowing the golden of his cat, his nearly white hair pushed back from his healed, beautiful face. Had he been this pretty before he was burned? I didn't rightly think so. "Go on. Take her down. But if you'un get hurt, I'll skin your cat hide offa you'un in punishment," I threatened.

He grinned, his teeth flashing, reflecting distant lights. "Duly noted, plant-woman. But don't worry. Lainie gave us obfuscation charms if we need 'em." He kissed me quick and slipped from my car.

I sat and watched as Unit Eighteen and the two Irish witches talked, came to an agreement, and separated, approaching Carollette's home from oblique angles, moving tree to tree, house to house, using what they had for cover.

Occam raced cat-fast to the far side of the porch, into the dark. Out of my sight.

Rick was in front, carrying a gun with a huge barrel, big enough to be a small cannon.

Margot carried a target pistol with a long barrel and moved into range, half-hidden behind a car.

FireWind was carrying an old hunting rifle. He positioned himself at a different angle from Margot's. His job was to take Carollette down permanently if the other means didn't.

The three witches spread out in a triangle, Etain moving to the far side of the porch, T. Laine on the near side, and closer to their target. There wouldn't be time or opportunity to create a circle around the house. They would be using a triangle to cast their working, and with T. Laine the only powerful witch, the working could be limited in scope and power.

I wasn't wearing an earbud, but I understood. Because she was so dangerous, there would be no warnings. No chance to give up. No chance for the suspect to place a weapon on the ground and raise her hands. No chance. Because Carollette *was* a weapon.

FireWind and Rick shared a look and FireWind gave a single jutting nod, his lips saying, "Go." Rick aimed, took a breath, released half of it, and fired. A beanbag filled with steel pellets hit our suspect in the left chest. She rocked in her chair, her head whipping side to side.

Rick fired again, hitting his target. Carollette fell to the porch, her hands to her chest, her breath knocked out twice.

T. Laine threw all the null pens at the porch. They landed around the downed *ajasgili*.

T. Laine and FireWind raced in, the big boss with his weapon aimed at Carollette's head. T. Laine secured Carollette in official steel cuffs and then in silvered null wrist cuffs. While she was still trying to recover, T. Laine bound her head in silver skull cuffs, two of them, taking no chances. They backed away and the three witches cast a ward around the downed woman, a small but powerful *hedge of thorns*. The ward was so strong it cast a bright red glow in the night, something I hadn't seen before.

The body language of the surrounding unit and witches relaxed, the witches blowing out hard breaths.

FireWind backed away, his weapon pointed at the ground.

Margot, who was closest to me, chuckled and stood, her words carrying to me. "Well, that was easy."

But it wasn't easy. It wasn't over.

The earth trembled.

Death and decay began to rise.

Everything happened, almost too fast to follow.

FireWind raised his hunting rifle.

Catriona, Etain, and T. Laine whirled and began pouring energies into the *hedge*.

Margot bent over the hood of the car she had hidden behind. Aimed her target pistol.

FireWind aimed.

Rick dropped the beanbag gun. Pulled his service weapon, racing in.

The *hedge of thorns*, intended to enclose the necromancer and contain her *death and decay* energies, sparked and stuttered. The energies died.

FireWind fired.

Occam raced toward the porch, his eyes glowing in the night. His service weapon out in front. Holding the remains of the potted cabbage in the crook of my arm, I opened my car's passenger door, falling as the earth shook. I landed on my knees. Made it to my feet, clutching the car door. Gasping.

There wasn't much Soulwood soil left in the pot. There wasn't much of me left. I couldn't do this. I couldn't. And I had to.

Gunshots sounded, cracking on the night.

Tears raced down my face.

More shots sounded.

The earth rolled and shook.

My feet dragged as I approached the porch. More shots sounded. *Death and decay* roiled and stretched, aiming at our witches. Aiming at Occam, who fired from the far side of the house. When the porch was thirty feet ahead, I tried to say, "It's not going to be enough." But they didn't hear me over the weapons' fire.

Carollette rose from the porch floor and screamed, "Die!"

The ground rippled. The dead body of Ethel Myer rocked. Her body bent forward and she stood. Dead. Standing. She lurched off the porch.

FireWind shouted, "Retreat!" No one ran. He aimed his weapon. Rick and Occam aimed theirs. They fired at Carollette. But the *ajasgili* didn't fall.

"PsyLED! Carollette Ames, stop your magic attack, now!" FireWind shouted.

Rick raced to the side. Trying for a better shot.

The ground shook.

Ethel's dead body grabbed T. Laine into a hug, crushing her. T. Laine gagged and fought, thrusting her defensive magic agaisnt the dead body.

FireWind raced in and shoved Etain and Catriona toward the cars. "Run!" he screamed, and he leaped to the porch.

T. Laine moaned. A sound like death.

The tremor in the land went deep and wide. Trees shook. Windows in nearby houses popped and shattered. Margot raced toward the house, tripped, and fell. The porch where T. Laine, prisoned by the dead, stood, along with the *ajasgili*/necromancer and FireWind, juddered. One corner support dropped, crumbled. The porch cracked like a shotgun blast, the roof falling at an angle. Occam turned toward me, searching for me in the darkness.

I dropped the potted plant. Fell beside it. Shoved my hands into the soil spilled on the ground. Beneath the ground, the darkness roared and shimmered. *Death and decay* attacked. Everything, everyone began to die.

T. Laine was suffocating in the dead embrace. Her ribs popped. Her breath stopped.

Rick screamed, a cat scream in a human throat. Agony of death. *Death and decay* had touched him. He was dying.

The ground trembled.

Occam raced toward me, eyes glowing, claws at his fingertips. I felt his feet as they hit the earth.

I called on Soulwood. Light and warmth filled me. Tender branches whipped at the house. Roots exploded from the ground. Vines rippled across the porch. They tangled themselves into Carollette's white hair. Roots and thorns tore into her body. Blood splattered.

FireWind fired. Margot fired. Multiple gunshots tore through Carollette.

Rick fell to the ground.

The *ajasgili* screamed. My roots and vines tightened around her neck. She screamed and gurgled. Called on her dark power.

More shots echoed in the night, FireWind and Margot firing.

The house began to collapse. The dead body Carollette was riding slid to the porch floor, taking T. Laine with it into an oozing heap. Rick tried to shift. Writhing on the ground.

I fell forward. My vision was of my leafy hands in Soulwood soil. The light telescoped down, smaller and smaller, into two pinpoints. Everything went dark, but I wasn't totally out. I still *felt* the battle. Felt the power in FireWind as he tossed boards away. Tore the dead body from his agent and threw it. Lifted T. Laine. He leaped away from the house and landed on the ground hard, his arms cushioning Lainie. She whimpered. Took a faint breath.

Death and decay shriveled. Quivered. Hesitated.

And died.

Occam's strong arms were around me. His body heat burning. With my last thought, I sent health and life into them all. Healing. Warmth. *Life*.

I was awake. Sort of. Sitting in my car with the engine running, the heater on. Occam's arms were around me. I was sitting on his lap. I was safe. He was safe. The *death and decay* was gone. Carollette was dead, truly dead. My magic knew all this.

I was draped in an unfamiliar sweater. Cold shook me. Nausea rose in my throat, acidic and rancid. I was alive. In some kind of exhausted fugue state from healing the land at Hugo Ames' and defeating an attack of *death and decay* at Carollette's home.

Leaves rustled and fluttered across my fingers and through my hair.

Ambulances and first responders were everywhere. There were gas leaks from the small, localized earthquakes. People all through the town were injured. A fire was spreading down the street and residents were being evacuated. As if he knew I was awake, Occam's arms tightened about me.

T. Laine was on a stretcher, wheeled past me to an ambulance, Margot trotting at her side. "Where?" I croaked.

Occam cat-growled in my ear, "Heading to UTMC. She suffered a crushing injury. FireWind called Gonzales to meet her there."

"He's turning into a softie," I whispered. I was cold. So cold. I closed my eyes, pulling the sweater around my shoulders with my leafy fingers. I didn't know when or how the sweater had gotten here, but it was warm and fuzzy and comforting. The heat blew across me. I slept.

"Nell?"

I woke again, this time from a confusing dream full of angry people teetering on the edge of violence. I got my eyes open and blinked, confused. I was at HQ. I didn't remember getting here.

"Nell?" FireWind asked. He had used my first name. That was enough to wake the dead from sheer shock. He was kneeling in front of me.

Occam's arms were no longer around me, but he knelt beside my chair, his paws—*paws*—on my hands, his eyes the brilliant gold of his cat. He was . . . part cat. That was strange.

I looked around, discovered I was in HQ's conference room, with no idea how I had gotten there. "Occam?" I whispered. He cat-hissed. "Boss?" I whispered.

"Kahwi. Asvhvsga," he said.

I smelled coffee. There was a mug of coffee in FireWind's hands, extended to me. *Kahwi.* Cherokee for coffee? I had no idea of the other word. I accepted the mug, warm in my icy hands, and drank. There was sugar and creamer in it, a lot of both, and the sweets and the caffeine and the fat of the creamer went to work. When the mug was half-empty, I looked around the room to see JoJo, Occam, and my boss, who was still kneeling in front of me. "I'm okay," I said. I wasn't. I was lying. FireWind knew that. "T. Laine? And Rick? And . . . Carollette?"

The skin around FireWind's eyes tightened ever so slightly.

I remembered the vines wrapping around her neck. "Did I kill her?" I asked.

Occam's arms tightened around me. He snarled silently at our boss.

FireWind stood and moved away from me. "No," he answered. "Lainie is alive, at UTMC. After undergoing treatment she will be spending a few days here at HQ in the null room."

He called her Lainie, not Kent. Did that indicate she was in very bad shape? Or was FireWind softening?

"LaFleur was down, but shifted in time to survive," FireWind said. "Carollette Ames survived, with six rounds in her and her throat crushed by vines. She is in custody. And we are all alive, thanks to you."

"Where?" I managed, sipping again. My throat was raw, and my hands were leafy, though not so leafy as I remembered them being. Occam must have groomed me. Cat mating ritual. I softened all over and rubbed my jaw against his furry forehead, knowing I'd have to deal with this weird partial-cat-state at some point.

"She is on her way to New Orleans. Catriona and Etain borrowed the portable null trailer from UTMC, put her in it, wrapped her in a dozen null cuffs and all of the unit's null pens."

"She shouldn't have been able to survive being shot."

"No." He smiled slightly. "Which is why she is being trailered directly to New Orleans and the null prisons kept by the witch council there."

"No trial?" I asked.

"No," he said again, the word sharp. "She admitted nothing, but our investigation amassed enough evidence to make sure she is never released."

"The deaths had nothing to do with Stella," JoJo said. "And everything to do with her. Everything went back to the commune and the relationships that Stella forged there. And the kind of human jealousy that kills instead of walking away." Jo pulled on her earrings, stretching her ear. "Carollette deserves to be dead, not in a null room."

"Not our call," FireWind said. "She may not read as a witch, but she is *ajasgili*. She is *death and decay* and they think only the strongest witches are capable of restraining necromancy."

"The trigger in the T-shirt box?" I asked. "Was that set by Ethel?"

FireWind shifted his position on the edge of the conference table where he was propped. "Similar elements of the trigger were found in the remains of Ethel Myer's house, her fingerprints on a bottle of absinthe. Kent believes that Ethel helped Carollette build the power sink to contain her death energies at puberty. If so, that was a brilliant, though temporary solution to control such dangerous magics." His mouth turned down, a frown that said he was thinking. "It worked until Carollette was betrayed and found a use for her magics, to get back at her cheating husband. Conjecture. But it seems to fit the evidence that Carollette took the power into her own hands and Ethel assisted. But we may never know everything. *Death and decay* is destroying the evidence."

JoJo said, "The witches will probably study Carollette for the next fifty years, until she dies. Let me play my tiny violin."

There were still things that didn't add up. I knew I'd be asking questions for a while, as would all the team. "What about the dead plants?" I asked.

FireWind said, "Verna Upton cared for the houseplants. I am speculating that Carollette brought contaminated dirt from her *death and decay* circle and sprinkled some in each pot in the studio to act as a focal, to contain the energies to the house."

The part of me that was attached to Soulwood wanted to shrivel at the very thought. I should have been able to sense the soil in the pots. I looked at my fingertips. They were leafy yet still not fully healed from touching the *death and decay*.

Gingerly, FireWind asked, "Will you be able to dissolve all the shielded energies?"

Occam growled and moved as if to attack. I caught his hair in one leafy hand, stopping him. "I think so," I said. "Maybe?" I put my head on the conference room desk and yawned. Closed my eyes. "Eventually. After I get some sleeee . . ."

Less than a week later, Occam and I pulled up to Stella Mae's horse farm. It looked the same as the first time I'd come, except for the pasture where I had found Adrian's Hell covered in green froth. That entire field was barren, brown, dead. I may have groaned in pain because Occam took my hand.

"You could say no, Nell, sugar. Or that you need a break. You don't have to fix this. Not today."

"If not me, then who? If I don't fix it or at least help to fix it, then who will? And if it enters the water table, then what?" *What if it kills the somnolent presence in the deeps of the Earth?*

I shoved my viny scarlet hair out of my eyes, shifted my body away from the devastation, and looked at Occam. His eyes were glowing the gold of his cat. His emotions were high. I hadn't spent a lot of time in the office in the last few days, traveling with one or another of Unit Eighteen's agents, healing various energies, and sleeping a lot in between. I had lost track of the phase of the moon, but I knew the werecats had hunted, taking down a big buck.

My magics and the magics of Soulwood had healed him. His blond hair was lighter. His scars were gone. His movements were the lithe and graceful speed of the were-creature fully integrated with his cat, like a ballet dancer but faster, stronger, with far more stamina. People watched him when he stalked down the street. He drew the eye. When he and Rick were together, were-magic sparked, the leftover magic of Soulwood giving them a keen awareness of each other. They no longer seemed to be sparring for alpha status. They seemed content. When Margot was with them, they had magic even humans could feel.

"Play your antishift music," I suggested. "I have work to do." I opened the car door, my feet crunching on the gravel as I slid under the fence boards and into the dead field.

I didn't bring the faded, patched, and sewn blanket, which I had salvaged, nor did I bring a potted plant, but I had brought a lancet and a plastic bag of Soulwood soil from the garden. I had figured out the procedure to heal the earth of the necromantic energies. It wasn't easy, but I could do it, and without turning into a tree.

I found the place where Adrian's Hell had died and I sat just outside of the depression of death where his body had lain. Unlike last time, the grass crunched beneath my feet and my backside, dead, as I wriggled into a comfortable spot.

I dumped out the soil and pricked two fingers, index left and index right, and let blood collect in my palms. When there were tiny pools of thick, bright red, I slammed my hands against the earth, one against the dead dirt, across the dead grass. One against the Soulwood soil. Pushing with my magic.

I called on life. I called on the green, green, *green* that was life. I fed the faint spark of life in the deeper roots, in the far-away roots, in the rare still-living grasses that had once been so plentiful and healthy here. I pushed my own life force into the land. *Pushed*. Called on life. Gave the land my own. I reached out to Soulwood, to the life that was twined with mine. I wrapped the *death and decay* in the life of Soulwood. I claimed the land, but with only the faintest of leashes. I pushed with my magic. And I made the land grow.

ΝINETEEN

Mud had taken the bus to school. Esther was at the church, packing up her belongings, probably ordering all the Nicholson menfolk around, telling them how to load things into the moving van Daddy had rented, driving everyone crazy with her complaints. It was just Cherry and me on the front porch, sitting in the swing in the cold and fog of morning, my human-skin hands wrapped around a warm tea mug. Cherry put her head on my thigh and breathed out in contentment. "Me too," I said to her. "It's nice to be alone."

I was wearing flannel pants, wool socks, fluffy slippers, and layered sweatshirts against the cold, having learned how comfortable store-bought, modern clothes could be. Inside, my gardening bib overalls were folded neatly on my bed, my work boots beside the back door. I was off for a few days, healing my own body before I would try to heal the land at the power sink. I needed, almost desperately, to have my hands in Soulwood soil, my spirit in Soulwood's warmth and power. But first, strong tea and quiet time.

Cherry yawned as I rubbed behind her ears and along her skull. She closed her eyes in bliss. And I felt his car turn onto the road at the bottom of the mountain, Soulwood warning me, and then curling like a contented cat. Heated warmth spiraled up from inside me. "My cat-man is here," I told the dog. "Musta come straight from work."

Cherry didn't seem impressed.

I thought about running inside and putting on makeup, pulling on a dress, but I had brushed my teeth and combed my ridiculously curly hair. I had groomed my leaves. I wasn't a girly-type girl. I was a plant-woman. This would do. Coffee and a pot of tea waited. And eggs if Occam was hungry.

But that warmth grew, and when he turned into the short drive, I felt as if I was glowing with it. My cat-man was here.

He stood from his fancy car and walked around it, his long legs steady, his blond hair bright in the foggy day. Cherry dropped to the porch and met him at the top of the stairs, where he paused, one foot on the top step, one on the porch, leg bent, stroking her head the way she liked. He was wearing jeans and a denim jacket, and his eyes were glowing gold. "Morning, Nell, sugar."

The warmth inside me unfolded and spun and whirled and gamboled across my land. And I was ready.

"Morning, cat-man. I like the fog."

"I like it too."

"And I like tea in the mornings, sitting on the porch."

"I like that too."

"I'm getting chickens."

"I'm right fond of eggs, chickens, and eating both."

"I'm gonna have Mud living here. She's a handful. You okay with that?"

He chuckled and my skin rose in goose bumps. "Yeah. She is. And she belongs here. So does Esther, God help us, her and her baby, when it comes."

I remembered my vision of a spotted leopard curled around a plant-baby. "Occam? Will you marry me?"

His hand stilled on Cherry's head. His smile went from amused and happy to blazing. Softly, as if he was scared I might run away or change my mind, he said, "Yes. Right now? Tomorrow? I'm free the day after too."

I laughed. "Let's get through the full moon and then we can pick a date. Jist a warning, though. Even though I'm a widderwoman, Mama will want a full God's Cloud of Glory Church wedding. They're kinda overwhelming."

"I'd fly to the full moon and back if that's what it took to marry you, Nell, sugar. Besides. I'm marrying your family too. I'm smart enough to know that."

I held out a hand. He took the last step to the porch and sat beside me on the swing, sliding an arm along the back of the swing to cradle me. He pushed off with a toe and I rested my head on his shoulder. We rocked. The day brightened as the sun rose.

* * *

The sun was falling toward the west, scarlet clouds limned with gold. The moon was up, though clouded over. The air was cold.

My two sisters and I were sitting, carefully positioned on my mended faded pink blanket, not in any kind of circle that Esther might construe as witchy. She was propped by pillows I had carried from the house, grumpy as usual, difficult to maneuver in her huge state, but not impossible to be around.

At the edge of the blanket was a small packet of blood-drawing supplies: sterile lancets, gauze, alcohol wipes in foil packets, Band-Aids. There was a bag of Soulwood soil too, because though I could see my house if I looked over my shoulder, this wasn't my land and I might need it.

We were sitting near the road, my house behind us, in a small copse of trees. Or tree. Vampire tree. Thankfully there were no dead animals being devoured on the thorns. Dark green leaves rustled overhead and vines seemed to wave. I hoped I was the only one to realize that there was no breeze. The tree seemed almost curious, attentive, if not helpful. I hoped this would be easier than last time I had tried to talk to the tree, when I had threatened to kill it.

"I still don't understand how I'm'a claim some trees," Esther complained.

"We're plant-people," Mud said. "All you gonna do is tell it which plant is boss."

Esther shook her head at the absurdity, but we had gone over this several times. I knew Soulwood through the wood of my house. Esther needed to know her land through the wood of her house too, so that she would know when danger was approaching, so she could call on the plants and trees around her for protection. To make sure she was safe, we were going to claim the tree, then the land where her house would be built. I had carefully considered the visions and concepts I would use to talk to the Green Knight.

I pricked my finger, dumped the soil, and let a few drops of my blood run into it. Not sure what would happen, not sure if the tree would try to hurt me, I reached out and touched the trunk with my bloody palm. Nothing happened, just my palm against the cool bark. I closed my eyes.

In my vision, the Green Knight stood in a pasture, his hand on the pale green horse's neck, the mane tangled with flowers. He was unarmed, though still armored. Waiting. Attentive.

I showed the knight myself, my sisters, and, just across the road, two massive warcats, one spotted green, the other a green so dark it was nearly black. They were crouched on the three grassy acres, taking up all of the empty land, their tails coiled around the house and in the trees on the far side. Foot-long fangs; claws like curved blades, extended. This was an image of my power, my threat, the power of Soulwood.

The horse leaned down and grazed, chomping. The Green Knight stroked the neck of his horse, his hand in the mane.

Just like last time, I sent it images of the vampire trees being cut down, shaped into logs, some cut into boards. Of being made into a house, just there on the bottom of my property. Beside the house I envisioned a tiny vampire tree growing and spreading its leaves over the house, protecting it. This was my offer. The Green Knight would accept a job to do, to become a house, perhaps more than one, in return for being allowed to live.

The Green Knight and the horse simply stood there, the horse grinding tender shoots of grasses. This was not agreement, but it was better than a vision of it attacking, the vision of its anger, of dragging me under the surface of the earth and killing me.

Without opening my eyes, I said, "Your turn, Esther."

Paper crinkled. "Ouch! Dagnabbit! You'un sure this ain't witchcraft?"

"I'm sure. It's simply plant power. Put your hand beside mine on the tree. Close your eyes. Tell me if you see anything."

"Mama would be having kittens."

"Mama ain't here," Mud said, her voice hushed, awed. "Ouch! Okay. I got blood too."

I felt Esther lean near me. Place her palm beside mine. Mud's bloody palm went beside Esther's.

In my vision, the Green Knight looked at the hands, his helmet moving slightly side to side. He removed his gauntleted fist from the horse's mane. Slowly, as if he feared we might harm him, he reached out with both open hands. Gently, he placed his palms against Esther's and mine. The wood beneath my hand instantly became smoother, slicker, not quite the warmth of flesh or the smoothness of steel, but something in between.

Beside me, Esther gasped. "You'un feel that?" she whispered.

"Yes," I said. "You see anything?"

"A meadow full of tall grass. And one tree smack in the middle of it. Kinda looks like a live oak from the shape, but its leaves are paler, softer, and shaped like maple—" Esther inhaled fast. "It's like my leaves. Is this *my* tree?"

"It could be. We have to claim the land, and claim anything we grow on the land. We're plant-people. Our true home is the land and the trees that grow on it."

"I like it. It's pretty. It's growing flowers in big white bunches."

"Mud?" I asked.

"I don't see nothin' but a green horse. It . . . Ohhh. It put its head against my hand."

In my own vision, the Green Knight stepped back and looked at his blood-coated palms, shocking scarlet with blood. He bowed his head.

The horse stepped back, tail switching. A scarlet handprint marked his face, where a blaze might have gone. Mud gasped, "I got me a tree horse."

"Okay. On three," I said. "One, two, three."

We removed our hands. Opened our eyes.

"That right there was amazing," Esther murmured, her eyes lit with wild joy. "Okay. Let's go claim my patch of land."

We rode down the hill in John's old truck and sat on the small grassy area where the house would go, a ways away from the raw dirt of the septic system and downhill of the well. Esther pricked her skin again and placed her hands on the ground, mingling her blood with the earth. A small vine unfurled and twisted from the ground and around Esther's wrist. Her eyes closed in ecstasy.

Mud and I watched as thin vines crawled over her hands, encasing them like gloves. And over her belly, touching her gently. Esther claimed the land and it claimed her.

* * *

The next morning I rocked back and forth on the porch swing, one toe controlling the movement, watching as Sam and the churchmen in his faction, including my daddy, discussed which trees to take first. They were gathered on the Vaughn farm's downhill side of the road, visible from this vantage. There were a lot of shouted instructions and disagreements about where to drop the trees on the slanted road. There was even more fussing and discussing about how to get the cut logs onto the logging truck, to the construction site where they would be rough shaped, and then under the temporary shelter waiting for them. Further discussion followed about how long the logs would need to cure before they could be used for construction.

I had received the Vaughns' wildly enthusiastic permission to thin the vampire trees that had encroached on their farm, despite Brother Vaughn's antipathy to me personally. The tree, the creation of which had, thankfully, not been attributed to me, had a reputation on church lands as a devil tree. It was a well-deserved reputation, the tree having killed a rooster, a puppy, a full-grown dog, and a cat, as well as numerous squirrels. And a man, though no one had mentioned that in my hearing.

"Men take forever to do *anything*," Esther commented from the rocking chair near the door. Her hands were scratching lazy circles on her rounded belly, her housedress stretched tightly across her. "If women were doing this, all that other stuff woulda been decided long afore we got here and we'da started cutting two hours past."

I smiled, watching the arm waving, foot stomping, and general air of disagreeable excitement among the men. "That's true. But they're having fun. Look at Daddy." Old Man Nicholson, as Daddy had begun to be called since he'd been shot and the subsequent surgeries, was perched in a lawn chair. He had one leg propped on a stump and was contributing to the conversation with much cane brandishing and general gesticulation.

Esther slid her hands to her lower spine and pushed, her eyes pensive, not meeting mine. "You'un sure that wasn't witchcraft, what we done last night? Pricking my finger and bleeding all over tarnation felt a lot like devil stuff."

"It wasn't witchcraft," I said placidly. "No witch circle, no spells. It was just sharing your blood-scent with the tree, so it would agree to become your house."

"Tree smelling my blood. Strange things you do, Nellie. *Humph.*" The sound was a lot like Mama's and my smile grew. Mama was planning her next grandbaby. To make sure there would be no baby-killings should Esther's child be born with leaves, Mama had hired an outside midwife to be on-site when Esther went into labor.

"Get away from me, dog," Esther grouched, nudging Cherry with a toe. The springer had become overly protective this morning, when Esther had hard contractions and the baby started kicking in seeming retaliation. I stopped the swing and patted the seat beside me. Cherry whined but leaped obediently up beside me and lay down, her chin hanging off the seat, her eyes on my sister's belly.

Out front, the logging trailer had been leveled, the crane that lifted the logs to the trailer was in place, and the lumbermen secured goggles to protect their eyes. The roar of multiple chain saws commenced. Cherry whined louder and shoved her nose under my hand; I covered her ears. Sam had tied plastic ribbons around each tree to be taken: the four biggest were tied with blue, to be shaped and used as the floor girders. The red ones were the next size up, to be left whole and round for the outer walls. The odd-sized ones were to be cut into boards for inner walls, window casings, door casings, and such.

That is, if the blasted tree allowed the men to cut them without a fight and if the men didn't run scared when the cut wood bled red. I had warned them about that, insinuating that the vampire tree was a new, fast-growing, invasive tree and they needed to get out in front of the infestation and find a use for it before it took over the world. Having seen all the invasive plants and animals from Asia and South America, they were in complete agreement about tree culling, but I had a feeling they thought I was joking about the bloody sap.

The chain saws bit in. I half expected that the vampire tree would grow vines and attack the lumbermen, but the trees—tree?—stayed quiescent. Blood sprayed everywhere. The chain saws went silent. The roar died away and a peculiar quiet settled.

A crow cawed, the repetitive sound like insulting laughter. The men looked at the mess on their clothes and their skin.

Sam called out, "Nellie, will this stuff stain?"

I thought about the few times I had broken off a leaf or a thorn. "Shouldn't," I answered back.

"What the tarnation is this stuff?" Ben Aden yelled. "Begging your pardon, ladies," he added for church-cussing.

I pushed off with my toe and called back, "Because its sap is red, the tree's called a Bloody Nickelodeon."

Sam gave a quick start and barked a laugh at the Nicholson reference.

"It ain't poison, is it?" Ben asked.

"Nope," I called. "So get to work, boys."

The men with the saws shook their heads at the vagaries of women and restarted the chain saws. Trees began to fall.

By midafternoon, they had cut enough wood for a twenty-eight-by-twenty-four-foot log cabin and had rough shaped the logs. By the next evening, the wood had been transported to the house site. And no one was bitten, stabbed by thorns, or eaten. I counted that as a win.

The traditional rule of thumb for air-drying lumber was one year of drying time per inch of wood thickness. The vampire logs dried far faster than anyone expected. Within weeks the wood was ready for use. The dried pinkish wood had a lovely grain that didn't need staining and a scent reminiscent of cedar. The wood chinked well and held pegs and nails perfectly. It was easy to work, it took a shine with a simple polish, and the trim took the white paint well. The shakes for the roof splintered off as if they were waiting on the ax. The house went up in record time before Thanksgiving, and a CO—certificate of occupancy—was granted. I felt as if the universe and God were finally helping out.

At six a.m. on the first day of the first full moon before Thanksgiving, my sister started moving in, planning to spend her first night in her own home. She was hugely pregnant, as if she might bust at any moment. Her feet were swollen, her face was swollen, and she had more leaves than I'd ever had, even when I was a tree. It was a major chore to keep her groomed. *Pruned?*

Not that I said that. I was too busy following orders, as were Mud, Mama, Sam, Priscilla (my older true sister), Judith (a younger true sister), a half dozen half sisters and half brothers, and everyone else Esther had berated into helping. Lainie and JoJo had dropped by with a baby gift and skedaddled as fast as they could when my bossy preggers sister tried to put them to work.

It was a long day.

A *loooong* day.

Long after dark, it was just Esther, Mud, and me. Two of us were still working, sweating in the cold of the new house with the windows open, because Esther was hot-flashing. Esther was demanding, criticizing, bossy, and so grumpy I wanted to tear my fading scarlet hair out by its curly roots.

I made Esther's bed to her exacting specifications, swept, mopped, dusted, and washed dishes. Mud folded clothes precisely and put them *exactly* where Esther wanted them. Then refolded them. Twice. I arranged Esther's kitchen dishes where she pointed, while she sat in her rocking chair, giving orders. When the mama-to-be got hungry, I heated housewarming soup and rewashed the supper dishes. When I was done, I said, "Mud, go to the car."

"You'un ain't finished," Esther said as Mud ran out of the house like a cat with her tail on fire.

"Oh yes we are," I said.

"Fine." She gave me the Nicholson scowl and said, "This is pretty. Get on out. I need to shower off the stink and put on my nightgown."

I pulled the new curtains over the windows and left, locking the door behind me. Fast. Before she could change her mind.

Through the open window, I could still hear Esther fussing, talking to herself.

John's old truck, which I had driven laden with Esther's things, was now empty and it was light as a feather as it bumped back along Esther's new driveway to the road and then up the hill to home. In blessed silence.

We were halfway there when Mud whooshed out a breath and stated, "I ain't never *ever* having no babies. They make people crazy."

I chuckled unwillingly. I didn't really want to laugh at Esther, but Mud had a point.

"And you'un—you—know what she's gonna do, don'tcha? She's gonna call every hour all night long, not able to sleep, keeping you awake, complaining about funny noises the house makes as it settles, complaining that werecats are hunting in her yard. And they will be, you know that, prowling in the woods, caterwauling, what with it being the full moon. There's the cars on the side of the road," she pointed out.

She was right about the werecats, but I said nothing, not even correcting Mud's grammar. I fully believed my younger sister was right and I'd have calls all night.

But for two hours there was nothing, not a single call. Mud, the dog, the cats, and I ate popcorn, watched a Disney movie about Aladdin, and went to sleep early, our home feeling like our home again. Just ours.

It didn't last.

At two a.m., Esther called my cell, in high dudgeon. "You'un get your'nself down this hill to my house right this minute," she demanded. "You'un need to talk to the trees."

"The trees?"

"Get on down here and see for your'nself." The call ended in a huff I could feel through the airwaves.

I shoved the cats off me, got up, dressed in jeans, boots, and a T-shirt with a sweatshirt over it. I clomped up the stairs and looked in on Mud, who was sleeping, limbs sprawled across the covers. Back down the stairs, I checked the banked coals in the stove, which were keeping the house a little too warm tonight, and cracked a few windows to let out some heat. Satisfied that the house was safe, and that I had no other legitimate reasons to dither, I stared at my PsyLED gear and debated taking my official weapon. This was a private issue, not a law enforcement one—I hoped—so I settled on John's shotgun, loaded it with ammo big enough to take down a deer, and trudged outside.

The night air smelled of woodsmoke, winter foliage, fresh-cut hay from somewhere, and chickens. Putting my hand to the earth, I inspected the property, discerning only creatures who belonged, including a leap of werecats off on the church boundary eating a deer they had taken down. I paid them no mind, looking for unexpected or strange things. Found none. Mud was safe, so I got in my car.

I passed Unit Eighteen's cars as I drove down the hill and was surprised to see FireWind's car too. I hadn't counted the cats, but he must be with them. That was interesting, especially as Soulwood was treating the new cat like one of the weres. I would have to pull all the info about the hunt out of Occam come morning.

I eased down the hill, whipping the wheel into my sister's drive. I braked, the tires grinding in the gravel, the house illuminated by headlights.

The house was . . . different. Crazy different.

The horizontal logs had put out roots, long, sinuous roots, trailing and draping to the ground, thickening into trunks. They were also growing up, becoming tall like saplings, and out, like living siding, with branches all sprouting leaves. Not the dark green leaves with red petioles of the vampire tree, but burgundy, five-pointed leaves, edges serrated like maple leaves, growing in pairs, one pair one way, the next pair the other, so they appeared in a round fan. The leaves on the bottom were huge; near the tops of the new trees, which were still sprouting, they were smaller. The treetops curled, rising above the roof, where they spread out, forming what looked like an unopened tulip-blossom-shaped framework. A roof of living wood.

Vines with the same leaf positioning were growing all around the trim on the windows and around the doorway like decorations. Saplings had sprouted around the periphery of the house. Every branch and twig was flowering bunches of pretty, tiny white flowers. Like a fairy house.

"Oh. Dear," I said aloud to the night.

I parked on a gravel area where no saplings grew and got out. I left the shotgun. There was no need for it. I kept a flashlight in my glove compartment and I turned it on. The bright beam tossed images of intense illumination and deepest shadows, bouncing off the window glass.

My sister opened the back door and waddled onto the stoop. "You'un make this here tree stop doing all this," she demanded, pointing all around as if it was my fault. "It's gonna bury the house and me with it."

"Ummm. It's your tree, sister mine. You make it stop."

She stomped her foot. "I can't—" She froze. Grabbed her belly. Looked down.

I walked closer and directed the light at her feet. Pouring over the blossoming boards was pale green liquid. Esther's mouth opened. Closed. Opened again. I reached her and took her hand. Turned off my light.

We stood there, hand in hand, beneath the last of the night's full moon. I let my consciousness move down, through the land, into the deeps of Soulwood. Into the intertwined roots of the tree growing here. Searching. And I found him.

The Green Knight was fully armored, his sword drawn, a shield on his left arm. He was sitting on his paler green horse, who now had a blaze down his face in purest white, shaped like a handprint between his eyes, with a trailing wrist to his nose. The steed stomped, the vibration reaching me. He snorted, horse breath like a bellows blowing. The knight planted his halberd in the ground with a thump. Beside them was a pole flying a swallowtail pennant, centered with a dark green tree with tiny white flowers. As I watched, white flowers burst into bloom everywhere, in the grass beneath him, from the halberd's hardened shaft, from the top of the pennant pole, from the knight's hands.

"I'm having a baby," Esther whispered.

"Yes," I breathed, pulling myself back to her. "And the trees must have known it. I think the growth is a protection and a gift."

"You'un gonna call Mama?"

"I'm gonna call all the mamas, and the midwife, and Mud. And we're gonna make tea and tell stories and sing songs, and welcome your baby into this world, right here in your magical tree house."

Esther nodded. "That's good. That's real good." She let go of my hand, gathered up her soaked nightgown skirt, and bunched it beneath her. She waddled back inside. And called over her shoulder, "Clean up that mess, you'un hear?"

I laughed. From the ground beneath the porch, tendrils were rising, bursting with pale green leaves and minuscule white flower buds. The vines sucked up all the fluid, and the white flowers burst open. "I think your land is taking care of any mess, sister mine." I pulled my cell and started making calls. The first baby plant-person was about to be born.

* * *

My cell rang, and Occam's name was on the display. I stepped outside my sister's house into the bright light of late dawn and went down the steps to the ground. I answered, saying, "Hey, cat-man."

"You're on speaker to all the cats, Nell, sugar. That was amazing." A peculiar joy sounded in his voice. "Soulwood's practically dancin' with joy. We take it you're an aunt again?"

"I am." I closed my eyes and thought about the land beneath my bare feet, and realized that he was right. The land was singing, a warm vibration like spring and growth and all things good.

In the background I heard Rick say, "We all sense it. Something special in the land. Even in our human forms, we still feel it."

"Boy or girl?" Margot asked. "And how are they?"

"Both. We got us some twins." I knew what she really wanted to ask and so I said, "And they're all right as rain. And the babies have skin, not bark and leaves. They look human."

"That right there is good news, Nell, sugar. Hang on. I'm setting us to private. Okay. You tell your family we've set a date?"

Joy filled me, stronger than an ancient oak, but I wasn't really feeling strong. It had been a long night, and I was worn slap out. I leaned against the outer wall and rested my head on the pinkish logs nestled between bunches of white flowers. I dug my bare feet into Esther's land and it recognized me, accepted me. "Esther's had a rough night. Two babies in four hours was fast. I thought we'd let her have the spotlight for a few days and tell the Nicholsons at Thanksgiving."

"Tell us what at Thanksgiving?"

I whirled and saw Mud, her head sticking out of the door. "Shhh," I said. "None a your'un business."

Her eyes went wide. "Mama!" she hollered. "Nell's getting hitched! We'uns having twins *and* a wedding!"

"Cat's outta the bag, Nell, sugar."

I groaned at his joke. And at the screams from inside the house.

"You best be picking out your wedding dress," he said. I didn't reply, because womenfolk were descending around me, squealing and all talking at once. Barely audible, Occam said, "I love you to the full moon and back, Nell, sugar."

"I love you too, cat-man. To the deeps of the roots and the heights of the trees."

Acknowledgments

Brooks Prater, endurance rider, for all the horsey stuff.

Teri Lee, timeline and continuity editor extraordinaire.

Mud Mymudes for all things planty and doggy, and for beta reading and PR.

Let's Talk Promotions at http://www.ltpromos.com for getting me where I am today.

Lee Williams Watts for being the best PA a girl can have.

Beast Claws! Best Street Team Evah!

Mike Pruette at http://www.celticleatherworks.com for all the fabo merch.

Lucienne Diver of The Knight Agency, as always, for applying your agile and splendid mind to my writing and my career, and for being a font of wisdom.

Many thanks to my copy editor, Sheila Moody.

Thanks to Katie Anderson for the glorious cover design.

Thanks to Miranda Hill, editor at Penguin Random House/Ace, for all the answered questions.

As always, a huge thank-you to my longtime editor, Jessica Wade of Penguin Random House. Without you there would be no books at all.

Read on for an excerpt of the first book
in Faith Hunter's *New York Times* bestselling
Jane Yellowrock series,

SKINWALKER

Available wherever books are sold!

I wheeled my bike down Decatur Street and eased deeper into the French Quarter, the bike's engine purring. My shotgun, a Benelli M4 Super 90, was slung over my back and loaded for vamp with hand-packed silver fléchette rounds. I carried a selection of silver crosses in my belt, hidden under my leather jacket, and stakes, secured in loops on my jeans-clad thighs. The saddlebags on my bike were filled with my meager travel belongings—clothes in one side, tools of the trade in the other. As a vamp killer for hire, I travel light.

I'd need to put the vamp-hunting tools out of sight for my interview. My hostess might be offended. Not a good thing when said hostess held my next paycheck in her hands and possessed a set of fangs of her own.

A guy, a good-looking Joe standing in a doorway, turned his head to follow my progress as I motored past. He wore leather boots, a jacket, and jeans, like me, though his dark hair was short and mine was down to my hips when not braided out of the way, tight to my head, for fighting. A Kawasaki motorbike leaned on a stand nearby. I didn't like his interest, but he didn't prick my predatory or territorial instincts.

I maneuvered the bike down St. Louis and then onto Dauphine, weaving between nervous-looking shop workers heading home for the evening and a few early revelers out for fun. I spotted the address in the fading light. Katie's Ladies was the oldest continually operating whorehouse in the Quarter, in business since 1845, though at various locations, depending on hurricane, flood, the price of rent, and the agreeable nature of local law and its enforcement officers. I parked, set the kickstand, and unwound my long legs from the hog.

I had found two bikes in a junkyard in Charlotte, North Carolina, bodies rusted, rubber rotted. They were in bad shape. But Jacob, a semiretired Harley restoration mechanic/Zen Harley priest living along the Catawba River, took my money, fixing one up, using the other for parts, ordering what else he needed over the Net. It took six months.

During that time I'd hunted for him, keeping his wife and four kids supplied with venison, rabbit, turkey—whatever I could catch, as maimed as I was—restocked supplies from the city with my hoarded money, and rehabbed my damaged body back into shape. It was the best I could do for the months it took me to heal. Even someone with my rapid healing and variable metabolism takes a long while to totally mend from a near beheading.

Now that I was a hundred percent, I needed work. My best bet was a job killing off a rogue vampire that was terrorizing the city of New Orleans. It had taken down three tourists and left a squad of cops, drained and smiling, dead where it dropped them. Scuttlebutt said it hadn't been satisfied with just blood—it had eaten their internal organs. All that suggested the rogue was old, powerful, and deadly—a whacked-out vamp. The nutty ones were always the worst.

Just last week, Katherine "Katie" Fonteneau, the proprietress and namesake of Katie's Ladies, had e-mailed me. According to my Web site, I had successfully taken down an entire blood-family in the mountains near Asheville. And I had. No lies on the Web site or in the media reports, not bald-faced ones anyway. Truth is, I'd nearly died, but I'd done the job, made a rep for myself, and then taken off a few months to invest my legitimately gotten gains. Or to heal, but spin is everything. A lengthy vacation sounded better than the complete truth.

I took off my helmet and the clip that held my hair, pulling my braids out of my jacket collar and letting them fall around me, beads clicking. I palmed a few tools of the trade—one stake, ash wood and silver tipped; a tiny gun; and a cross—and tucked them into the braids, rearranging them to hang smoothly with no lumps or bulges. I also breathed deeply, seeking to relax, to assure my safety through the upcoming interview. I was nervous, and being nervous around a vamp was just plain dumb.

The sun was setting, casting a red glow on the horizon, limning the ancient buildings, shuttered windows, and wrought-iron balconies in fuchsia. It was pretty in a purely human way. I opened my senses and let my Beast taste the world. She liked the smells and wanted to prowl. *Later*, I promised her. Predators usually growl when irritated. *Soon*—she sent mental claws into my soul, kneading. It was uncomfortable, but the claw pricks kept me alert, which I'd need for the interview. I had never met a civilized vamp, certainly never done business with one. So far as I knew, vamps and skinwalkers had never met. I was about to change that. This could get interesting.

I clipped my sunglasses onto my collar, lenses hanging out. I glanced at the witchy-locks on my saddlebags and, satisfied, I walked to the narrow red door and pushed the buzzer. The bald-headed man who answered was definitely human, but big enough to be something else: professional wrestler, steroid-augmented bodybuilder, or troll. All of the above, maybe. The thought made me smile. He blocked the door, standing with arms loose and ready. "Something funny?" he asked, voice like a horse-hoof rasp on stone.

"Not really. Tell Katie that Jane Yellowrock is here." Tough always works best on first acquaintance. That my knees were knocking wasn't a consideration.

"Card?" Troll asked. A man of few words. I liked him already. My new best pal. With two gloved fingers, I unzipped my leather jacket, fished a business card from an inside pocket, and extended it to him. It read JANE YELLOWROCK, HAVE STAKES WILL TRAVEL. Vamp killing is a bloody business. I had discovered that a little humor went a long way to making it all bearable.

Troll took the card and closed the door in my face. I might have to teach my new pal a few manners. But that was nearly axiomatic for all the men of my acquaintance.

I heard a bike two blocks away. It wasn't a Harley. Maybe a Kawasaki, like the bright red crotch rocket I had seen earlier. I wasn't surprised when it came into view and it was the Joe from Decatur Street. He pulled his bike up beside mine, powered down, and sat there, eyes hidden behind sunglasses. He had a toothpick in his mouth and it twitched once as he pulled his helmet and glasses off.

The Joe was a looker. A little taller than my six feet even, he had olive skin, black hair, black brows. Black jacket and jeans.

Black boots. Bit of overkill with all the black, but he made it work, with muscular legs wrapped around the red bike.

No silver in sight. No shotgun, but a suspicious bulge beneath his right arm. Made him a leftie. Something glinted in the back of his collar. A knife hilt, secured in a spine sheath. Maybe more than one blade. There were scuffs on his boots (Western, like mine, not Harley butt-stompers) but his were Fryes and mine were ostrich-skin Luccheses. I pulled in scents, my nostrils widening. His boots smelled of horse manure, fresh. Local boy, then, or one who had been in town long enough to find a mount. I smelled horse sweat and hay, a clean blend of scents. And cigar. It was the cigar that made me like him. The taint of steel, gun oil, and silver made me fall in love. Well, sorta. My Beast thought he was kinda cute, and maybe tough enough to be worthy of us. Yet there was a faint scent on the man, hidden beneath the surface smells, that made me wary.

The silence had lasted longer than expected. Since he had been the one to pull up, I just stared, and clearly our silence bothered the Joe, but it didn't bother me. I let a half grin curl my lip. He smiled back and eased off his bike. Behind me, inside Katie's, I heard footsteps. I maneuvered so that the Joe and the doorway were both visible. No way could I do it and be unobtrusive, but I raised a shoulder to show I had no hard feelings. Just playing it smart. Even for a pretty boy.

Troll opened the door and jerked his head to the side. I took it as the invitation it was and stepped inside. "You got interesting taste in friends," Troll said, as the door closed on the Joe.

"Never met him. Where you want the weapons?" Always better to offer than to have them removed. Power plays work all kinds of ways.

Troll opened an armoire. I unbuckled the shotgun holster and set it inside, pulling silver crosses from my belt and thighs and from beneath the coat until there was a nice pile. Thirteen crosses—excessive, but they distracted people from my backup weapons. Next came the wooden stakes and silver stakes. Thirteen of each. And the silver vial of holy water. One vial. If I carried thirteen, I'd slosh.

I hung the leather jacket on the hanger in the armoire and tucked the glasses in the inside pocket with the cell phone. I closed the armoire door and assumed the position so Troll could search me. He grunted as if surprised, but pleased, and did a thorough job. To give him credit, he didn't seem to enjoy it overmuch—used only the backs of his hands, no fingers, didn't linger or stroke where he shouldn't. Breathing didn't speed up, heart rate stayed regular; things I can sense if it's quiet enough. After a thorough feel inside the tops of my boots, he said, "This way."

I followed him down a narrow hallway that made two crooked turns toward the back of the house. We walked over old Persian carpets, past oils and watercolors done by famous and not-so-famous artists. The hallway was lit with stained-glass Lalique sconces, which looked real, not like reproductions, but maybe you can fake old; I didn't know. The walls were painted a soft butter color that worked with the sconces to illuminate the paintings. Classy joint for a whorehouse. The Christian children's home schoolgirl in me was both appalled and intrigued.

When Troll paused outside the red door at the end of the hallway, I stumbled, catching my foot on a rug. He caught me with one hand and I pushed off him with little body contact. I managed to look embarrassed; he shook his head. He knocked. I braced myself and palmed the cross he had missed. And the tiny two-shot derringer. Both hidden against my skull on the crown of my head, and covered by my braids, which men never, ever searched, as opposed to my boots, which men always had to stick their fingers in. He opened the door and stood aside. I stepped in.

The room was spartan but expensive, and each piece of furniture looked Spanish. Old Spanish. Like Queen-Isabella-and-Christopher-Columbus old. The woman, wearing a teal dress and soft slippers, standing beside the desk, could have passed for twenty until you looked in her eyes. Then she might have passed for said queen's older sister. Old, old, *old* eyes. Peaceful as she stepped toward me. Until she caught my scent.

In a single instant her eyes bled red, pupils went wide and black, and her fangs snapped down. She leaped. I dodged under her jump as I pulled the cross and derringer, quickly moving to the far wall, where I held out the weapons. The cross was for the vamp, the gun for the Troll. She hissed at me, fangs fully extended. Her claws were bone white and two inches long. Troll had pulled a gun. A big gun. Men and their pissing contests.

Crap. Why couldn't they ever just let me be the only one with a gun?

"Predator," she hissed. "In my territory." Vamp anger pheromones filled the air, bitter as wormwood.

"I'm not human," I said, my voice steady. "That's what you smell." I couldn't do anything about the tripping heart rate, which I knew would drive her further over the edge; I'm an animal. Biological factors always kick in. So much for trying not to be nervous. The cross in my hand glowed with a cold white light, and Katie, if that was her original name, tucked her head, shielding her eyes. Not attacking, which meant that she was thinking. Good.

"Katie?" Troll asked.

"I'm not human," I repeated. "I'll really hate shooting your Troll here, to bleed all over your rugs, but I will."

"Troll?" Katie asked. Her body froze with that inhuman stillness vamps possess when thinking, resting, or whatever else it is they do when they aren't hunting, eating, or killing. Her shoulders dropped and her fangs clicked back into the roof of her mouth with a sudden spurt of humor. Vampires can't laugh and go vampy at the same time. They're two distinct parts of them, one part still human, one part rabid hunter. Well, that's likely insulting, but then this was the first so-called civilized vamp I'd ever met. All the others I'd had personal contact with were sick, twisted killers. And then dead. Really dead.

Troll's eyes narrowed behind the .45 aimed my way. I figured he didn't like being compared to the bad guy in a children's fairy tale. I was better at fighting, but negotiation seemed wise. "Tell him to back off. Let me talk." I nudged it a bit. "Or I'll take you down and he'll never get a shot off." Unless he noticed that I had set the safety on his gun when I tripped. Then I'd *have* to shoot him. I wasn't betting on my .22 stopping him unless I got an eye shot. Chest hits wouldn't even slow him down. In fact they'd likely just make him mad.

When neither attacked, I said, "I'm not here to stake you. I'm Jane Yellowrock, here to interview for a job, to take out a rogue vamp that your own council declared an outlaw. But I don't smell human, so I take precautions. One cross, one stake, one two-shot derringer." The word "stake" didn't elude her. Or him. He'd missed three weapons. No Christmas bonus for Troll.

"What are you?" she asked.

"You tell me where you sleep during the day and I'll tell you what I am. Otherwise, we can agree to do business. Or I can leave."

Telling the location of a lair—where a vamp sleeps—is information for lovers, dearest friends, or family. Katie chuckled. It was one of the silky laughs that her kind can give, low and erotic, like vocal sex. My Beast purred. She liked the sound.

"Are you offering to be my toy for a while, intriguing nonhuman female?" When I didn't answer, she slid closer, despite the glowing cross, and said, "You are interesting. Tall, slender, young." She leaned in and breathed in my scent. "Or not so young. What are you?" she pressed, her voice heavy with fascination. Her eyes had gone back to their natural color, a sort of grayish hazel, but blood blush still marred her cheeks so I knew she was still primed for violence. That violence being my death.

"Secretive," she murmured, her voice taking on that tone they use to enthrall, a deep vibration that seems to stroke every gland. "Enticing scent. Likely tasty. Perhaps your blood would be worth the trade. Would you come to my bed if I offered?"

"No," I said. No inflection in my voice. No interest, no revulsion, no irritation, nothing. Nothing to tick off the vamp or her servant.

"Pity. Put down the gun, Tom. Get our guest something to drink."

I didn't wait for Tommy Troll to lower his weapon; I dropped mine. Beast wasn't happy, but she understood. I was the intruder in Katie's territory. While I couldn't show submission, I could show manners. Tom lowered his gun and his attitude at the same time and holstered the weapon as he moved into the room toward a well-stocked bar.

"Tom?" I said. "Uncheck your safety." He stopped midstride. "I set it when I fell against you in the hallway."

"Couldn't happen," he said.

"I'm fast. It's why your employer invited me for a job interview."

He inspected his .45 and nodded at his boss. Why anyone would want to go around with a holstered .45 with the safety off is beyond me. It smacks of either stupidity or quiet desperation, and Katie had lived too long to be stupid. I was guessing the rogue had made her truly apprehensive. I tucked the cross inside a little lead-foil-lined pocket in the leather belt holding up my Levi's, and eased the small gun in beside it, strapping it down. There was a safety, but on such a small gun, it was easy to knock the safety off with an accidental brush of my arm.

"Is that where you hid the weapons?" Katie asked. When I just looked at her, she shrugged as if my answer were unimportant and said, "Impressive. You are impressive."

Katie was one of those dark ash blondes with long straight hair so thick it whispered when she moved, falling across the teal silk that fit her like a second skin. She stood five feet and a smidge, but height was no measure of power in her kind. She could move as fast as I could and kill in an eyeblink. She had buffed nails that were short when she wasn't in killing mode, pale skin, and she wore exotic, Egyptian-style makeup around the eyes. Black liner overlaid with some kind of glitter. Not the kind of look I'd ever had the guts to try. I'd rather face down a grizzly than try to achieve "a look."

"What'll it be, Miz Yellowrock?" Tom asked.

"Cola's fine. No diet."

He popped the top on a Coke and poured it over ice that crackled and split when the liquid hit, placed a wedge of lime on the rim, and handed it to me. His employer got a tall fluted glass of something milky that smelled sharp and alcoholic. Well, at least it wasn't blood on ice. Ick.

"Thank you for coming such a distance," Katie said, taking one of two chairs and indicating the other for me. Both chairs were situated with backs to the door, which I didn't like, but I sat as she continued. "We never made proper introductions, and the In-ter-net," she said, separating the syllables as if the term was strange, "is no substitute for formal, proper introductions. I am Katherine Fonteneau." She offered the tips of her fingers, and I took them for a moment in my own before dropping them.

"Jane Yellowrock," I said, feeling as though it was all a little redundant. She sipped; I sipped. I figured that was enough etiquette. "Do I get the job?" I asked.

Katie waved away my impertinence. "I like to know the people with whom I do business. Tell me about yourself."

Cripes. The sun was down. I needed to be tooling around town, getting the smell and the feel of the place. I had errands to run, an apartment to rent, rocks to find, meat to buy. "You've been to my Web site, no doubt read my bio. It's all there in black and white." Well, in full color graphics, but still.

Katie's brows rose politely. "Your bio is dull and uninformative. For instance, there is no mention that you appeared out of the forest at age twelve, a feral child raised by wolves, without even the rudiments of human behavior. That you were placed in a children's home, where you spent the next six years. And that you again vanished until you reappeared two years ago and started killing my kind."

My hackles started to rise, but I forced them down. I'd been baited by a roomful of teenaged girls before I even learned to speak English. After that, nothing was too painful. I grinned and threw a leg over the chair arm. Which took Katie, of the elegant attack, aback. "I wasn't raised by wolves. At least I don't think so. I don't feel an urge to howl at the moon, anyway. I have no memories of my first twelve years of life, so I can't answer you about them, but I think I'm probably Cherokee." I touched my black hair, then my face with its golden brown skin and sharp American Indian nose in explanation. "After that, I was raised in a Christian children's home in the mountains of South Carolina. I left when I was eighteen, traveled around a while, and took up an apprenticeship with a security firm for two years. Then I hung out my shingle, and eventually drifted into the vamp-hunting business.

"What about you? You going to share all your own deep dark secrets, Katie of Katie's Ladies? Who is known to the world as Katherine Fonteneau, aka Katherine Louisa Dupre, Katherine Pearl Duplantis, and Katherine Vuillemont, among others I uncovered. Who renewed her liquor license in February, is a registered Republican, votes religiously, pardon the term, sits on the local full vampiric council, has numerous offshore accounts in various names, a half interest in two local hotels, at least three restaurants, and several bars, and has enough money to buy and sell this entire city if she wanted to."

"We have both done our research, I see."

I had a feeling Katie found me amusing. Must be hard to live a few centuries and find yourself in a modern world where everyone knows what you are and is either infatuated with you or scared silly by you. I was neither, which she liked, if the small smile was any indication. "So. Do I have the job?" I asked again.

Katie considered me for a moment, as if weighing my responses and attitude. "Yes," she said. "I've arranged a small house for you, per the requirements on your In-ter-net web place."

My brows went up despite myself. She must have been pretty sure she was gonna hire me, then.

"It backs up to this property." She waved vaguely at the back of the room. "The small L-shaped garden at the side and back is walled in brick, and I had the stones you require delivered two days ago."

Okay. Now I was impressed. My Web site says I require close proximity to boulders or a rock garden, and that I won't take a job if such a place can't be found. And the woman—the vamp—had made sure that nothing would keep me from accepting the job. I wondered what she would have done if I'd said no.

At her glance, Tr—Tom took up the narrative. "The gardener had a conniption, but he figured out a way to get boulders into the garden with a crane, and then blended them into his landscaping. Grumbled about it, but it's done."

"Would you tell me why you need piles of stone?" Katie asked.

"Meditation." When she looked blank I said, "I use stone for meditation. It helps prepare me for a hunt." I knew she had no idea what I was talking about. It sounded pretty lame even to me, and I had made up the lie. I'd have to work on that one.

Katie stood and so did I, setting aside my Coke. Katie had drained her foul-smelling libation. On her breath it smelled vaguely like licorice. "Tom will give you the contract and a packet of information, the compiled evidence gathered about the rogue by the police and our own investigators. Tonight you may rest or indulge in whatever pursuits appeal to you.

"Tomorrow, once you deliver the signed contract, you are invited to join my girls for dinner before business commences. They will be attending a private party, and dinner will be served at seven of the evening. I will not be present, that they may speak freely. Through them you may learn something of import." It was a strange way to say seven p.m., and an even stranger request for me to interrogate her employees right off the bat, but I didn't react. Maybe one of them knew something about the rogue. And maybe Katie knew it. "After dinner, you may initiate your inquiries.

"The council's offer of a bonus stands. An extra twenty percent if you dispatch the rogue inside of ten days, without the media taking a stronger note of *us*." The last word had an inflection that let me know the "us" wasn't Katie and me. She meant the vamps. "Human media attention has been . . . difficult. And the rogue's feeding has strained relations in the vampiric council. It is *important*," she said.

I nodded. *Sure. Whatever. I want to get paid, so I aim to please.* But I didn't say it.

Katie extended a folder to me and I tucked it under my arm. "The police photos of the crime scenes you requested. Three samples of bloodied cloth from the necks of the most recent victims, carefully wiped to gather saliva," she said.

Vamp saliva, I thought. *Full of vamp scent. Good for tracking.*

"On a card is my contact at the NOPD. She is expecting a call from you. Let Tom know if you need anything else." Katie settled cold eyes on me in obvious dismissal. She had already turned her mind to other things. Like dinner? Yep. Her cheeks had paled again and she suddenly looked drawn with hunger. Her eyes slipped to my neck. Time to leave.

Ready to find
your next great read?

Let us help.

Visit prh.com/nextread